BLINDED

BLINDED

KIM PRITEKEL

SAPPHIRE BOOKS

SALINAS, CALIFORNIA

Blinded
Copyright © 2016 by **Kim Pritekel**. All rights reserved.

ISBN - 978-1-943353-53-8

This is a work of fiction - names, characters, places, and incidents are the product of the author's imagination or are used fictitiously. Any resemblance to actual persons living or dead, business, events or locales is entirely coincidental.

All rights reserved. No part of this publication may be reproduced, distributed, or transmitted in any form or by any means, including photocopying, recording, or other electronic or mechanical methods, without written permission of the publisher.

Edited by Nikki Busch
Cover by Michelle Broduer
Book design by LJ Reynold

Sapphire Books Publishing, LLC
P.O. Box 8142
Salinas, CA 93912
www.sapphirebooks.com

Printed in the United States of America
First Edition – November 2016

This and other Sapphire Books titles can be found at
www.sapphirebooks.com

Dedication

This novel is dedicated to anyone who has had to pick themselves up from the ashes and start over.

Chapter One

2010 – Atlanta, GA

"Burton Blenday?"

Burton Blinde glanced up from her phone where she was seated in a comfortable chair in the lobby of CNN headquarters. "It's pronounced blind," she said with a smile as she pushed to her feet. She pulled the strap on her purse to her shoulder before reaching down to make sure her A-line skirt was adjusted correctly.

"My apologies," the woman said with a quick smile from where she stood at the entrance to the lobby. "I guess I was trying to make your name a bit more exotic than it really is. Please follow me." She peeked behind at Burton. "Burton. Is that your given name or your TV persona?"

"My given name," Burton said with a smile. "Burton Elizabeth Blinde."

"Well," the woman said, turning back around, "at least part of your name is interesting."

Burton followed the woman who wore well-fitted slacks and an off-white silk blouse. She appeared to be in her mid-forties and led Burton through a maze of hallways. Familiar faces in huge framed posters smiled at Burton along the way: Wolf Blitzer, Anderson Cooper, and others. She slowed her pace, rubbernecking at her idols.

"Miss Blinde?"

"Sorry," she murmured, hurrying as fast as she

could in high heels after her host.

They ended up in an office decorated in paisley prints mixed with modern furnishings. It was interesting, and Burton did her best not to stare. She was directed to sit at the desk, which was essentially a thick slab of glass that seemed to float over a huge wood block painted black.

She scooted the chrome-and-black-leather chair away from the desk and sat down, placing her purse on the floor next to the chair, her hands clasped in her lap. To her surprise, the woman in the silk blouse took a seat across from her.

"So," the woman said as she settled into her own chair. She opened the screen of the laptop computer that sat at the center of the desk, which seemed to already be set to Burton's information. The woman's dark eyes immediately tracked across the screen. "I'm Martha Tillman," she said absently, "and I'm your absolute last roadblock to becoming part of the CNN family." She spared a glance at Burton, the red slash of her lips curving up into an icy smile.

Burton swallowed, her fingers twitching nervously in her lap before she sent them a direct command to stop. "It's a pleasure to meet you, Miss Tillman," she said, proud of herself for the fact that her voice sounded even and confident. It was the rare specimen that intimidated her, but this woman was certainly one of those. Perhaps, she thought, it may just be that she held the future of her career in her talon-like fingers.

"I have to admit, Burton, I'm quite impressed with your body of work thus far," Tillman said, her hand on the cordless mouse, finger running over the ball as though scanning through Burton's extensive resume. Her eyebrows shot up. "The William J. Murray award in journalistic excellence, very impressive." She glanced over the top of her computer, sitting back in her chair. "I watched your tape this morning, and I won't lie, I was fairly amused."

Burton tried not to react. Somehow, the word "amused" didn't seem like a positive in what she viewed was her best work, all edited into a single film, her greatest hits, as it were. "Oh," was all she could manage.

"The way you went after that dog catcher guy." The HR supervisor clapped her hands once as she let out a cackle. "I thought that guy was going to pee himself."

Burton nearly burst into song at her relief. "Yes, well he wasn't giving me what I wanted, so—"

"And the way you wormed your way into that school to get the interview with the janitor. Stroke of brilliance."

"Thank you. I was trying to—"

"Listen," Martha said, shutting her laptop with finality. "You've been through this twice on the phone and once over Skype. We didn't fly you all the way out here just to split hairs." She pushed back from her desk and walked to the office door, pulling it open and standing next to it. "We'll be in touch within the week with an offer."

Burton remained seated, her mind spinning, trying to make sense of what she'd just heard. "What?"

"Probably by Thursday, if not Monday," Martha said, pulling the door open a bit wider. "You remember how to find your way out, don't you?"

Her brain kicking into gear, Burton grabbed her purse and pushed to her feet, although a bit unsteady as her heart began to race. She wobbled her way toward the door, enough brain power remaining to extend her hand. "Thank you, Miss Tillman. I look forward to it."

Burton managed to make two turns in the maze before it hit her. She dropped her purse and her head fell back. "Holy shit!"

※※※※

Denver, CO

The passengers were jostled as the wheels touched down on the runway, once then a second time before finally, the rubber took to the tarmac and the plane began to slow its taxi into Denver International Airport.

Burton glanced out the window, the tarmac wet from recent rains, which Simone had texted her about. She pulled out her phone and powered it up. She knew her friend was already waiting for her, notoriously early, in direct defiance of Burton's constant tardiness. It was usually because she'd seen a story in the making and therefore followed the crumb trail, working or not.

The flight attendant made her announcement, welcoming everyone to the Mile High City. A symphony of random buzzes and noises accompanied her when everyone throughout the cabin powered on their phones, Burton included. She quickly sent off a text to Simone, letting her know they'd landed. She was not remotely surprised to receive an instant message that her friend was already there and waiting for her at baggage claim.

Simone Townsend was Burton's closest friend—as close as Burton would allow a friend to become—and was the makeup girl down at KNWZ, Denver's Channel 6 News, where Burton had worked as an on-camera reporter for six years. She loved her job and most of the people she worked with, but it was time for bigger and better things, and the past twenty-four hours had been all about that.

Burton couldn't help the smile that broke out across her face as she remembered her exciting, albeit short, final interview in Atlanta. Depending on what the offer amounted to, this would be the new start to the next phase of her life, and it couldn't happen soon enough.

She reached under the seat in front of her to drag out her laptop, setting it in her lap as she waited for her chance to get her carry-on from the overhead compartment.

Twenty-five minutes later, after her stop was announced by the recorded voice, she stepped off the tram that took weary travelers from the terminals to the baggage claim and exit doors. She'd signed a few autographs along the way, but now she was ready to get home to Cricket, her beloved tabby. The escalator she took slowly rose to the landing where she caught the second escalator that finally brought her to the baggage claim floor, as well as where a gathered crowd waited to meet their traveler.

It wasn't hard to pick Simone out. As her colleague John Lemmon always said, she was a tall drink of water. Standing close to six feet tall, she was a fashion plate at any given time with her sophisticated style, cat-like gray eyes, and modern shoulder-length hairstyle that was at the moment dark blond with caramel highlights.

"What happened to the plum?" Burton said, laughing as she moved into the hug Simone offered. She stepped back and looked at the hair her fingers reached for. "I've been gone for not even two full days."

"And?" Simone retorted with a raised eyebrow. "Do you honestly expect me to not change it up for you?"

Burton chuckled, shaking her head. "Come on, let's get out of here. I need food!"

"Oh, thank you, love," Simone gushed as the waiter set the glass of red wine before her.

Burton watched, sipping from her chocolate martini. "We've been here for fifteen minutes and you're already on your second glass. Do I need to drive us home?" she asked, slightly amused.

"It's about time you invite me to come home with you," Simone said, not missing a beat as she wrapped elegant fingers around the stem of the glass, lifting it to painted lips. "Or we can go to mine."

Burton rolled her eyes and returned her attention to her menu. She couldn't remember a day that Simone hadn't hit on her since they'd met two years before. "Ain't gonna happen," she said in a sing-song voice before shooting her friend a sweet smile.

"So you say. All right." Simone sat back in her chair, her wineglass in one hand while the other tossed her hair back away from her face. "So, are you going to tell me what happened?"

"I can't tell you," Burton said, sipping from her drink. "Not until I give my two weeks'—"

Simone let out an embarrassing cry and set her wineglass down so hard and quickly that the red liquid sloshed onto the table before she hurried around to Burton's side, hugging her painfully tight. "You got it!"

"Okay, uh, honey, okay. I know you're excited, but I can't breathe," Burton managed to say, trying her best not to spill her drink all over herself.

Simone released her from the hug, but before Burton could react, her friend took her face into her hands to steady it for the lingering kiss to the lips that followed. Anger quickly overtook her shock.

"Simone!" she hissed, looking around the crowded restaurant to see if anyone had seen. "You could ruin my career!" She glared at the woman who was now sitting back in her chair across from her. "Damn it. People could think I'm a damn lesbian and bam"—she snapped her fingers—"forget CNN or even Channel 6."

Simone gave her a contrite look. "I'm sorry. I'm just excited for you." She took a sip of her wine. "And, hey, it's not like you're going to Fox News or something. Hell, you'll be working with Anderson Cooper, for crying out loud! Gayest and *whitest* boy on TV."

At the mention of her future colleague, Burton's anger instantly drained. She raised her glass. "To change."

Simone clinked her wineglass against it. "To change."

❧ ❧ ❦ ❦

"Okay, okay, I hear you," Burton cooed to her little girl who followed her through the small apartment to the bedroom. Even after five minutes of loves at the door, Cricket hadn't had enough and was letting Burton know it with her chirps, which had earned her her name three years before.

Burton flicked on the light, which showed her bedroom exactly as she'd left it, save for the throw pillows which were scattered, thanks to the petite cat's inclination to burrow. She placed her carry-on roller bag on the bed, Cricket jumping up to sniff.

"Were you a good girl?" she asked, using the baby voice that nobody in the world would ever hear except her baby. "Mommy's girl, yes you are," she murmured, picking up the cat and nuzzling the soft fur of her neck. She smiled at the vibration of Cricket's silent purr. Giving her a loud kiss, she sat on the bed and unzipped her bag to sort out laundry from items that needed to be put away or rehung.

Her mind began to wander as she hung up clothes, put away cosmetics, and readied herself for bed. She thought about the new opportunity to move up to a much larger market with CNN, which of course would require her to leave Colorado. She'd been born in the small town of Pueblo, living there until she'd moved to Boulder to attend college on a full scholarship to Colorado University, otherwise known as CU. Right out of college, she'd landed the job she currently held with KNWZ.

She'd risen through the ranks, taken her lumps, and ultimately was seen as one of the best in her business in the market she was in. The best part of it was she'd been able to work with not only the greatest cameraman in the world, but the greatest man in the world, Roger Eggleston.

At the age of seven, Burton had become an orphan after her mother's mysterious death, her father long disappeared from their lives. She'd never received satisfactory answers from her Aunt Carol, who had taken her in and raised her along with her cousin, Lewis, who was now her only living family. At an early age, Burton had honed her curiosity and investigatory skills, trying to find answers to her troubled childhood.

The magical turning point had come in seventh grade when a reporter and cameraman arrived at Pleasant View Middle School to awe Mr. Brotherton's social studies class. A thirteen-year-old Burton hadn't been able to take her eyes off the massive camera the bulky man hefted upon his massive shoulders as she was handed the microphone from the reporter, the logo for KOAA News 5 out of Colorado Springs on it. She stared into the unblinking eye of that camera as she pretended to be a reporter live on scene. The truth, however, was in that moment, she wasn't talking to a piece of equipment, she was speaking to the world—telling her story and sharing her views.

The man behind that camera had been Roger Eggleston, a kind man in his later forties with large, calloused hands; leathery skin; and gentle blue eyes. He'd answered every single question from a girl who had endless curiosity about his camera, his craft, the TV station, and how it all worked. She had so many questions, in fact, that he'd been willing to give her his e-mail address so she could continue to ask. Those e-mails continued on through high school into college with advice for the best course of study in journalism and then a place to stay in Littleton with his family after that curious girl had turned into a newly hired reporter with KNWZ.

Now, she and Roger were four years partnered as the news crew on the go, covering every story from a rogue dogcatcher to the grand opening of a new hair salon in Five Points. The patient kindness of a middle school guest had become the father that Burton never had, his wife, Theresa, a mother and dear friend. Burton had joined the Eggleston family for every holiday dinner and celebration since her sophomore year in college and even babysat their grandchildren on several occasions.

After washing her face and brushing her teeth, Burton pumped a bit of lotion onto her palm and rubbed it into her face and hands. She examined her reflection in the bathroom mirror, noting the shoulder-length, straight dark brown hair and shiny and large hazel eyes that sometimes looked green, sometimes had hints of gold. She was told they were beautiful, that she was beautiful, but all she saw was a twenty-eight-year-old woman whose ambition often outweighed her common sense. She was a searcher, and she knew full well that rather than searching within and finding that very lost little girl, she searched for others, finding their truth and avoiding her own.

After one last look into her own eyes, Burton turned off the bathroom light and headed to her bedroom where Cricket had already taken her place on the unused pillow, the very tip of her tail twitching like a rattlesnake, making it quite clear she was irritated Burton was taking so long to finally turn off the light and go to sleep.

Burton smiled down at her furry companion as she kicked off her slippers and climbed under the covers. "Good night, pretty girl," she murmured, giving her cat a kiss on the head before turning off the lamp and settling in.

Chapter Two

Burton weaved her way through the maze of desks in the newsroom, her messenger bag slung over her shoulder. Today, she wore a well-fitted pantsuit in deep purple, her blouse cream, and her hair up. She waved to a few colleagues and said hello to others until she reached her desk. Since she'd missed the previous day, she had a stack of messages waiting for her and the voice mail light was blinking on her desk phone.

Allowing the strap of her bag to slide down her arm, she pulled open the mostly empty bottom drawer of her desk and placed it inside before shrugging out of her suit jacket and placing it on the back of her chair.

"Welcome back."

She glanced up from where she'd sat down at the desk, an instant smile coming to her lips, though she wasn't sure if it was more for the man or for the large Starbucks cup he held out to her.

"Mocha breve, just the way you like it," he said, handing it to her.

"Bless you, Roger. You know I'm always a complete airhead on my Monday," she said, removing the plastic green plug from the drinking hole in the lid before taking a careful sip.

"I do"—he nodded—"even if it is Wednesday."

"Be nice to me," she said with a playful pout.

"I am, thus why I just paid seven bucks for coffee and whipped cream." He leaned against the desk as he sipped his daily Americana.

Burton looked him over, noting the worn blue jeans that sagged on his behind from an oversized belly pushing down the waistline, the old beat-up brown work boots, and the ever-present flannel shirt rolled up at the elbow. His salt-and-pepper hair was shaggy as always, sideburns a bit too thick and long to be fashionable. "Why does Theresa let you leave the house?"

Roger looked down at himself. "What?"

"Need some new duds there, partner," she said, tugging lightly on the baggy jeans.

"Hey, I hear it enough from my wife, I don't need you nagging on me, too." He took a long sip from his drink before slamming the paper cup down on the corner of her desk. He leaned down toward her. "So?" he said quietly. Apparently the huge smile she gave him said it all as he grabbed her in a quick but tight hug. "I'm so proud of you!"

"Thanks. She said I should hear from them later this week or Monday with an offer." She checked to make sure they weren't being overheard. Before she had a definite offer and accepted it, she couldn't say anything at work except to those she absolutely trusted, like Roger and Simone.

"Why don't you come over this weekend?" he said, picking his cup up again and pushing away from the desk. "We'll celebrate." He raised the cup in salute then headed toward the editing bay.

Burton watched him go, mixed feelings washing through her. How would she handle not working with him every day? Not seeing him or Theresa on a regular basis? She let out a heavy sigh as she powered on her computer. As she waited for the ancient machine to sputter to life, she grabbed the messages and mail, sorting through it all. Much of it was callbacks for stories she'd reached out to cover, others updates on previous stories people wanted done. Then there was the crazy stuff—fan mail.

In the beginning, fan mail used to be fun and quite the ego boost. Unfortunately, over the years and as the public felt they "knew" her better, it had gotten downright weird and once in a great while, creepy. In today's pile included cards and handwritten and typed letters and notes. One was even an offer for a free vacation in Ireland as long as she agreed to cover Don Hesten's pub in LoDo forever.

Rolling her eyes, she tossed that one aside. A few letters later, she felt the smoothness of the picture side of a postcard.

"Didn't know they still even make these," she muttered, looking at the picture. The shot had been taken on a long, obviously old street, the buildings on either side beautiful with ancient architecture, even as a young woman dressed in present-day clothing sat forever frozen on a modern bicycle. "Chilvokia," she read aloud. "Where the hell is that?" She turned the card over to see there was no message, name, or anything other than the address for the station and Burton's name.

Shaking her head, she tossed the picturesque postcard aside into the trash pile. She only had a few more minutes before the morning meeting when assignments would be discussed and ultimately doled out.

≈≈≈≈

"You think he's guilty, don't you?" Burton asked, sitting in the passenger seat of the station van that Roger drove, the back filled with monitors and editing equipment as well as his camera gear.

"As sin," he said, flicking on the turn signal as he pulled up to a red traffic light.

"I don't know," she said, shaking her head as she reviewed the notes she'd just taken after interviewing the police officer who was accused of murdering his wife. KNWZ had been granted an exclusive jailhouse interview. "My gut tells me there's more to this story than meets the eye."

"Speaking of more to the story"—Roger pulled the van into the parking lot of St. Luke's Medical Center—"you ready to take on Dr. Feelgood?"

"Let's do it," Burton replied, stowing her notes in her messenger bag and pulling out her notebook for a new set of notes. The question was whether they'd be able to find the elusive doctor.

One of Burton's many sources had sent her an e-mail regarding the plastic surgeon, claiming he was quietly selling pain medication out of his office to patients or anyone who was willing to pay. After doing some research and digging, the intrepid reporter felt she had enough to confront Dr. Dennis Fiducci.

As Roger parked the van, Burton pulled down the sun visor to use the mirror on the opposite side. She checked her makeup and hair, making sure she'd look good on camera. She was about to put the visor back when her phone buzzed as a text came in. She pulled her phone out of her bag and looked at it. Her eyebrows rose.

"Looks like Senator Rodriguez is in town."

Roger, who stood by the opened driver's side door, stared at her. "No."

"Come on, Rog!" she whined. "I know if I can only get to talk to him—"

"No," Roger said again, closing his door only to open the double back doors moments later to grab his camera gear. "Everett told you specifically to let Paul handle that."

"But, Paul sucks," she said under her breath, pushing open her own door and climbing out of the van. She walked around back to help her partner gear up. "Want me to take the battery pack?" He handed her the heavy bag in lieu of a verbal response. "Just because he so *happens* to be the political reporter."

Roger pulled the heavy camera out of its Pelican case. "Honey," he said quietly, his colleague persona gone and replaced by the protective father figure he was outside of work, "just because you see a potential for a story doesn't mean you have to chase down each one." He met her wounded gaze. "Listen, Burt, you're the best journalist I've ever seen in my thirty-two years in the business. You're bright and your instincts are usually always dead-on. But sometimes you have to know when to let someone else do their job."

Though she knew he was right, she was a bit stung by his words. She gazed down at the battery bag she held only to see one of his big hands enter her line of vision as he lifted her chin with two fingers beneath it. She met his gaze.

"I don't want to see you burn out before you really take off, Burt," he said gently. "I've seen it happen time and time again in this business."

She let out a sigh and nodded. "I know. You know your advice means the world to me, Roger."

He gave her a soft smile then returned his attention to getting his gear ready. "Let's bag us a crooked doctor."

The lobby doors whooshed open as Burton and Roger stepped up to them and entered. They instantly got looks—they always did. Most people were either excited or nervous to see a news crew on-site. Burton ignored the stares; she had one thing in mind and one thing only. Once she was in work mode, nothing else mattered.

The loud clicks of her high heels on the linoleum tile announced their arrival at the surgeon's office door, which was closed. Burton glanced at Roger before raising a fist to knock. With no response, she knocked again, a bit louder.

"He's not here," she murmured, disappointed. She knew it was likely they'd have to hunt him down but was hoping it would be nice and easy for once.

"And the hunt continues," Roger said, readjusting the camera on his shoulder.

"Let's head to the third floor where the surgery ward is," Burton suggested, leading the way toward the bank of elevators.

She reached out a finger to press the elevator button. A moment later, it arrived with a ding. When the door opened, there were two people already inside: a tall man wearing a low-slung baseball cap and a woman dressed professionally.

The pair seemed to be together and stood closely side by side. After giving them a polite smile, Burton wouldn't have given them another thought. But something about the woman caught her attention. She was beautiful, but there were attractive women and men around all the time. Her hair was blond and cut in a stylish bob that ended at her jawline. Her features were delicate, lips full and slightly pouty. But what caught Burton's attention the most were her eyes. They were the deepest, most intense color of green she'd ever seen in human eyes. If she wasn't able to see the vibrant life behind them, she would have thought they were colored contact lenses.

Their gazes met briefly, but in that moment, Burton felt like she'd been struck by lightning, a strange jolt passing through her so strongly that she had to look away. She stared straight ahead, facing the shiny metal doors of the elevator without actually seeing them. Her heart raced and she felt as though her suit was constricting her. She tugged lightly on the simple gold chain she wore, which settled at the hollow of her throat.

The elevator stopped at the second floor and, to her shock, when the doors opened for whoever had beckoned the second-floor stop, Dr. Fiducci stood directly in front of her. He gave her a quick once-over before stepping inside the car and joining their little party.

Instantly, Burton went into investigative mode, tossing aside anything she'd been feeling mere moments before.

She turned to the doctor, who stood next to her. "Dr. Fiducci, I'm Burton Blinde from KNWZ, Channel 6 and I'd like to ask you some questions."

The scrubs-clad surgeon looked at her, surprise in his brown eyes as his eyebrows drew together. "Yes, I recognize you from the news, but why do you want to talk to me?" He peered at the other three people in the car with them, especially Roger, who had raised the heavy camera to his shoulder and was shooting. "What is this? What do you want?" he asked, a bit of panic tinging his voice no matter how much Burton could tell he was trying to retain his calm.

"I'd like to ask you about your connection with the Leland Group," she said, referring to the pharmaceutical company he'd been linked to in her research. She watched him carefully, looking for the slightest change in his face or body language.

"I'm sorry, Miss Blinde, but I have no idea what you're talking about," he said, though the tone of his voice had lowered substantially as he eyed the pair standing at the back of the elevator. "I think you have me confused with someone else."

"What would you say to Ruth Horton?" Burton pressed him, naming a woman who had died of a drug overdose the previous September. Dr. Fiducci had been her doctor.

"I had nothing to do with her death!" he exclaimed, his face red and veins popping from his neck. He took a deep breath and ran a hand through his graying hair, making it stand up slightly in the back. "I only heard about that on your news program. She wasn't a patient of mine."

"I believe she was, Doctor," Burton said, seeing her opening to move in for the kill. She came slightly closer to him, trying to bring down his anxiety by making him feel safe, like it was just a little conversation between them. "Listen, Dennis," she said softly, "We both know this story is going to come out. Why don't you let me help you—tell me *your* side so the truth comes out on your terms. Hmm?" She gave him a comforting smile once he met her gaze. She could see the wheels in his head turning.

"Meet me in my office in half an hour," he said as the elevator stopped on the third floor, the doors opening with a ding.

Burton glanced at Roger who was lowering the camera, a triumphant moment shared between them. She felt eyes on her and peeked over her shoulder to see the blond woman watching her intently. Burton quickly turned away and walked out of the elevator, not because she had any business on the third floor now, but because she needed space from those haunting green eyes.

Chapter Three

Roger sat perched on Burton's desk as together they watched news coverage of Dr. Fiducci turning himself in to the police as it aired on one of the many TVs in the newsroom. Burton was filled with a mixture of pride and guilt. She wanted no part of ruining someone's life, but at the same time, the story she broke was getting what amounted to a greedy drug dealer off the streets.

"You did good, kid," Roger said softly, a hand on her shoulder.

She reached up and covered it, squeezing lightly before dropping her hand back in her lap.

"Special delivery!" Simone exclaimed as she walked into the newsroom, a wrapped box in her hand with a card taped to it. She walked over to Burton's desk. "For you."

"Who from?" Burton asked, taking the slightly heavy box from her.

"No idea. It came in with the mail."

The paper the box was wrapped in was sky blue and the satin ribbon tied around it was white. She lifted it to her ear.

"Is it ticking?" Roger said with a chuckle.

"Very funny, and no." She set the box in her lap and removed the card. The envelope wasn't sealed and the small greeting card was blank on the outside. She flipped it open to see a single word written in beautiful and flowing handwriting.

Congratulations

"Do you trust it?" Simone asked, plucking the card from Burton's fingers.

"I have no idea." Burton tugged the end of the ribbon, pulling it off from around the box. She set it on the desk behind her then removed the paper. It was a plain, square box, the ends taped shut. She pulled a letter opener from her desk drawer to slice through it then tugged the box ends open. Inside was a bottle wrapped in several layers of Bubble Wrap.

"Oh my! You made someone happy," Simone said, eyeing the bottle.

"Why do you say that?" Burton asked, realizing that what she held was a short, round bottle of vodka, N7 vodka, to be exact.

"We used to use this stuff back in my bartending days. This little baby is a ninety-dollar bottle," she explained, tapping the crystal bottle with a painted fingernail. "It's made in this tiny little country up near Russia that I can't remember the name of now, but it's good stuff."

"You're still coming to dinner Saturday night, right?" Roger asked, pushing to his feet.

"Yes," Burton said, looking the bottle over. She'd never heard of the brand before, though since she wasn't that much of a drinker, she wasn't much of an aficionado.

"Bring the booze," he said before heading off toward the editing suite.

She smiled and set the bottle on her desk. "Want to grab some lunch?" she asked her friend.

"Yeah, sounds good. Let me get Claire and Rick ready for their noon broadcast, then we can go."

Burton watched her friend walk away, wishing not for the first time that she had Simone's confidence and self-awareness of herself and her body. Simone was a beautiful woman, for sure, but it was more about her aura that drew people to her. She was never left wanting for attention or a date.

Swiveling in her chair, Burton faced her desk. Her gaze fell to the bottle of vodka and she wondered who had sent it and why. Part of her wanted to know if it had been sent from someone at CNN, but it looked as though it had been hand-delivered and not mailed—the mailman just got the task of bringing it inside. Perhaps it was from her managing editor at KNWZ. Maybe he'd heard about her job offer, which she was waiting on pins and needles to get.

She glanced up, startled when her name was yelled from her boss's office. Pushing back from her desk, she got to her feet and walked across the newsroom to the opened doorway. "What's up, Everett?" she asked, leaning her shoulder against the doorframe.

"Sit down and shut the door," he grumbled, waving her in.

"In that order?"

"You're killin' me, Smalls!" he said, slapping his hand on his desk in mock amusement. The rail-thin man with unquestionably effeminate mannerisms removed his glasses and rubbed his eyes with his fingers. She noticed his short brown hair was a bit spikier than normal as though he'd used a bit too much product that morning. "So, I just spoke with Joel," he said, his hands falling back to the desk. "Seems CNN wants to buy out your contract."

Burton felt a quick moment of giddiness and nearly jumped to her feet to dance a jig around the cluttered office. Instead, she remained calm and professional. "Yes, I've had several interviews with them and was told I'd be getting an offer."

"And, you hadn't told me this, why?" Everett asked, grabbing his glasses and replacing them on his face.

"Because I had no idea if I was going to get what I want," Burton said, feeling slightly defensive. Even though Everett looked like he was fourteen, he was actually a seasoned journalist and story editor in his mid-forties, and he'd always been very good and supportive of her. She felt guilty as though by pursuing this other opportunity, she was stabbing him in the back.

"Well," he said, letting out a heavy sigh. "As sad as I am to see you go, and Joel's freaking out, by the way, congratulations. Nobody deserves it more than you, Burt."

She graced him with her biggest smile. "Thank you, Everett. I'm excited and nervous to see what they're going to offer me."

"Well, since they've already talked to our GM, I'm guessing you'll be getting that call soon." He leaned forward in his chair, clasping his hands on the desk. "I have to know, how the hell did you get that doctor to fess up and then go to the cops?"

She grinned. "They're called boobs, Everett."

"Okay, fine Erin Brockovich," he muttered, rolling his small, gray eyes. "Whatever you did, great job. Guy's career is shot, that's for sure."

"Speaking of ruined careers, Everett, Senator Rodriguez is in town—"

"No."

"Everett!"

"Burton! I'll give you some cheese with that whine." He sat back, once again removing his glasses. "He's in town for a fundraising dinner next Wednesday, and Paul is already going."

"But, Paul sucks."

He shook his head as he laughed. "No, Paul may not have as much experience as you do, but he'll do fine. It's a simple dinner. I'm sure he can handle it."

"But, you know there's a bigger story there than a simple dinner for the DNC, Everett. I've been trying to get you to let me talk to him since rumors began flying nine months ago."

He smirked. "Yeah, but honey, somehow I don't think your boobs are going to do much to help you this time."

She snickered. "You made a good funny, Everett. I knew you had it in you. So, can I go?"

"To the dinner?"

"Yeah."

"Absolutely not." He shook his head. "I'm not yanking our political reporter off a political story. That's not fair to Paul. Your beat is crime, Burton, you know that. Despite what some may think, this story with Senator Rodriquez is not crime."

She let out a heavy sigh, frustrated. Finally, she placed her hands on her thighs and pushed up to her feet. "All right, Everett. You win. Maybe CNN will let me do the story," she said with a grin before opening the door and leaving the office.

≈≈≈≈

"Hello, hello, hello!" Burton called out, entering the Eggleston residence, which was a comfortable thirty-year-old house in Littleton, Colorado, about twenty minutes outside of downtown Denver.

"In the kitchen, hon!" Theresa Eggleston called out.

Burton shrugged out of her jacket and hung it along with her purse in the guest closet before making her way through the living room into the kitchen. "Smells amazing," she said, looking around. The counters were covered with fresh vegetables that needed to be chopped, a plate of raw hamburger patties, and various other things to go with dinner.

Roger's wife of thirty-four years stood at the stove stirring a huge pot of baked beans. "Hey, hon. Glad you're here," Therese said, sending a kind smile over her shoulder to Burton. "Give me just a second."

"Sure, no problem. What can I do to help?" Burton asked, walking farther into the kitchen.

"Well, first you can give me a hug," Theresa said. "Then you can cut up the veggies for the salad. Roger is getting the grill ready for the burgers."

"Only Roger would barbecue on a cold April afternoon," Burton said with a chuckle, walking toward the older black woman who she deeply respected and admired. She gave her a one-armed hug, as Theresa had to continue stirring her homemade baked beans.

"Congratulations," she said, leaving a peck on Burton's cheek. "I'm so proud of you, though I have to say, we're going to miss you something awful. Can't you work for them from Denver?"

Burton grinned, making her way over to the vegetables as she grabbed the cutting board from the cabinet near the sink. "It doesn't work that way, though I wish you guys would move to New York with me."

Theresa laughed. "Can you imagine Roger in downtown Manhattan?"

"In a flannel," Burton added, both women laughing at the image and idea.

"You'll just have to come back here to visit us, honey. We can't do Christmas without you." They worked in companionable silence for a moment until Theresa spoke again. "Does Tim know?"

Burton let out a small sigh. "I haven't spoken to Tim in months."

"I still hold out hope you two will find your way back to each other," Theresa said, placing the lid on the pot of beans and holding the mixing spoon out to Burton, a bit of the baked beans on the end. "Tell me what you think."

Burton took the spoon from her and blew on the hot mixture before taking a taste. Immediately her eyes closed in pleasure as the explosion of flavors filled her mouth. "So good," she said, handing the spoon back to Theresa, who rinsed it off before adding it to the pile of dishes she needed to wash. "I know you really liked him," she said, continuing their conversation, "but, there just wasn't anything there anymore." She shrugged. "He was a good guy, but I just wasn't in love. Not like I've always hoped I would be." She met Theresa's gaze. "Like you and Roger. That connection you two have. That's what I want, and I knew it wasn't going to happen with Tim."

"What are you going to do in that huge city all by yourself?" Theresa asked.

Glad the subject had been changed from her ex-boyfriend, Burton answered, "Work my butt off and win a Pulitzer."

Eyes twinkling, the two women burst into laughter.

≈≈≈≈

Burton pulled her red 2009 Jeep Wrangler Unlimited, her baby outside of Cricket, into the parking space assigned to her at her apartment complex. She killed the ignition and grabbed her purse. She had absolutely nothing planned for Sunday and couldn't wait to do nothing other than work out.

Locking her Jeep, she walked up the path to the stairway that led to her third-floor apartment. Once she mounted the final few stairs to her floor, a short breezeway led to her apartment at the back of the building.

She sorted through the various keys on her key chain until she found her house key. She inserted it into the dead bolt when suddenly someone grabbed her from behind. A large body pressed behind her and a bruising hand covered her mouth. She tried to fight against it, but the grip was like iron.

Whimpering in absolute terror while completely pinned against the person who held her, with no way of getting free, she held still. She felt hot breath near her ear as words were whispered.

"You listen and you listen good," he said, an accent that she couldn't place tinging his words. "You get in the way, you die. Understand me?"

Before she could even respond, she was grabbed by the hair and her head was drawn back just before her forehead was slammed into her front door. All went black.

❧❧❧❧

"Is there anything else you can remember?" the policeman asked gently.

Burton, who sat on her couch with Cricket tucked in her lap and a bandage on her forehead administered by the EMT, shook her head. "No. What I told you, that's all I remember."

"Can you think of anyone who would want to hurt you, Miss Blinde? Boyfriend, perhaps someone you've covered on the news?"

She shook her head and trembled. Her head

throbbed. "I'm not working on any controversial cases or anything." She glanced up when there was a knock at the door. The partner of the interviewing officer opened it. Burton was beyond relieved when she saw Simone. She set Cricket down on the couch and hurried over to her friend. She'd called her once she'd come to while waiting for the police.

"Hey," Simone said, pulling her into a tight hug. "What happened?" She examined Burton's face, her own wincing in sympathy at the huge bruise on Burton's forehead. "I should have something that can cover that."

Burton returned to her place on the couch, Cricket jumping down and disappearing into the kitchen. Simone sat down next to her and grasped her hand with both of hers, holding it in her lap.

"Sorry," Burton said to the officer. "This is my friend, Simone. She works down at the station, too."

"Can you think of anyone who would want to hurt or threaten your friend?" he asked the makeup artist.

Simone shook her head. "Nobody."

"All right." The officer closed his notebook and stood. "If you remember anything else, Miss Blinde, or anything else happens, give us a call."

"Thank you."

"We'll see ourselves out," he said and grabbed his hat before the two men left the apartment.

Simone jumped off the couch and locked the door behind them. "That is some crazy shit," she said, returning to the couch. She sat so she could face Burton, her knees touching the side of Burton's thigh. "Are you okay? What happened?" She reached up a hand and brushed some dark hair away from Burton's face.

"He came from out of nowhere. Scared the hell out of me," Burton said, letting out a shaky breath. "Maybe he had the wrong person. You know how dark it is in that breezeway."

"I know. You really need to get on the landlord to get those fixed. This was bad, but it could have been really, really bad."

"I know," Burton sighed, running a hand through her hair and wincing, as even that made her head hurt worse."

She felt the sting of tears as everything began to sink in. Her face crumbled as the sobs came hard and quick.

"Come here," Simone murmured, holding her and rocking her gently as she ran soothing circles over Burton's back.

Three and a half hours later, Burton's eyes flew open, her heart racing and head pounding. She lifted her head from her pillow, her eyes as big as saucers. She realized she wasn't alone, and for a second, swore he'd come back, but this time he had gotten inside. Turning to her left, she was relieved to see Simone sleeping soundly wearing a borrowed T-shirt.

Sitting up in bed, Burton looked around her bedroom, noting that everything seemed just fine, including a sleepy Cricket eyeing her from the foot of the bed. She took a deep breath and decided to get up. Her alarm clock read almost four-thirty, and it was a dark and chilly morning.

Padding through the apartment in a pair of sweatpants and an oversized T-shirt, she headed to the kitchen, feeling restless and anxious. She thought that perhaps if she made some hot Sleepytime tea, it could help her calm down enough to go back to sleep.

After having such a wonderful time with Roger and Theresa, she'd been excited to return home for a relaxing evening with Cricket and to catch up on some of her shows. The last thing she expected was to be attacked by a stranger and threatened. She could still smell his breath and feel its wet hotness on her ear and the side of her face.

Bracing her hands on the counter as she leaned against it, her eyes squeezed shut, she felt that terror grip her again. She felt short of breath, her breasts heaving so harshly she thought she'd hyperventilate. She tried desperately to calm herself down, taking in cleansing breaths.

In that moment, she felt utterly alone. She wished so badly that she had someone special in her life she could give her full trust to but figured that was not possible. She'd been told by more than one ex that she had abandonment issues, and those caused her to keep everyone at arm's length. She knew they were right. In truth, it was only Roger and his family and Simone, to an extent, who had ever truly been able to reach her.

Pushing away such morose thoughts, she gathered what she'd need to make her tea, smiling when she felt Cricket weave between her ankles before heading off for an early morning snack.

She walked over to the breakfast bar where her laptop sat and powered it on. She tapped the bar top as she waited then headed back to the stove when her tea kettle began to whistle, steam flowing out of the spout. She poured some into her mug and dipped the tea bag in, watching the absent motion of her hand.

Wanting to get her mind off the events of the night, she took her mind where she always did when she wanted to find peace: work. She thought once again about the good senator, who had been in office for more than a decade and was popular in Democratic politics with his handsome looks and notorious flirtations with the press. The only problem was, there was a nasty little rumor floating around for nearly a year that he'd had a long-term affair with a male intern, and now that man was looking to cash in.

She had to smile at her own thoughts as she squeezed in some honey when she considered asking Paul if he'd bring her with him as his guest to the fundraising dinner Wednesday night. Something, however, did occur to her. She had an interview with the District Attorney regarding some parole hearings that were to take place that same day. Maybe she and Roger could just do a wee bit of overtime and see if they could catch Senator Rodriguez either entering or leaving the event, a complete coincidence, of course.

She sipped her tea as she walked over to the breakfast bar, taking a seat on one of the stools as she logged into her work e-mail. She read a couple, deleted a couple more. One caught her eye and she clicked on it. The subject line was: *Do the right thing*. Upon clicking on the e-mail, the return address had been blocked. There was a simple message in the body of the e-mail: *We all have a destiny in life. Yours is to bring light to the truth.*

She was baffled. It made no sense and seemed pretty much like nonsense, so she deleted it.

"What are you doing?" Simone asked, yawning as she padded into the room, her fingers running through her hair to put it in some semblance of order.

"Did I wake you?" Burton asked, reaching for her mug to take a sip.

"I had to pee and saw the light on in here. How are you feeling? Did you sleep at all?" She walked up behind Burton and wrapped her arms around a trim waist.

Sometimes it bothered Burton how affectionate Simone insisted on being with her, but she knew it was just her way, so she allowed it. She patted Simone's hands before gingerly moving out of her embrace as she stood. "I did, for a few hours, I think. My head hurts, but I'll live. Want some tea?" she asked, refilling the kettle under the faucet.

"No, it'll keep me awake." Simone let out a loud yawn. "God, it's already nearly quarter after five. "

"I know. I'm sorry I've ruined your weekend, Simone. I never wanted any of this to happen," Burton said, brushing her fingertips across the deep bruise on her forehead.

"Not your fault, sweet pea. Listen, I think I'm going to head home," Simone said, walking toward Burton. She rubbed her hands up and down her arms a few times. "Is that okay? I have a photo shoot I have to do makeup for tonight, and I want to be able to fully crash."

"No, that's fine." Out of character, but her gratitude overrode her norm, she initiated a tight hug, which her friend immediately returned. They held each other for a long moment. "Thank you for everything, Simone. It means the world to me that you were here."

"Of course! I'm here for you anytime, you know that."

"I do," Burton said, surprised by the lingering kiss Simone left on her lips. Her surprise left her frozen, and when Simone leaned in for a second kiss, her surprise grew as she felt herself responding.

The events of the past six hours had left her in such a state of shock and trauma that now she found herself standing in her kitchen making out with her best friend. She couldn't wrap her mind around her own actions even as she felt Simone deepen the kiss and bury one of her hands in Burton's hair. Burton's hands remained on the makeup artist's upper arms, but what brought her back to reality was when she felt one of Simone's hands cup her left breast.

"Wait," she said, chest heaving from her increased breathing. She took a step back and several deep breaths. "Wait."

"I'm sorry, Burt. Really," Simone said, seeming to be quite nervous as she reached up a slightly trembling hand to tuck her hair behind her ear.

"It's okay, don't be sorry. I just...I just can't," she said, hoping that somehow her friend could understand. If she were ever to be with a woman, it would likely be Simone, but she just didn't see that in her future. More often than not she felt her destiny was to be alone and have only her work for companionship.

"Well, I'm going to go," Simone said, entering the living room to grab her purse and keys. She'd already changed back into her own clothes from the night before. Burton followed. "If you need me today, don't hesitate. You're welcome to go to the photo shoot with me, see a couple gorgeous, yet utterly shallow people at work."

Burton returned the smile she was given. "Nah, that's okay. I see enough shallow people at work every day."

"This is true, me among them." She leaned over and, as she often did, left a quick peck on Burton's cheek before she left.

Alone, Burton looked around her apartment, hands on her hips. Though tired, she didn't feel comfortable going back to sleep while the world beyond her windows was still dark. She decided to catch up on those shows she'd wanted to watch the night before until she fell asleep. Besides, she needed a distraction to keep her from thinking about what had just happened.

Chapter Four

"Listen, Burt," Everett said gently, "I absolutely cannot allow you to head back out there after this." He leaned forward in his seat, glasses pushed atop his head. "You got your offer this morning and accepted it. We got the offer for your contract and have accepted it. Honey"—he reached across the desk and took her hands in his—"why don't you take this time, two whole weeks, to get your life in order here in Denver. It's a big move ahead of you, lots to do…"

"I can't just walk out on my job because of some lunatic, Everett." Burton shook her head as she pulled her hands out of his. "No. I have two weeks left and I refuse to leave everyone here hanging."

"Roger announced at the meeting this morning that he's going to retire. I can get Jane and Troy to cover your beat—"

"No, damn it!" she exclaimed, pushing to her feet and pacing in the small space in front of the editor's desk. "I'm not going to let that 'lunatic,' as you call him, determine how I end my time at KNWZ. I won't and I can't."

Everett sighed, removing his glasses from his head and tossing them on the desk. "Fine. You have the parole story you're working on with your interview with DA Sparks Wednesday. How about after that you work on putting together a good-bye story for yourself? I can't put you on another story after Sparks because there will likely not be time for you to complete it. Deal?"

Burton brought her hand up and placed it on a flat stomach as she headed back to her chair and sat down. "Okay," she said, nodding. "Deal."

※ ※ ※ ※

"All right, I think that went really well," Burton said, glancing over at Roger from the passenger seat of the station van. "Sparks was totally on and charming and gave some excellent answers. I think this will make a great story. I'm excited to put the package together tonight."

"I agree," Roger said with a nod, slowing the van as they neared a red traffic light. "You did really good, Burt. You should be proud of your final story with KNWZ." His smile to her was all proud and paternal.

"Eh, you helped, old man," she said with a chuckle, touched by his words of praise.

As they drove, she noticed the time on the van's dashboard and realized they weren't far from the convention center where the fundraiser was going to be held. Something in her gut was begging her to go rogue and follow this story to the end.

"Hey, Rog?" she said, her voice sweet.

"You know, I really hate it when you use that tone with me," he said, shaking his head. "Just like Justine when she was a kid."

"Well, your daughter is as sweet as I am, so..." She sent a disarming smile his way. "You know we're awful close to the convention center and it's almost eight-thirty..."

He glanced at her, heavy eyebrows drawn. "You're serious? Haven't you seen enough trouble for a while?" he asked, reaching over to place a gentle thumb on her bruised forehead to take the sting out of his words. "It's late. We've had a long day. Let's just go back to the station, get this packaged up and—"

"Roger, you know how badly I want this story. I'm not going to get another chance. With CNN, I'm going to be based in New York, not DC. I won't see Rodriguez again, likely."

"Why are you so determined to nab this fish, huh?" he asked, moving the van forward again once the light turned green.

"Because that's what I do," she said simply, the strange and random e-mail from the other night coming back to her. "I'm a truth seeker." She smiled at his look of disbelief but did a little cheer in her seat as he turned the van in the right direction for the convention center.

※※※※

"I'm telling you, next time we need to see if we can grab the leftovers," Roger muttered from where he'd been sitting behind the wheel for forty-five minutes, his left elbow resting on the van door arm, his fingers brushing over his lips absently.

Burton chuckled, her head leaning against the headrest. "I can text Paul and see if he'll bring us some hors d'oeuvres." She grabbed her messenger bag from the floor by her feet. "Let me see what I have in here." She dug through it, finding an unopened Snickers bar. "You really should eat one, Rog," she said, her eyes squinting with mischief. "You're just not yourself when you're hungry."

Bursting into laughter, Roger snatched the candy bar from her hand and ripped open the wrapper. "I like the old slogan better: 'Snickers really satisfies you.'"

"Yes, well you're old, so you remember those."

"You know, considering I'm doing you a favor

stalking this senator, you're being a little brat," he said around a mouthful of chocolate, caramel, and nuts.

Smiling, she turned her attention away from her coworker and back to the lit confines of the parking garage before them. It had been a long night and she was tired and definitely ready to go home. Even still, she was absolutely determined to get her fish on the line before calling it a day, no matter what. That dogged tenacity is what had gotten her where she was.

"Paul said he should be leaving the dinner around nine-thirty," she said, leaning forward in the passenger seat to try to get a better look at the bank of elevators where the Democratic politician would likely exit in order to meet his waiting limousine.

"You do realize we've already had a fourteen-hour day, right?" Roger murmured, his head back against the headrest and eyes closed, the crumpled candy wrapper stuffed into the cup holder in the console between them.

Burton took in her friend's grizzled face, barely visible in the dim cab of the van. "Come on, Rog. Just a little longer?" She batted her big, pretty eyes at him, knowing full well it got him every time. "Pretty please?"

Like clockwork, he shook his head and began to whistle his ever-present little tune between his teeth, a sure sign he was irritated.

"You know you want to stay," Burton whined.

"Burton," he whined back, "I wanna go home. Theresa made salmon for me."

"Oh," Burton nearly drooled. "The baked salmon?"

"The very one."

"Damn. Love that stuff." She barely got the words out when she saw movement. "Oh! Here we go."

Out of the van like a shot, the clicking of her high heels echoed across the cement of the parking garage as she hurried to the elevator the senator had just exited, his driver beside him.

"Senator Rodriguez!"

The married forty-three-year-old turned at the sound of her voice. Dark eyes sparkled when he saw her. "Miss Blinde," he said, his deep voice rich, even as he once again insisted on accenting her last name so it sounded like blenda, rather than blind. "I thought you would've been at the dinner. Imagine my disappointment when I saw Paul instead. I've already answered his questions. The press conference was an hour ago."

"Yes, well, it turns out I'm not assigned to cover politics anymore, Senator," she teased, walking alongside him, the driver walking ahead to get the black stretch ready for its occupant.

The politician chuckled, bringing well-manicured hands up to adjust the gray London Fog he wore over a black striped Armani suit with red tie. He definitely cut a handsome and powerful profile.

"That would explain why I've missed the pleasure of your company, Miss Blinde."

"I'm here now," Burton said, turning on the charm to hopefully take the sting out of what she was about to say. It certainly got his attention, as he stopped in his tracks. "I want to talk to you about Ron Golderman."

Twinkling Spanish eyes turned hard and predatory. "I think you should be careful, Burton," he said, voice dropping. "You may have stopped covering politics, but be careful. You can still be eaten alive."

Burton's much shorter legs had to hurry to keep up with the Democrat's long strides. "Senator," she called after him, barely catching him before he climbed inside the long black car, his driver holding the back passenger door open for him. "Senator," she said again, nearly falling as one of her heels caught in a crack in the cement. She teetered but stayed upright. "Tim, you know the story is going to get out."

He glared down at her, one hand resting on the frame of the door, the other atop the roof. "I don't know what you're talking about. There is no 'story.'"

"You and I both know that's not true." She also placed her hand on the doorframe, but more to stop him from closing it than anything else. "You know I'll do it, right?"

He studied her for a long moment with hard eyes. "Why?"

"Off the record?" she asked, quirking a small smile, which he responded to with a ghost of one of his own.

"Off the record."

"Because I think you can win Minority Leader from Reed, that's why. I think you've got the backing and I think you have some damn good ideas," she said, speaking the truth as she saw it. "But, if Golderman gets his side out before you do, you're finished. You will never survive a gay scandal, even with Obama in the White House and you know it."

The senator let out a heavy sigh and looked around the parking garage. He glanced at his Rolex. "Get in. You have as long as it takes to get me to the hotel and that's it."

"Okay." Burton let out a relieved breath and wide smile. "Let me just get my guy—" she began to turn toward the direction of Roger and the van.

"No cameras," Rodriguez said, grabbing her wrist in a light grip. She met his gaze. "Just you."

"Okay. Just me." She gently pulled her wrist out of his grasp. "Let me tell Roger." Burton hurried as fast as she dared back to the van, Roger rolling the driver's side window down as she neared. "We're in," she said softly so the senator wouldn't hear.

"Is he going to sit down with us?"

"Yes and no."

"Yes and no?"

"He agreed to sit down with me," Burton said, knowing what was coming.

"No way, Burton," Roger said, shaking his grayed head. "I'm going, too."

"He won't let you, Roger. I'll be fine."

"That guy is a snake!" Roger hissed, blue eyes darting to where the politician was stepping into the car. "He's had how many complaints of inappropriate behavior with female journalists, huh?"

Burton smirked. "Somehow I don't think I'm exactly his type, Rog."

The older man rolled his eyes. "You don't actually believe that nonsense, do you?"

"Yeah, actually I do. I smell something here, Roger. I'm not walking away from this." She reached up and covered his hand, which rested on the opened frame for the window. "Go home, Roger. Okay? Go get your salmon dinner. I'll be fine."

He let out a heavy sigh, glancing toward the limousine with drawn eyebrows. Slowly shaking his head, he returned his gaze to her. "I don't think I should leave you alone. How are you going to get back to the station?"

"Don't worry about it. I'll call a cab or something." She leaned in and left a quick peck on his unshaven cheek before taking her purse, which Roger handed her through the open window.

"I'll follow to make sure you get there," the cameraman growled, before quickly rolling up the window to stop any arguments.

"Thanks, Dad," Burton sighed, shouldering her

purse as she turned to head back to the sleek car, the driver opening the door for her.

The interior of the car was as elegant as the outside, with leather upholstery and any and everything the taxpayer could provide. Timothy Rodriguez was on his phone when she slid onto the warmed seat. He ended the call as the door was closed behind the reporter and tucked the device into the inside pocket of his suit jacket.

"So," he said, resting his hand on one of his thighs. "You've got me here, what will you do with me?"

Burton ignored the innuendo in his tone, not worried about this guy for a second. She didn't have a lot of time and wasn't going to waste any on games. "So, no cameras," she began, knowing she had one shot at this.

"No cameras."

He hadn't said a thing about recorders, so she figured the little one in her pocket that she'd hit the record button on before getting in the car wasn't against the rules.

"Okay," she said, turning in her seat so she was sitting three-quarters toward him, looking him in the eye, skirt pulled taut just above her knees, revealing shapely calves. "Ron says the two of you allegedly had relations during your senatorial reelection campaign run in 2006. He says he was organizing more than just your daily schedule."

The muscles in Rodriguez's jaw began to pulse as he looked away from her, the car beginning to move. A quick glance out the window showed Burton that, sure enough, Roger was following in the van. She returned her focus to the senator, not wanting to miss a single expression or clue in his body language.

"I can't believe he's opened this can of worms," he murmured, seeming to be speaking more to himself than to Burton. Clearing his throat, he met her penetrating gaze. "It's true," he said flatly. "It's true and it was stupid and trust me, there isn't a day I don't regret it."

The car came to a sudden halt, throwing its two occupants a bit. Rodriguez glared up the long way to the front seat.

"Are you trying to give me and the lady whiplash back here?" His booming voice easily carried the distance to the driver.

"Sorry, Senator Rodriguez," the man behind the wheel said, looking back at them through the rearview mirror. "Some guy just ran out in front of the car. I had to hit the brakes."

"Well, get the fucking thing moving again! I have somewhere I have to be." The veins in his neck were bulging a bit as he reached up to straighten his tie.

"How long did it last?" Burton asked, noting the car had begun to lurch forward again. She shut it out and focused on her quarry. "Is he the only man you've been with?"

"It lasted for about six months, give or take. Manuella has no idea," he added, meaning his wife of thirteen years.

"And, before Ron?" Burton asked carefully.

"That's not relevant here, Miss Blinde."

"Does Ron know of anyone else? You know that's going to come out in the wash, too, Tim."

His mouth opened as though to respond when he looked past her through the window behind Burton. "What did that guy just throw?"

There was a loud thump on the car door then suddenly an ear-splitting explosion rent the underground garage, ripping the car to shreds like a tin can, sending bodies, car parts, and cement chips flying. The last thing Burton knew, her head was slamming into a thick, cement column. She heard a crack then nothing.

※※※※

"My God." EMT, Cheryl Compton glanced over at her partner as they did all they could to stabilize their patient before loading them into the ambulance for transport to St. Luke's Medical Center.

The blood and gore of the scene were of nightmarish proportions. The area was filled with police, FBI, the bomb squad, architects to ensure the integrity of the structure, and EMTs trying to save the life of the one person who was still alive, though barely.

The siren of the ambulance screamed through the night, the team inside fighting to bring their victim back to life after a flatline.

"Come on," Cheryl yelled, administering CPR for a second time.

"We've got signs," her partner Dave said, glancing up at the screen of the monitor for vital signs. "We're almost there."

※※※※

Back at the scene, the FBI agent in charge stood with the head of the bomb squad. "Car bomb?" he asked.

"Nah, I think it was a grenade."

He looked at him with surprise. "Grenade? Where on earth would someone get a grenade?"

"Black market, former military. But, from the destruction pattern and what was left behind, I'd put money on it. From what was left, looks like an M26. I haven't seen one of those in thirty years. Used during Korea and Vietnam. Known as the 'lemon grenade' because of its shape. Interesting."

The FBI agent whistled through his teeth. "All right. We'll start looking in that direction, then." He tucked his hands in the pockets of his trousers. "How many dead?"

"Right now, looks like three dead, the fourth en route to St. Luke's."

He ran a hand through his hair. "What a goddamn mess. We'll have to get someone on the phone to Washington."

Chapter Five

"As you can see, the procession has begun winding its way into the cemetery, Senator Rodriguez's body carried in the black hearse there, followed by President Obama's limousine," the CNN reporter commented. "A large gathering here at Arlington. The senator, of course, was a former Marine, having fought in Desert Storm before retiring in 2002.

"We showed you images of the very touching funeral yesterday for Roger Eggleston, the cameraman of local station, KNWZ, who was also caught in the car explosion that took the life of the senator and his driver, Edward Bardoon and critically wounded reporter, Burton Blinde, who was just about to begin her tenure here in New York with CNN.

"Later today, after the televised funeral, we'll be discussing—"

Everett Timpton set the television remote down on the roller table that could extend over the bed. He gazed down at the figure lying there, the wrappings covering so much of her body that little was left bare. He focused on the one eye that wasn't covered, long lashes resting on the deeply bruised cheek. It hadn't opened, nor even fluttered since he'd arrived.

"Don't think we need to see any more of that," he said softly, lowering his tall frame into the one chair next to the bed. He rested his hands in his lap and looked over at the woman he'd just spoken to about her final assignment a week before. He scanned over the petite frame, made bulky and shapeless from the protective wrappings. The true extent of her injuries had yet to be fully assessed as doctors said the burns needed to heal more before anything permanent could be declared.

The level of guilt he felt had kept him up nights and in tears since he'd received the horrifying news by the station's GM. Though he'd told her in no uncertain terms that she was absolutely *not* to pursue the Rodriguez scandal, he knew her better than that. In the six years she'd worked for him, he had learned all too well how stubborn and tenacious she could be.

He wasn't sure what he could have done differently, but he felt it was solely in his hands that one of his people was dead, and the other lay in the bed next to him, fighting for her life every day.

He let out a heavy sigh. "I spoke to Jan Austin today," he continued, speaking of the head of HR. Though his silent companion was asleep, he felt the need to break the silence with words for fear he would with tears. "She said all your medical costs will be picked up, so no worries there." He picked at a tiny piece of lint on his pant leg, not entirely sure what to do with himself. "Oh!" he said, perking up. "Not sure if they told you, but the president himself called a few days ago. You were kind of out of it, but he did. Yup, he sure did." He glanced over at her. "I have to admit, Barack has a sexy voice." He smiled, knowing that Burton would have been amused by that.

Everett wasn't entirely sure what to say next. He was never a man who lacked things to talk about, but he almost felt like he was sitting in a room with a dead body. He wasn't sure what to feel, besides guilt, and they knew so little about her chance of beating this, it was difficult to be hopeful.

Ran into Simone when I came in." He checked to see if there was a reaction. Everyone knew how close the two women were, some even wondering if it extended beyond friendship. "Yeah, she said she'd been here for an hour or so before work. Not sure if you were awake." He studied what was visible of her face and the mass of bandaging over her body. "Oh, sweetie," he whispered, feeling the stinging behind his eyes as his emotion rose yet again.

Pushing to his feet, he grabbed a tissue from the box on the moveable table and dabbed at the tears that managed to escape.

"It's going to be okay, sweetie," he whispered with a nod, more to convince himself than the sleeping woman before him. He smiled down at her. "I'll leave you alone for now but will be back tomorrow, okay?"

With a very light squeeze to her shoulder, Everett gathered his peacoat and folded it over his arm. Taking one last look over his shoulder at the still figure, he left the room, wiping his eyes as he entered the hall and walked away.

Her high heels clicked on the linoleum floor as she made her way from pediatrics to ICU. Her hands were tucked in the deep pockets of her lab coat, a name tag pinned to it that read Dr. Lilli Lange. She brought a hand up to tuck jaw-length blond hair behind her ear before pressing the elevator button to head to her desired floor.

Once there, she exited the elevator and clicked her way to a specific room, a room she'd visited every day for the past week. She pushed open the heavy, hydraulic-hinged door, which slowly closed behind her. The room was dim, television off. The figure lying on the bed was still, heavily bandaged.

Walking over to the bed, she reached out a hand, using the gentlest of fingertips to touch the small bit of exposed skin on the patient's face. She said nothing as she leaned down and placed the softest of kisses upon her bandaged forehead.

"I'm sorry," she whispered.

As quickly as she'd come, she left the room.

❧❧❧❧

Burton felt herself beginning to come somewhat to the surface, the painkillers easing through her system via drip keeping her drowsy most of the time. She was just cognizant enough to hear footfalls walk away from her bed, though she had no idea whom they belonged to. She heard a door open then slowly close. What seemed in her pickled brain was hours later, she heard the door open once more.

Though it sounded muffled and far away, she could hear someone enter, the click-clack of high heels. A moment later, a cool touch brushed across her cheek before even softer lips pressed briefly against her forehead. She could smell the most wonderful perfume, a floral scent with a slightly musky undertone. It was feminine yet exotic.

That soothing scent and touch sent Burton back into blissful sleep. Before the darkness once again consumed her, she heard the whispered words.

"I'm sorry."

❧❧❧❧

The air hung heavily between them, Simone's words almost physically hovering in the air, as though stuck in a dialogue bubble floating over their heads. Burton lay in the hospital bed, Simone's hand cradling her own. Her mind was still fuzzy from all the medications they had her on, though they'd stopped the morphine. Despite everything, she could still feel emotion somewhere deep in her soul. Her heart was broken by the news Simone had so delicately given her. After being essentially taken from her three-day medically induced coma to get her brain swelling down, she'd been highly sedated to help her body heal and to keep the pain of her burns at bay.

It had only been three days since she'd been allowed to gain full consciousness, and from what she'd been told, thirteen days since the explosion. She had no memory of it, but doctors warned her that bits and pieces—if not the entire thing—may come back over time. Today, Simone had arrived as she did every day, but said it was time Burton knew the whole of it.

"What are you thinking, honey?" Simone asked gently, unwittingly bringing Burton's fuzzy thoughts back to the present.

Burton stared past her friend to the window behind her. It was a sunny day out, from what she could see. What was she thinking, indeed? Tears stung behind her eyes, now both uncovered, though bandages remained over much of the left side of her body, her left leg with the worse injuries.

"It's my fault," she whispered. "Because of me, Roger is dead."

"Oh, sweetheart," Simone whispered, leaning forward in her chair. She caressed the back of Burton's hand with her thumb. "No. You didn't do this."

"Yes, I did," Burton insisted, tears falling freely now. She knew she wasn't feeling the full brunt of her heartbreak and anguish simply because of the medications they had her on. She dreaded later on when it would hit her fully. She glanced at her friend. "I made him go there, Simone. He didn't want to." She turned away, sniffling. "He wanted a baked salmon dinner," she whispered. That was the last thing she remembered, that snippet of conversation with him.

"Baby," Simone murmured, standing and leaning over Burton to hug her, cradling her head against her chest. "I'm so sorry."

"Theresa must hate me," Burton whispered, allowing Simone to hold her. "God, she must absolutely hate me."

"No," Simone assured her, running her fingers carefully through Burton's hair, now short and ragged. Half of it had been singed off, so the nurses had cut the remainder to even it out. "She's been here to see you. Spent a lot of time with you, actually."

"Really?" Burton asked, almost afraid to believe those words.

As if a message from the angels, Simone's phone chirped to life to denote an incoming text message. Simone grabbed the phone from where it sat on the sliding table. She brought the phone in front of Burton.

From Theresa:
How's Burt? Tell her we love her.

Burton burst into fresh tears, holding on to Simone, her relief and grief coming out all at once. After a long moment, she suddenly felt utterly exhausted and wanted nothing more than to give in to the sleep that beckoned her.

Pulling away from Simone, she lay her head back down on the pillow, her eyes heavy from exhaustion as well as the many tears she'd just shed. "I'm so tired," she said, meeting Simone's gaze.

"Okay, I'll leave you alone to rest." The makeup

artist brushed some strands of dark hair off Burton's forehead. "It's a trip seeing you with such short hair," she said quietly. "You look like a cute little androgynous lesbian."

Burton gave her a ghost of a smile, all she could manage as she began to doze, drifting into the peaceful darkness. "You're determined to bring me over to the dark side," she murmured as sleep overcame her.

༄ ༄ ༅ ༅

Burton squeezed her eyes shut, her chest heaving and body covered with sweat as she did her best to push against the physical therapist's hand with her left foot.

"Come on, Burton," he urged. "Come on, baby. You're almost there, almost…"

Burton yelled out in exertion, her leg nearly straight against the padded bench on which she lay. Her body fell limp, a whimper escaping her lips in frustration and pain.

"You did good, Burt. You did real, real, good." Keith, her physical therapist, patted her leg affectionately as he sat on the padded bench next to hers. "How you feeling, Boss?"

"Like I want to hit you," she managed between heavy breaths.

The black man chuckled. "I'd welcome that. We're done for the day, champ. You outdid yourself. By far, you made more progress than Monday." He pushed to his feet, reaching a hand down to help her sit up, which she did. "I want you to keep working on those stretches and exercises I showed you, get that leg strengthened. Friday we'll get you up and walking on the treadmill again."

"Oh God," she breathed, eyes closed in dread.

Finally, she let out a heavy breath and nodded as she opened her eyes. "Okay. Thanks, Keith." She reached up and slapped the hand he held out for her, high-five style. "Thank you."

Left alone in the hospital's gym, Burton reached for her cane, using it to help her stand. Wincing in pain as she did, she managed to make it to her wheelchair and lowered herself into its trusty seat, placing the cane across her lap. With her hands on the rims of her wheelchair tires, she turned the chair around to head to the elevators and back to her room.

She'd now been in the hospital for twenty-one days and was definitely ready to go home. The burns on her left leg had long passed; the fear of infection had lessened and skin grafts had taken well. Now, after two surgeries—with many more to come—she was left with awful scarring, though she was told plastic surgery in the future would be able to minimize it to a point. The scarring on her left arm wasn't as bad, just a patch of it on her shoulder. Needless to say, her days of wearing tank tops or strapless dresses were over.

At this point, she was just glad to get out of ICU and into her own private room. Once there, she wheeled herself to the bed, the heavy room door sliding shut behind her. She glanced at the bedside table and just as it had happened a few times before, she saw a vase of fresh flowers, always a mixed bouquet and always absolutely exquisite.

She locked the wheels of her wheelchair, eyes never leaving the fresh blossoms as she took the handle of her cane in her right hand and, with a grunt, slowly got to her feet, waiting until she felt solid before she slowly made her way over to them.

She'd asked Theresa and Simone—even Everett. Everyone denied they were the secret deliverer of the random bouquets, which never had a card attached. This time, however, they did. Surprised, she plucked the small white envelope out of the clear plastic trident that held it and made her way over to the bed, taking it slow as she lowered her body to sit, tucking her bottom lip in concentration to master the simple move.

Seated safely, she leaned the cane against her right leg then opened the envelope and pulled out the card, which was blank, save for the message written in beautiful, sprawling penmanship inside:

I'm so pleased you're healing nicely. Please take care and never give up on your passion.

It was not signed.

She examined the flowers again, eyebrows drawn. Her thoughts were interrupted by the knock on her room door.

"Come in," she called, setting the note on the table next to the flowers.

The door opened and her doctor entered. "Good morning, Burton," he said, stepping into the room. "How did PT go today?"

"I think Keith Princeton should be tortured slowly," she said with a bright smile.

Dr. Bernard Heaton chuckled. "I wouldn't expect any other answer. Let's get a good look at you, okay?"

The door opened and the doctor entered with a female nurse who stood silently by. Burton endured his examination. Though he was very gentle and sensitive with her, it was embarrassing and she was over it. He explained to her what he was seeing, how she was healing, and what he thought of her progress. Her injuries had been substantial, with a skull fracture, second- and third-degree burns over 15 percent of her body, all on the left side, with minor burns to her face. She'd received four broken ribs, two broken fingers, and a bruised heart. In short, she was a mess and lucky to be alive.

Every day she thought about the other three men who had died, especially Roger, always Roger. She swore she'd seen him in her dreams, but she figured it was just guilt and missing him. She'd only seen Theresa once, and it had been awkward, no doubt most of that coming from Burton herself. She had no idea what to say to her, no idea how to apologize, no matter how much everyone kept saying she didn't need to, that it hadn't been her fault.

She'd been given very little information on the investigation that had taken place and couldn't get up the courage to turn on the news. She hadn't asked Simone any questions, though she sensed her friend was willing but was waiting for Burton to make the first move.

"Does that sound good?"

Burton was shaken out of her thoughts, realizing the doctor had stood from where he'd been kneeling in front of her, his hands in the pockets of his white lab coat. "What? I'm sorry," she said, shaking her head to clear it. "What did you say?"

"I said, everything looks fantastic and, other than you continuing your PT, I'm ready to clear you to go home."

※ ※ ※ ※

Burton could feel Simone's eyes on her as together they packed up her hospital room. After nearly a month's stay, she had many books, clothes, and gifts from visitors to gather and stuff into duffel bags that her friend had brought. She went about her task with an empty heart and even emptier soul. Something had been badly broken inside, far more than her body had been broken. She checked herself in the mirror and no longer saw what she'd seen for nearly twenty-nine years. Yes, other than shorter hair and a few mild scars, she still looked like the same woman, but her eyes told a very different story.

"Burt?" Simone said. "Burt?"

"What?" Burton snapped, irritated at being bothered.

Simone stared at her with wide eyes. "Uh, what do you want done with these?" she asked, holding up the vase of flowers that Burton had found after her PT two days before.

"Oh," Burton said, feeling contrite. "Um, I guess we can take them with us. They've still got a week or so before they should be tossed."

Simone nodded, eyeing her friend before turning away, moving the flowers to the mobile table. "So," she said conversationally, "when do you start the new job? I'm assuming they've given you a later start date with all that's happened—"

"I'm not," Burton interrupted, her own voice flat.

"What?" Simone walked over to her, placing a hand on her arm. "Burt, that was your dream job!"

"And I can't do it anymore!" Burton raged, pulling her arm out of her friend's grasp. "How the hell can I go out on the streets and do stories and interviews when just the other day I knocked down an entire fucking medicine cart after someone dropped something at the nurse's station and I flipped out like a fucking freak?" She challenged surprised gray eyes with the fire in her own. "I can't go through my day without thinking it's happening again, Simone, okay? I told CNN to go fuck themselves"

Her heart was pounding and she felt the infuriating

sting of tears behind her eyes. She felt bad about erupting on Simone, the one person in the world who didn't deserve it. She was getting frustrated as she tried to zip one of the duffel bags, but her broken fingers ached and she was having a problem.

"Damn it!" she exclaimed, shoving the bag to the floor and walking to the bathroom where she slammed the door behind her.

As she braced herself against the sink, she felt so out of control of her body and of her life. She wasn't surprised when she heard a quiet, almost timid knock on the door. Bringing up a hand to swipe at the tears that had fallen, she pulled the door open, a sympathetic Simone standing on the other side.

Burton fell into her arms, her emotions finally catching up to her. She was no longer on the medications they'd given her, and it seemed the dam had finally broken. Everything she'd been able to hold back over the weeks came at her like a wild animal, clawing at her very soul.

"I've got you," Simone whispered, rocking her gently as she held her. "It's okay."

Burton allowed her emotions to fully drain, feeling exhausted and embarrassed. She pulled away, reaching over by the toilet to tug a long strip of toilet paper to wipe at her eyes and nose.

"Listen," Simone said, her hand still on Burton's back. "Why don't you come stay with me for a while? Cricket is already there, so…"

Burton blew her nose and tossed the soiled tissue in the trash before meeting Simone's kind eyes. Without a word, she nodded.

☙❧❧❧

"Make yourself at home, sweetheart," Simone said after unlocking the front door of her three-bedroom house. She pushed it open, a chirping Cricket waiting for her.

"Hi, baby!" Burton exclaimed, immediately falling to her knees—as quickly as she could—to gather the feline in her arms. It was the longest she'd ever gone without seeing her furry baby, and Cricket seemed to be equally excited as she purred, rubbing her face all over Burton's.

On shaky legs, and with help from Simone, she got to her feet with her cat in her arms and entered the house, which she'd visited many times before. Much like its owner, it was sophisticated and beautiful, though not too much for one person to take care of. She walked over to the couch and sat down, already out of breath from her journey from the hospital to Simone's car, from her car to the house.

"Why don't you rest, okay?" Simone said, walking over to her and placing a hand on her right knee. "I'm going to bring everything in from the car."

"If you give me a sec to breathe, I can help you," Burton said, absently rubbing Cricket's head as she looked up at her friend.

"No, don't worry. It'll take me just a minute. I'll get you set up in the guest bedroom."

Left alone, Burton hugged her cat to her, closing her eyes at the little body that vibrated against her with the intensity of Cricket's purring. She'd missed her cat so much, one aspect of her life that made it feel normal, despite the fact they weren't at home. They would be soon enough. She agreed with Simone that it wasn't a good idea for her to be alone right now.

They sat in Simone's car where she'd parked it on the street, the station just down the way. Simone had offered to park in the parking garage where employees usually did, but Burton declined. She wasn't entirely sure she'd ever be able to enter one again. She felt a hand rest on her arm. She glanced over at her friend's beautiful face.

"Are you sure? I can run in and get your stuff if you want to wait."

Burton let out a shaky breath then shook her head. "No. I'd like to do it myself. I think I need to." She gave her a sheepish smile. "That's what Dr. Rose said, anyway," she added, referring to the therapist she'd been seeing for the two weeks since she'd been out of the hospital, twice a week an hour each day. It was helping, but she still couldn't seem to find herself.

She reached for the door handle and, after a truck drove by, pushed it open and exited the 1961 candy apple red Stingray convertible, Simone's baby. Her father owned his own body shop, so he'd rebuilt the gorgeous little car for his little princess as a college graduation gift. Normally Burton would ask to drive it, but her left leg and foot were still too injured to operate pedals. Her Jeep had been parked outside Simone's house since the day after the explosion instead of being parked at her complex. Everett and Simone were worried that, unsupervised, it would be stolen or vandalized.

Burton gratefully accepted her cane, which Simone produced from the trunk. Feeling somewhat stabilized, she felt a hand on her arm.

"Are you ready?"

With a nod, Burton and Simone made their way down the sidewalk to the building that a month ago was a place of joy and excitement. Burton never knew what would meet her on any given day, what she'd find, and what she'd uncover. Now, all she wanted was to know what *exactly* was around every corner.

Together, they entered the fourth floor, which was where the newsroom was. Along the way she'd received stares, polite hellos, and a couple hugs. Most, though, just looked at her as though they weren't sure what to say. It made her feel awkward and conspicuous, especially with the do-rag on her head to cover the areas that were splotchy from the burns but were growing back. Simone had given her a wonderful haircut that helped cover it, but when going out into the world, she was still very self-conscious. The slight limp she had, which the doctor said she'd likely always carry, didn't help, either.

When she pushed open the glass doors that led to the newsroom, she had no idea what to think. Every one of her former coworkers was there waiting for them, and as she entered the room, they all began to clap, standing along the main aisle where she made her slow, measured way down, Simone following behind.

Burton looked from one person to the next, noting some had tears in their eyes, others all smiles and cheers. She didn't know what to think. Some of these people she knew by face but not by name, others she'd only worked with a time or two. What got her, though, was when Everett stepped out of his office and into the line of KNWZ employees, whooping her on with a fist in the air. She laughed even as tears sprang to her eyes.

"Hey, hon," he said softly once she reached him, accepting his hug. He lifted her slightly off the ground before setting her gingerly back on her feet. "I'm so glad to see you up and walking."

"Me, too," she said, trying to add levity to a serious moment, but it didn't work. Instead, she received another hug. Released, she turned to all her former coworkers who'd gathered around them. "Thank you, everyone. Not sure what I did to deserve that reception, but I'm touched."

"I have your things in my office," he said, hitching a thumb in that direction. "I wanted to talk to you, too."

"Okay."

Everett led the way to his office, Burton getting hugs and good wishes along the way. Finally, she was able to take a seat across from him at his cluttered desk, the bank of monitors behind him showing various reporters out in the field as well as the noon cast that was underway.

She tore her eyes from it all and cleared her throat. "So, you have my things?" she asked.

"I do." He swiveled his chair around so he could get up and walked over to one of the many bookcases in the office. A white box with a lid sat on the floor and he picked it up, walking it over to the desk and setting it down. "I'm sorry we had to do this," he said, sounding sheepish. "But, Gregory was starting and…"

"No, it's okay," Burton said, glancing at the box before returning her gaze to him. "What did you want to talk to me about?"

"I hear you turned CNN down. I'm not going to ask as it's your business and I think I understand. But, I spoke with Joel. If you want to come back, Burt—"

"Everett," she breathed, sitting back in her chair.

"Wait," he said, raising his hands in supplication "I'm just putting it out there. If you ever want a job… okay?"

She met his gaze for a long moment, his unwavering. Finally, she dropped hers. "Okay."

Chapter Six

Burton lay on the bed in Simone's guest bedroom absently stroking Cricket's back. The box of her gathered belongings from her desk at KNWZ sat on the floor next to the dresser. It had been a trying day, though admittedly good to say good-bye to those she'd shared her day with. The hardest part, however, had been seeing Roger's editing bay and the young buck they'd hired to take his place as he'd sat back in his chair, *Roger's* chair, his feet up on the desk.

She lay with an ankle crossed over the other, her gaze focused on the ceiling above her. It took a moment to realize there was a knock at the door. She glanced at it. "Come in."

Simone opened the door and entered the room, lit only by a lamp on the dresser. She wore an oversized T-shirt that canted slightly off one shoulder and thin cotton shorts, which showed off long, shapely legs.

"How goes it?" she asked, walking over to the bed and sitting on the side.

Burton shrugged a shoulder, she herself dressed for bed in a T-shirt and Denver Broncos pajama pants. "Okay. Just thinking about today. You arranged all that, didn't you? Told them we were coming," she said.

Simone let out a tired sigh and tilted her head slightly as she studied her friend. "I knew a lot of people wanted to see you. They wanted to be able to say good-bye and see that you were all right. You've become quite the legend down there, don't you know."

Burton laughed ruefully. "I should be more notorious than legendary."

"Oh, stop," Simone said, slapping her playfully on the foot. "Come on. I'm going to watch some TV in bed. Come watch with me."

Burton studied her for a moment and seeing the sincerity in her friend's eyes, she agreed.

They sat up against stacked pillows in Simone's giant king-sized bed. Simone clicked on various programs, nothing appealing to either of them.

"*Home Alone*?" Simone asked, referring to the movie that was half over on the screen.

"Sure," Burton said, partially interested in the antics of the boy left alone at home and the two burglars intent on getting their bounty.

Simone set the remote control on her bedside table and settled in. Burton could feel Simone's gaze on her from time to time and finally glanced over at her.

"What?"

"I think you should become a go-go dancer," Simone said, a grin quirking her lips.

"What?" Burton exclaimed, eyes wide. "Are you out of your mind?"

"You so should, though," Simone said persistently. "You're hot as hell, I mean those eyes alone will get you loads of lap dances."

"What the hell have you been drinking? I mean what, should my stage name be—Gimpy?" Where initially Burton had felt offended, wondering illogically if Simone was making fun of her, suddenly she found humor in the situation. "Or, should I make it sexier. Something like, Gimpy Rose?"

Simone dissolved into giggles. "I'd call myself Annie Oakley," she said, pushing the covers off her and getting to her knees. She cupped a breast in each of her hands and with accompanying shooting sounds, lifted each breast accordingly.

It was Burton's turn to lose herself in laughter, which felt good, she had to admit. Slowly, she too got to her knees. She cupped her own breasts. "Hello, Annie," she said, bobbing the flesh with each word. "I'm Gimpy Rose."

Simone moved a bit closer. "Nice to meet you. Give us a kiss."

Burton gasped slightly; she felt her nipples grow rigid when Simone pressed their breasts together, both still cupping their own. But, it was when she rubbed them together slightly that a jolt shot through her body. All amusement gone, she searched Simone's eyes and saw a deep desire in them.

Over the past six weeks, Burton had felt utterly alone, even though she'd been surrounded by friends and medical personnel. She desperately needed to feel connected to someone because she certainly didn't feel connected to herself. She also owed Simone so much. Nobody had been there for her the way her friend had. She didn't move, didn't flinch when Simone moved a bit closer, her hands coming up to cup either side of her face. Burton's eyes fell closed as she felt Simone's lips lightly touch her own, their play over.

Burton's eyes remained closed and Simone teased her slightly with her bottom lip before leaving a lingering kiss. "My leg hurts," Burton murmured as her left leg began to ache from the position she was kneeling in.

Without a word between them, Simone moved away and helped her lie back on the mattress, both slipping beneath the covers, though Simone remained close by on her side, next to where Burton lay on her back. She leaned down again, returning to their kiss.

Burton was nervous, not entirely sure what was

about to happen. She responded to the kiss, opening her lips to Simone, which pulled a sigh from her friend. She could feel Simone's breasts press against her arm, and she had to admit, the softness was interesting and beautiful.

The kiss deepened and, to Burton's surprise, she found herself bringing up a hand to bury in Simone's hair, their kiss intensifying. It felt so good to be touched, to be wanted and, just for a moment, not to feel alone.

A surprised gasp escaped when she felt questing fingers run down her belly and rest against her pubic bone atop her pajama pants. Simone broke the kiss and pulled back just enough to look down at her, a question in her eyes. Burton knew she needed to do this, for so many reasons. Without allowing herself to overthink it, she pulled Simone down once more to continue their kiss, sighing as Simone's fingers found the waistband of her pants.

※※※※

The room was dark when Burton's eyes opened. She lay on her side with her back to Simone who slept on her stomach, arms tucked under her pillow. They were both naked, and the weight of what had happened hours before suddenly hit her like a ton of bricks

As quietly as she could, Burton slid out of bed and found her clothes; she tugged them on, not sure if things were inside out or backward. Once dressed, she quietly closed Simone's bedroom door then hurried to the room she'd been using for the past couple of weeks. As quickly as she dared, she packed all that was at the house and gathered Cricket, who, true to her namesake, chirped at her in sleepy irritation.

Faced with a chilly May night, Burton loaded her

Jeep, then, holding her breath in hopes she wouldn't get into an accident, she started the SUV and used only her right foot to drive.

≈≈≈≈

Westcliffe, CO – Present Day

"Okay, Mrs. Hollis, I have your new Nora Roberts in…Yes, ma'am. Okay, yes…yes, I know, I won't tell Mr. Hollis." Burton chuckled into the phone. "I'll have them at my desk and yes, as always, I'll check them out for you ahead of time. You have a good day, too. Good-bye."

Burton replaced the phone in its cradle and then with fingers flying across her keyboard pulled up Helen Hollis's library account and scanned the paperback books to her account, accepting the printed-out due date ticket and placing it inside one of the three books, utterly amused. Helen's husband, Wayne, hated her reading the romance author—he felt it gave her unrealistic expectations of him.

"Burton, did you get my e-mail about Smithy Pollack?" Burton's boss, Sally Estrada asked, stepping up to Burton's desk, which sat in the middle of the West Custer County Library.

"I did," Burton said, looking up at the older woman, who was the director of the library system. "I'm going to give him a call to get some more information before I start on his case."

"Wonderful. All right, I'm leaving for the day. See you tomorrow."

Burton watched her leave then returned to what she'd been doing.

Four hours later, Burton drove her Jeep down a rutted dirt road to the house she'd rented four years before. After the owner had died six months ago, her son had sold it to her for a steal just to get it off his hands.

Now, she was fighting the county to get the road paved, as well as slowly working to renovate the 120-year-old home she'd given her heart to. The two-story house was set off by itself on two acres of land, not all of which was usable by her, but that was all right; she was making a small amount of rent from the acre the neighbor used as part of his small farm, inherited from Mrs. Stover, who had owned it before. She also got fresh vegetables out of the deal.

The house was in the tiny mountain town of Westcliffe, which lay in the Wet Mountain Valley between the Wet Mountains to the east and the Sangre de Cristo Range to the west. Winters could be brutal, but it was all worth it for the view and the anonymity she craved. Here, there were no questions, there was no recognition, there was no remembering.

Pulling the Jeep into the weed-strewn dirt driveway that led to the detached garage at the back of the house, she pulled the brake and killed the engine. She smiled when she heard the howl of her Japanese Akita, Ajax, from inside the house. She could easily picture him sitting next to Cricket, waiting for her to open the back door to the kitchen.

She gathered her purse and keys then climbed out of the Jeep, not even bothering to lock it as she made her way to the back of the house, her limp still present, though more subtle now, six years after her injuries.

She reached up to adjust her long ponytail—it had come a bit loose during her workday. Though Sally was the library director, Burton was the head librarian. She hadn't earned an MLS, but the area couldn't get the qualified personnel to apply, so her double degree in Journalism and Poly Sci had gotten her the job, which she enjoyed.

She walked up to the glass-paned back door that led to the kitchen, her furry babies on the other side barking and whining. She stopped just shy of unlocking the door and leaned in, listening, a mischievous smile on her lips. She brought up a fist and knocked lightly on one of the panes. Her babies grew silent before all hell broke loose with Ajax's loud, mournful howl and Cricket's chirps barely audible above the racket.

Unable to torture them anymore, she unlocked the back door and braced herself. Ajax nearly took off, his curled tail wagging so fast she worried it would launch him off into space. Cricket did her dance, moving back and forth in order to not get stomped on by big dog paws, waiting for her attention.

Managing to make it inside with loves, licks, and pets given and without falling, Burton placed her purse on the counter next to her keys and sunglasses. It was Friday, and she was glad for the weekend. Now that the house was hers, she'd focused her attention on a different room every weekend, tugging down shelving she didn't want, pulling down paneling, painting, or whatever she could do without bringing in professionals. She was leaving those types of jobs for later.

The kitchen was her least favorite room of the house at the moment. The house had been a rental for years, and unfortunately, the last owners had attempted to do renovations in the 1970s, and it looked it. Renters throughout the years hadn't done anything to it, other than not take care of the house. The reasons she bought it were, yes, she got a great deal, but also the house had such great bones. She knew that though it would take time, love, and money, she could turn it into her dream home.

"You guys hungry?" she asked unnecessarily as

Ajax trotted up to her with his empty food bowl in his mouth. She smiled and reached down to rub the top of his head. "All right, come on, let's feed you."

The utility room was off the side of the kitchen in an enclosed porch where the washer and dryer were, as well as the animals' food bowls and Cricket's litter box. It was a large area, granting her room to scoop the box while her dog and cat ate their dinner.

Finished with that, she headed back to the kitchen to grab her purse and walked to the front door of the house; it was a beautiful heavy wood door with an oval-etched glass centerpiece. She hung her purse up on the coat hook just inside the door before she unlocked and opened it, allowing the early evening light in. It was late July, and the nights were beginning to cool down in the mountains, which was nice. But, up in the mountains, it never got as hot as it had in Denver and certainly not in her hometown of Pueblo, where she'd lived for a year before moving to Westcliffe.

She gazed out at her front yard. It needed some work—like everything else—and she intended to dedicate time to it come spring. For now, she opened some windows as she made her way up to her bedroom on the second floor. She balanced a hand against the hallway wall and reached down to remove her high heels one at a time, holding them by their heels as she padded into her bedroom. There were three bedrooms upstairs; one was her home office and the third a guest bedroom, though it had never been slept in during her residency in the house.

Her bedroom was at the end of the hall and was the only room in the house that was exactly how she wanted it. She'd restored the crown molding, original to the house, and had done the same in a few other rooms, too. She was proud of the room, decorated with rich dark wood furniture, and enjoyed spending time in it. For the first time in her life, she hadn't settled for whatever furniture she could get her hands on or that someone she knew was selling or giving away.

When she was living in Denver, she'd been so devoted to her career at the station that her home wasn't really connected to her and said little about her. She never intended to stay put, so furnishings or paint color—let alone owning a home—were far down on her list of priorities. She wasn't sure if it was her age now as she entered her mid-thirties or perhaps because she was simply hiding from herself, as her therapist had once told her. No matter the reason, her home had now definitely become her castle.

Her adopted hometown was less than two square miles, and she had grown to enjoy and appreciate the small town and had become a homebody, something she'd never knew she was capable of. When she became lonely, she delved into the work she did outside her day job: genealogy. She found it interesting, but most of all, it allowed her to use her natural curiosity and investigative mind in a positive way. She also did cases for the library, but she most enjoyed the private ones she did from home. On occasion, she dabbled a bit in helping a private investigator out of Colorado Springs find background information for her clients.

Now, she shrugged out of the suit jacket that was part of the skirt suit she'd worn to work, tossing the garment on the bed, then unbuttoned her blouse, the silky ends falling away to reveal bra-clad breasts. She caught her reflection in the mirror above the dresser and allowed herself a brief perusal of her torso.

Her own body—other than working out—wasn't something she contemplated much. She had a road map of scars all along her left leg, which she only looked at while bathing or shaving. Many of the scars were still sensitive and couldn't take too much touch or pressure. There had been far too much nerve and muscle damage for the leg to ever feel or fully look the same again. Her left thigh was thinner than the right, and there was a patch of angry pink skin along the left side of her calf.

She didn't want to think about her leg. She was reminded of her injuries every day, whether she looked at her leg or not. There were still times that she had to pull her cane out. She kept one at the house and one in the back of her Jeep, just in case.

Now, as she studied her torso, she saw what she'd once been, which was a young, attractive woman. That is if she allowed herself to think that way. She didn't often because she saw that part of her life as very much over. That last night at Simone's house, what she'd allowed herself to do for so many of the wrong reasons, she couldn't do to someone again. After she'd left the house, she'd gone to her apartment, packed up only what she'd absolutely needed or wanted, then left a note and the next months' rent under the door of her landlord's office, and she'd gone. She'd even left her phone in the apartment. She didn't want to be contacted by anyone from that old part of her life. It was too painful.

The hardest part had been the e-mails she'd received from Simone, Theresa, and Everett. She'd ignored them for a while, but when she realized they were beginning to think the worst, she'd responded with a simple note, the same to all three: *I'm fine. Please leave me alone.*

The coward's way out. She knew it and hated herself for it. But, she didn't know any other way. She didn't know who had been hurt more, Theresa or Simone, but to have either of them in her life again wasn't an option. She'd come to terms with that, and almost as a penance, she allowed nobody else into her life, her bed, or her heart.

Turning away from a woman in her prime, she shrugged her blouse off her shoulders, tossing it to the bed where it floated down to land on her jacket. She reached behind her as she walked to the bathroom, her bra, skirt, and panties all following suit, though her panties didn't quite make it and slid to the floor where Ajax sniffed them before he followed her into the bathroom.

Burton was craving a nice, lengthy shower. It had been a long day and it was her night off from working out, so tonight after her shower, her intent was to make herself some dinner then get to work on her newest case.

An hour later, Burton padded into the kitchen wearing a pair of shorts and T-shirt as she brushed her long dark hair, still damp from the shower. She set the brush on the counter before investigating her cabinets, trying to decide what she had and what sounded good. Carefully kneeling down, she pushed the lazy Susan to see if she still had the box of pasta salad to make. She noticed her tiny stash of alcohol in the back, which included a three-year-old bottle of wine and the unopened bottle of vodka she'd been given as a gift during her last days at KNWZ. She studied it for a moment, considering a small drink with dinner.

"Nah," she said, grabbing the box of pasta salad and closing the cabinet.

≈≈≈≈

The helicopter slowly lowered to the roof, its single passenger removing her headset and tossing it to the empty seat beside her before touchdown.

"Thanks!" she called out over the roar of the rotors

overhead. She got a salute from the pilot in return and slid the side door open on the metal bird.

"Glad you're back!" Ivan exclaimed, the slender man waiting for her.

"Thanks."

She climbed out of the chopper, she and her young assistant hurrying away from the helicopter to get out of its deadly wind grasp on the roof of the Spiritan Hotel. Long auburn hair blew every which way until they reached the door that would lead to the metal staircase and down into the fifteen-story building.

Once they'd entered, she let out a breath. She hated getting on or off one of those things, but it was the only way. She attempted to bring some semblance to her hair before she and Ivan headed down the long staircase.

"Is it going to work?" he asked, following behind, his military-cut blond hair not even ruffled by the intense wind they'd just been in.

"Yes," she said as they reached the landing that led to the fifteenth-floor hallway. She pushed her hair behind a shoulder before unzipping her jacket and shrugging out of it to reveal a fitted army-green T-shirt beneath it. "I'm going to get showered," she announced, reaching into the pocket of her black BDU pants and retrieving her room key. "Tell my father I've returned and to meet me in twenty minutes."

"Okay." Like a shot, Ivan was gone.

Watching him go, she inserted her key in the door lock and turned it, pushing the door open before entering the room. Door closed behind her, she stripped as she walked the short distance to the bathroom. She was exhausted and wanted nothing more than to go to bed, but that wasn't an option. She had a debriefing to do and a plan to share.

Once in the bathroom, she glanced at her reflection in the mirror. Intense green eyes looked back at her; throughout her entire life, people had commented on the unusual vibrancy of the color. She'd even had those who asked if they were fake.

Turning away, she readied her shower.

Chapter Seven

Burton stood dressed in shorts and T-shirt, her long hair pulled back in a tight ponytail as she surveyed the small room she was about to paint. It was the guest bedroom. She'd taken down the bed the night before and had struggled and grunted as she removed it, the frame, mattress and box spring leaning against the wall out in the hallway next to the single nightstand. She didn't have a dresser for the room quite yet.

She checked her supplies, noting she had two cans of paint, painter's tape, and paint tray and roller. She realized she hadn't grabbed one of the several packages of drop cloths she'd been hoarding over the months until she could finally paint.

"Damn it," she muttered, heading out of the bedroom and climbing past the mattress and box spring and furniture to reach her home office. Inside the tiny closet was a somewhat hidden door that she'd accidentally discovered led to a second room, which she called Xanadu. She used it for storage.

Heading inside, she tugged on the chain until the lightbulb clicked on. Moving a few boxes around, she found the drop cloths, but she also found the box Everett had given her that last day at the station. She had never looked through it, never emptied it, and obviously hadn't thrown it away, though she'd considered it.

Drop cloths in hand, she was about to leave the small storage room but stopped. Turning, she glanced once again at the white box with the lid and handles

built into the cardboard.
Again, she was about to walk out, but for a second time she stopped. With a sigh, she placed the packages of drop cloths on top of the cardboard lid and grabbed the box, bringing it out of the darkness of storage and her memory and into the light of day.

Sitting at the center of the bedroom waiting for the paint to dry, Burton lifted the lid off the white box and, after so many years, was curious to see what lay within. She smiled when she pulled out her favorite coffee cup, a huge white mug with, *SPEAK INTO THE MICROPHONE, BITCH!* written on it in huge block letters. It had been a graduation gift after college.

Setting the mug aside, intending to use it the following morning, she reached in to see what else she would find. She pulled out various little stuffed animals and knickknacks she'd been given by fans over the years that she'd kept on her desk, all of which brought a smile to her face. She also found a stack of unopened mail, all dated during the weeks she'd been in the hospital.

She was about to toss it all aside to be shredded when something caught her eye. Letting the rest fall to the drop cloth-covered floor beneath her, her eyebrows drew together as she studied the glossy picture on the postcard. It was a frozen-over ocean scene with a huge merchant ship cracking through the ice. It was beautiful in its frightening way. Above the ship was the message: *Come Visit the Beauty of Chilvokia.*

Something struck her about that...something clear back in her memory. She turned the card over and saw beautiful handwriting. The top message was written in another language. She wasn't entirely sure

what it was:
Бог правду видит, да не скоро скажет.
Beneath it in English read:
Your truth is our salvation.
"What the hell?" she murmured, flipping the card over to look at the picture again and the words. A second look at the handwritten message and something occurred to her.

Setting the postcard down, she tugged the box closer to her and began to dig through it until she found what she was looking for.

Congratulations

It was written on the simple card that had arrived along with the bottle of N7 vodka. Picking up the postcard, she eyed the two handwritten messages, and it was very clear the two were identical and written by the same hand. She suddenly remembered that she'd received another postcard with the strange Chilvokia on it, though that one had been blank and long ago thrown away.

Tapping her leg with the postcard as she stared off into space thinking, she decided to check something on a whim. Taking the postcard with her, she stood and made her way downstairs to the kitchen. Once there, she walked over to the lazy Susan and turned it until the bottle of vodka was visible and she grabbed it. She stood and examined it, not entirely sure what she was looking for. Finally, she found it at the bottom of the label.

Made in Chilvokia since 1741

She gasped, shocked. Though she knew what the result would be, she looked at the postcard then at the bottle—same place. Her investigative mind began to churn. She brought up a hand and absently played with her bottom lip as she considered what she'd learned.

It could be nothing, it could be something. Setting

the bottle on the counter, she hurried as fast as her leg would allow to the stairs and up to her office computer.

Plopping down in the chair behind the desk, she tapped her fingers on the desktop as she waited, studying the handwriting on the postcard, including the one written in a language she didn't recognize. She thought it may be Russian or some sort of derivative, but wasn't positive.

Once her computer was ready, she immediately went to Google and typed in the name on the bottle and postcards. She leaned her chin on an upturned palm as her eyes scanned what came up on the screen:

...tiny island nation near the Kara Sea...
...less than one hundred miles from Russia...
...conquered by King Ravika in 1217...
...vodka producer...
...sovereign nation since 1463...
...quiet and peaceful people.

Burton chewed on her bottom lip in contemplation. Nothing was standing out to her as a smoking gun, red flag, or even anything interesting.

Disappointed and a bit confused, she shut down the page she was reading and closed the lid of her laptop so she could return to painting.

※※※※

Ajax looked around at his surroundings, eyes squinted against the wind as he sat in the front seat of Burton's Jeep, the top left back at the house in Westcliffe. It was a gorgeous day and Burton knew how much her dog loved the hour-and-a-half trip to Colorado Springs, where she was headed to meet with Lee Ann, the private investigator she did side work for, and had information to share with her.

She stopped the Jeep at a traffic light on Academy, humming softly to Sarah Brightman's haunting song, "Gloomy Sunday." She peeked at Ajax, who leaned over and gave her nose a quick lick before he was once more surveying his mobile kingdom.

Ten minutes later, she pulled the Jeep into the parking lot of the small, squat building that housed L. M. Investigative Services. She pulled the brake and killed the engine.

"Come on, Ajax," she said, unbuckling her seatbelt. Lee Ann loved the dog and he was always welcome inside her office.

The space was an old building with wood-paneled walls, worn carpeting, and old metal desks rescued from a school that was about to be demolished. The artwork on the walls was negligible, but Lee Ann was the best in the business. She was a former NYPD detective with eighteen years under her belt, but after she'd been shot during a takedown, she'd been injured too badly to return to service so had retired and moved out west with her husband and son to be closer to her parents.

"Look who's here!" Lee Ann boomed, standing up from her cluttered desk and walking around it to pull Burton into a painfully tight hug.

Burton winced, but accepted it, patting her friend on the back before escaping her clutches. "I've got some good stuff for you," she said, following the tall woman, who most would call "big boned," to her desk where she took a seat across from her. Ajax walked around the desk to plop down next to Lee Ann's feet where he let out a loud groan before falling asleep.

"Excellent!" The older woman rubbed her hands together in anticipation. "Show me."

Burton opened the flap of her messenger bag and pulled out three manila folders, each marked with the individual client's name. She tossed them onto the pile of papers already sitting on the desk blotter. "Tell me what you think."

Looking like a kid in a candy store, Lee Ann opened the first folder and flipped through the pages.

Burton sat back in the chair, glancing around the office with its covered cardboard boxes stacked against one entire wall and a row of mismatched filing cabinets lining the other. She glanced back at her friend upon hearing her name.

"So, this Hammond character, Regina's grandfather, yeah?"

"Yup. He's dead, as you can see there, but his fourth wife is still alive. I figured it might be a great angle for you to take."

"Most definitely," Lee Ann said her nose still buried in the files.

As Burton sat there watching, she mulled over whether to mention the Chilvokia situation or not. It had been a week since she'd put the few little crumbs together, only to come up with nothing. She chewed on her bottom lip for a moment then cleared her throat.

"Lee Ann?"

"Hmm?" her friend hummed, setting aside the first folder only to dig into the second. "What's up?"

"Have you ever heard of a place called Chilvokia?"

"Chil-who?" she asked, sparing a glance at Burton before returning dark eyes to the provided files.

"Chilvokia. Apparently some tiny little country up in the Russia area, known for good vodka…"

Lee Ann chuckled. "There's your problem. I'm a beer girl."

"Cute."

"Sorry. No, I've never heard of it. What about it?"

Burton took a moment. It wasn't something

she enjoyed talking about, her past at the station, but she knew there was no other way. "When I was still with KNWZ, I began getting these crazy and random postcards from this place, at least with the name on it. Sometimes blank, sometimes with handwritten messages. Then I got a bottle of N7 vodka, which I'd never heard of, and come to find out, it's produced in that place."

"Do you have any of the stuff with you?" Lee Ann asked, setting aside the files Burton had brought.

Burton hesitated for only a moment before she went back to her messenger bag. The truth was, that morning she hadn't been entirely sure what prompted her to bring them, but she had. She reached in and produced them, handing the items across the desk along with the congratulations card.

Lee Ann examined all of it, shaking her head after a long moment. "You know what I think, Burt?"

"What?"

"I mean, none of this makes sense. It really rings as a bunch of cryptic nonsense." She tossed the postcards and card on the desk as she sat back in her chair. "You know, what I think is this: Back in the day you were well known, one of the best. You had quite the oyster as far as public goes. I think it's the maker of that stuff," she said, tapping the card that had come with the bottle of liquor. "I think it was a pretty damn clever attempt at free publicity and marketing." She shrugged. "You were an investigative reporter, my friend. What better way to catch your attention than with a little manufactured mystery, right?"

Burton shook her head, unable to keep the smile from her face. "I feel like such an idiot," she murmured, gathering the postcards and card and dumping them into the metal trash can next to Lee Ann's desk. "You're right. Why the hell didn't I see that?"

"You're rusty."

"Something like that." She pushed up from her chair. "Come on, Ajax."

The dog lifted his head then got to his feet, tail slowly wagging as he walked around the desk to her.

"I better get going. Let me know if you have questions on any of that stuff," Burton said, indicating the files.

"Will do. I'll PayPal ya some cash this week."

"Sounds good."

Burton accepted a hug then she and Ajax were on their way.

※ ※ ※ ※

Burton sat on the couch holding Cricket who purred away as she got loves. As Burton scratched between the cat's ears and under her chin, she smiled. She thought back to when she'd gotten the petite feline as a three-month-old kitten. Now, she was eight years old and still going strong.

When Burton had gotten Ajax, she'd been worried as Cricket had never seen a dog in her life, but Burton just didn't feel safe living out as far as she did without a little extra added protection. Now, she felt completely safe, half the time not even bothering to lock her car, but in the early days she'd been lonely and had felt vulnerable.

"Been through a lot together, you and me." She placed a kiss on top of her head before laying the cat down on the couch and getting to her feet to put coffee on. Lee Ann would be there within a few minutes, her friend having called her the night before to ask if she could swing by, that she had some information for

Burton. Lee Ann and her husband, Phil, loved to fish at a lake nearby, so it worked out well for everyone.

She filled the carafe with water as she glanced out the kitchen window and saw the dust cloud as a car made its way up the road to her house. She finished with coffee preparations around the same time Lee Ann's Tundra was pulling into her driveway.

She took out two mugs and the flavored creamer. Lee Ann had said she wouldn't be there long, but Burton knew better than to not get her coffee-addicted friend her fix before they got back on the road for the final forty-five minutes to their destination.

She walked over to the back door, hipping a barking Ajax away as she unlocked the door and opened it to allow Lee Ann in. "Hey!"

"Hey you," Lee Ann said, handing Burton her laptop bag so she could kneel to give the whimpering dog attention. "Hello, baby," she cooed.

"Sometimes I think he loves you more than he does me," Burton chuckled, carrying the laptop to the breakfast bar and setting it down next to Lee Ann's mug and the container of creamer.

"Of course he does!" Lee Ann stated as though everyone knew that. With a final pet and kisses to Cricket, she got to her feet and joined Burton, taking a seat. "Oh, thank you," she said as Burton poured the freshly brewed coffee into the mug.

"Absolutely." Burton poured herself a cup then returned the carafe to the warming plate on the coffee maker. "So, whatcha got for me?" she asked, stirring some Hershey's and caramel creamer into the black brew.

"Okay, here's the deal," Lee Ann said, putting her coffee aside in order to pull her computer out of the bag. "Back in the day, you were a hell of a reporter.

Hell,"—she shrugged—"you still are." She eyed Burton who stood at the bar beside her. "That info you brought me last week was beyond helpful, young lady."

Burton grinned with pride. "Great."

"Anyway, so I guess what I'm trying to say is, you've got the nose for a good story or when something just doesn't smell right, and I have a feeling that's the case with this Chilvokia stuff. After you left, I got to thinking and did a little research of my own." She brought out a printed page from the bag and handed it to Burton before she pulled the computer out and opened the screen. "I had that translated. It's Russian, apparently some sort of Russian proverb or something."

Burton looked at the page, noting the familiar line from one of the postcards.

Бог правду видит, да не скоро скажет

"Basically," Lee Ann said, logging onto her laptop, "it's saying God sees the truth, but just isn't going to tell anytime soon."

Burton stared at her for a long moment, the page still in her hand. "I got an e-mail," she said, racking her brain as she tried to remember exactly when it was. "It was sent to my work e-mail around that time. Basically it had some cryptic message like, my passion is to find the truth, a truth seeker or something."

Lee Ann stopped what she was doing and met Burton's gaze. "Do you think it could be connected?"

Burton tossed the page on the bar and ran her hands over the smoothed-back hair that ended in a long ponytail. "At this point, I wouldn't be surprised. I don't believe in coincidence."

"Me neither. So, look at this," Lee Ann said, finger moving around on the touchpad until she clicked on a file. "I talked to my buddy Ryan at the National Weather Service. He got us some satellite images of this place."

Intrigued, Burton moved to stand behind where her friend was seated on a barstool.

"Now," the older woman began, bringing up the picture of a specific part of the globe, an image taken from space. "This here," she said, a finger making an imaginary circle at the top right of the image, "is our little piece of heaven, otherwise known as Chilvokia. It's dark, all seems well in the neighborhood, yeah? This was taken February of 2000."

Burton nodded, bringing her fingers up to nervously tug at her bottom lip. "Yeah."

"Okay, so let's zoom ahead to 2007." She opened up a second photo of the same satellite position. This time, the area wasn't dark but had a bit of a glow to it.

"What is that?" Burton asked, leaning forward over Lee Ann's shoulder to get a better look.

"Who knows. Could be a forest fire, anything." She looked back at her friend. "When did you start getting the postcards and stuff?"

"Twenty-ten."

"And," Lee Ann said, opening a third photo. "Here's our motherland in 2010."

Burton gasped, her hand covering her mouth. What had been a small bit of orange three years before nearly covered the entire area. "What the hell?"

"Lit up like a goddamn Roman candle. I showed this to Phil to get his thoughts after so many years as a navigator in the Air Force. He said to him it looked like a battle zone."

Burton stood upright again, her eyebrows drawn. She met the steady dark gaze of her friend. "What does this mean?" she asked quietly.

"I think someone was sending you an SOS, Burt."

Chapter Eight

Burton took several deep breaths, hoping that her makeup had held up since she'd left her Jeep. She wanted to look her best, her hair down and curled, professional makeup, and a fitted emerald-green skirt suit. Her heart was pounding and she was about ready to bolt when the elevator dinged the arrival of the newest car.

"I'll be damned."

She glanced over and rose slowly to her feet, not sure what to do. She watched as Everett walked toward her. He appeared haggard, his hair peppered with more gray than it had been six years before. His expression was stern and his shirt and loosened tie were wrinkled. In short, he looked like a busy story editor.

"Hi," she said, not sure what else to say. She extended her hand, which he looked at, then a moment later he pulled her in for a tight hug.

"Where the hell have you been?" he murmured.

She nearly burst into tears, so relieved at his reception. She swallowed a few times before pulling out of the hug. "Been around," she said with a small smile.

"When Billy called up and said someone was here to see me, I had no idea who it could be."

"Just little ol' me," Burton said nervously.

"Come on. Let's head up to my office."

Burton grabbed her messenger bag and hiked it up on her shoulder before following her previous boss into the elevator. Arriving at the fourth floor, they made their way through the familiar maze of hallways until finally they reached the glass doors of the newsroom. She looked around, saddened though not surprised to see mostly new faces. Those who had been there back when she was, were far too busy with their midday story research and trying to contact sources to bother looking up.

"After you," he said, allowing her to enter his office first.

She stepped in, amused. It was as cluttered as ever, and part of her wondered if some of the clutter dated back to her tenure at the station.

"Have a seat."

Burton did as asked and made herself comfortable, one leg crossed over the other, her bag resting on her lap. "I figured you'd be a GM or on the production team by now," she said, looking around.

"What, and leave all this? Not in a million."

She chuckled, remembering the banter between her and Everett, both film buffs, when they used lines from movies. This time, *Pretty Woman*.

"No, I guess I just prefer knowing exactly how the beating is going to feel before testing out a new master," he answered, sitting back in his chair and removing his glasses, which he tossed on the desk. He studied her for a long moment. "Six years, Burt," he said softly. "You gave us all a good scare. I wasn't sure if you were still alive, you know? You didn't leave in the best frame of mind."

"I know. I'm truly sorry for that. I think I just needed to hit the reset button, and I realized I couldn't do it here or anywhere near here."

He nodded, bouncing lightly on the springs of his desk chair. "Where's home?"

"Westcliffe. I'm the librarian there," she said, not sure whether to sound proud or ashamed.

He nodded, his response noncommittal. "So, why are you back here, then?"

Why, indeed? She felt the weight of what lay across her lap and, for the first time, thought that maybe this had been a terrible mistake. She was about to say as much when something stopped her. She opened her mouth to speak and again, something stopped whatever she was about to say.

She gazed up into a patient face. Though he'd aged surprisingly in six years, she saw her old friend in those small, gray eyes. She cleared her throat and opened up her bag. "I've brought something to show you." She began pulling out all the printouts she'd prepared and brought with her. For a moment she felt like her tongue was two sizes too big and she'd swallowed a bag of cotton. She felt so out of practice in pitching a story. She spared him a glance before shutting her emotions off and shifting to reporter mode.

She glanced at Everett's face often, making sure he was engaged in what she was telling him, that he was following the trail of crumbs she was leaving for him, and that he saw the value in the story that she did. She felt her confidence grow with every point she made, with every raise of Everett's eyebrows, and every time they dropped again.

At long last, she was finished, all of her evidence spread out across his desk, every piece explained, every point made, and every reason why this was a good story that needed to be told given.

Finished with her pitch, she sat in her chair, carefully watching Everett, who sat back in his chair with a heavy sigh. He stroked his chin as he studied all that lay before him, seeming to look beyond it.

"What are you wanting, exactly?" he asked at length, looking Burton in the eye.

"I'm not entirely sure, to be honest. I just know this story needs me."

"Are you saying you want a job back with KNWZ?" he asked, an eyebrow raised.

"Well, you once told me I'd always have one here, but I have a life in the mountains, Ev. What about maybe a freelance situation just for this story?"

Everett continued to stroke his chin. "I'd have to talk to Joel."

"Did anything else ever come here for me? Anything at all?" she asked, curious if any more postcards or anything else relating to the strange case had shown up, the sender oblivious to the fact that she'd left the station.

"Nope," he said, reaching out and tapping his fingertips on the pages splayed out on his desk. "After the incident, nothing came." He pushed up to his feet and walked around his desk to Burton. "I'll talk to Katherine Dennison, our GM now. Stay close and I'll call you with whatever she says."

"Okay," Burton said, grabbing one of Everett's business cards and a pen from his desk. "I've got myself a room here in Denver, so here's my phone number." She scribbled her information down and handed it to him, tossing the pen back on the desk. She stood up next to him, shaking her head as a slow smile crossed her lips. "It's so good to see you."

"You, too." He gave her another bone-crushing hug and left a kiss on her cheek.

She left Everett's office and pushed through the glass door, leaving the newsroom. She was about to head to the bank of elevators but stopped, her gaze turning down the hallway in the opposite direction. Standing at the intersection of the hall, she made a decision.

She walked down the hall she'd walked down

every single morning for six years at what they all called "butt crack a.m." But, it was a necessary evil. Now, it was to ease her curiosity and her conscience.

She slowed her pace as she neared the room with all the mirrors and round lights. The room with tons of random tubes, canisters, and brushes lying around, none of which made a lick of sense to Burton back in the day, but to the magician that was Simone, they were her props and magic curtains.

"I don't know, Todd," a familiar woman's voice said from around the corner, which would be the makeup room. "I think this little rug you've got going on your chin ain't your thing."

"Aw, come on, Simone! My girlfriend wants me to grow a beard.," a man whined.

Burton smiled, rounding the corner and entering the room.

"Yeah, well tell her you're not quite—" Simone stopped midsentence as her gaze followed the newcomer into the room. She appeared shocked and turned away. "Uh, tell her you're not so good at it," she finished, putting a few touches on the man who sat in her chair. "All finished." She gave him a smile, which Burton knew well enough was as fake as they come, but said nothing and stood aside.

The man glanced at her as he stepped down from the raised chair and left the room. Burton waited until he was gone before she looked to her old friend, who was cleaning up the mess of tubes and such she'd used on him.

To alleviate her discomfort in the quiet, Burton examined the room, noting a snapshot tucked into the side of the mirror with a smiling Simone cuddled up to a beautiful Asian woman, their heads pressed together on what looked to be a back patio or someone's backyard.

They appeared as though they'd been caught forever in the middle of a laugh.

Something caught Burton's eye and she noticed something on Simone's left ring finger. The ring was classy and elegant, not too extravagant, but a statement piece, just like the woman herself. There were diamonds and a beautiful ruby, whose glint in the light had captured Burton's attention.

"Can't say I ever thought I'd see you here again," Simone said quietly, pulling Burton away from her examination of the ring.

She cleared her throat, walking a bit farther into the room. "Neither did I, to be honest."

Simone wasn't looking at her, instead wiping down her work space. She remained quiet, as though waiting for Burton to make the next verbal move. Burton knew it was hers to make.

"I'm sorry, Simone. I'm really sorry," she said, though it sounded lame to her own ears. "I couldn't handle being here anymore, around everyone."

Simone nodded, though still didn't look at her. "It's okay," she said flatly. "We all have to do what we have to do, right?" She graced her with a small, tight smile.

"No," Burton said, able to see just how deeply she'd hurt her friend. She took a step closer but stopped when she saw Simone stiffen a bit. "Simone," she said softly. "I ran away, there's no other way to say it. It was a cowardly thing to do, but I truly believe it saved my life."

For the first time, Simone looked up and met her gaze but said nothing.

Though it was hard for Burton to go back there, to bring back those memories and emotions, she knew Simone deserved nothing less. "Every day that I stayed here, a little bit more of me died." She let out a heavy breath with a little shrug. "I had to start over. I had to find me again, and I knew there was no way I could do it surrounded by people who...people who were there, people who knew a part of who I was before and during that time." Simone had returned her focus to wiping down the tabletop, but Burton could tell she was listening. "I know it probably makes no sense to you, and that's okay, I accept that." She looked down at the messenger bag slung over her shoulder as her fingers played with the flap. She let out a heavy sigh and regarded her old friend again. "I'm sorry."

Burton turned and began to head out of the small room until she was stopped by the sound of her name. She turned to see Simone standing by the makeup chair, a hand resting on the back of it.

"I have the same e-mail, if you want to ever catch up, that is," she said, her tone sounding weak and nervous.

Burton sent her a grateful smile. "Okay. I'll do that."

≈≈≈≈

The hotel room was like any other she'd ever been in. A queen-sized bed, dresser top with a flat-screen TV on it, bathroom with crappy towels, and a table with an armchair in front of the window.

Burton set her overnight bag on the bed, placing her hands on the scratchy comforter and pushing down to test the mattress. It wasn't horrible but certainly wasn't her pillow top back home. She tossed the suit jacket onto the bed, too hot to wear it. Though the day hadn't been long in hours, it had been endless in emotions.

She kicked her high heels off and let out an obscene

groan at the relief of her bare feet on the Berber carpet. She padded to the bathroom, unbuttoning her blouse as she went. She wanted nothing more than to take a long, hot shower and crawl into bed. She allowed the billowy material to flow down her arms, gathered the blouse, and tossed it onto the vanity top, which stretched the length of the bathroom wall.

Checking her reflection, Burton saw a woman who appeared tired. She unzipped her overnight toiletry case and withdrew her brush, wincing slightly as she brushed through tangles and hairspray.

Finished with that, she stripped off the rest of her clothing and moved under a hot spray. She relished the seemingly unending supply of water in the hotel, taking her time in washing. Finished, she stood under the spray for several minutes before the guilt of wasting water forced her to turn off the tap and step out.

She wrapped her long hair in a towel and her body in a second towel, which left a nice little space open for anyone who wanted a peek. She moved to the bedroom portion of the room, grabbing the remote off the dresser top and flicking the TV on. She searched through the guide to see what sounded interesting when "Wishing You Were Somehow Here Again" rent the air, Burton's ringtone a song from the Broadway musical, *Phantom of the Opera*. She turned the TV off and hurried over to the bed where she'd left her phone. It was Everett.

"Hello?...Hey, Everett. What's the good word?... Okay, yeah, sure. I'm here overnight, so not a problem... eleven-thirty," she said, hurrying over to her purse and digging until she found a pen and pad of paper. She wrote down what he was telling her. "Absolutely...Okay. Me too, quite honestly." She chuckled into the phone. "I wasn't expecting to be back here, that's for sure. But, I'll be there...Okay, bye."

She ended the call and set her phone back down on the bed with a heavy breath. Everett and the GM wanted to meet with her tomorrow to discuss the path forward with the story. She'd be lying if she didn't say part of her hoped the GM would pass on it. Burton knew she wouldn't, though. Katherine had been in the industry too long, and she knew a good story when she saw one, or as Lee Ann said, when she smelled one.

She glanced at the mirror above the dresser and let out another deep breath. "Okay," she said to her reflection. "Here we go."

༺༻༺༻

The sky overhead was as blue as a robin's egg, not a cloud in sight. The vibrancy of it was almost unsettling, as was the lush green at Burton's feet. Wild grass blew gently in the softest of breezes that gently ruffled her hair, which hung loosely around her shoulders and down her back.

She walked along the edge of a rocky cliff. What lay below she had no idea. She couldn't bring herself to go near enough the edge to find out. The summer dress she wore blew gently around her calves, her bare feet enjoying the coolness of the grass. She felt light and free.

Suddenly, she knew she wasn't alone. Turning around, she was overjoyed to see Roger walking toward her, with his ever-present flannel, jeans, and working boots. He opened his arms to her and she ran, swooped up in them.

Burton's eyes squeezed shut as she was held close. She took a deep breath, inhaling Roger's scent: leather, flannel, and Old Spice. She'd never felt happier as she rested her head on a broad chest, able to feel his belly—which she used to jokingly call his thirteen-month pregnant belly—press against her. It was such a comforting part of him, like a giant teddy bear.

After a long moment, she pulled out of the hug and looked up at him, noting his grizzled face, the hard lines softening instantly with his gentle smile.

"I've missed you," she said, stepping back but keeping her hands resting on strong forearms.

"I've always been here," he said, his deep voice a balm to her soul. "I always will be. But," he added, lifting her chin slightly with two fingers, "you've gotta let me."

"I don't understand."

"Don't walk away from what makes you you. Celebrate your passion and spirit, Burt."

She looked into his eyes, noting the absolute vibrancy of the blue color, never remembering them being so blue. "I can't," she said, shaking her head.

"Oh, I don't buy that for a single solitary second," he scolded her gently. "Believe in yourself like I do. Don't hide from what makes you great."

Burton's eyes slid closed as he leaned forward and placed a soft kiss on her forehead.

"Don't hide from yourself," he whispered. "Come out of the shadows..."

≈≈≈≈

Burton woke up with a gasp, her heart racing and eyes wide open as she gazed around the darkened hotel room. She was disoriented for a moment, not entirely sure where she was until she heard the light hum of the air conditioner running from beneath the window.

Once she had her bearings, tears instantly sprang to her eyes and she sat up, burying her face in her hands. After long moments, her grief lifted and the tears slowed then stopped. She used the sheet to wipe her eyes and face.

Looking around the room again, she was surprised to not see Roger leaning against the wall, grinning at her. The dream had been so vivid, so real. She took several deep, calming breaths and squinted at the alarm clock. It was nearly six-fifteen, so she decided to get up, as there was no doubt sleep wasn't coming back anytime soon.

Pushing the covers off, she got up and turned off the AC. The morning air was cool and crisp. She pushed open the heavy drapes and viewed the dawning day. It was a beautiful early Wednesday morning, her room overlooking downtown Denver. Traffic was already in play, the beginning of rush hour. She remembered those days, and in truth, didn't miss them. That was one thing she enjoyed about her slow, lazy little life in Westcliffe.

She headed to the bathroom to get ready for her day. She had to meet Everett and Katherine at eleven-thirty, so she decided to go out for a bite to eat and make a stop before she headed to the station.

☙☙❧❧

Burton pulled her Jeep to a stop on one of the many winding paths throughout Fort Logan National Cemetery in Littleton. She peeked out her passenger window to see row upon row of the bright white gravestones, marking the fallen of America's military. She glanced at her watch to see that she was a few minutes early and sat quietly behind the wheel with her own thoughts.

She'd been near comatose on the day of Roger's funeral, and even after she'd been released from the hospital and continued on with her life, she'd never been able to say a proper good-bye. She'd never been to his grave, never been able to face—truly face—her guilt. It, like so many other emotions, had been pushed down over the past six years to the point of living life effectively numb, not feeling much of anything except love for her animals and simple enjoyment for her job and her home.

Today, she had to face it, really look what had happened in the eye. She felt her dream had told her as much the night before.

Something caught her eye and Burton saw a figure in the distance walking up to a stone. She knew in her gut that it was Theresa, arriving a bit earlier than their planned nine-thirty meeting. She felt her stomach reel a little as she hadn't seen Theresa in all that time.

Deciding it was time to face the music, she grabbed her purse and the flowers she'd purchased on the way to the cemetery and exited the Jeep. The grass was green and lush as she walked between the seemingly unending rows of graves, careful not to step on any of them. As she came closer, she saw that Roger had been buried near a tree, which made sense, she thought, considering he'd looked like a lumberjack most of his adult life. She smiled at the thought.

Theresa stood at the foot of Roger's grave, looking as beautiful and vibrant as ever, though she had more gray in her hair and was noticeably thinner. Burton met her gaze as the older woman turned to watch her approach. No words were spoken as the two moved into each other's arms, holding on for a long moment.

Burton's eyes closed at the warm comfort of the woman who had been a mother figure to her for so many years. Being in her presence, she realized just how much she'd missed it. She smiled as Theresa began to rub soothing circles over her back until finally she pulled out of the hug.

"I'm so glad you called," she said quietly.

Burton nodded, not trusting her voice for a

moment. "Me, too," she managed at length.

☙☙❧❧

Burton had been buzzed in by the security guard in the lobby and was told to go to what they called the "story room" on the fourth floor, where all the reporters, producers, and editors gathered in the morning to discuss what stories would be covered by whom. She knew the room well.

Now, she sat at the huge table in the glassed-in room, looking out over the newsroom. There were only a few people at their desks, none of whom she knew. She hadn't been surprised the previous day by the new faces. The news business—be it print or TV—was a fairly transient business. Talent was always looking to move on to a bigger market or bigger title. Her old station, KNWZ, was no different.

She caught movement out of the corner of her eye and saw Everett walking toward the room followed by a middle-aged woman with a tight blond perm and a no-nonsense expression. He pulled the door open and held it for her then followed, closing the door behind them. Burton swallowed her nerves and smiled at the duo.

"Thanks for coming in, Burton," he said, taking a seat next to her while the woman sat perpendicular from her at the head of the long table. "This is Katherine Dennison, General Manager of the station, Katherine, Burton Blinde, former investigative reporter for us."

"Yes," the GM said, extending her hand. "I remember your work, Miss Blinde. It's unfortunate you're no longer in the industry."

Not entirely sure how to respond to that sanitized comment, Burton simply smiled politely.

"Well, that brings us here, Katherine, as you know. Burton," Everett said, turning his focus to her, "I shared your evidence with Katherine last night and we're interested in taking this further."

"Yes," Katherine said, taking the baton from Everett, even if he hadn't exactly handed it to her. "Here's what I'm thinking. We get in touch with Chad Andrews, who is essentially our international correspondent in London. Have you work with him, get him caught up, and he can take things from there. It saves us the cost, and, quite simply, he's employed with a news organization there."

"Well," Everett added, bringing a finger up to push his glasses a bit farther onto the bridge of his nose. "All due respect, Katherine, but I think Burton should take this one to the finish line."

"Everett, she runs a library in the mountains," Katherine pointed out.

Burton felt like she was caught up in a tennis match as the two talked about her as though she weren't there.

"I understand that, but Burton is the best in the business, Katherine. I worked with her for six years, and if…things…hadn't happened, she'd be the jewel in the CNN crown by now."

Katherine gave him a hard look before turning her gaze to Burton. "Miss Blinde, would you mind waiting just outside for a moment, please?"

"Of course." Burton pushed back from the table and stood, leaving the room and the tension which could be cut with a knife.

Standing just outside, Burton could see that Everett had scooted over to her abandoned chair and he and Katherine Dennison were leaning toward each other, heads close and mouths working nonstop, her former boss gesticulating dramatically. She knew he was fighting for her, and in truth, she wasn't sure what she thought of it all. The former reporter in her was feeling territorial over what she'd uncovered, but who she had become was terrified that he'd win.

She walked across the small space toward an unoccupied desk and sat down, crossing one leg over the other. As she glanced around the newsroom, a small part of her twitched with the need to belong again, to be part of a team. She eyed her old desk and saw the typical mess of a harried reporter but also a framed picture of a handsome black man smiling with a beautiful black woman and a baby who looked to be no more than a year. She warmed at that, wondering if a young reporter—either the man or the woman—had gotten their shot with her absence.

"Burton?"

Startled, her head swung around to see Everett standing in front of her. "Hey. Yeah."

"Be ready to head out in two weeks."

Chapter Nine

They sat in what used to be a robust and lively room with endless productivity, continuing a tradition that was hundreds of years old. Now, machines sat silent, the conveyor belts covered with dust.

He inserted the earpiece with attached microphone, which was attached to an arm that extended out near his mouth. He adjusted a few knobs and tweaked the volume.

"Testing, testing," he said. "Can you hear me okay?"

"Yes, I can hear you," came the voice that sounded so far away. "There's a bit of static, though."

"Okay. Let me see what I can do." He nearly jumped off his stool at the sudden whine that blasted his ear. He frantically changed the pitch and tone, slowly lowering the volume and bass. The whine lowered then was gone. "Better?"

"Much, though I think I just lost about three octaves of hearing," the voice complained in his earpiece.

"I know. Sorry. Okay, is that good, then?" he asked, hands braced on his thighs as he listened for any imperfections.

"Yes, we're good."

"Wonderful. I'll be here. Good luck."

"See you soon enough."

Burton stood in the doorway of her kitchen, feeling a bit overwhelmed. She'd just finished being mauled with kisses by her babies after returning from Denver. She'd been gone for a day and a half and in that time, her world had changed.

Everett assured her a freelance contract would be sent her way within the next day or so and she should be on the lookout for it. In the interim, she was to get her life ready to report to Denver International Airport on September 3 to catch an 8:15 a.m. flight to Heathrow. There, she'd meet up with Bishop Fromminger, her accompanying cameraman who was from the British affiliate. The two stations had decided to split the cost and both would benefit from the world-exclusive story, the pair slated to spend three days in the strange little island nation—it was all the Chilvokian government was willing to give them, with a day of travel on either end.

An entire week she'd be gone. She hadn't spent that much time away from her animals since she'd been in the hospital and Simone had kept Cricket for her. Burton knew exactly who to ask to take care of them now, and that was Lee Ann. She had the space and loved the animals as much as they loved her.

As Burton looked around her house, she was mentally going through her closet upstairs, trying to decide what she wanted to take with her. She felt overwhelmed and profoundly out of practice. She was used to teaching new shelvers the Dewey decimal system, not finding out what was bringing a foreign land to possible war.

Running a hand through her hair, she shook herself out of her fear and hurried upstairs to begin sorting what she wanted to pack so she could make sure it was washed or dropped off at the dry cleaners.

She had so much to do. She needed to learn

absolutely everything she could about Chilvokia, which would not be an easy task, considering how limited the available information was. The Department of Tourism promised to send her some information; it would be helpful, but purely biased, so she hoped to be able to meet with Bishop and nail down their assignment 100 percent.

☙☙☙☙

Burton was almost in tears as she headed northeast of Colorado Springs to the town of Falcon and the relatively new subdivision called The Gables. It was a bit out of the way but was beautiful and the mountain view was uncompromised. Lee Ann and Phil had settled there when they'd moved to Colorado, one of the first residents in the budding neighborhood.

She easily navigated the maze of winding streets until she pulled up in front of the spring-yellow house with the white trim and porch, a swing moving slightly in the evening breeze. Burton pulled her Jeep onto the rocks to the side of the driveway, not wanting it to be in the way since it would be parked there for a week. She'd be spending the night with the Pollack family, leaving her beloved animals as Lee Ann gave her a ride to DIA in the early hours of the morning.

She decided to stow her luggage in the Jeep; they'd gather it before leaving in the morning. Instead, she grabbed her overnight bag and Cricket in her carrier. Ajax ran ahead, barking as he met her at the front door, looking up over his shoulder, waiting for Burton to let him in.

She reached over Ajax and rang the doorbell. A moment later, the door was opened and a smiling Lee Ann greeted them.

"Come on in."

After everyone was settled and Cricket and Ajax had calmed down, Burton sat with Lee Ann in the downstairs family room, a cup of decaf for Burton, a glass of wine for the investigator.

"I can't believe you're going," Lee Ann said, sipping from her Riesling.

Burton smirked. "You? I don't know, as crazy as it sounds, I figured this would all just blow over and go away."

Lee Ann studied her. "Then, why did you ever bring it to the light of day? It would have been easy to bury, you know. Not like anyone would have known any better."

"Except for whoever sent those postcards," Burton said, sparing a glance at her.

"Except that, yes." She gazed down into her coffee cup. "My old boss said no other mail came for me."

"After what?"

Burton shrugged a shoulder. "After I left, I guess." She sipped from the hot brew. "Maybe they changed their mind." She stared off into the distance for a moment before meeting her friend's gaze. "You don't think this is a mistake, do you? I mean, what if I arrive and find absolute Utopia?"

Lee Ann grinned. "Then you've got a new vacation destination."

༄༅༄༅

Burton glanced out the window she had been sitting next to for nearly nine hours. Her butt hurt, her leg hurt, and after all the reading and updating herself on the current story she'd been doing, her brain hurt. As she watched the ground get closer and closer, the airplane made its way through the fog to touch down on the tarmac of Heathrow Airport, arguably the busiest airport in all of Europe.

The flight attendant made the announcement that they'd landed in London and gave the temperature as eighteen degrees Celsius. Burton had to scramble to figure out what that was in Fahrenheit. She turned to her phone, which had been in airplane mode, and switched it over to active so she could see that it was a pleasant sixty-five degrees.

Gathering her belongings together, she waited until she could disembark. Luckily, her seat was somewhat near the front of the 747. She was ready to get off that thing, considering she still had almost five hours to go before reaching her final destination.

She'd received a text from her travel companion telling her where he'd meet her. She searched for the restaurant he'd mentioned. Making her way through the throngs of people, she finally spotted it and was relieved to see the short, thin black man standing out front waiting for her. They'd texted each other a picture of themselves the night before so it would make connection easier.

"Bishop?" she said, walking up to the man who was dressed casually in stylish blue jeans and a red button-up shirt, sleeves rolled up to just below his elbows.

"Lovely to meet you, Burton," he said, his British accent charming and utterly disarming. "I figure we can grab a bite to eat since we have just over an hour before our flight."

"Perfect, yeah. I'm sorry, but a small bag of four peanuts doesn't do it over a nine-hour flight," she said, following him into the restaurant where he'd already gotten them seats.

He chuckled. "Isn't that the truth? Rubbish, if you ask me." He sat down, a beer already in front of him. Within moments, a waitress was at their table waiting to take Burton's drink order.

"Just a Diet Coke, please."

"So," he said, once they were left alone. "Tell me about yourself outside of what I know already."

"Well," she said, letting out a long breath. She was glad to see he was personable. She'd worked with some real jackasses in her career, which made getting a story difficult and beyond unpleasant. "Currently, I'm the head librarian of a small library in a mountain town and have a cat and a dog."

He leaned forward in the booth, dark eyes wide. "A librarian, eh? That's bloody fantastic! And here I thought I was lucky, being a bloke with a Polaroid as a kid."

They shared a laugh at that.

"No, I was in this business for quite a while before I left," she said, not giving an explanation beyond that.

"I know who you are," he said gently with a kind smile. "Even over here, we were all shocked. Kind of like your Alison Parker and Adam Ward, shot on live TV last year."

Burton nodded. "Just awful."

"Did they ever catch the bastard who did it? With you, I mean?" he asked, sipping his beer.

She shook her head. "No. It's assumed it was to shut the senator up, but I guess we'll never know."

"A load of bollocks, you ask me."

She smiled. "So," she said wanting to change the subject. "You texted you had some new information for us. What you got?"

"Yes. I've got an old buddy from Moscow who was able to shed a bit more light on this place." He reached into the computer bag he had tucked beneath the table and unzipped a side pocket to remove some sheets of paper. "I printed us both out a copy so we could study it." He handed her one. "So, it looks like this bloke"—he reached across the table to tap the colored picture with a finger—"is the king of Chilvokia, as was his father, and his father and so on. He's been on the throne for twenty-two years."

Burton stared down at the man with blond hair and blue eyes. "He looks like Luke Skywalker," she muttered.

Bishop burst into laughter, a few patrons around them glancing over at their table. "Oh, that's priceless. Not sure good ol' King Arvid of the House of Berg would be so thrilled at that comparison. Here's the interesting thing," he added, leaning forward slightly. "My friend tells me that though Chilvokia is largely Russian in culture, even the language is close, the ruling class for a couple hundred years has been more Nordic."

She met his gaze. "A mixture of two totally different cultures."

"Definitely."

༄༅༄༅

The flight from London to Moscow was nearly four hours, and to say that Burton was sick and tired of being on an airplane was an understatement. She was tired, nervous, and just wanted to be home with her babies. Since that wasn't an option, she decided to try to get some sleep. Bishop was already dozing beside her.

She peeked at him, envious at his seeming ease in falling asleep. She'd never been able to sleep on planes, but also, her mind was alive with nonstop thoughts about what she was about to do. She was trying to come up with a plan of attack. One of the biggest problems was, she had no idea what was wrong or what they were heading into. There was absolutely no recent or current news on Chilvokia and its people. Planning for the unknown was one thing, but this felt like planning to pack for an alien planet.

"Trouble sleeping?"

She glanced over to see that Bishop's eyes were still closed, but he was facing her direction. "Yeah. Did I wake you?"

"Nah," he said, shaking his head. "Just too wound up to really drift off."

"Me, too."

"You know, I'm going to miss my son's birthday while we're there." He opened his eyes and ran a hand over his closely shaven head.

"Oh no! I'm so sorry, Bishop. How old?"

"Three." He gave her a sad smile. "Apple of my eye, that kid. Things didn't work out so well with his mum, but she's good about bringing him to my flat. Keep 'im most weekends since she works."

"What's his name?" Burton was charmed, able to hear the love in his voice.

"Jonathan, but we call him Johnny. Greatest bloke, ever." His smile was wide and bright, which she returned.

"Well," she said with a yawn. "We'll get you back home to Johnny as soon as we can."

※※※※

It was the middle of the night by the time they reached Sheremetyevo International Airport in Moscow. They were ushered to a private jet for the final forty-five-minute flight to their ultimate destination.

Burton met Bishop's gaze for a moment as they boarded the plush ride. Inside, they discovered white leather La-Z-Boy-type seats that offered plenty of leg room, each furnished with its own small, moveable round table next to it, either to place refreshments or laptop computers, and so on.

"My, my," Burton muttered, choosing a seat. They were the only two on board, other than a woman who was to serve them during their flight and the two pilots.

"Indeed."

They were offered champagne and hors d'oeuvres. Bishop devoured them. Burton, who was entirely too tired to eat, sipped her champagne sparingly, knowing that with her level of exhaustion and lack of food in her system, it would be potent. She needed to keep her wits about her as they headed to where she felt she should have been six years ago.

An uneventful fifty minutes later, the luxury jet landed on a lit runway, though as Burton looked out the window, it seemed to be the only lights on in the entire place. She and Bishop gathered their carry-on luggage and disembarked with a smile from their flight attendant.

They walked up the familiar tube that connected the plane to the gate, only to enter a completely abandoned, dimmed airport. Burton felt uncomfortable as her gaze swept the wide hall, gates dotting either side. The airport layout reminded her of the Colorado Springs airport, which had one terminal and a dozen gates.

Even so, to see the digital signs above each boarding station dark, only a row of recessed lights on above their heads, it felt surreal and like a horror movie. They reached the escalator that the flight attendant had told them to head for, which wasn't running, and walked down the metal stairs. She told them a car would be waiting for them just beyond the glass exit doors.

"I feel like I'm in a bloody horror flick," Bishop murmured, "waiting for the goddamn zombies to attack."

Burton smiled, mostly to make herself feel better by using brain power to react to something rather than the fact that she actually thought what he'd said was humorous. She thought it was a smidge too close to reality.

Sure enough, just as the flight attendant had said, there was a black town car waiting for them at the curb. The driver, dressed in a black chauffeur's outfit, was loading the trunk with their luggage from the belly of the plane. He said nothing, nor did he open the door of the shiny car for them.

Again, exchanging a look, Burton tugged open the back door and climbed in followed by Bishop. As the car left the ghost town of an airport, they were serenaded to arias from Verdi's opera, *La Traviata*, which the driver felt the need to add his own unique baritone to.

Burton wanted to laugh—she felt as though she were in the middle of some weird *Candid Camera* moment. She looked around the backseat of the car, searching for a camera or listening device. She had no idea what to think, but it was certainly making her anxiety level rise.

The car took a winding path through the dark countryside, though now and then they seemed to be passing through a town. More than once, the smoldering remains of a building could be seen, as well as houses on fire and riots in the streets. Burton watched in horror as one man was beaten by three other men, a woman holding a child to her chest crying mere feet away.

Next to her, Bishop flinched when something was

thrown at the car, hitting his window as they drove past a group of young men who were keeping themselves warm around a burning pile of what appeared to be furniture. They yelled things at the passing car, none of which could be heard above the music and certainly not understood.

Finally, the car made its way toward a long drive that led to a guard post. The driver turned the music off before pulling to a stop. He rolled down his window and exchanged a few words with the guard who came out of the small guard shack. The guard went back inside and the imposing iron gates before them slowly opened, allowing the car to pass.

The sprawling grounds weren't quite as impressive as the sprawling Greco-Roman-style building before them. Lights strategically placed along the grounds shined beams of light up onto the columned building with a circle drive in front and a massive portico to double front doors.

The town car pulled in front of the impressive spread of stairs that led up to the building, once again the driver ignoring his passengers in favor of opening the trunk and removing their luggage. He left their bags at the foot of the stairs.

As soon as Burton and Bishop let themselves out of the car, the driver climbed back behind the wheel and the car pulled away.

"I guess we're the bell boys," Burton murmured, walking over to her large roller bag and tugging the handle up from its hiding place. Bishop did the same as the two began to mount the stairs.

Once they reached the top, they were surprised to see a man standing there waiting for them. He had wavy, shoulder-length brown hair and long, thin sideburns, a look that was a bit too youthful for a man who appeared to be in his later fifties. Though there was no gray, his face told the story. His eyes, however, caught Burton's attention. They were a vibrant blueberry blue.

"Welcome, Miss Blinde, Mr. Fromminger. It's a pleasure to have you here," he said in accented English. It sounded German. "I am Heinz Bergman, head of the Ministry of Socialization here in His Majesty's court." He shook Bishop's hand and kissed Burton's knuckles. "You may leave your luggage here," he said, turning to head toward the impressive building behind him.

Burton and Bishop exchanged a look of uncertainty before following.

Stepping inside, Burton felt like she was more in a museum than a residence. Artwork was hung everywhere in gold frames, sculptures set on marble pedestals. The marble floor of the lavish entryway was inlaid with what appeared to be the Crown's code of arms.

They were led up a winding staircase to the second floor, the ceilings standing at least thirty feet above their heads.

"It's very late, so I figure you two can slumber and we can begin in the morning," he said, glancing over his shoulder at the two who followed him. "Well," he added with a charming smile, "that is, later in the morning." Bergman stopped at an opened doorway. "Mr. Bishop, this is your room," he said, extending an arm of invitation toward the cameraman.

"Thank you," Bishop said, glancing briefly at Burton before entering the room.

Left alone with their host, Burton followed him about four doors down the hall before he stopped, her door also left open for her.

"Miss Blinde. Your things will be brought up to you shortly." He gave her a smile then closed the door behind her once she'd gone inside.

Left alone, Burton moved farther into the large, extravagant room. She felt extremely vulnerable, nothing with her except her laptop, purse, and cell phone. The thick carpeting at her feet was red, the walls white with gilded accents. The furniture was large and lavish in dark woods, the four-poster bed literally having a small step stool next to it for her to use.

There was a bathroom attached, nearly as large as her old apartment in Denver, with a sunken tub, separate shower, and a water closet. The mirror above the double sinks was gilded in gold and, though garish, was beautiful in its own way.

Burton was startled by a knock at the door. When she opened it, there was no one there, only her roller bag. She pulled it inside the room and closed and locked the door. She had the feeling that, regardless of how exhausted she was, sleep was going to be long in coming.

Chapter Ten

Burton slowly came to the land of the awake, her eyes blinking open a few times before they stayed that way. It was daytime, sunlight coming in through the gauzy curtains at the other end of the large room. Something caught her eye and she saw that on the small bench placed at the end of the bed was what appeared to be a gift basket. She had no idea when it had arrived or even what time it was.

Glancing toward the bedside table, she saw her phone. She tried to roll over, as the bed was entirely too large for her to reach it, but she'd sunk so deeply into the cloud-like mattress that it took her three tries to even sit up. She felt like Johnny Depp in *Nightmare On Elm Street* when he was being sucked in by the water bed.

Finally able to climb to the side of the bed, she sat on the edge and grabbed her phone, sending a quick text off to Bishop. She also saw that it was just after eight-twenty local time, which meant it was almost eleven-thirty at night. She felt out of it and definitely was suffering from jet lag.

Burton: Good morning, Bishop. Are you awake yet?

Bishop: Mornin'! Yes, I am. I'm munching on the killer cheese from this gift basket.

She eyed her own gift basket again, her hunger suddenly making its appearance known. She slid off the bed and walked over to it, untying the silver bow and pushing the colored plastic wrapping away to show a minibottle of N7 vodka.

"I can't get away from this stuff," she muttered, pushing it aside.

She found a wrapped smoked sausage and the cheese Bishop had mentioned, as well as crackers and a box of scones.

She ripped open the cheese log and took a bite, moaning at the explosion of flavors.

Burton: Have you seen anyone?

Bishop: Only what I guess is a servant-type person. Def not the typical maid outfit!

As if on cue, there was a knock on her room door. She put her phone and the basket aside and padded across the thick red carpeting, unlocking the door and pulling it open. In the doorway was one of the stranger things she'd ever seen.

Standing before her was a woman who wore a head covering, much like a burka, but a strip across her face revealed only her eyes and some of the bridge of her nose. The strangest part, however, was it wasn't the all-covering gown that was usually part of the Islamic garb. The head scarf was flipped back over her shoulder, and her top was a fitted three-quarter-sleeve shirt that hugged her breasts and revealed her midriff, her belly flat and somewhat muscular. Her skirt flowed around her legs like a hundred silken scarves sewn together in every hue. Her barely visible feet seemed to be clad in sandals.

"Hello," Burton said, assuming this must be the strange "servant" Bishop was speaking of in his text.

"Good morning, Miss Blinde," she said, her words accented, though Burton had no idea from where. "Minister Bergman would like to invite you to breakfast so your day might begin."

"Oh, all right. That would be great."

"Wonderful." The woman held her hand out

where Burton saw she held a folded piece of paper. "It will be served in an hour." With that, she turned and walked away.

Burton watched her go, mystified before she unfolded the paper. She saw that it was a map of the palace with a large red X at the dining area.

"I guess X marks the spot," she murmured, then closed the door to get ready.

🕮🕮🕮🕮

Showered and dressed in a midnight blue pantsuit, Burton applied camera-ready makeup but didn't overdo it. Simone had taught her well over the years. Her hair was down and slightly curled. She felt good and ready to begin whatever journalistic journey she was supposed to take with Bishop, who of course was dressed as casual as possible, as most cameramen were. He had his equipment with him when they met at the dining room.

The dining room was something to behold. Huge state dinners could obviously be held there, with the elaborate table able to seat fifty and room to extend it for an additional twenty. Many of the outlying furnishings in the room were original to the palace and absolutely exquisite. Burton stood aside as Bishop grabbed some b-roll to be edited into their story later.

"Got it?" she asked once he lowered the camera from his shoulder.

"Got it."

"Good morning!" Heinz Bergman's voice boomed as he entered the cathedral-like room. "I'm so pleased you found it all right. I hope you're hungry."

He clapped his hands and a small army of the headdress-clad women entered, each carrying tray upon tray of food—from the recognizable eggs and sausage to entrees that looked downright frightening.

Burton watched the women, feeling as though she'd just been transported back to a 1985 Robert Palmer music video with all the women dressed identically playing the guitar. It was unsettling but she pushed it aside and walked over to the chair Heinz had pulled out for her. She sat and gave him a polite smile as he pushed it in. He took the chair at the head of the table to her left and Bishop sat on her right.

The minister insisted on preparing a plate for Burton, piling on the food and explaining each dish, many local to Chilvokia. She willingly played along, even if some of it looked like it would make an encore appearance after it went down.

"Minster Bergman," she said, deciding to get things started, "when driving here from the airport last night, there were some frightening scenes we passed. Violence and obvious distress. In a nutshell, what's happened here? Can you give me some background?"

Bishop had set up a shot with the camera on a tripod on the other side of the table so he was not on screen.

Bergman let out a sad breath as he chewed his food. He nodded as he blotted his mouth with the cloth napkin by his plate. "We have a happy, peaceful country, and kingdom. And, unlike some western countries, our king is the head of the power, not just a figurehead. However," he said, holding up a finger, "our king has abandoned his people, his country, and his ancestors."

Burton's fork stopped halfway to her mouth, some egg falling back on her plate. She lowered the fork and rested it back down. "Can you explain?"

"Let us finish eating and then I have things to show you," he said with a smile.

Burton nodded in agreement. The last thing she needed was a shot of her with green pepper falling out of her mouth. She looked around the room where half a dozen of the masked women stood, seemingly waiting for any need they may have.

"Why the head scarves?" she asked.

Bergman followed Burton's gaze before returning his focus to his meal. "Hundreds of years ago, it was tradition for servants to be covered head to toe. The purpose was for them to disappear like a ghost, only to appear when they were needed. Over time, it's become a rite of passage and an honor."

She eyed the women then their host, who was focused solely on his food. It sounded odd, but this place was quickly turning out to be a strange place, indeed.

※ ※ ※ ※

Bishop followed the pair, camera on his shoulder, as the minister walked down the ancient halls of the palace, hands tucked behind his back. As they talked, Bishop moved around, getting varying shots.

"I'll give you a bit of history," Bergman said.

"All right," Burton answered, walking alongside him, sensing he was leading them to a specific location. She decided to ask a broader question about him. "What exactly is the Ministry of Socialization?"

"Well," he said, glancing at her, "this was a position created out of desperation due to the situation I'm about to explain to you."

Heinz led them into a massive room with thirty-foot ceilings and red-painted walls with gold accents. Life-sized painted portraits lined the walls, men and women staring down at the three, wearing garb representing many decades and hundreds of years.

"This," he said, walking backward into the room with arms spread, "is the history of our kingdom and our land. This is the oldest room in the palace, built in 1329."

Burton listened to him drone on and on about the history of the building, the history of each and every person in the portraits, and every little fact about the beginnings of Chilvokia. It was difficult to feign interest when none of this had a thing to do with why she and Bishop had flown so far to a land of mystery and seeming craziness. But, she figured if she listened and let him get through what he felt the need to tell them—his pride in his country and its history obvious—perhaps they could get down to brass tacks. Besides, she thought, glancing over at Bishop, it would help give the story dimension as a solid piece.

Finally, she was led toward a set of two ornate chairs upholstered in red velvet. They were oversized and Burton, who was a woman of average height, felt like a little girl, just the tiptoes of her high heels touched the floor.

"You ask what the Ministry of Socialization is," Bergman said, crossing one leg over the other, his fingers running along the sharp crease in the pant leg of his trousers. "Technically, our King, Arvid of the House of Berg, has been on the throne for twenty-two years." His voice was even and serious. His bright blue eyes were focused to an almost unsettling level on Burton. She forced herself to meet that gaze. "However, he abandoned his people about four years past."

"What do you mean by, 'abandoned'?" she asked, head slightly tilted to the side as she listened. Out of the corner of her eye she could see Bishop moving around to set up a shot on a tripod.

"Well, let me go back a bit. Arvid is a good man,

but he could never measure up to his father and just how beloved he was. But, I think he tried. He took the throne at a young age, which no doubt was daunting for him." He let out a heavy and sad sigh, glancing over at the portrait of Arvid, whom Burton still thought looked like he belonged in *Star Wars*. "Suddenly, maybe oh, ten, twelve years ago, he changed. Greatly changed. He began to systematically rid Chilvokia of all that made it great. We are a country of agriculture, fine artistry, and of course"—he grinned over at her—"our famous N7 vodka."

"I've heard a lot about it," Burton responded with a knowing little smile. "What does the 'N' stand for?"

"Novikoff, the family that has been making it for centuries. But, eventually, once it began to be sold outside of Chilvokia, it was difficult for folks to remember what to look for upon a second purchase, so to modernize it, about thirty years ago, they changed it to a make it new and, what do you call it, hip?"

Burton chuckled and nodded in understanding.

"But," he said, holding up a manicured finger, "what he did that hurt us the most was to start limiting tourism, which has been a large industry for us for years. Many people come from Russia and other places. We are not communists here, so it's an open and free place to come."

"In what way did he begin to limit tourism?" Burton asked, intrigued by this new information, trying to connect any dots she could in her head.

"He put limits on flights that could come in, put limits on how many days a week the airport could be open. Until it is what you saw last night." He shook his head, heavy brow drawn. "It's empty. Shops inside were forced to close, eateries...All those people lost their jobs and their businesses."

Burton could see the pain in his eyes and concern for the people. "What do you think caused this change in him?"

He shrugged. "We've wondered if it was drugs of some sort, mental illness or if he'd simply tired of his role and wanted out." He leaned slightly over the arm of his chair closer to her. "The country began to fall apart at the seams, Miss Blinde. People rose up and began to rebel. I cannot tell you how many thousands have been slaughtered in the past decade of chaos, oppression, and confusion." He chuckled ruefully. "We've reached out, trying to get help for our tiny nation, but even Putin, our closest neighbor, wants nothing to do with this mess."

Bergman turned away from her, bringing a hand up to smooth over his hair and clear his throat. He let out a heavy breath before looking at her again.

"I apologize. This is an upsetting topic for me."

"It's okay," Burton said, understanding in her voice. She let him get himself back together before she asked, "Where is the king as we speak?"

"That, I cannot tell you. Literally, one night he disappeared and took a goodly amount of the treasury with him." He shrugged with wide eyes. "We were left to pick up the pieces."

"And, so this new position you hold does what?"

"Ah, yes. With the killings and displaced people. It's been up to me to figure out what to do with them, what to do with their children, what to do about their destroyed schools." He slapped his hands on his thighs before he stood. "Tomorrow, I'll share more of that with you. Now, I must leave you as I have a full day of meetings and work to do." He took Burton's hand, bringing it to his lips as he had done when they'd arrived. He looked her in the eye, that same intense look in his own. "It's been a pleasure, Miss Blinde." He kissed her knuckles then was on his way.

Burton watched him go before she turned to Bishop. "Let's cut it."

He hit stop on the large camera and shook his head. "What a wanker, this king."

Chapter Eleven

Burton sat at the desk tucked in the corner of her room with her laptop, typing up a detailed e-mail for Everett. She was working out the angle of her story and wanted to make sure he approved before she got too far in her strategy. After all, they only had another day and a half there before heading back.

She completed the e-mail and hit send then closed her e-mail. She sat back in her chair and chewed her lower lip as she stared at the wallpaper on her laptop, which was an adorable picture of a sleeping Ajax wrapped around a glaring Cricket. She thought back over what she'd been told that day, a tremendous amount of information that she was trying to sort out. One thing she planned to ask Heinz the next day was who had sent her the postcards and vodka, who within the kingdom was trying to get her attention.

She'd considered bringing them with her—to see if perhaps somebody would recognize the handwriting or would cop to writing them—but in the end had decided against it.

She glanced out the window and saw that the sun was beginning to fall. She felt sleepy, her body's clock still back in Colorado, but she didn't' want to waste any time. She still had the map she'd been given by the woman that morning and decided to take advantage of it.

She had changed out of her suit after dinner and now wore a pair of jeans, tennis shoes, and a T-shirt from her alma mater, CU-Boulder. Her hair was pulled back in a ponytail and her face was washed clean of makeup. She slid her phone into the back pocket of her jeans.

Map in hand, she pulled the door to her room open, looking right then left before heading into the dim hall. The wall sconces were lit every third one, casting eerie shadows across the floor and walls. Glancing down at her map, she noticed that there was nothing on the map to the right of her room, only to the left, which led to the stairs and lower levels.

Curious, she headed right. The farther down the hall she traveled, the more spaced out the light was until she was nearly in the dark in the seemingly endless hallway. It was almost like a fun house; every closed door looked like the dozens of others she'd passed. She stopped and had tried a couple only to find them locked.

She checked around her, feeling uncomfortable and absolutely as though she were being watched. She reached behind her and tugged her phone out of her jeans pocket, illuminating the flashlight app. The ghostly image of a woman appeared before her, and she gasped in surprise, her heart racing. A second later, she rolled her eyes, hand resting on her chest as she realized she was looking at a reflected image of herself in a mirror.

"Like a goddamn fun house," she murmured, turning away from it.

She found herself toward the end of the long hallway that extended about two or three hundred yards. Something strange had occurred, though. As she'd walked, she'd gone from clean opulence to dirty, dark, cobweb-covered furnishings and dirty carpet. It was as though she'd walked through some sort of time portal.

Walking to the end of the hall, she noticed yet another door, though this one appeared to be different. It was narrow with no doorknob nor a place where there should have been one. She walked over to it and, with a light touch, pushed on it. It moved slightly, and when she pushed slightly harder, the heavy wood stubbornly opened with a groan of its hinges.

Beyond the door was a steep staircase with stone walls and stone stairs. She reached her arm out as far as she could to shine light within the narrow, dank space to ensure it would be safe to continue. Although not a structural engineer, she decided it looked safe enough and followed the first and second steps down. Upon reaching the third, she cried out when the door behind her slammed closed. She leaned against the cold stone wall, taking several deep breaths before continuing on.

The narrow stairs wound down; they looked like something more from a twelfth-century castle than the palace she was in. The stairs continued farther and farther down for about two stories before Burton finally reached the floor.

She flashed her light in every direction, noting more stone walls, and she could distantly hear the dripping of water. It seemed as though she were literally inside the walls of the palace, with pipes running along the ceiling, some exposed wire work running along the wall to her right. To the left was a closed wooden door; directly ahead was a closed wooden door, and just past the wiring to the right was yet another closed wooden door, each reinforced with an iron arm across it. They appeared extremely old, again something more from a castle. She decided to start from the left and move right. As she got closer to the door to her left, she realized it had a square hole cut into the thick wood;

iron bars, spaced a few inches apart, were bolted to it. She hadn't noticed it initially because of the thickness of the cobwebs entwined in the bars, forming an almost full wall in the square opening. Even the bright LED light of her phone wouldn't penetrate it.

She noted the iron doorknob and grabbed it. It turned ever so slightly but seemed to be stuck. It didn't look like the room—or perhaps cell, she wondered?—had been used for decades if not longer, so she decided to leave it be.

Moving on to the center door, she found it unlocked and it opened easily. The room beyond was pitch black, the light of her phone flashlight barely making a dent in the midnight thickness. She stepped in, noting a large rock sitting by the wall to her left. She grunted as she maneuvered the heavy stone to hold the door open—she figured that's what it was there for. The last thing she needed was to get trapped.

The room was square and no bigger than the average bedroom. She noted, however, two-thirds of it was filled floor to ceiling with wooden crates, some stamped with N7, others Novikoff & Co. She walked over to a crate that lay on the floor, its top removed. Squatting down, she reached in and dug through the straw filler until her fingers came in contact with something smooth.

Pulling it out, she saw that it was a round bottle with the tall, narrow neck, just like the bottle she'd received six years before. The label was the exact same as was the bulbous cork wrapped in silver foil.

She took in the room as she squatted there, wondering how many thousands upon thousands of bottles surrounded her. Putting the bottle back, she walked to the door, using her right leg to shove the big rock back to its place by the wall, the door slamming shut, nearly taking her fingers with it.

"The hinges in this place. Jesus," she muttered.

She walked over to the final door, and like the second, it opened easily. She gasped in surprise, however when she saw that it didn't lead to a room, but a tunnel. There was no rock to put in the door, so she stood outside it and closed it again checking to see how hard it would be to open it once she was on her way out. There didn't seem to be a problem, but she'd find out.

With a big breath for courage and a little prayer sent out to whoever was listening, she guided the door to slowly close and headed down the long tunnel with arched ceiling, all of it made of stone.

The light was dimming somewhat, so Burton checked her battery life. "Shit," she growled, noting she had less than 35 percent life left. Deciding to conserve, she turned off her phone and used her hand to glide along the damp and somewhat slimy stone of the tunnel. She stopped when her fingers trailed over hinges. Using the light briefly, she saw that it was yet another cell door, much in the state of the first.

Creeped out yet determined, she continued on. Her fingers trailed along the curve in the tunnel as it turned to the right. Following along, she came to three more cell doors along the way, the final one allowing a glimpse in between the bars. She shivered when she noted the shackles bolted to the wall.

Shaking it off, she continued on until she reached the end of the tunnel, which ended at a steel, riveted door. She clicked on her phone flashlight and examined it, thinking it would take a bomb blast to get through it.

"Damn." She sighed. Then, she realized the door wasn't fully closed. "Oh!"

She had to tuck her phone back in her back pocket in order to use her full strength to open the door, which easily weighed a hundred pounds. Once it was open enough for her to slip through, she noted she was safe: it wasn't moving anytime soon.

Grabbing her phone again, she illuminated the huge room though was surprised to see that this one had been updated in recent times. The floor and walls were all cement, the ceiling so high above that the light of her flashlight couldn't breach the distance. What she could see, however, were metal shelves lining three of the four walls and boxes on the floor.

After a cursory inspection, she realized she'd found an armory. Boxes of pistols and rocket launchers lay on the shelves along with endless boxes of ammunition, rifles, and other long-barreled guns. She also saw three huge boxes of hand grenades, M26 stenciled on the outside.

"Yikes," she whispered.

Something else caught her eye and when she walked over to it, she realized that tucked in the corner was some clothing. Squatting next to it, it seemed to be a folded pair of black pants, perhaps cargo pants, and what seemed to be a folded-up camouflage jacket. From the condition of everything in the room, they appeared fresh, so to speak, as though they hadn't been there long.

About to pick up the jacket, her head jerked to the side when she heard something. Pushing to her feet, she remained as quiet as she could as she walked toward the partially opened steel door. She heard a man crying and pleading in a language she couldn't understand before the distinct sound of a key sliding into a lock and turning. It sounded like the closest cell to her, the one she'd passed coming in.

She held her breath, eyes huge as she turned off her phone, praying the door to the room she was in wouldn't be seen.

A second man yelled at the first in a similar language before she heard the sound of flesh being struck and hard. The whimpering man cried out, again more pleas, which seemed to be ignored after more sounds of a beating were followed by the sounds of metal squeaking then clicking.

Burton remembered the bolted shackles and felt sick as she wondered if that's what she was hearing.

More beating and crying then all went silent for a moment. Finally, she heard the sound of the door slamming closed and the lock being engaged then heavy footfalls against the stone leading away from Burton's direction until they were gone.

She stood there, frozen. Her heart was racing and sweat ran down between her shoulder blades and breasts. Her breath caught when she heard something behind and to the right of her, in the area of the clothing she'd found. It sounded like the scuffling of a shoe.

Hurrying out of the room, she winced with the exertion as she pushed the door closed then scurried off down the tunnel. She dared not use the light of her phone, so she ran blind, desperately trying to use her fingertips as her eyes as they grazed the wall. She gasped when she reached the cell and was startled by a whimper from inside.

Terrified, she hurried on, eyes huge as she tried to see through the darkness. After what seemed like hours, she reached the wooden door that led to the open area with the three doors. She was nearly whimpering herself as she got it closed, only then bringing her phone back out, the light dim as her phone battery was dying.

"Please, please," she pleaded with her phone to get her back to her room.

She ran to the narrow winding staircase and

slipped, falling and hitting her chin hard on one of the stairs. She bit her tongue in the fall and instantly tasted blood. Dazed, she lay there for a moment before she scrambled to her feet and continued up the stairs. She stopped halfway up, thinking she heard something. Back pressed to the rounded wall and hands flattened against it on either side of her hips, she tried to hold her breath, listening.

"Oh God," she breathed, clearly hearing one of the three doors from below opening.

She ran up the rest of the way, swearing she felt breath against the back of her neck, though she knew it was only in her mind. She nearly cried in relief when she reached the narrow wooden door that led to the same floor as her room. Holding the door until it silently closed behind her, she took off on a dead sprint down the carpeted hallway, her left leg killing her and her lungs burning, but she didn't dare stop until she reached her room.

She almost overran the door, barely managing to stop as she grabbed the doorknob and turned it, pushing inside and slamming the door behind her. She leaned against it, her chest heaving and eyes closed. She screamed when there was a knock at her door.

Trying to pull herself together, she took several deep breaths and ran a hand over her discombobulated ponytail, escaped strands of hair hanging down in her face. She moved away from the door and put as calm an expression on her face as she could before opening the door.

One of the covered servant women with large brown eyes stood on the other side, a tray held in upturned palms. Upon the tray was a steaming ceramic teapot and a petite teacup sitting upside down on a saucer with a spoon and wedge of lemon lying beside it.

"Good evening, Miss Blinde," the woman said in her accented English. "A nightcap for you, as no doubt you still suffer from jet lag."

Burton glanced down at her offerings, up at the woman's eyes, then back to the teapot. She felt like she was in the Twilight Zone. The offering was so incongruous after the last hour's events.

"Oh. Um, thank you." With a smile, she took the tray. "I appreciate that."

After the woman walked away, Burton closed the door, walking deeper into the room, which looked exactly as she'd left it, and set the tray down on the dresser top. Her heart was still racing and tears were threatening to fall. She was doing her damnedest to hold them at bay. She was on assignment and there was no time for tears.

There's no crying in baseball... she heard in her mind, which made her smile. Movies, were always her go-to when she felt nervous. Her whole childhood had been made up of movies and a pretend world.

She closed her eyes and let out several deep, calming breaths. This was one time she wished she knew how to do yoga—the calming effects would certainly be welcome. Instead, she opened her eyes and poured herself a cup of the beautifully fragrant tea. What a wonderful idea, she thought, grateful for the thoughtfulness of whomever.

The tea bags had already been placed inside the teapot, allowed to steep, so the tea was ready to pour and drink. She squeezed the slightest bit of lemon into the cup, noticing curiously a bit of fizz that quickly dissipated as she stirred.

Teacup in hand, she walked over to the bed where she took a sip then set the cup down on the bedside table. She reached behind her head and tugged the band that held her ponytail free, allowing the long strands to fall around her shoulders.

She grabbed the teacup and took another sip, enjoying the warmth that spread down her throat and throughout her body, especially after spending the past hour in the dank depths of the palace.

Lowering the cup, she began to feel lightheaded, her lips beginning to become slightly numb. She tried to lick them but her tongue wouldn't work. She turned to set the cup on the nightstand, but it slipped, hitting the floor, the brown liquid spraying the carpet and side of the comforter on the bed.

Bracing herself with a hand on the tall mattress, Burton felt a numbness spread from her lips down through her arms and her legs. She tried to focus on the wall opposite the bed, but she couldn't keep her eyes focused on a single point. She felt nausea prick at her stomach as she tried to take a step forward and fell to her knees.

As though a thousand miles away, she heard voices, a woman's and a man's.

"Pack up everything you can," the woman said.

Burton tried desperately to get to her feet only to fall flat on her face, her arms giving out. She tried to fight as she was grabbed under the arms and picked up. She couldn't speak, her tongue feeling as though it were twenty times too big for her mouth.

"Hurry!" someone hissed.

Burton's vision was becoming nothing more than a tunnel, the end growing farther and farther away. She felt her body give out and suddenly she was lifted and heaved up onto someone's shoulder. Her mind screamed at her to fight against whoever was carrying her away, but it was impossible. She was too tired, too weak.

"No," she managed to slur, no idea what she was even saying. "No."

A moment later her stomach revolted and she felt her body betray her, even as she was bounced and carried hurriedly out of the room.

"No," she managed one more time.

Chapter Twelve

Burton woke up when her stomach began to heave. By instinct, she raised herself to her hands and knees and retched, her throat burning and back hunched as dry heaves wracked her entire frame. Finally, she was able to fall over to her side, panting and exhausted. She brought up a hand and swiped it across her mouth, stomach roiling again when she felt that her lips were covered in slime.

Opening her eyes, she moved into a seated position, her mind fuzzy and head pounding. She was shocked to find herself sitting on the floor of a large shower stall in her panties and bra. Her hair hung in her face and she was surrounded by vomit smears. The smell was ungodly.

She stood slowly, weak and confused. She couldn't think straight enough to wonder why none of this made sense. Instead, she turned on the hot and cold spigots, wincing when the cold spray roared down on her. After a moment, it began to warm, the mess on the floor swirling around the drain at her feet until it was gone.

On unsteady feet, she managed to balance one foot at a time to remove her panties, which had spots of vomit on them, followed by her bra, the front covered with it. She slung them to the far end of the shower where they hit the floor with a sickening splat.

Looking around, she noticed that the shower was fully stocked with shampoo, conditioner, and body wash, the double glass doors frosted strategically. She closed her eyes and stood under the hot spray, which felt amazing and helped her head to clear a bit.

She smoothed her hair back, grimacing at the knots that were in it from dried vomit. Once it was all wet, she washed it three times with the fragrant shampoo before she felt satisfied. It took her a moment to realize the shampoo she was using was her own, bought at the airport in Moscow. She turned and examined all the products on the built-in shelf in the wall and realized they were all hers.

She walked to the shower door and opened it just enough to peek beyond it. She was not in the palace bathroom anymore. The bathroom door was closed, but the bathroom itself was modern, though a bit run-down with chipped granite countertop and stained tile on the floor.

She closed the shower door again and returned to cleaning herself. She felt a little better with each product she used. She was surprised when she lifted her arm to shave to see the level of growth of her underarm hair. It had to have been about two or three days since she'd shaved.

Feeling like she could faint for a moment, she braced her forearm against the tile wall and rested her head on it. She took several deep breaths, waiting for it to pass. Once it did, she resumed showering, desperate to shave, even if she did a horrible job in her current state. She also managed to nick herself in the sensitive flesh of her armpit.

After she felt clean, she stood under the spray for a few more moments before turning the water off and pulling one side of the shower door back to step out. The entire bathroom was filled with steam as she grabbed one of the folded bath towels lying atop the bathroom vanity and slowly dried herself off, taking it slow. Her overheated skin was making her feel faint again.

Towel wrapped around her, she staggered to the door and pulled it open, a rush of cooler air washing over her. She leaned against the doorframe for a moment, enjoying the cooldown before she stepped out of the bathroom.

She found herself in what seemed to be a hotel room if the placard on the closed door was any indication. There was a full-sized bed that was unmade, the comforter halfway on the floor, and one of the three pillows was on the floor in the foot of space between the bed and the wall. The bedside table next to the bed had an illuminated lamp on it, as well as her cell phone, which was plugged into its charger. There was also an alarm clock that read 7:55.

She walked over to the bed and sat down on the end. She couldn't get over how weak she felt. She also couldn't get over how she could be nauseous and hungry at the same time. Spotting her brush on the dresser with a bolted-down TV, she pushed up from the bed and walked over to it, grabbing the brush and slowly brushing through the intricately tangled strands.

The mirror above the dresser showed her the reflection of a woman she didn't know. She was incredibly pale and her face was thin. Her lips were chapped, which she had to assume was from the dehydration of so much vomiting, if the shower floor was any indication.

She turned away from the mirror to see her roller bag tucked against the wall in the corner, her laptop in its bag leaning against it. She was relieved though couldn't manage even a smile. Instead, she brushed her hair through a couple of times before tossing the brush on the bed and padding over to the roller bag, struggling with its heft to lay it on its back on the floor. She unzipped it and opened the flap for the main compartment where she kept her clothes.

Checking inside, Burton was surprised to see the condition of things. It literally looked as though everything had been thrown in, nothing folded like it had been when she'd packed it. She sorted through the mess, finding her comb, her high heels, and her pantsuit shoved inside. She winced, thinking about how long it was going to take to iron out her blouse. Pushing it aside, she found a pair of panties and the other bra she'd packed, as well as a pair of sweatpants and the CU T-shirt she'd been wearing during her last memory. She brought it up to her nose, noting that it smelled of laundry detergent. It had been recently washed.

She chose it to wear and zipped the bag shut. She tugged on her clothing, an activity that drained her of all energy. She made her way to the bed and collapsed, closing her eyes and falling fast asleep.

≈!≈!≈!≈!

Burton's eyes blinked open and she found herself in a bed in a hotel room that seemed somewhat familiar. She was relieved to see Bishop sitting in a chair in the corner. A weak smile came to her lips.

"Hi," she said, voice raspy.

His smile, however, was wide and bright as he sat forward in the chair. "Aren't you a bloody sight for sore eyes," he said. "I cannot even tell you how good it is to see you awake and coherent."

"Hear, hear," Burton murmured, trying to lighten the heaviness in the air. She still felt a bit groggy but far more clearheaded than she had when she'd glanced at the bedside clock—three hours before. "Where are we? What happened?"

"You were given a noxious chemical which, the

doctor said, is essentially an enhanced version of the date-rape drug. Potent and brutal."

Burton nodded, sitting up and running her hand through her hair. "I guess." She was glad to see she still wore the sweats and CU T-shirt, no vomit to be found.

"She was here just a bit ago," he added, pushing up from the chair and walking over to the dresser where a bottle of water and an apple sat. "Doctor's orders, drink as much as you can and get the fruit down and you're cleared to travel."

"Where are we going?" Burton asked, slowly making her way out of the bed.

"Home," he said simply. "We're in grave danger here, my friend." He moved aside as she grabbed the water bottle, but she was unable to do the simple task of twisting the cap off. He took it from her and did it for her, handing the bottle back. "We've got just a bit before they're going to load us up in their helicopter and fly us to safety to catch a flight back." He checked his watch. "I'll leave you to get ready and eat and drink, okay? Be back to nab you half past the hour."

Burton nodded, still unsure of anything that was going on, but trusting him. She accepted a quick hug then was left alone. As much as she wanted to guzzle the water, she knew her stomach would revolt at that, so she sipped the cool liquid. She processed what she'd been told and tried to think of when she could have been drugged. All she could think of was the hot tea, but she would have thought it would have taken more time to enter her system than it had, if that was the cause.

She noticed that her phone was still plugged into the charger on the end table and grabbed it so she could text Everett and Lee Ann to let them know what the hell was going on, to her best knowledge, anyway. No doubt they were scared to death. She should be typing up her story by now and working over e-mail with Everett on putting the story together.

With a heavy, tired sigh, she unplugged the fully charged phone and unplugged the charger from the wall and set it beside her so she wouldn't forget it. She swiped her thumb over the lock screen and went to her text messaging screen. She was shocked to see that texts had been sent back and forth between Everett and the doctor who was treating her in Chilvokia. She scrolled through them, reading:

Burton: Hello, Mr. Timpton. My name is Dr. Liliya Novikoff, a General Practitioner here in Chilvokia. I am using Miss Blinde's phone to communicate with you because she is currently under my care. I believe at this time she has come down with a virus that has rendered her profoundly nauseous and exhausted, often losing consciousness.

She is resting comfortably at the moment, so she and Mr. Fromminger shall not be returning this evening, as planned. I will contact you when I have more information.

Everett: I really appreciate you contacting me on Burton's behalf, Dr. I won't lie, I'm extremely concerned. Please keep me posted!

Burton: Good news after my text two days ago. Burton has begun to regain consciousness on a regularity that makes me more comfortable. I've also administered an IV drip to combat dehydration. I should be able to clear her for travel soon.

Everett: Wonderful news!

For a moment she wondered why the doctor had told him she had a virus, but then she figured it was so Everett wouldn't be completely freaked out, no idea what was going on. She turned her phone off and gathered her things. She decided to keep her sweats and T-shirt on to travel; she wanted to be as comfortable as possible, especially by not having anything too tight against her stomach.

She walked to the bathroom, grabbing her brush on the way, and stood in front of the mirror brushing her hair out so she could pull it back in a ponytail to get it out of her face. Having fallen asleep with wet hair, it had dried wonky, so pulling it back was definitely the best way to go.

She checked around the bathroom to see what was hers and needed to be packed. Her gaze landed on the shower and her soiled bra and panties lying in the corner. Revolted, she quickly snatched them and shoved them into the trashcan before she grabbed her toiletries, placing them in a side pocket of her roller bag in the sleeping area of the room. While there, she sat on the bed and tugged her tennis shoes on, looking around the room in general to make sure she hadn't missed anything.

Shrugging into a hoodie, she grabbed her bag and heard a knock at the door. She pulled it open to see Bishop standing on the other side as well as a blond man who was small in stature, much like Bishop, with the kindest brown eyes she'd ever seen. Something about him was so gentle, almost like a child in a man's body.

"Burton, this is Ivan. He's going to help us get everything up to the roof," Bishop said, grabbing her attention.

"The roof?"

"Chopper."

"Oh, okay."

Burton watched as Ivan moved past her into the room and gathered her belongings before giving her a big smile and hurrying back out, disappearing down the hall. She turned to Bishop.

"Where are we? Who are these people?" she asked, her brain finally clearing enough to absorb actual information and to understand the situation they were in.

"I've not been told much," he said, stepping into the hall and allowing her to leave the room. "But, from what I've gathered, the rebel stronghold."

Their attention was grabbed by Ivan's voice at the end of the hall, hollering in Chilvokian, which neither of them understood, but the tone wasn't hard to miss.

"Come on," Bishop said, "let's go. We can talk on the flight home."

The two hurried down the hallway where Ivan waited for them; then they followed him up a flight of stairs and down another hallway. Burton's lungs burned and her chest heaved, her energy draining fast after her body had fought so hard against the drug that had been given to her.

Finally, they mounted one final staircase, a narrow set of metal stairs that led to a door at the top. Burton's breath caught when she realized that door led to the roof of a fifteen-story building. She was terrified of heights, and it took everything in her being not to turn and flee back down the stairs.

The helicopter was already there, the roar of the engine and deadly spinning rotors awaited them. The sliding door of the chopper was open and Ivan ran ahead, ducking as he got closer, tossing in Burton's roller bag and setting her laptop on one of the seats before he ran back to grab Bishop's bag.

"You ready?" Bishop asked, yelling above the cacophony.

Burton viewed the metal bird, her eyes huge. She

was admittedly terrified. She hated flying in airplanes, let alone her first time in a tin can with windows.

"Let's go, mate!" Bishop yelled, taking her hand and tugging her behind him.

She climbed up the steps before moving into the belly of the helicopter, placing her laptop in her lap as she sat. Ivan came up and belted her in before giving her a smile and a thumbs up. Bishop followed, getting settled in the seat beside her, belting himself in.

The pilot, who wore a visored helmet with headset, turned back to look at them from his place behind the controls. "Ready?" he asked, his English surprisingly good.

Burton stared out the helicopter window at Ivan. Hands tucked into the pockets of his leather jacket, he stood watching by the door that led back into the building. Gazing out the other way, she saw a dark landscape. It was the middle of the night, though the orange of a fire burning far away lit up that distant area. As she watched, an explosion turned the night golden, the sound deafening, even from what seemed to be a long distance away.

"Let's go, man!" Bishop yelled, using hand gestures to emphasize his words.

She turned away from her friend and gazed back out at the burning night, only to cry out in surprise at a second explosion that rocked the night, this one closer. She saw that Ivan was thrown back slightly against the door. He collected himself then turned and bolted inside.

Burton's stomach lurched slightly as the helicopter lifted from the landing pad, straight up like an elevator. She saw the door next to her was still open then glimpsed the ground, about five feet below them. She turned to look at a visibly frightened Bishop.

She reached over and grabbed his hand in hers. When he met her gaze, she smiled. "Go home to Johnny," she said.

Seeing Roger's face before her mind's eye, she smiled. *Your death will not be in vain!*

She kicked her roller bag out of the helicopter where it landed on its bottom before flopping down on its side on the rooftop. Quickly, she unbuckled her seatbelt and jumped. She landed on her feet on the landing pad before she fell to one knee. Looking up, she watched as the helicopter continued to rise farther and farther away into the fire-filled night sky.

She slowly stood, never taking her eyes off the helicopter until it was safely on its way and raising a hand to wave good-bye.

Chapter Thirteen

Burton woke up, happy to report that she was feeling better than she had since everything had happened. Her head was clear, her stomach had settled, and she was quite hungry. She'd never gotten around to eating the apple Bishop had brought her the night before. She glanced over at the dresser and was excited to see it was still there.

Pushing back the covers, she hurried over to it, taking a healthy bite as she hurried to the bathroom to do her morning business.

After she'd made the self-admitted absolutely, incredibly stupid decision to jump out of the helicopter and once she was relatively sure Bishop was safe, she'd headed back inside and hurried back to the only place where she felt somewhat safe: the room she'd been in the past few days. She still had no idea where she was, besides what Bishop had told her was the rebel stronghold. What that meant exactly, she had no idea. Other than Ivan, she hadn't seen a soul.

For now, she intended to get the apple and the rest of the water down, shower, then go exploring. She had no idea if she was even welcome to stay here, taking a lot into assumption. But, at the end of the day, she was a reporter; investigation and getting down to the truth were in her blood, and she was determined to follow her heart.

Finishing the apple, she wrapped the core in toilet paper and tossed it in the trash on top of her soiled bra and panties. She'd have to find a dumpster to get rid of all of it, or it would be an incredibly unpleasant stay in that room.

She took a large drink from the bottle of water, noting her reflection in the vanity mirror. She had far more color in her face, though she was surprised at how much weight she'd lost in the few days since she'd been so violently ill. It wasn't hard for her to lose weight when she put her mind to it, but this was a bit much. She could tell by the way her T-shirt and sweats fit her, as well.

Turning away from the mirror, she walked back into the bedroom part of the room and retrieved the toiletries she'd just packed the night before. She put them back where they'd been then turned the shower on, testing the temperature of the spray with her fingertips. She wanted to be completely fresh and on her game. She had no idea where to begin, but after her shower, she'd start to check out the hotel—the Spiritan Hotel—according to the huge letters she'd seen on the roof.

Shedding her clothes, she stepped into the large shower and slid the glass door shut. She let out a satisfied sigh as the hot water fell over her skin. She was so happy to feel more like herself, even though she was in the strangest situation she'd ever been in, one which she'd put herself in.

Her mind wandered to what her next move would be. She considered calling Bishop to see who he'd spoken to since they'd been there and to get any sort of name or direction to go. She thought about asking him what he'd seen of the stronghold, how many were there, what ideas he might have—

"Why are you still here?"

Burton cried out in surprise, her arms automatically coming up to cover her naked breasts as she faced the woman who stood at the opened glass door to the shower. She had long auburn hair and fierce green eyes. She was dressed in black battle dress uniform pants, or BDUs and a fitted olive-green T-shirt.

Mortified, Burton could only stare at the woman, trying to cover her nakedness in vain. The woman looked her over then met her eyes with a little smirk.

"You have nothing I haven't already seen," she said before the smirk fell from her lips. "Why are you still here?" she demanded again.

Burton was speechless, with no idea what to say or how to react to what felt like an attack during a most vulnerable moment. All she could manage was, "Can I please get dressed?"

To her relief, the woman closed the glass shower door and turned and exited the bathroom, slamming the door behind her. Burton was left startled and shaken, a hand resting on her chest. She took several deep breaths before she pulled herself together, turned off the water, and dried herself before tugging on her sweats and T-shirt again.

The woman sat in the chair Bishop had been sitting in earlier, one leg crossed elegantly over the other, even as her arms stretched out along the length of the chair arms, her fingers tapping endlessly against the wood.

Burton felt admittedly intimidated by the sheer intensity of energy that came off the woman in waves. Even though the reporter was dressed, she still felt the humiliating vulnerability of moments before. She could feel that sharp gaze on her as she made her way to the bed and sat down, not more than ten feet away from the strange woman.

Settled, she garnered the courage to look her unexpected guest in the eye. "My name is Burton Blinde," she began, knowing the woman spoke English from her outburst in the bathroom. "And you are?"

"It doesn't matter," the woman said, her English very good, only slightly accented. "With your recklessness, you likely won't be alive long enough for me to bother with proper introductions."

Burton was stung by those words but chose to push them aside. "I don't know who you are or what your problem with me is, but someone tried to get my attention years ago, obviously wanting to expose whatever is happening here," she said, proud that her voice sounded far calmer and firmer than she actually felt. "I was...delayed, but here I am."

"Why on earth would you send your cameraman off and you jump out of safety?" the woman asked, sitting forward in her chair, crossed foot falling to the floor and her elbows resting on muscular thighs. "What were you thinking?"

"That I wasn't going to lose anyone else because of me again!" Burton exclaimed, immediately ashamed at her tone. She looked away for a moment, taking a deep breath to calm herself down. "I'm sorry," she said, forcing herself to look at the woman once more. "I came here to investigate a story," she said, voice calmer. "And, that's exactly what I intend to do."

The woman let out a heavy sigh before she pushed to her feet, heading to the hotel room door. "Well"—she turned at the door to face Burton, who had also stood—"the helicopter won't be back for five days, so that's exactly how long *you* have to investigate your story and how long *we* have to try to keep you alive."

"Wait," Burton said, taking a step toward her. "What's your name? I'll need someone who can speak English to help me to talk with others."

The woman with the unusually green eyes studied her for a moment before responding. "You can call me

Lilli." With that, she left, closing the door behind her.

Burton stared at the closed door, reeling. Something about the woman gave her the strangest sense of déjà vu. She shook it off and quickly locked the room door before heading back to the bathroom, also locking that door behind her.

❦❦❦❦

Burton would be lying if she tried to say she hadn't been standing at the door to her room for twelve minutes, trying to get the courage to open it. She was showered, dressed, hair brushed to a shine, and makeup artfully applied. She didn't bother with one of her suits—wrinkled or not—as she had a strong feeling it wouldn't be appropriate anymore. Anything she'd learned in her years as a reporter and in her years in college no longer applied. She was on her own, learning as she went.

So, in a pair of jeans, T-shirt, and hiking boots, she was ready to go—sort of.

"This is ridiculous," she whispered, eyes closed as she lightly banged her head against the solid wood of the door. She cried out at the responding knock.

Unlocking and opening the door, she saw Ivan standing on the other side, his ever-present smile shining. He spoke, but since she couldn't understand a word he was saying, she shook her head with a shrug. Instead of repeating himself, he gestured for her to follow him.

"Here we go," she whispered. She'd realized belatedly that the hotel was old-school and didn't have doors that locked automatically upon closing and actually needed a little metal thing called a key, which she'd found on the dresser top. She locked the door before she hurried after Ivan.

He led the way down the hall, once again past the elevator to the stairway. She did her best to keep up with him. The apple had been great, but it only provided so much energy. He stopped glancing back at her as she'd fallen back as they headed down from the twelfth floor. She finally caught up and offered an apologetic smile. He gave her one of his winning smiles and slowed down, the two making their way to the fourth floor together.

He held the door open for her and Burton stepped into the dim hallway, much like her own up eight flights of stairs, then followed Ivan to a room with opened double doors where she could hear lots of talking and laughter, as well as dishes clanging. Her stomach growled in response.

They reached the doorway to see a cafeteria-type setup in what looked to have once been a ballroom or conference room. Dozens of round tables that sat ten were positioned all over the room along with buffet-type food stations like those found at a self-serve restaurant. Burton glanced at the tables; they were filled mostly with men, a woman peppered in from time to time. But, as she and Ivan entered, she could almost hear the scratch of the needle taken off the record.

All laughter and conversation ceased and two hundred pairs of eyes were on her. She could feel herself being visually undressed many times over and swallowed her nerves. Most were dressed in casual clothing, though some were dressed as Lilli had been earlier, in BDUs or military garb.

She was startled when she felt something cold touch her arm. Ivan held out a food tray for her, the various food compartments already carved out. It reminded her of the trays she used to use during her days in school. She took the tray with a smile, her hunger from earlier somewhat leaving her as nerves took over.

Little by little, conversation began again, all in Ivan's language, and she wondered how much was about her. She got that answer somewhat as she and Ivan walked past a table where a group of eight men talked, one gesturing at her with his head as he said something that made the entire table erupt with laughter.

Letting out a nervous breath, she followed Ivan to the end of the line. It felt like the first day of high school all over again. She felt an intense gaze on her and peeked to her right. About halfway across the room, sitting at a table with three empty seats was Lilli, and she was looking right at her. The woman's presence should have made Burton feel more comfortable, if not safer, but it didn't. It amped up her anxiety level, instead.

She turned away from the redhead's unwavering gaze and focused on the bounty before her. She looked up to see a mountain of a man standing on the other side of the buffet table filled with fragrant food under warmers. He was at least six-and-a-half-feet tall and built like he should be playing for the Denver Broncos. He wore jeans that hugged massive thighs and a black T-shirt that was stretched dangerously tight over biceps larger than Burton's waist. Tattoos covered his arms and part of his bald head.

What grabbed Burton's attention, however, was the fact that he wore an apron tied around his narrow hips and was watching her with a wide-eyed intensity. She met his dark gaze.

"Hello," she said with an uncertain smile.

"Eat!" he said in extremely accented English.

She was startled when he snagged the tray from her hand and went down the line, moving another food worker out of the way to load it up with fried chicken, Swedish meatballs, vegetables, sweet potatoes, and even shrimp, which was not a favorite.

"Eat!" he said again, shoving the tray back at her with an expectant expression on his chiseled face.

Burton stared down at the mountain of food, wondering if perhaps this guy was the cook. She had to admit it all smelled amazing. When she hesitated, he grunted in disdain and grabbed a bundle of silverware wrapped in a napkin and tugged out the fork. Using it to stab a healthy portion of the Swedish meatball, he held it for her, his eyes indicating there was no room for argument and that she was expected to eat from the fork in his hand.

She hesitated for a second longer before she leaned forward, taking the succulent meat from the fork with her teeth. Instantly, flavors exploded in her mouth, causing her to close her eyes and let out a small moan of approval.

"Is good, yeah?" he asked, eyebrows raised like a child awaiting approval from his parent.

"Mmmhmm," she said around the food she chewed. She brought up her hand and gave him a thumbs up, which he responded to with a smile that lit up his entire face and a responding thumbs up. He handed her a fresh bundle of silverware and sent her on her way.

She grabbed one of the dozens of cups filled with something that smelled like fruit punch from a table tucked against the wall. She scanned the dining room, again the analogy of a first day at school popping into her mind as she sought a place to sit. It didn't seem any of these people spoke English, so without a person to translate, talking with them would be a Herculean task.

She set her sights on a random table, deciding to take a chance when her shirt sleeve was tugged lightly. She turned and nearly broke into tears of relief at seeing

Ivan's welcoming smile. He said something to her that she recognized from other times when he wanted her to follow and she assumed it meant come or follow, so she did.

He weaved his way through the tables, again the room going silent as they made their way to the table where Lilli sat with six men, all of whom continued to eat, even as they followed Burton's every move.

"You're making yourself into a target," the redhead said, sipping from her cup as Burton sat down in the chair next to hers. "You look scared to death."

"I *am* scared to death," Burton whispered, eyeing those around them who stared at her.

"Well, you made the choice to stay," she reminded her, sparing her a glance before she stabbed at the salad on her plate. "Perhaps you should have gone home with your colleague after all, hmm?"

"No," Burton said, shaking her head as she tried to make heads or tails of the mishmash of food that had been piled on her plate. She did, however, know that Lilli was right. She needed to reach down deep and find some confidence so she could do her job. "Somebody wanted me here, so I'm here."

Lilli shook her head with a little laugh. "Well, then let me introduce you." She looked at Burton, making sure their gazes met. "These are proud men and women. You are not a reporter, do you understand?"

Burton met that gaze, and yet again, she found herself getting lost in a memory she couldn't make out as she stared into their grass-green depths. She nodded. "I understand."

Lilli looked away. "They're good people just trying to survive."

Burton nodded, sipping from her drink, which was cloyingly sweet. She shivered as the sugar passed through her system and put the cup down, craving cold water. She focused on her food, taking a big bite out of the fried chicken, which could have been made by the Colonel, himself.

"Good cook, isn't he?" Lilli asked, grinning.

Burton nodded, unable to speak, her mouth full of chicken. She swallowed and had to force herself to take another drink of the punch then wiped her mouth with the napkin that had been wrapped around her silverware. "So, are you going to introduce me to these guys who are glaring at me?"

Lilli glanced at her before turning her attention to the men at the table, all focused on the two women, eyeing Burton suspiciously. She said something to them in their language, indicating Burton and saying her name, obviously making introductions to them. She looked at the reporter and began to introduce them one by one, some ignoring the introduction altogether, some nodding in acknowledgment, others giving her a wave and a charming smile. The last to be introduced was the large, muscular man sitting on the other side of Lilli.

"This is my brother, Alexey," she said, the young man glancing briefly up at Burton, his light blue eyes hard and cold. He wore a baseball cap backward, but from what could be seen of his hair, it was short and strawberry blond, though more blond than strawberry. "You're not likely to hear much from him," Lilli said, sipping from her drink.

Burton's head turned to three men sitting on the other side of Ivan, who sat next to her. They were giggling like schoolboys as they spoke in their language. One was using his hand to make an obscene gesture as he spoke. Burton turned to Lilli as the redhead barked out something to them that caught their attention. One of the men had one last thing to say, his eyes on Burton before he smirked and focused on his food.

"What did he say?" she asked, glancing at the man then at Lilli.

Lilli looked at her briefly then back at her food. "He said, 'Welcome.'"

Chapter Fourteen

After breakfast, as unorthodox as it was, Burton was headed to the stairway, intending to return to her bedroom and send an e-mail off to Lee Ann and Everett. She was stopped, however, by Lilli's voice. Hand on the handrail, she turned to see the other woman walking up to her.

"I want you to switch rooms," she said.

"Excuse me?" Burton asked, turning to fully face Lilli. "Why?"

Lilli waited until a few of the men passed before responding. "Because you'll be safer that way. I'm on the third floor and the room next door is free."

Burton crossed her arms over her chest. "Safer? From what?" Another couple of guys passed them, one eyeing Burton. "Or, should I say from who?"

Lilli looked away from her for a moment before she ran her hand through her hair and let out a heavy sigh. "You have to understand what these people have been through, Burton," she said, her tone somewhat defensive. "Many of their wives have disappeared, their children gone. They've lost everything, forced to live here," she added, holding her hands out to indicate their surroundings. "Many of us don't even know what we're fighting for anymore."

Burton was touched by Lilli's words and the truth she could see in the depth of her eyes. She could see a woman who was tired...soul tired. "Okay," she finally said. "I'll move."

Twenty minutes later, Burton checked out her new digs—a smaller room than the one she'd had on the twelfth floor, but she didn't care. She still had a full-sized bed but had lost the desk and chair. She was also sharing a bathroom with Lilli, both with a locking door at either end of the bathroom that led to their individual rooms.

She shrugged the strap of her laptop bag from her shoulder and set the computer down on the bed, which was currently a bare mattress. She turned at the knock on the bathroom door. "Yeah?"

The door opened and Lilli entered, a pile of linens in her arms. "They don't match, but they're clean."

Burton walked toward her, taking the burden from her arms. "Thank you, I really appreciate it. I grabbed the pillows from upstairs like you suggested," she said, hitching a thumb over her shoulder in the direction of the pillows stacked on the dresser.

"Well," Lilli said, looking around the room. "I'll leave you to it."

"Wait." Burton took a step toward Lilli's retreat. When she had her attention, she spoke. "After I get settled in, would you mind sitting down with me and helping me understand what's going on? What's happened? From what the minister said, after the king abandoned his people—"

"That's what he told you?" Lilli asked, surprise in her voice. "And, that's what he's calling himself now, huh? Interesting. And, yes, we can talk." With that, she was gone, closing Burton's bathroom door behind her.

Burton pulled her computer out of the bag and powered it up. She set it on the dresser to load and go through the long process of snagging a Wi-Fi signal, which she'd learned could take some time in Chilvokia.

She turned to the bed and made it up, amused

by the purple flowers of the fitted sheet and the zebra pattern of the top sheet, all topped with a thick lime-green blanket.

"Very nice," she chuckled.

Her laptop ready to go, she quickly sent off the e-mails she wanted to and added a few notes to the document she had saved to her desktop for that reason. Later, she'd organize all her notes into a cohesive story.

As she did so, she thought about the e-mail she'd received from Bishop. She was beyond relieved to find out he'd reached London safely, and sure enough, went directly to see his son. He told her he fully intended to go through the footage he'd shot while there and asked for her to send him any footage she could get on her phone so he could mix it in for a complete addition to the story.

All that was wonderful, but what truly touched her heart was to know he was okay. "He made it," she whispered, letting out a happy sigh.

She shut her laptop off and closed the lid, business taken care of. Ready to head out for whatever Lilli had planned, she climbed off the bed and walked over to the bathroom, knocking on the door. With no response, she opened her side of the bathroom to indeed find it empty. She knocked on Lilli's side, again no response.

She tucked in her bottom lip, glancing behind her into her own room before knocking softly again. No response. She hesitated for just a moment before she reached for the doorknob and turned it, gasping when it pushed open. She glanced behind her one more time to make sure she was alone on her side then pushed the door open.

The room was identical to hers, only the furnishings were set up on opposite walls. She noticed what appeared to be a pair of pajama pants folded at the end of the hospital-corners bed, and intrigued, she decided to step inside. The room was very neat, the bed made, the two visible pairs of shoes lined up neatly against the wall next to the bed.

Her gaze fell on the dresser top where she saw a few bottles of lotion and body sprays. Curious, she sniffed each one, deciding Lilli had good taste. Next to the TV, she saw a bottle of perfume, about two-thirds used. She removed the cap of that and spritzed a bit, leaning in to take in the fragrance. Her eyebrows drew as she knew the floral-musk scent from somewhere. It was unique, but she couldn't place where she'd smelled it before.

As she replaced the cap and set the bottle down, she noticed black material peeking out of a drawer that seemed to have been hastily shut—in complete opposition to the rest of the neatly organized room. Glancing around the room again, she slowly pulled the drawer open. She reached in and took hold of a black knit shirt that seemed to be an extremely fitted, short midriff. She felt her heart race slightly as she put it aside, noting a long, black scarf beneath it, the cotton easily malleable. It would be very easy to turn it into a burka-type head scarf.

She dropped the material back in the drawer, taking a step back in surprise, unable to take her eyes off it. Suddenly, she heard a key in the door.

"Shit," she growled, shoving the scarf and shirt back inside the drawer before slamming it closed and sprinting back to her side, closing Lilli's bathroom door behind her.

Heart racing, she took several deep breaths, trying to calm herself down. She buried her face in her hands.

"How did I get so damn out of practice? I'm a reporter, for crying out loud!" she hissed to herself.

She didn't have much time to beat herself up before her side of the bathroom opened, Lilli standing there. She expected to see the emerald fire of accusation shoot from those eyes, but instead it was just a harried expression.

"Hey. I have some rounds to make then I'm going to see my father. Do you want to come along?"

"Uh, yeah, absolutely." Burton gave her a smile and grabbed her phone, tucking it in the back pocket of her jeans as she followed her suite mate out the door.

※※※※

Burton sat on the bike, her mouth gone dry. She glanced at Lilli who was staring back at her with an amused expression on her beautiful face. "Um, okay," Burton said, swallowing hard. She looked down at the Kawasaki dirt bike she straddled. "Now what?"

"Put it in neutral," Lilli said, reaching over from her own bike and showing Burton how to do it. "There, on the right-hand side down by your foot, flip the kick starter lever out—perfect. Okay, quickly push down on it, good, good! Now, rev your throttle with your right hand, hurry, hurry!"

The bike died.

"It's okay," Lilli said, a small smile on her face. "Let's try it again."

Eventually, Burton got it together and they were on their way. She had to admit, she definitely planned to get herself one of those things once she made it home. But, for the meantime, she had to focus on what she was doing. It was obvious why a two-wheeled vehicle was necessary. The roads were clogged with debris from buildings, burned-out and broken-down cars, and trash. She knew better than to take her mind or eyes off the road or she'd be head over rear wheel.

She followed Lilli, neither wearing a helmet, their dirt bikes whining their way across the moon-like landscape. From the hotel, they'd ridden a long way on desolate, cluttered roads, but now they were entering what looked like it had once been a thriving village.

She was awed at the destruction. Where houses had once stood were piles of rubble and ash. Ruins remained in stark contrast to the bright blue sky, the beauty of the day mocking the damage to a thriving society. She was surprised to see what appeared to be a tent city of sorts set up in the shadow of what had once been a three-story building but was now nothing more than a shell providing a bit of shade.

Astonished and shocked, she pulled her bike to a stop next to Lilli's. She and Bishop had seen plenty of destruction in the middle of the night when they'd entered the country, but she hadn't seen it in the light of day.

"My God," she said, shaking her head. She felt Lilli's gaze on her and met it. "Unreal."

Lilli nodded. "It's all over the country. You figure Chilvokia is a country of about sixty thousand people on a good day." She shook her head with a heavy sigh as she sat in the saddle of her bike. "Now"—she met Burton's gaze—"many are dead, but far too many are missing. We honestly aren't even sure what we're dealing with."

Burton studied Lilli's profile as the redhead stared out over the tent city again. She was yet again struck with déjà vu, and it was driving her crazy that she couldn't put the pieces together. "Lilli," she said, garnering the other woman's attention. "Your accent, it's relatively, I don't know," she shrugged a shoulder, "light I guess you'd say. Compared to the others I've spoken to who speak English. Almost as though you've been away from here for a while."

Lilli shifted her gaze for a bit before she cleared her throat. "Come. I've got work to do."

Burton was surprised that her observation was completely ignored but went with it. She was just excited that she got her bike going again on the first try.

They parked their dirt bikes just outside of the tent city, and instantly people began to run out calling a word that sounded like *vrahch* with a rolling 'r.' Burton looked to Lilli for clarification.

"What does that mean?" she asked. "Is that some sort of nickname for you, or something?"

Lilli smirked. "Of sorts."

"What does it mean?"

Lilli glanced at her. "Doctor."

Burton stared at her. "You're the doctor? As in, the doctor that Bishop talked about and who texted my boss?"

Lilli said nothing as she dismounted her bike and put the kickstand down. She walked toward the group that was gathering.

Burton watched as Lilli shrugged out of the stuffed backpack she'd been wearing. She unzipped it and walked over to a table and removed various basic medical supplies, such as bandages, bottles of medications, and the like.

As Burton watched, a memory came back to her, sharp and abrupt:

She reached out a finger to press the button. A moment later, it arrived with a ding. When the door opened, there were two people already inside: a tall man wearing a low-slung baseball cap and a woman dressed professionally.

The pair seemed to be together and stood closely side by side. After giving them a polite smile, Burton wouldn't have given them another thought. But something about the woman caught her attention. She was beautiful, but there were attractive women and men around all the time. Her hair was blond and cut in a stylish bob that ended at her jawline. Her features were delicate, lips full and slightly pouty. But what caught Burton's attention the most were her eyes. They were the deepest, most intense color of green she'd ever seen in human eyes. If she wasn't able to see the vibrant life behind them, she would have thought they were colored contact lenses.

Their gazes met briefly, but in that moment, Burton felt like she'd been struck by lightning, a strange jolt passing through her so strongly that she had to look away, unable to look at the woman again. She stared straight ahead, facing the shiny metal doors of the elevator without seeing them. Her heart raced and she felt as though her suit was constricting her. She tugged lightly on the simple gold chain she wore, which settled at the hollow of her throat.

She gasped with full recognition of the woman who checked temperatures, gave out vitamins, and chatted with the people. Through the throngs of people that surrounded her, Lilli's gaze found Burton's astonished one.

Even from thirty yards away, something told Burton that Lilli saw the recognition in her eyes, the ghost of a smile on the doctor's lips seeming to cement Burton's suspicion.

Burton shook herself out of her shock as she realized she was being incredibly rude. She dismounted her own bike and walked into the crowds, intrigued. The people looked at her with curiosity but not one with suspicion or menace. There wasn't a person there who spoke English, but they talked to her anyway. When they realized she didn't speak their language, they had fun with it and with her.

Soon, Burton found herself in the middle of what seemed to be a cultural dance, one of the women singing lyrics that had those around her laughing and singing along. A young man grabbed Burton by the hands and dragged her to the center of the circle. She tried to follow his steps but was failing miserably, the gathered group joining her in laughing at her ineptness

She pulled her hands free from him and stepped back, watching his footwork, a moment later attempting to replicate it, only to fail miserably. She burst into laughter as he teased her, mocking what she'd done.

"Hey, now!" she called out through her laughter. She felt an intense gaze on her and glanced to her right. Lilli was standing in the crowd, an amused expression on her face as she watched.

≋≋≋≋

By the time they'd returned to the Spiritan Hotel, Burton had figured the dirt bike thing out and was hooked. She followed Lilli to the parking garage beneath the hotel and pulled her bike to a stop in the same parking space she'd taken it from hours before. After the first village, they'd headed out to half a dozen just like it, though not all were in as good a shape as the first.

Now, she was exhausted, both physically and mentally. She and Lilli had grieved with some of the people that day who'd lost loved ones or those who "just didn't have a chance," said the good vrahch. Though she guessed that she and Lilli were around the same age, she had the deepest respect for her. She'd watched her with the people, her gentle touch and deep concern. She'd even assisted her a few times that day with minor procedures that needed to be done.

"Tired?" Lilli asked as they headed toward the door that would lead inside the building.

"Very."

They walked together in silence, Burton's mind racing a million miles an hour, so much information gathered in that day, so many images she couldn't wait to commit to paper. She'd gotten some on film on her phone with permission from those who were okay with hamming it up.

She was humbled by what she'd seen and participated in, and part of her was filled with anger at what the people were forced to deal with, and for what? For who? To what end?

"Listen," Lilli said as they found their way to the lobby. "Why don't you head up and I'll scare us up some dinner?"

Burton nodded. "Great idea, I'm starving!"

"Me, too. See you in a bit."

They parted ways and Burton walked to the staircase. She was tired and desperately wanted a shower. She almost whimpered as she had to bypass the elevator, still not entirely sure why it was avoided.

She hit the second-floor landing and began her ascent for the final floor when she heard the second-floor door open behind her and the talking and laughter of a group of men. She felt slightly nervous, especially when she heard the catcalls behind her, but kept going, trying to ignore them.

She was halfway to the third-floor door when they caught up to her, one of them pinching her behind. She wanted to slap him but again tried to ignore it. They weren't going to allow that as she found herself cornered on the landing, three of the five men blocking her way. She noticed that out of the two men who stood back, one was Alexey, Lilli's brother. She sent pleading eyes his way, but all he did was smirk at her in return.

Realizing she was completely alone in this situation, she eyed the three men who surrounded her. "Please, just leave me alone," she said, attempting to keep her voice as calm as possible. She knew they couldn't understand her, but hoped something in her tone would get through. "Leave me alone," she said with a firmer tone, slapping away the hand of one of them who tried to grab one of her breasts.

His face became the mask of rage as he raised his hand high in the air. She winced at the backhand that never came.

Burton's eyes snapped open at the shout that came up the stairs, two of the men roughly shoved aside, including the one who had tried to grope her. Lilli stood in front of the huge men, all five-feet-four inches of her. With her green eyes shooting emerald fire and a sweeping halo of auburn hair, she looked like some sort of ethereal creature.

Balancing two Styrofoam containers in one hand, Lilli grabbed the man by the front of his shirt with her free hand, shaking him as she yelled in their language. Not for the first time, Burton wished she understood what was being said and happening. She glanced over at Alexey to see muscular arms crossed over his barrel chest, his light blue eyes chips of ice.

Burton's attention was snagged back to Lilli when the man she was pushing around fought back verbally, gesturing toward Burton. Burton watched, afraid for both her and Lilli. She was surprised when Lilli shoved the two containers into the man's hands then turned to Burton, cupping her face roughly and taking her in a deep, possessive kiss. Burton was even more surprised when she found herself fully responding to it.

Lilli pulled away, leaving Burton reeling. She was

in a confused daze as the redhead grabbed their food from a stunned Chilvokian man, leaving him and his comrades behind as she grabbed Burton's hand and led her out of the stairwell and to their floor.

Stopping in front of her own door, Lilli dropped Burton's hand, leaving Burton to walk the few feet to her own door. She was still stunned as she tugged her room key out of her pocket. She glanced at Lilli who was unlocking her own door.

"Why did you do that?" she asked, accepting the container of food that Lilli extended to her.

Lilli met her gaze before pushing her room door open. "They'll leave you alone now," she said quietly, closing her door behind her just as quietly.

Burton stood there for a long moment before she headed into her own room.

Chapter Fifteen

Sitting on her bed alone, eating from the container Lilli had given her, Burton couldn't get her mind to calm down after what had just happened in the stairwell. This, of course brought her full circle to that kiss. She understood why Lilli had done it, and the instant change in the men's body language told her she was essentially safe, basically "claimed" by Lilli, as far as they knew.

As she picked at her dinner, she had to admit, she'd been scared to death. What if Lilli hadn't come along? She shivered thinking about what could have happened, the incredible danger she'd been in.

Feeling lonely and vulnerable, she glanced at the closed bathroom door and decided she didn't want to be alone anymore. She closed up her container and grabbed her plastic fork and bottle of water she had in her room and climbed off the bed. She opened her side of the bathroom and knocked on Lilli's closed side. With the invitation to come in, she opened her side.

"Mind if I join you?" she asked, noting Lilli was sitting in basically the same position she had been moments before.

"No, come on in," Lilli said, moving her dinner container to one side of the bed to make room.

Burton entered the room feeling slightly guilty, knowing she'd just been poking around in it that morning. She climbed onto the bed and got settled, tucking her feet under her as Lilli had. They ate in silence for a moment before Burton spoke again.

"Thank you for dinner and thank you for...well, that could have been bad."

Lilli sipped from her own water bottle, twisting the cap on before setting the bottle down, silent the entire time. She put her food aside and climbed off the bed, walking over to the very drawer that Burton had been snooping in earlier that day. For a moment, Burton's heart stopped.

"Do you know how to use a gun, Burton?" Lilli asked, surprising Burton with the non-sequitur.

"What?"

"A gun," Lilli said, reaching into the drawer and pulling something out. She returned to the bed holding a 9mm pistol. "Do you know how to use one?"

Burton's eyes were glued to the firearm, unease filling her. "No. I don't like guns."

"Neither do I, but unfortunately they're a necessary evil here sometimes." She scooted over so she was sitting so close to Burton their thighs brushed. "Let me show you."

Burton gave Lilli her full attention, watching and listening as she was shown how to load, unload, and use the safety on the weapon. She took the heavy pistol from Lilli, not liking the feel of it one bit, but after what she'd just experienced, she had the idea that perhaps this wasn't such a bad thing.

"Do you feel comfortable?" Lilli asked. "Why don't you go through the process of loading and unloading a couple times, just so you're okay if you need to do it without thinking."

Burton did as she was told, feeling better about using the gun but still not thrilled about having it. "Why are you showing me all this?"

"I want you to keep that on you at all times,"

Lilli said, returning to her dinner. "A lot of these guys working with us are ex-convicts, released from jail when everything went down."

Burton's eyes grew wide. "Why?"

"They needed the help, trying to build reinforcing walls with sandbags, muscle, all of it. The truth be told, it's worked out pretty well, but you unfortunately have some loose cannons, like Lev in the stairwell." She met Burton's gaze. "I'm really sorry he did that to you."

Burton nodded, returning her gaze to her dinner. She set the gun on the bed beside her and began to eat again. She didn't want to think about it or talk about it anymore. "You were at St. Luke's, weren't you?" she asked, finally able to give voice to what she'd realized earlier that day while out in the field.

Lilli's head snapped up and she stared at Burton with surprise in her eyes. "What?"

"In Denver. I remember you, in the elevator. You had short blond hair, though. That was you, wasn't it?"

Lilli looked away, a smile on her lips. "I was told blondes have more fun in America," she said.

Burton grinned, happy that she'd remembered correctly. "Do they? I wouldn't know," she added, running her fingers through her dark locks.

Lilli smiled. "Well, my first foray in America didn't go so well as a redhead, so for my second, I decided to try something a little different."

"How did you end up there at all?" Burton asked, finishing her meal and her water. She tucked the empty water bottle into the container and closed the lid, setting it aside.

"My mother is an American," Lilli said softly.

Burton was surprised as she scooted farther onto the bed to lean back against the pillows. "Really?"

"Yes, really. My father, Grigoriy, traveled to

Colorado in 1980 for 'research,'" she said, using her fingers as air quotes.

"Research for what?"

Lilli shrugged, moving their empty food containers to her bedside table. "Research for new ways to distill," she said. "He was considering adding beer to the business, and with Coors made in Golden, Colorado, he wanted to tour the plant, get some advice."

Burton shook her head, confused. "What business? What do you mean?"

Lilli smiled, seeming amused. "You don't know? I'm part of vodka royalty here in Chilvokia, Miss Blinde."

More confused than ever, something occurred to her. Burton pulled her phone out from her back pocket and opened up her text messages. She reread those sent to Everett. Slapping her forehead, she rolled her eyes. "Dr. Liliya Novikoff," she read. "I'm such an idiot. How didn't I put that together?" She looked at Lilli. "You're a Novikoff?"

"I am," Lilli said with a nod. "Nice investigation, reporter." She smiled. "Though I practiced under my mother's maiden name in America, Lange."

"Why?" Burton asked, setting her phone on the bedside table on her side.

"Easier for my instructors, classmates, and patients to say," she said with a laugh.

"Oh, do I understand that. Try going through life with a first name like Burton. Good times."

Lilli smiled, though it quickly left her lips. "But, also, I suppose I was hoping someone would see it, notice."

"Notice what?"

"The last name, the resemblance," Lilli said softly, almost shyly. She picked at some lint on her sock. "Alexey and I left here for America with our mother,

Allison, when I was around seven and he was five. Her mother was sick with breast cancer, I guess. I don't remember her, though. So, we left our father here since he really couldn't leave the business, and one day she took us to the store to buy new shoes." She stopped her story and smiled the saddest smile Burton had ever seen. "Alexey and I had both picked out a pair, really excited to bring them home so our father could see them, *American* shoes." She met Burton's gaze. "Like they didn't sell the same thing here."

Burton gave her a small smile, sure she wasn't going to like what she was about to hear.

"So, there we were, standing at the register with our new shoes and our mother realized she'd forgotten her wallet in the car. She told us to stay put and she'd be right back."

When nothing more was forthcoming, Burton reached over and placed a hand on Lilli's knee. "Then what, Lilli?" she asked gently. "What happened?"

"She never came back," Lilli whispered. "She got in her car and drove away."

Burton's heart ached for the young girl she saw the woman before her melt into. She scooted closer to her. "Where did she go?"

Lilli shook her head, taking a deep breath. "We never saw her again. The clerk at the store called the police after we'd been waiting there for a couple hours. The store was about to close, I'll never forget that. The young man working there was complaining that he had a date and couldn't babysit a couple of brats."

Burton sat there for a long moment, speechless. She shook her head and glanced over at Lilli. "I honestly don't know what to say. I'm sorry seems so weak. But, I am sorry. Is that why Alexey hates me so much? Because I'm American?"

Lilli let out a heavy sigh and met Burton's gaze. "He's a very hard man. To be honest, I don't understand him half the time. My father is so gentle and Alexey is always looking for the fight."

"So, did you go back to America to practice?" Burton asked, stretching her legs out and crossing one ankle over the other. Her left leg ached so often, she frequently had to change its position.

"After a lot of arguing, my father finally agreed to send me there to go to college and medical school. He wanted me to go in London or Spain, but I insisted."

"In hopes you'd find her," Burton said, echoing her own heart with her mother, dead so long but no real answers why.

Lilli nodded. "Yes."

※※※※

Later that night, lying in bed, Burton had her computer resting on her lap as she quickly typed up an e-mail to Lee Ann. She added any and all information she could remember, starting with Allison's name, year she'd met Lilli's father, and years she'd given birth to her two children. She added the town she'd grown up in, which she'd learned was the mountain town of Evergreen, Colorado. She'd also learned that Allison had allegedly abandoned her children at a shoe store outside of Aurora, Colorado.

She chewed on her bottom lip as she tried to think of any other information that would be needed. She typed it all out then added a note of thanks for taking care of her babies for longer than expected and that she owed Lee Ann a good steak dinner when she returned in a few days.

Hitting send, Burton waited until the e-mail was

sent successfully then shut her computer down and went to sleep.

※※※※

They rode up to a large square building built of concrete blocks with a metal roof. Huge, heavily stained windows marred the lines. Enormous bay doors dotted the side of the building and a person-sized entrance lay in front, where Lilli pulled up, followed by Burton.

Dismounting her bike, Burton brought up a hand to shield her eyes from the sun above as she took in the building's height, noting it was quite obviously a factory of some sort, though there was no longer a sign announcing what the building had been. She did, however, notice huge tanks out back that were connected with a labyrinth of pipes to the building.

"Come on," Lilli said, leading the way, her backpack in place.

Burton followed, today her messenger bag strapped across her chest, the unsettling weight of the 9mm inside.

Inside the door was an office with old computers that appeared to be thirty years old, all the monitors covered with a thin layer of dust. The brown Berber carpeting was thin and worn, various stains peppered throughout the room. Burton noticed the banner that was proudly plastered across the back wall:

N7 Vodka. The world's finest.

The familiar bottle was pictured under the slogan, surprisingly printed in English.

"Is this the vodka place?" Burton asked, her eyes everywhere as they headed through a hallway that passed offices and a bathroom and finally to a windowed door that led to a huge open space with cement floors and walls.

"It is," Lilli said, pride in her voice.

Huge machines sat silent with conveyor belts stilled possibly forever, covered in the same layer of dust as the computers in the office.

"So sad to see it all at a standstill," Burton said, walking in a small circle to take it all in. She could easily imagine workers in hard hats coming and going, yelling instructions or conversation at each other over the loud engines, bottle fillers, and label machines, all piped in from the distilleries outside.

"I'd love to see it all come back to life someday," Lilli said, glancing around, as though seeing it for the first time through Burton's eyes.

Burton noticed a small desk off by itself that had a small audio control panel atop it with knobs and levelers to adjust volume and noise quality. A headset straddled the back of the office chair that was pulled up to the desk.

"Come on," Lilli said, tugging lightly on Burton's shirt sleeve to get her attention.

The two women headed to the freight elevator at the back of the factory. Once they were inside, Lilli pulled the gate closed and hit the button that would take them down.

"It's nice to not have to use stairs." Burton grinned.

"Yes, well early on someone sabotaged the elevator cables at the hotel sending four people to their death," Lilli explained absently, glancing up at the panel of lights above the elevator door.

"Oh," Burton said simply, wishing she hadn't known that.

When the elevator clanged jarringly at its final destination, Burton wondered if they were about to enter the dragon's lair in a role-playing game. Lilli peeked at her as she tugged open the gate, laughing. "There's no monster down here."

Burton glared at her, irritated that she was so easily read. She froze when she heard the very obvious sound of a shotgun pumped into action. A man of medium build stepped out of the shadows with short grayish-blond hair and ice-blue eyes, the gun held at chest height. Once he set eyes on Lilli, he instantly lowered the gun and cold chips turned to joyous blue.

"Liliya!" he exclaimed, the arm that didn't hold the gun extended toward her.

Lilli walked over to him and wrapped her arms tightly around his neck before leaving a loud kiss on his cheek. They exchanged a few words in Chilvokian before Lilli glanced at Burton. "Burton Blinde," Lilli said. Burton noticed the man's expression was that of recognition of her name and surprise. "Burton, my father, Grigoriy."

Burton came forward and extended her hand to him, which he took.

"Come." He beckoned to her, his arm still around his daughter's shoulders.

Burton followed, taking in her surroundings as they went. It was a typical basement-like tunnel with exposed pipes and heating system. They passed several open rooms with shelving units, most empty. It was much cooler down there, so she figured that's where they used to store the alcohol after it was bottled. It made her sad to see there was none left in the factory. But then she remembered the seemingly endless boxes of it in the palace.

Lilli's father shouldered the barrel of the gun and slid open a large steel door, allowing both women to pass before he pulled it shut with a loud clang. The room beyond looked nothing like the rest of the building.

Burton had no idea what it had been originally, but its purpose now was quite obviously a living space, replete with living room furniture, kitchenette, and round kitchen table with four chairs. There was an entertainment center filled with books, DVDs, and a large flat-screen TV and various equipment plugged into it.

"It's been a while since I've had to speak to American clients, Miss Blinde, but I'll do my best," he said in heavily accented English.

Burton smiled. "I appreciate it, sir. I've been in the dark pretty much my entire trip."

He chuckled at that. "What can I get you girls? Food? Drink?"

"No, Papa, we're okay," Lilli said, even as they were shepherded over to sit at the table.

"How are things?" he asked, bustling around the small kitchen, eventually producing a tray of sliced cheese and crackers and two tumblers of clear liquid with ice cubes clinking.

Burton eyed her drink, suspecting strongly it wasn't ice water. She took a surreptitious sniff and was nearly sent flying backward from the strength of what was no doubt N7.

"It's hard, Papa," Lilli said, sadness in her voice. "Supplies are getting low, and as winter is coming, I'm worried."

Grigoriy joined them, his own drink set before his place. He said to Burton, "Is there nothing you can do about this?"

Burton looked from one to the other. "Well," she said, not sure what to say, "I'd like to help. This has definitely been eye opening and unbelievably disturbing."

"Well," he said, taking hold of his glass. "That's

why my...eh, what it is?" He brought a hand up to his head as he seemed to be concentrating on something. "Angle—"

"Angel, Papa," Lilli said with a smile.

"Yes. That's why my angel contacted you for help!" Grigoriy exclaimed, raising his glass. "To us," he said, looking at the two women.

Burton felt as though she'd been hit in the gut. She looked at Lilli with huge eyes, the redhead meeting her gaze briefly. Trying to get her breath back, Burton raised her glass but said nothing.

"To us," Lilli said quietly.

Chapter Sixteen

Burton was quiet as they went out into the afternoon sun. Her mind was still a bit fuzzy from the drink they'd shared with Lilli's father, no matter how much she'd allowed hers to get watered down by the melting ice. Now, as it was just her and Lilli, Grigoriy's words from a couple hours before bounced around in her head.

As she grabbed the handlebars of her bike and flipped her leg over the seat, she could feel her companion's eyes on her. Burton looked at Lilli, saying nothing; she wanted Lilli to speak for herself.

"It's true," Lilli said at length.

Burton fingered the rubber that covered one of the handlebars, not looking at the other woman, sensing she wasn't finished.

"It was I who tried to get your attention." She let out a heavy breath. "I sent you the postcards, had my father send me a bottle of N7 to send to you. Hoping."

Burton smiled. "I still have it." She glanced at the redhead. "What were you hoping?"

"I don't know, honestly," she said, meeting Burton's gaze. "Hoping you'd figure it out, thought I was being quite the cloak-and-dagger." She viewed the pitted terrain. "I didn't know things would happen as they did." She brought a hand up, looking away as she seemed to be wiping at a tear.

Burton climbed off the bike and walked over to her, surprised when Lilli gave her back to her. "What?"

she asked softly. "Why are you crying?"

"I'm so sorry," Lilli whispered.

"Talk to me," Burton said gently, moving around Lilli so she could see her face.

"I almost got you killed, Burton!" Lilli erupted. "Do you get that? Your friend died! Because of me." She turned away again, swiping at the endless stream of tears that flowed down her cheeks. "Every day," she said. "Every day, I sat with you."

Stunned, Burton's mouth fell open. "At the hospital?"

Lilli nodded, using the sleeve of her T-shirt to wipe her face only for more tears to come. "Some days I could only stop by, bring you flowers." She met Burton's gaze, her green eyes tortured. "I'm so sorry. I didn't know it would lead to that."

Burton could feel Lilli's heartbreak. Without a word, she gathered her into her arms and held her, Lilli crying against her neck. Burton felt her own emotions stinging the backs of her eyes. So much pain, so much loss all around. "It's okay," she whispered, stroking soft strands of auburn. "It's okay."

It took several moments, but finally Lilli calmed and pulled away. "I'm sorry," she whispered, wiping her face again. She took several deep, calming breaths. She met Burton's gaze. "Can you ever forgive me?"

Burton smiled. "I already have."

Lilli gave her a blinding smile. "Come on. I have one stop I need to make before we can head back to the hotel. Ivan is supposed to meet us."

Twenty minutes later, they reached what was left of a medium-sized town, more of the buildings still intact than Burton had seen the previous day. The people weren't living in tents, but some were living in second-floor apartments where the outside wall was missing, their entire homes revealed as if a giant had come along and used a butter knife to slice away that fourth wall. Burton found it utterly surreal as she pulled her bike to a stop in front of a shop that used to sell fish.

She noticed Ivan standing with a few men on what was left of the sidewalk, talking and laughing. She turned to Lilli, who came up beside her. "He's such a sweet guy."

"He is."

"You guys seem close. Is he a brother or cousin or something?"

Lilli shook her head, shrugging her backpack down her arms. "No, but he may as well be. My father basically took him in when he was about twelve." She met Burton's gaze. "He's been with us ever since. Just a gentle soul. He was in a horrible car accident a couple years later and it did some brain damage."

Burton nodded, now understanding that difference she'd detected in him. She raised her hand and waved when Ivan noticed them and gave the two women a winning smile. He said something to the men he was talking to then left them and walked over to Burton and Lilli.

Lilli grabbed him in a quick hug. To Burton's surprise, he turned and gave her one as well. She smiled at him, patting his back once they parted.

"Burdon," he said, so much concentration on his face at trying to say Burton's name that she didn't have the heart to correct him.

Instead, she nodded and gave him a thumbs up. "Ivan," she said, poking his chest playfully. He grinned, poking her back. Within seconds, it had become the poking war of ten-year-olds.

"All right, you two!" Lilli exclaimed, a hand on each of their chests to playfully separate them. "We've got work to do." She turned to Ivan, speaking to him in Chilvokian.

Pretty sure he was getting the same lecture, Burton chuckled and walked away, noting with a smile that the town was coming alive, everyone spilling out into the streets. Every town they'd come to had been overjoyed to see Lilli and this one was no different.

Lilli began to mingle with the people, chatting as she examined mouths and ears and felt foreheads, obviously checking their basic needs.

Burton turned when she heard the tip-tip-tip-tip of helicopter blades slicing through the air. She spied a speck in the distance quickly growing larger and larger. Dirt and rocks sprayed as tiny bits of lightning hit the ground. She watched in horror when a man was cut in two as rounds sprayed his body, smoke rising as the corpse fell to the dirt.

Instant chaos ensued as people screamed, the entire town dispersing as they ran for their lives.

The helicopter made a pass over the crowd, spraying them with lead death, cutting people down where they ran and stood.

"Run!" Lilli screamed.

No need to be asked twice, Burton took off down the street only to see a man dressed head to toe in black roaring toward her on a motorcycle, the man sitting behind him armed with an AK-47, bullets spraying.

Burton threw herself to the ground behind a barrel filled with rainwater, bullets exploding the wood into splinters that showered over her head, which was covered by her hands. She peeked out to see the pair race by her, plowing through terrified townspeople. She watched in horror as a man was mowed down, his back exploding into ribbons of the material of his shirt and blood before he fell face-first into the street, the small child who had been running alongside him crying by his feet.

Burton crawled out from behind the barrel, relieved to see that Ivan and Lilli were hiding behind a broken-down truck. She met eyes with Lilli briefly before returning her focus to the carnage.

The helicopter flew off in the distance only to make a sharp turn and return, guns blazing. Burton watched in horror as a trail of bullets tore up the earth until it reached a woman running, holding an infant to her chest. The child's head exploded in a fountain of gore, the woman falling to her knees as bullets raked up her back until the back of her head disappeared. Her body fell on top of that of the infant.

"Jesus Christ," Burton whispered, horrified. Her attention was grabbed when she saw a little girl, no older than five or six, begin to run out to the body of the woman. "No!" she screamed when Ivan began to run out after her. She saw the two on the motorcycle turning around at the end of the street, the driver putting the bike into gear as it headed back in their direction.

As Burton watched, everything slowed down, her brain seeming to have a full minute to process everything it was seeing. She tore the messenger bag off her shoulder and reached inside it, feeling the cold steel of the gun on her fingers.

Ivan had nearly reached the child as the motorcycle bore down on him, the driver seeming intent on running him or the child over.

With an inhuman roar, Burton stood and aimed the 9mm, clicking off the safety with her thumb as she fired three rounds, hitting the driver in the chest. He reacted to each one, the bike giving in to gravity and skidding as the back wheel continued to turn. The man with the AK-47 fell to the ground and rolled, his gun flying in the opposite direction.

"Die, you fucker!" Burton screamed, firing the remainder of her clip into the gunman, his body jumping with every shot that hit its mark.

Out of the corner of her eye she saw the helicopter circling back, headed right to the center of town where Ivan was grabbing the little girl and turning, about to run. The guns let loose on either side of the chopper, sending a deadly trail over the two men in black, their bodies jumping in reaction to the shots.

Burton raised her pistol and to her horror, all she got was a clicking sound. "Fuck!"

She watched as the bullet trail reached Ivan, catching his right calf and sending him and the girl to the ground. More movement caught her eye and she watched as Lilli ran out to the bull's-eye and grabbed the AK-47. She raised it and pulled the trigger, the sound deafening as she riddled the helicopter with bullets, the gunman screaming as he fell out of the bird, landing in a bloody heap on top of a car. The helicopter trailed off, only to crash moments later when the rotors stopped spinning.

Out of breath and her heart racing, Burton felt like she was in a nightmare, her brain unable to absorb everything that had just happened. Suddenly, she couldn't hear anything and the color seeped out of the images she was seeing. She staggered over to a building, reaching out a hand to brace herself as her legs began to give out on her.

"Burton!"

Somehow, as through water, she heard her name. Slowly she turned her head, unable to focus.

"Burton! Damn it, I need you!"

Everything came back with a rush of sound and sight, leaving Burton breathless. She pushed off the building and ran as best she could to Lilli, who was kneeling next to Ivan; he was screaming in pain.

"Wrapping!" Lilli yelled. "I need something to wrap his leg!"

Looking around, Burton saw some wash hanging on a line and ran over to it, snagging the shirt and ran back to Lilli, falling to her knees as she reached them.

"Good," Lilli said, holding the pressure with her hands. "Tie it right there, tight!"

Burton did as she was told, glancing into Ivan's pain-stricken face. She gave him as encouraging a smile as she could before returning her full focus to her task.

"Good."

Burton stopped, surprised when she felt an iron grip on her arm. She stared into Lilli's eyes, which bore into her own.

"I need you to ride back to the hotel. Tell them what's happened and send help. We need to get some of these people out of here and to a more sterile environment."

"Lilli, I'm not leaving you—"

"Go!"

Burton slowly backed away, looking over the horror film in front of her before she turned and ran toward her bike. She jumped on and was off like a shot.

The dust stuck to the trails of her tears as she rode hard, her heart aching and mind reeling from both what she'd just witnessed and participated in as well as all the horrors it had brought back. Her left leg ached, though she knew it was more likely psychological than physical.

She almost cried in relief when the hotel loomed up ahead. She peeled into the underground garage, nearly running over a man who was taking out a huge bag of trash. He yelled at her, raising his fist.

Ignoring him, she parked the bike and jumped

off almost before it was stopped. She had no idea how she was going to relay her message, but she had to. Suddenly, a thought occurred to her.

Standing in the lobby, she pulled her phone out of her bag and, fingers racing across the touch screen, pulled up a translator site. She hoped that Chilvokian was to Russian like Spanish was to Italian. She typed out what had happened and what was needed then thrust the screen in the face of the first person she came across.

At first, he tried to bat the phone away but when she thrust it in his face a second time, he took it from her and read it. His eyes bulged and he threw the phone back at Burton, who barely caught it before he took off at a sprint, calling out as he went.

Chapter Seventeen

Burton hurried up to the fifth floor, looking left and right for the closet Lilli had mentioned on the phone. She'd called and told Burton to get two hospital stations ready. She'd never forget Lilli's last words:

"The good news is, there are only two coming in. The bad news is, there are only two coming in."

She found what she thought was the storage closet Lilli was talking about and hurried over to it, tugging it open. It was the size of a large walk-in closet and held supplies for the hotel, such as toilet paper, mini bottles of shampoo with the hotel's logo on them, and extra towels.

"Bingo," she said, grabbing as many of the towels as she could. She found a roll of trash bags so opened those and began to fill them with towels, washcloths, and anything else she thought would be useful to Lilli.

Loaded up, Burton left the supply closet and headed toward the stairs but then noticed a second closet and decided to check it out to see if she could find anything else. Lilli had only mentioned the one, but in this case, too much could never be too much.

It took some tugging, but the door finally opened. Inside, she found several folded mobile beds that could be requested if say the person renting the room for the night needed extra sleeping space for guests. The beds could be rolled to their destination then unfolded to reveal a twin-sized bed.

Seeing nothing useful, she was about to close the door when something at the back of the closet caught her eye. It was a black duffel bag stuffed full with something. She squeezed her way to the back, pushing one of the beds out of the way before squatting down next to it. The bag was bulky, something hard within, or more accurately, what felt like *lots* of hard somethings inside.

She glanced over her shoulder to make sure she was still alone and her loaded trash bags sitting out in the hall hadn't been spotted. Alone, she returned her focus to the duffel and unzipped it. Burton gasped when she realized it was loaded with grenades that looked like little lemons from their shape. She recognized them instantly for those in boxes at the palace.

Sitting back on her haunches, she stared down into the bag, her heart racing. She chewed her bottom lip and decided to leave them where they were and perhaps talk to Lilli about them. Zipping the bag back up, she pushed to her feet and left the closet.

৶৶৶৶

Ivan was screaming in agony as he was rolled in on a luggage cart. His pant leg had been ripped open, the denim saturated in blood, the white shirt Burton had tied around it crimson.

The man wheeling the cart around like a madman was barking out orders, and as the gathered crowd moved aside, Burton had to assume he was telling them to get out of the way.

Lilli was guiding the cart, both she and the man running with it through the lobby and back to the room Burton had set up for the incoming patients. Behind Ivan, another man ran in carrying the limp body of a child in his arms, the child's head and dangling feet jostled with the motion.

No idea what to do, Burton sprinted down the hall ahead of them to make sure everything was still set up and ready for them. The two beds in the hotel room had been covered in plastic to protect the mattresses from any blood or other bodily fluids. An IV stand had been set up and any and all of the medical supplies the hotel had to offer, including a defibrillator and heart monitor, were at the ready.

Burton heard the commotion coming closer so pressed herself against the wall to stay out of the way.

"Burton," Lilli called out when she glanced over at her as the luggage cart was wheeled inside. "I forgot to ask you to get my medical bag from my room upstairs. It's in the closet."

Burton managed to get through the crush of people gathered at the doorway until she ran into the human wall that was Alexey Novikoff. She stopped short and stared up at his face with wide eyes.

"Excuse me," she said, figuring he'd move aside, but instead he continued to stare down at her, his eyes their typical chips of ice. "I need to get through, please excuse me," she said again, not entirely sure if he spoke English anymore or not. Finally, with a smirk, he moved aside, letting her pass. She was shaken a bit but had to let it go as she continued on her mission.

❦❦❦❦

It had been an extremely long and traumatizing day. Burton and Lilli had said a very quiet good night to each other before each woman went her own way. Burton needed space for a moment to reflect and feel. She'd had a good cry, reliving what she'd seen, what no human being should ever have to witness.

Of course, it had brought back that night in the back of the limo with Senator Rodriguez. Though she was lucky in that she remembered nothing of what happened after getting settled in the long car, in her heart she knew what happened, and her friend was gone to her forever.

So were those fourteen people who lost their lives that day, including three children.

Lilli had managed to get the little boy stabilized and she said she felt comfortable going to bed. Ivan was fine, though it was still a question if he'd keep his leg. He was comfortable and on pain medication to get him through the night.

Now, she lay in bed, a hand behind her head and sleep entirely too elusive. She was upset, lonely, and really wished she was in her own bed.

Burton glanced toward the closed bathroom door when she heard the soft knock. She pushed the sheet and blanket back and, wearing simple cotton shorts and a T-shirt, she walked over to it, pulling it open. Lilli stood on the other side dressed similarly. She took one look at Lilli and held her arms out, the doctor falling into them. In that moment, Lilli seemed to have the weight of the world on her shoulders, and the depths of her eyes were so terribly haunted.

Burton cupped the back of Lilli's head as she rested her head on the reporter's shoulder. Burton's eyes slid closed as she felt the wetness of silent tears against her neck. Her emotions rose as she held the other woman, trying as best she could to offer her comfort and solace with her touch.

They stood there for long moments, just holding each other, basking in the comfort that only another human could bring. Seconds passed and Lilli pulled away, a sheepish smile on her lips as she used her shirt sleeve to wipe at her eyes.

"Sorry."

"Don't apologize. It's been a trying day," Burton said gently, her hand resting on Lilli's shoulder.

Lilli chuckled ruefully. "It's been a long three years."

Burton returned her smile. "Why don't you lay down with me? Let's try to get some sleep."

Lilli nodded, following Burton to the bed. She walked around to the opposite side, climbing in. They both lay on their backs, Burton staring up at the ceiling. She had to admit it was nice to have Lilli's presence beside her, to feel the faint warmth of her body heat a foot away. She turned her head to study Lilli's profile for a moment, noting the delicate features and just how beautiful Lilli truly was, not to mention the heart she was proving to have. She seemed to feel Burton's gaze on her as she too turned her head, their eyes meeting.

Burton honestly had no idea what possessed her to do what she did next, but she turned onto her side and propped herself up on her elbow so she was leaning over Lilli. She tilted her head down, their lips barely touching. She wasn't sure what Lilli's reaction would be. She needn't have worried, though, as Lilli's hand reached up and buried itself in Burton's hair, guiding her down a bit for a more substantial kiss.

Lilli turned to her side, Burton lowering her head back to the pillow as the kiss continued. It was so delicate, so gentle, unlike anything Burton had experienced. Even with her one other time kissing a woman—Simone—this was worlds apart in every way.

The first touch of Lilli's tongue brushing against her own brought a soft sigh from Burton, her hand running down Lilli's side to rest on her hip. She was surprised when Lilli's hand found its way beneath her T-shirt to rest on the heated skin of her lower back.

Burton could feel her body responding in ways she'd never responded to anyone in her sexual history. She pulled away from the kiss and looked into Lilli's eyes, both women breathing hard. She saw so much passion and need in those emerald depths. It was a need no doubt reflected in her own eyes.

Lilli pushed her to her back then moved to straddle her hips, gazing down at her. She lowered her upper body, their cotton-covered breasts pressed together as she left a soft, lingering kiss on Burton's lips. She pulled back a bit as if to examine Burton's face. She brought up a hand, fingers lightly caressing the side of her cheek and down her neck.

Again, surprised at her own actions, Burton's hands found the hem of Lilli's T-shirt; she wrapped her fingers in it before she gently tugged upward. Lilli sat upright, raising her arms so the shirt could pass, then shook long auburn strands free. The shirt was tossed off into the shadows.

Burton devoured the woman sitting atop her hips with her eyes, stunned at the beauty before her. Her gaze settled on Lilli's naked breasts, so perfect and beautiful, the light-colored nipples hard against the moonlight coming in through the window, their contours painted silver. Her hands were taken in Lilli's warm ones and brought up to cup those very breasts, the rigid tips pressed against Burton's palms.

Lilli moaned, her head falling back as Burton massaged her breasts, Lilli's nails trailing down along Burton's forearms. Burton was lost, her thumb and forefinger gently tweaking the nipples, which hardened further, goose bumps erupting around the areolas. She gazed up at Lilli when the doctor took Burton's hands in hers, using them as leverage to pull Burton into a sitting position.

The kiss that greeted her was deeper than before, filled with even more passionate need. As the kiss continued, Lilli reached down and tugged Burton's own T-shirt up and over her head. Now, both topless, Burton moaned deeply as their flesh touched, the kiss fiery but quick.

Lilli moved off Burton, pushing the covers back off of them until the bedding gathered at the foot of the bed. She returned to Burton and pulled down her shorts and panties, tossing them aside before removing her own. Both fully naked, Lilli stared down at Burton, who lay on her back once more relishing Lilli's sitting form like she was the goddess she appeared to be.

Burton reached for her and Lilli lay back down on top of her, one thigh insinuated between the other. They began a slow, passionate kiss, hands caressing and touching, teasing and arousing. Lilli began to move her hips just slightly, Burton sighing at the new sensations that brought, her own hips beginning to move in tandem.

Lilli left Burton's lips and began to kiss and lick Burton's neck, leaving a trail of fire as she moved her way down until she caught one of Burton's nipples in her mouth. Burton's back arched, her fingers finding the thick strands of Lilli's hair, holding her in place as Lilli suckled her. She couldn't keep her hips still, her need and desire for the woman who was loving her breasts with her mouth so palpable and profound.

After giving both breasts equal treatment, Lilli kissed her way farther down along Burton's torso. She reached lower, urging strong thighs to part as she moved her body in between them. Burton's head tilted back as her legs fell open. The first touch of Lilli's tongue in her most sacred place brought a languid moan from deep in her throat. The truth was, she'd never allowed a lover such an intimate kiss. She couldn't wrap her mind around why she was allowing Lilli such access now.

Burton couldn't think, couldn't form a single coherent brain connection as Lilli gently and easily ran her tongue through saturated folds, seeming to know all the places Burton needed her most. Her breathing was quick and erratic, moans and whimpers renting the air as Lilli became relentless. A moment later, her entire body ceased, everything she knew about pleasure changed as her release exploded from her lips with a loud, high-pitched cry, her thighs closing against Lilli's head of their own accord, trapping her for a moment as her tongue continued to press against pulsing flesh.

Burton felt faint, her heart pounding so quickly. Vaguely she heard and felt Lilli move away from her and kiss her way back up her body. It was only when she tasted herself upon Lilli's lips that Burton felt like she was fully coming back into herself.

She pulled her down atop her once more, their kiss deep, but slow and exploratory. Burton felt a closeness to the woman in her arms that she didn't know was possible. After a lifetime of holding people at bay, it was a foreign feeling, but one she embraced as she pushed Lilli to her back, following suit.

As their kiss continued, Burton allowed her hand to wander, brushing against the rounded side of a breast, fingers trailing over a hardened nipple. She fed off Lilli's soft moans and sighs as she tasted the flesh of her neck and upper chest. Seeming on a mission of their own making, her fingers trailed down to find the closely trimmed hair between Lilli's opening thighs. The volcanic heat she felt there brought a moan from her own lips.

The truth was, she didn't entirely know what she

was doing but felt the need to allow her fingers to travel and experiment, listening closely to Lilli's responses. Together, they gasped as her fingers followed the line of Lilli's womanhood until they were tucked inside her.

Burton lifted her head from where it had been at her breast and met a hooded gaze. She saw absolute permission there and pushed two fingers in as deep as she could, Lilli's mouth falling open as her eyes fell closed. For a moment, Burton felt panic, but when Lilli's own hand reached down between her legs and wrapped around her fingers, Burton was guided to exactly what Lilli needed.

She initiated a slow, loving kiss as her fingers began to slowly pull out only to push back in, Lilli moving Burton's thumb to rub against her sensitive clit with each pass. Initially it was awkward, but once Burton got the hang of it, she felt it to her very soul, each one of Lilli's sighs, whimpers, and moans.

After a while, Lilli gripped Burton's bicep with a vice-like grip as Burton stroked her inside and out, their mouths within an inch of each other, both breathing hard. Burton could feel the slickness on her fingers and hand as she increased her thrusting until finally Lilli's head flew back and a loud gasp escaped her lips, her fingers painful upon Burton's arm as she released. Burton kept thrusting, only stilling when she felt the powerful muscles pulsing around her fingers.

She rained down kisses all over Lilli's face as the woman beneath her reacted to the intensity of her release. At last, Burton removed her fingers and pulled Lilli to her, burying her face in the warm softness of her neck. She felt Lilli wrap her arms around her in an almost painful hug, her chest heaving as she came down from her experience.

After several moments, Lilli loosened her hold,

her breathing calming as she left a kiss to the side of Burton's head. Burton pulled back just enough to look into that beautiful face, a smile coming to her lips when she saw the peace in her eyes and the contented smile upon her lips. She returned that smile, leaving a kiss there.

They moved so they were lying on their sides again, facing each other. Several moments of contented silence passed as they studied each other, gentle caresses and touches exchanged. As Burton searched her eyes, she was overwhelmed by how connected she felt to Lilli. She honestly didn't know how she was going to leave in just a couple days. How would she ever leave her behind?

Lilli leaned forward and left a lingering kiss on her lips. "Let's sleep," she whispered, then turned, presenting her back to Burton.

Burton scooted forward until their bodies were pressed together. She promptly fell into a deep sleep.

≈≈≈≈

Lilli's eyes blinked open a few times before they remained open. It took her a moment before she realized where she was. In their sleep, they'd changed positions, and she was now spooning Burton. She studied the dark mass of hair before her for a long moment before she scooted away as slowly as she could so as not to wake Burton.

As she slid out of bed, she was exhausted, but she knew she had to do what she was going to do. Looking around the room, she spotted Burton's cell phone on the dresser top. Getting to her feet, she glanced back to see if the woman she'd made love to mere hours before was still asleep. Assured that she was, she walked over to the phone and grabbed it, keeping her eyes on Burton as she made her way to the adjoining bathroom and to her own room. She closed the door silently before she turned on the light in her room and activated Burton's phone.

Chapter Eighteen

Burton awoke to find herself alone. The other pillow looked as though it had only just recently been abandoned. She didn't hear the shower going, and since both bathroom doors were open, she didn't see or hear any movement in Lilli's room.

Sitting up in bed, she realized she was naked, which was strange to her—she hadn't woken up naked in years, six years, to be exactly. She had to find it somewhat amusing that the last two times she'd been with someone, it had been a woman. She was surprised how differently she felt after both occasions, however.

As the sun shone through the curtains to her room, she felt happy, content, and couldn't wait to see Lilli's beautiful face. She was admittedly disappointed that she wasn't there, but she figured the dedicated doctor was probably already downstairs with her patients.

Pushing the covers off, Burton climbed out of bed and padded to the bathroom where she flicked on the light and glanced at her reflection on the way to the toilet. She had to chuckle; she looked like a woman who had been absolutely and thoroughly made love to the night before. Indeed, she had.

After showering and dressing, sure enough, she found Lilli in the make-do hospital room. She stood just inside the door and watched the beautiful doctor with the little boy. She was singing to him, her voice quite beautiful. From the child's reaction and the interplay, it seemed like it must be something along the lines of

"Itsy Bitsy Spider" in America. Even as the child was wounded and no doubt frightened, Lilli's interaction with him seemed to take all that away.

"Burdon!"

Burton started at the boisterous male voice. She turned toward the source and smiled when she saw Ivan grinning at her from his bed. His leg was heavily bandaged and he had far more color in his face than he had the day before.

"Ivan!" she said, just as excited. They shared a smile.

"Good morning," Lilli said, glancing behind her shoulder at Burton.

"Morning," Burton said, the two women sharing a long look before Lilli turned away to say something to the boy then walked over to her.

"Did you get some sleep?" Lilli asked quietly.

Burton nodded, tucking her hands in the back pockets of her jeans. "I did. Did you?"

Lilli grinned. "Slept better than I have in a long time."

Burton blushed, bringing up a hand to rub the back of her neck. "Well, good. I'm so glad."

"Listen," Lilli said, the playful tone disappearing as she lowered her voice. "After I'm done here, I need to talk to you."

Burton could see the seriousness in her eyes. "Okay. What about?"

"I'm getting you out of here."

"No! No, I'm not leaving—"

"You have to!" Lilli hissed, moving so she was within a few inches of Burton. "Something is telling me, Burton." She lifted her hand and briefly brushed her fingertips down Burton's cheek. "Please, just listen to me."

Burton looked away, surprised by the sudden emotion that rose within her. She turned back and felt Lilli take her hand with warm fingers.

"Give me another twenty minutes and we'll grab some breakfast and take it up to our rooms and talk. Okay?"

Burton nodded. "Okay."

Lilli glanced at her patients before quickly leaning in for a peck and walking back to the boy.

Burton watched her go then tossed a smile to Ivan before she left the room, headed for the cafeteria so she could grab a cup of coffee, and wait for Lilli to finish up. She figured while waiting, she could send some e-mails and jot down a few more notes on the Notepad app on her phone to transfer to the Word document on her laptop.

Entering the stairwell, Burton gazed down at her phone, about to open the text messaging app when she gasped as she was grabbed from behind, a firm hand covering her mouth painfully tight as an arm wrapped around her neck, cutting off her air supply as she was pulled hard back against a body. Her phone crashed to the cement floor as she clawed at the arm that only tightened as she fought.

"I told you," a voice whispered in her ear. "I told you long ago outside that shit hole you lived in not to get in my way."

Burton gasped and her eyes grew huge at the recognition of those words and the voice. She fought, trying desperately to scream, but could do nothing more than rasp out a plea to deaf ears. Suddenly she was turned around, her back slammed against the wall and a large hand grasping her throat. She was stunned to see Alexey Novikoff standing before her, hatred in his eyes.

"Just because my sister is willing to let you be her

little American whore, I'm not."

He brought his fist back and smashed it into her cheek, causing Burton's head to slam against the wall with the impact. She saw stars and everything went mute, even as she saw his mouth moving. She blinked several times, shaking her head to try to remain conscious. He struck a second blow, this one to her mouth. Blood flew as her lip and inside of her mouth were cut in the process.

"You fucking American bitch," he growled, so close spittle landed on her lip. "Why didn't you die?" He sent another punch her way, once again causing her world to dim for a moment.

To her further horror, she saw other men begin to gather, recognizing many from the breakfast table that first morning as well as from the stairwell two nights before.

Alexey didn't even bother looking at them. "Get the others ready to go," he said, the others scattering. He returned his full focus to her. "Now, I'm going to squash this bug," he said, a fourth punch sending her into darkness.

※※※※

Finished for the morning and feeling great about the prognosis of her patients, Lilli hummed a little tune as she headed down the hall to the stairs to reach the floor with the cafeteria. As she made her way down the main hall of the overtaken hotel, she thought about her night with Burton. Yes, she knew it had been a mistake. She had already lined up transportation for Burton to get out of Chilvokia and get home. She was thankful Everett had friends in the military. Soon, Burton would be gone, back to her world in the United States, and they'd never see each other again.

Her mind returned to the previous night. Even though it had been Burton who initiated what had happened between them, it was something she'd wanted for more than six years. Since she'd seen not only Burton's beauty but her dedication and tenacity on the news, she'd been drawn to her. Then, when she'd first seen her in person, when she and Alexey had been standing on that elevator with Burton and Roger Eggleston, her heart had begun to race and she'd been deeply moved by the brief encounter. What she'd suspected before was validated that day, watching Burton with the doctor—she was the one.

And then everything had gone horribly wrong.

The guilt of what happened would stay with Lilli as long as she was alive, which she feared would not be much longer. But, she had pushed that aside while making love with Burton, allowing her true feelings to come through in her touch and her kiss, hoping that Burton felt it.

Now, she was going to make sure Burton got out of this safely, never to be harmed by the chaos that was her country again.

She quickened her step to reach Burton, wanting to spend as much time with her as possible before she had to let her go. She reached the door to the stairwell and tugged it open, still humming her tune as she went inside. She glanced down at the ground then did a double take. Stopping, she squatted, reaching out to pick up what had caught her eye.

It was Burton's cell phone, the screen cracked from landing face down on the cement. She recognized the colorful rubber case the body was housed in. Confused, she checked around, glancing up the stairs to see if Burton had fallen. She then noticed something on the wall. Stepping closer, she realized it was fresh blood, and directly above where the phone had landed.

Heart racing, Lilli took the phone with her and ran up the stairs, bursting through the door to the third floor. She ran down the hall to her room, tugging the key out of her pants pocket and quickly unlocking the door. Both bathroom doors were open, so she ran straight through to Burton's room, stopping short.

The room had been ransacked. She could hardly breathe as she moved farther into the room, looking around. The bedding was on the floor, the mattresses turned over and halfway against the wall.

She saw Burton's roller bag suitcase, unzipped and on its side, clothing strewn everywhere. What she didn't see was Burton's ever-present laptop or its case. But, what hit her like a punch to the gut was what sat on the dresser top next to the smashed television.

Walking over to it, Lilli reached out and took it in her hand, smooth and the shape of a lemon, thus their nickname of the lemon grenade.

"Oh my God," she whispered, looking around again.

Grenade in hand, Lilli ran out of Burton's room, plowing through the stairwell door to the fourth floor and pounding up the stairs until she reached that door, then nearly took two men out as she bolted down the hall to the cafeteria. She knew her brother would be eating breakfast. She had to tell him, had to warn him that Burton had been taken.

Breathing heavily, Lilli stopped once she hit the doorway, her gaze touching every face as people talked over breakfast. Not one of them was Alexey, and even stranger than that, not one of them was her brother's close circle of friends. In fact, the table they always sat at was empty.

Something niggling at her gut, she hurried out of the cafeteria, ignoring the stares as she ran with a grenade, pin still intact. She sprinted up the stairs to the fifth floor and down the hall until she reached Alexey's room. She was gasping for breath by the time she reached the opened door. Leaning on the doorframe for a moment, she took several deep breaths to calm her racing heart a bit before pushing off of it and walking into the room.

The bed was neatly made, the curtains opened. The room appeared abandoned, the closet filled with empty wooden hangers, the bathroom looking as though it were waiting for the next guest to stay.

"What the hell?" she whispered, running a hand through her hair as she walked farther into the room, trying to wrap her mind around what she was seeing.

She stopped dead in her tracks when she saw something sitting on the dresser. It was lying on its side, but it was unmistakable what it was. She grabbed it, only too late to realize what she'd done.

The pin, which had been tethered to fishing wire that was trapped by the drawer below clanged to the wooden surface with finality.

Lilli turned and ran, screaming at the top of her lungs to evacuate as she did. The force of the explosion sent her flying, skidding along the carpeted hall on her shoulder before she slammed into the wall. Debris fell around her head, which she tried to cover with her hands.

She watched, horrified as the entire floor was on fire, flame fingers licking a trail along the walls and carpet, heading right for her. She ignored the pain of a dislocated shoulder and leapt through the door that sent her landing on the same shoulder on the hard cement of the stairwell landing. She cried out in excruciating pain as a fireball flew by, instantly heating the metal door.

She lay there for long moments, unable to move or even breathe, working through the pain. Finally, she was able to sit up, her mind fuzzy and confused. She crawled to the rail and used it to help her get to her feet. She hurried as quickly as she could down the stairs, tears streaming down her face and her jaw clenched as her shoulder screamed at her every move. She winced as another explosion rent the air on the floor above her.

"*Bhe!*" she screamed, her voice breaking with pain as she tried to get every person she saw out of the building. "Bhe!"

She reached her room, sweating profusely as she tried to breathe through the torture of her shoulder, her arm held close to her body. She grabbed a bag and stuffed what she could carry inside it, including the head scarf and accompanying outfit. Next, she'd have to get Ivan and the boy out of the building. Without help, they were sitting ducks.

"Liliya."

Lilli stopped, about to zip her duffel bag. She saw a man named Liev standing at the open door of her room.

"Everyone is just about ready to leave. The fire has spread to upper floors and we have some people who are missing."

Lilli closed her eyes, staving off her emotions. "All right. Someone needs to get Ivan and the boy out to safety."

"Done."

Left alone, Lilli nearly cried out in pain as she had to use the hand on her injured arm to hold the phone as she texted her father.

Liliya: Get prepared, we're all coming. I'll explain later.

Phone tucked in one of the pockets of her BDUs,

opposite side of her MP-443 Grach Russian-made pistol, she grabbed her duffel bag with her uninjured arm, nearly fainting from the pain as she heaved the heavy bag up and over her other shoulder. Taking several deep breaths, she waited for her vision to fully clear before she hurried out of the room. Once she made it to her father's distillery, she'd get his help to reset the shoulder and bind it.

Right now, she had to focus on getting her people out of the inferno that was gaining strength by the second. Her mind begged her to focus on the specifics of what was happening: Burton missing and likely hurt, Alexey's room booby-trapped, and the hotel literally coming down around her feet. She couldn't, however, because if she did, she'd break down and lose all control.

Leaving the room, she refused to glance over to Burton's side, her heart on the verge of breaking as it was. She hurried out, ignoring the nearly debilitating pain, instead using it to keep her going. It brought her back to the days of medical school, where she was working a full-time job on top of her punishing school schedule. She had to focus the exhaustion into determination. This was no different.

She ran down the stairs as quickly as she could, clenching her jaw as her shoulder was jostled. Finally, she reached the ground floor, the entire building beginning to fill with smoke as it entered all the vents. She brought her hand up as she began to cough, looking around to see people running toward the door which would lead to the parking garage, everyone carrying as many of their belongings as they could.

Liev stood at the door, barking out orders to try to keep everyone calm and organized. Lilli felt like they were trying to get everyone onto lifeboats as the *Titanic* went down. She hurried over to him to help—the man seemed overwhelmed.

"This way!" she called over the fray. "Everyone, stay calm!"

Suddenly, screams shattered the morning and people began trampling each other as they tried to get back inside the building. It was only then that Lilli heard automatic gunfire. She pushed past those trying to come back in, shocked to see men she knew behind the rampage.

"Oh God," she gasped, shoving her way back into the lobby, yelling for everyone to get down, Lilli ducking when bits of the wooden doorframe splintered around her as bullets ripped it apart.

She ran farther inside the building, grabbing her phone and speed-dialing her father, yelling into the phone that they needed backup before she tossed the phone aside and grabbed her gun, running back toward the doorway to the garage. If the two gunmen entered the building, very few would survive.

She fell to the floor, tears springing to her eyes and her breath leaving her body as she landed on her injured shoulder. All she could do for a moment was lie there and work through the white-hot pain. Another round of shots pulled her quickly into focus.

Rolling onto her stomach, she crawled to the door, which now hung limply against the outside wall, both from the crush of humanity but also from a couple of the hinges being shot out. Dead bodies were strewn across the parking garage floor, struck down in their attempt to escape the fire still licking a trail at their backs. It was like the purpose of the gunfire was to herd the cattle back inside to die one way or the other, either by gunfire or real fire.

Lilli knew the men were friends of her brother's, always with him. One of them had been in the stairwell the night they tried to attack Burton. Lilli's mind raced: was Alexey dead, his "friends" betraying him? Or, was it what she was terrified to even think of? Was the little brother she'd grown up with and helped to raise part of what was happening?

She swiped at the sudden tears that escaped her eyes, no time for that. She realized the gunfire had stopped and saw that one of the men was trying to make his way closer to the building through the maze of cars. She could see his boots beneath one of the cars he was walking past, hiding behind the tall SUV.

Closing one eye, Lilli grabbed her gun in both hands, aiming. With two quick shots, she heard him yell out then fall to the ground, grabbing at his shattered ankle. The other gunmen ran out of his hiding space, spraying bullets, causing Lilli to roll several times across the floor to escape the rounds coming through the opened door and through the wall, sending drywall flying.

A moment later, the roar of an engine rent the air, the massive body of a red Hummer screaming around the corner, taking the gunman by surprise. He didn't even have time to react or scream before his body was pushed beneath the massive tires, a trail of gore following the huge vehicle, dragging the AK-47 behind it as the gun belt caught on the back bumper.

Lilli's head fell to the floor in relief, her father's beloved Hummer pulling up to the door.

Chapter Nineteen

Burton's eyes slowly slid open, her entire body aching and jostled as she lay curled up in the wagon part of a station wagon. She looked around, the nauseating taste of copper in her mouth, dried blood on her lip and chin. She could tell it was daylight—the sight of the cloudless sky through the large back window told her as much.

She was in pain, her jaw and head throbbing, and, probing her mouth with her tongue, she was afraid she may have lost a tooth. She winced at the sudden pain so stopped, instead trying to get a better understanding of her surroundings and who was with her. She could hear the distinct voices of three men, one of them Alexey. They were laughing and chatting, and it sounded like a bottle was being passed around between them. She had to snicker inside as she wondered if it was vodka.

She was lying on her side, so from her position, she took in all that was around her. There was a stained green shirt that seemed to have been haphazardly tossed back there, as well as a few empty beer cans. The thin and scratchy maroon carpeting beneath her face smelled of locker room socks and urine. She didn't want to react or make any noise to alert the men she was awake, so she began to take shallower breaths as she continued her visual perusal.

There was nothing that could be used as a tool or weapon of any kind, no car tool kit, no flashlight. Just the shirt, cans, and a spare tire that was anchored to the wall of the car.

She glanced toward where her feet were braced against the hatchback door; it seemed to jiggle a bit when they hit a bump or rut in the road. Eyeing what could be the backseat, she was able to see the back of a dark head. Whoever was sitting there wasn't paying a lick of attention to her. In fact, as she watched him, he disappeared, as though he'd leaned forward in his seat. She heard someone say something, complaint in his tone, then the sound of the bottle passed and a swig taken.

Burton returned her focus to the hatchback, testing it slightly with a firm push of her tennis shoe. To her relief, she saw the smallest bit of daylight as the door latch was obviously damaged in some way and wasn't holding, or it simply hadn't been shut properly. The reason didn't matter.

Closing her eyes, she prayed there wasn't a car behind them, or she'd be instantly run over and possibly killed—if she could pull this off. Opening her eyes, she again glanced up toward the front of the car, but the man in the backseat hadn't yet returned to his previous sitting position.

She clenched her teeth and used the full force of muscular thighs and rubber-soled tennis shoes, kicking as hard as she could. The door flew up, the beer cans and T-shirt sucked out at the sudden change in air pressure. She looked for a split second and saw that they were, indeed, alone on the road. Gritting her teeth in anticipation for the pain to come, she rolled out of the back of the car, landing hard on the cracked pavement. Her body was sent rolling off onto the shoulder, her cheek bleeding and jeans torn from a nasty bash to her knee on the way out of the car.

She stopped, a gasp escaping her lips as pain

radiated from every part of her body. She felt like she'd broken at least one finger during her landing, as well. No time to consider, she heard a loud screech of tires and then men yelling.

Using every bit of adrenaline she had, Burton managed to get to her feet and ran off in the opposite direction, headed into the brush. She cried out when she heard a gunshot rock the afternoon, followed by what sounded like a thorough ass chewing from one of the men. Burton ran for all she was worth, her lungs burning, her left leg aching, and the rest of her flat-out throbbing.

She felt like she was trying to find a place to hide on the moon. The landscape was barren, out in the middle of nowhere. She waited for Mel Gibson to zoom over in some mutated *Mad Max* car, replete with the roaring engine, which she realized was the station wagon, flying over the terrain right toward her.

She chanced a glance over her shoulder, and sure enough, two of the men were running after her and the third was off-roading to her left, his obvious intention to cut her off. Suddenly, the car veered off and slowed down. It was only then that Burton realized she was running right toward a ten-foot-high chain-link fence.

"No!" she yelled, her heart falling as she slowed her own pace, knowing there was nowhere else to go. The men were gaining on her and the car could easily run her down.

Reaching the fence, she slammed her hands against it, the entire length of the fence shaking with her fury. She was about to turn and face her pursuers when something beyond the fence caught her eye. With shock and confusion, she realized the palace was not half a mile away.

"You stupid American bitch!" Alexey exclaimed,

breathless as he reached her and caught her with a backhand. He glared at her with absolute murderous hate in his cold eyes "Don't pull shit like this again. I don't care what Bergman wants. I'll kill you so fast your head will spin."

"What does he want with me?" she asked, truly terrified.

The smile that spread across Alexey's lips made Burton's heart nearly stop beating. "The only thing you're good for. Just like all the others."

He grabbed her by her hair and tugged her away from the fence, forcing her to walk over to where the station wagon was pulling up to them. He threw her into the backseat, scooting in beside her.

———

"Better?" Grigoriy asked, sitting back on the stool in front of the chair Lilli sat on.

She winced but was satisfied and impressed by the field dressing he'd given her arm after he'd helped her to reset it. He'd been a medic during a few smaller wars in the country in his younger years. His stories when she'd been a girl had been part of her inspiration to become a doctor.

Noticing that he was waiting for a response, she nodded. "Very good, Papa. This will do." She sat back in her chair, her injured shoulder tightly bound with her arm tied close to her body in a sling. She glanced at him, able to see the lines of his face hardened upon the full story of what had happened and the very real possibility that Alexey was behind every bit of it. "What do we do?"

"Well," he said, pushing to his feet and walking to the coffee pot, a fresh pot brewed as he'd taken care of

Lilli's shoulder. "We have to see who is left and willing to fight and what shape they're in," he said, pouring himself and Lilli a mug from his small apartment in the basement of the distillery. The fifty or so who had chosen to come with Lilli rather than disperse within their own villages had all settled in a makeshift dormitory in the bottling room above their heads.

"We've got to get her back, Papa. We've got to stop this before it's as out of control as the fire at the hotel." She studied his back as he prepared their mugs of coffee. "I have a plan, Papa. But—" She pushed up from the chair, wincing at the move, and walked over to him. She placed a hand on his arm to ensure she had his full attention. "I have a plan," she said again, "but I could end up dead, or, if Alexey is there, he could end up dead."

"He is there," Grigoriy growled, shoving the container of sugar away and pulling back from her. "I know it in my gut, he is part of this!" He raised his fist to the ceiling.

Lilli watched, heart breaking for her father and the difficult relationship he'd always had with his son.

"Every day, every day, I gave him love like I gave you. Every day, he had all the same chances and choices that you had. What did he do with it? Nothing! He got into fights with boys on the streets, he landed in jail for beating Anjelica." The pain was evident in his eyes. "When is it enough? When do you finally get all that anger and fire out of your soul?" He turned away from her. "Let him die," he finished quietly.

Lilli walked over to him and turned him around until he faced her; then she rested her head against his chest as she wrapped her one good arm around him. She could feel his pain and his profound disappointment, all of which mirrored her own. After a long moment, he responded, wrapping his arms around her and holding her close.

☙ ☙ ❧ ❧

A strange buzzing sound rang in Burton's ears, her mind beginning to focus in on it, her head feeling as though it were filled with cotton that happened to have a marching band hiding within its softness. Her jaw hurt terribly as did her left leg and right knee. But, as she took stock of her person, the buzzing began to slowly come into audio focus as male voices.

"Why do you always have to go after their faces?" one asked, his voice familiar, though in Burton's foggy state, she wasn't able to put a face to it. "Are you that small of a man that you have to go after their beauty?"

Burton started slightly when she felt fingertips on her chin, moving her head slightly this way and that. She was surprised the men were standing as close to her as they were since their voices seemed so far away.

"What does it matter? Her pussy is still intact. That's all you care about, isn't it?" the second man's voice said, again familiar to Burton.

The fingers on her face fell away. "Watch yourself, Alexey," the first man said. "You're not as necessary in this as you might fancy yourself."

"And you too should be careful, Heinz. I'm the one who leads this little army of yours. Just be glad the bitch is alive at all."

An uneasy silence filled the space, Burton keeping her eyes closed and not reacting as she listened, surprised they were both speaking in English.

"Don't get into a pissing contest with me, boy," Heinz said, his voice quiet and deadly. "I assure you, you will lose. But," he continued, tone brightening, "we're not here for unpleasantries, now are we? Wake her."

Burton gasped loudly as she was sprayed with incredibly cold water. She turned her head, trying to keep it away from her nose and mouth, even as she sputtered and spit out a mouthful. She was relieved when it stopped, though now she was freezing. She came to be more aware of her surroundings as her eyes opened. She was in a room made of stone with a single, low-watt bulb dangling from the low ceiling, which did more to create eerie shadows then illuminate the area.

To her horror, she realized she was shackled to the wall behind her by her wrists, which were chained a few inches above her head. She was fully dressed, though her T-shirt did very little to cover her as it was a light color and thoroughly soaked now. She faced the two men who stood before her, sure enough, Alexey Novikoff and Heinz Bergman.

"At last," Heinz said with a smile. "Our sleeping beauty awakes." He gave her a chilling smile as he walked up to her again, Alexey standing by with hose in hand. He brought up his hand, fingertips once again on her when Burton jerked her face away. The smile turned dark. The hand that would have been gentle now curled in a fist. It slammed into her midsection and stole her breath away, causing a sharp pain in her shoulders and wrists as her body tried to instinctually bend at the blow. "You see, Alexey," Heinz said, glancing at the other man over his shoulder, "there are ways to get your point across without leaving a mark."

Burton gasped for air, unable to fully fill her lungs. She took small gulps, trying to calm herself. She was in a pit with a snake, and she had to absolutely keep her wits about her at all costs.

Finally, she was able to speak. "What do you want with me?"

"Well," he said, reaching into the inside pocket of his impeccable suit jacket and bringing out a switchblade.

Burton gasped. He flicked the six-inch blade to life, the dull light above glinting off the sharp blade. Burton's eyes followed that blade as it got closer to her throat, the tip poking her slightly before the blade began to slice through the thin cotton of her T-shirt. She watched the progress, humiliated as her bra-clad breasts came into view, the nipples hard and pushing against the satin material that covered them from the water blast.

"Ah, yes," Heinz said with a smile. He met her gaze briefly before using the blade to push the sliced shards of her shirt further away to expose more of her torso. He glanced back over his shoulder again at Alexey, who observed with cold eyes. "Our first American. Even though she's not pure, we'll get good money for her."

Burton's eyes grew huge as realization of what Heinz intimated.

"This one is a lesbian whore," Alexey said, looking into Burton's eyes with hatred.

"Even better," Heinz grinned, looking back at Burton. "Even better." He leaned forward and inhaled. Burton was disgusted. He smiled, moving back from her to look her in the eyes. "You smell like blood, sweat and, soon enough, tears." He cupped a bra-clad breast, Burton bristling. "You left too soon, little dove. I thought you were a professional, hmm?" He met her gaze. "Our interview was not yet over, I assure you." He leaned forward and swiped her cheek with his tongue. "Get someone in here to take care of her wounds," he ordered, walking past Alexey.

Burton watched as the men headed out, Lilli's brother tossing the hose aside just before he caught the chain for the lightbulb, sending the cell into darkness.

She cringed at the clang of a heavy door slamming home and the sound of a lock turning. She could hear the footsteps of both men growing fainter and fainter. It took for the silence to ensue before she realized she wasn't alone. She felt fresh fear until she heard a sneeze coming from her left.

"You need to get out of here," someone whispered.

Burton tried desperately to see through the inky blackness but it was impossible. She was surprised by the male voice, which spoke English, though accented.

"Who are you? Where am I?" Burton whispered back.

"You need to get out," he whispered again. "Before it's too late."

He stopped speaking as the door was unlocked again, the light suddenly snapped on. Burton squinted slightly at the sudden burst of dim light, even if only moments after it had gone off. She saw a woman walking toward her, one of the creepy servant girls she remembered well. She wore the typical tight black top with revealed midriff, flowing skirt, and complete headdress.

Burton looked away from her, unable to take any more interaction with the craziness in the palace. As the woman began to gently clean up her face, Burton's gaze landed on her unwitting roommate. He was dressed in nothing more than rags, his body thin and beard long. He was shackled much like she was on the perpendicular wall. He met her gaze and she gasped.

"Luke Skywalker," she whispered.

Chapter Twenty

Lilli blinked several times, trying to get used to the brown contacts that she hadn't worn since her last foray into the palace mere days before. The unusual color of her eyes had certainly been an asset and gotten her attention over the years, but it was attention she couldn't afford to have going undercover. This was especially true if Alexey was, in fact, in the palace.

Kneeling in the dim corner of the armory wasn't the most sanitary place to get ready for her mission, but it would have to do. She didn't bother hiding a pile of clothes to change into to escape back through the underground tunnels like she did last time—no need, no time.

Two hundred years ago, King Sowell had the tunnels built. They extended all the way to the distillery for easier delivery of his favorite drink, tunnels that only the dead king and the Novikoff family knew about. They'd been sealed off years ago, only to be reopened two weeks prior for Lilli's undercover work, which was when she'd run smack into Burton and Bishop. She had planned to continue her reconnaissance, but when Bergman had ordered her to bring Burton the drugged tea, she knew the mission was over and she had to get the reporter and cameraman out of there.

The purpose of her first infiltration had been to fully understand what the government was up to and how to end the catastrophic killing and chaos in the country. Now, the time for understanding was over.

The message at the hotel had been plain and simple, the writing on the wall in blood: the stalemate was over and so were the games. The war was on.

Tonight, her one and only job was to get Burton the hell out of there. The others could sort everything else out.

Wearing the outfit she'd stolen from the house that the enslaved servant girls wore, she knelt down in a dark corner of the armory, doing her best to ignore her pain. She had nearly passed out when struggling to pull on the tight-fitting shirt back at her father's distillery. Her shoulder was in bad shape and it needed to be stabilized, not taken out of its bindings and allowed to move.

She favored her right arm, holding the left as close to her body as she could get away with, and grabbed her gun from the holster she had fastened around her thigh beneath the filmy skirt.

"I'm a doctor," she muttered, checking to make sure she had a full clip as well as a full spare. "When the hell did I become Lara Croft?"

"What's that, Liliya?" asked the tinny voice in her earpiece.

"Nothing, Papa," she said, grinning. She'd forgotten he was listening on the other end. "I'm going in."

"Be safe. *Ya lyublyu tebya.*"

Burton smiled. "I love you, too, Papa."

Returning her gun, she took a moment to put the complicated headscarf wrap in place before she made her way through the darkness with a tiny penlight so as not to run into anything. She noted the shelves full of weapons and boxes of ammo and grenades before moving on to the heavy steel door.

Holding her breath, she used all her strength to

pull it open with one hand, no way her injured shoulder would allow such abuse. The door opened slightly and she froze, listening. She heard nothing and pushed the door open a bit more, just enough to fit through. She aimed the beam of the penlight to the ground so it wouldn't easily be seen if someone came her way in the inky darkness of the tunnel. She ran her hand along the stone to help find her way.

Lilli stopped when her hand came in contact with the frame of another door. She knew it was the room with the boxes of stored vodka but decided to duck inside quickly to see if anything had changed in the few days since she'd been in the palace. Satisfied nothing had been changed or touched, she closed that door and continued down the tunnel only to stop not ten steps later.

She flicked the penlight off and pressed herself against the wall. The sound of coming footsteps echoed in the adjoining tunnel. She heard the clank of metal on metal, like a key inserted in a lock, and that lock disengaged before squeaky hinges announced an opening door.

She inched her way closer, knowing that was the last cell door around the corner and it was where the noises were coming from. She stopped again when she heard a soft voice, a woman's voice. There were the lower tones of a man's voice then another female's, and every single hair on Lilli's body stood at attention. She knew in her gut that was Burton's voice.

As silently as she could, she reached beneath her skirt and retrieved her gun, holding it tightly in her right hand as she stayed put for a moment. The knowledge that Burton was in that cell filled her with an almost debilitating fear and dread, but then there was equal relief. She was alive and just down the next tunnel.

"Papa," she whispered, hoping her father was listening. When she heard his voice in the affirmative, she smiled, relieved. "Extraction. I found her."

"The helicopter is here waiting," he assured her. "She'll be gone and safe."

She slid along the wall, following the rounded path into the tunnel with the cell. She could see buttery light flowing out of the room and spilling across the stones in the tunnel. She glanced down at it, noting the movement of a shadow within the room.

"Thank you," she heard Burton say softly.

Lilli again pressed herself against the wall. She heard footsteps coming closer to the opened cell door. Her heart was racing as she waited for someone to emerge. A moment later, she saw a servant woman dressed as Lilli was, holding an empty tray, just before the light inside the cell was turned off.

Before the woman could close and lock the door, Lilli pounced, wrapping a hand tightly over the woman's mouth, careful not to suffocate her considering she was wearing one of the crazy headdresses. She shoved the gun into her side and pulled her back toward the adjacent tunnel.

"Be quiet and I'll take my hand away," Lilli whispered, holding the woman's back firmly against her front until she felt the woman would cooperate. When the woman nodded in agreement, Lilli released her hand and turned the woman to face her.

She brought the penlight up in her left hand, wincing as pain shot through her arm at the movement, but ignored it as she flicked it on. The surprise in the servant's eyes would have been amusing if the situation wasn't so dire. Lilli tugged her own headdress off.

I'm here to help," she said in her native tongue since the woman had seemed to understand her words moments before. "What's your name?"

"Tasha," the woman whispered, looking over her shoulder. "They'll kill me if I'm gone too long."

Deciding there was no threat, Lilli lowered her gun and brought up her hand to remove the headdress. She gasped when she realized Tasha was a mere teenager. Not only that, but she sported a horrible bruise on her jaw.

"How long have you worked here?" Lilli asked, noting more bruises, though fainter, on her neck.

"I don't work here," Tasha said, tears coming to her blue eyes. "If I don't do what they ask, they won't let me see my son."

"Your son?" Lilli gasped, horrified. "You're just a child!" She took a steadying breath as the tears in Tasha's eyes began to flow down her cheeks.

"It wasn't my choice," she whispered. "But, now he's here and I'll do whatever I have to protect him."

Lilli felt sick, the weight of what was in front of her falling heavy on her heart. She could see the pain and suffering in this young woman's eyes. When she'd been here days before, she hadn't had long enough to find anything out of real value. She let out a heavy breath and ran a hand over the tight bun her hair was pulled back into.

Looking at Tasha, she asked. "Can you show me where your son is? Where the other girls like you are?"

Tasha nodded. "Yes."

Lilli put a hand on her shoulder, making sure she had her full attention. "I'm going to get you out of here. Okay? All of you."

"With my son?" Tasha asked, eyes wide.

"Yes. With your son."

"And all the other children, too?"

Lilli stared at her, shaking her head in confusion.

"What children? Those of the servant girls?"

Tasha nodded, then added, "And those taken. Those that are left, anyway."

"Wait, what do you mean?"

Tasha again glanced over her shoulder before lowering her voice. "There's a rumor going around," she said, grabbing both of Lilli's arms and shaking her slightly with the hiss of her words. Lilli winced as another wave of pain raced through her arm. Seeming not to notice, the teenager continued. "They've taken our children, many sold off to other countries for God only knows what purpose. I had to beg to keep my son here in the palace. The women, they're being sold, too! Like the American in the cell I just brought food to."

Lilli's attention was definitely caught at that last remark. "What about her?"

"She's to be made well again and fixed up, then"— Tasha glanced over her shoulder for a third time before returning her focus to Lilli, her words a whisper— "they're going to sell her. I've heard the ISIS militant group wants American women."

Lilli felt her heart stop beating for a moment. She took several steadying breaths, trying to stay calm. Losing control of her emotions now would get them all killed or worse, captured.

"I must go," Tasha said, about to turn away when Lilli caught her arm. She met her gaze, fear in her own.

"No. Come with me," Lilli said, taking the young woman's hand and tugging her back in the direction of the armory.

Chapter Twenty-one

Burton could still taste the chocolate shake on her lips, the servant girl holding up a small can of a supplemental drink such as Boost for her and her captive companion to drink through a straw. A bit before that, the same woman had helped with the absolutely humiliating process of urinating in a bedpan while standing up, shackled to a wall. It was obviously much easier for the man chained mere feet away from her, the ordained king of Chilvokia.

Left in the dark again, she hoped her blush had gone away. They'd both done their best to give the other privacy, but it just wasn't possible to shut your ears down, too. She was still in pain, even as she'd been tended to off and on in the many, many hours she'd been there. With no windows, it was impossible to know if it was day or night, one day or two days since she'd arrived, four hours. She had no idea.

"What have you done so terrible to end up in here with me?"

Burton peered through the dark in the direction of the other prisoner. He had said very little, his clothing hanging off his emaciated body, old and new wounds littering his flesh. Half the time he seemed to be partially unconscious when the light in the cell was turned on. His voice was thin and weak.

"Well," she said, "I think the better question is, what have *I* done to be thrown in with the scoundrel, King Arvid?" She heard his quiet gasp through the darkness.

"How did you know who I am?" he asked, nearly a whisper.

She smiled, even though it was unseen. "Any reporter worth her salt does her homework before going on assignment...what do I call you? I've never been around a king before."

He chuckled. "Arvid is quite fine. So, you're the one Liliya went after, I see."

Now it was Burton's turn to be surprised. "You know about that?"

"I know her family well, dealing with Grigoriy for twenty years on Novikoff vodka. For us, that's as much Chilvokia as apple pie is to America."

"Well, she sent me a bottle of it to get my attention." She smiled at the raspy laughter that garnered her. "What do you know about what they're doing here? Who 'they' is and what do they want?"

"Years ago," Arvid began, "Bergman was an assistant to me and nothing more, though he craved power." He laughed bitterly. "Should have seen that coming. When things began to become more and more unstable in the Middle East, he suggested we provide a safe place for refugees to land—for a price."

"Charge for admission" Burton said, nodding in understanding.

"Exactly. I said absolutely not. A few years after that, my wife had already died, my son off in England being educated. He disappeared and a fortnight later, so did I."

Burton was silent for a long time, allowing what she'd just been told to process. "You never abandoned your people, did you?"

Before Arvid responded, the cell door opened again and the light flicked on. Burton blinked several times at the unexpected light. She saw that it was one of the servant girls, but it wasn't the one from before. She watched as the woman walked up to her, large brown eyes focused on her. Something about those eyes was off, however. They looked dead in some way, as though they were glass eyes or contacts.

She tried to move away as much as she could tethered to the wall as the woman leaned in close. Her heart was racing and she felt nauseous, terrified what the woman was going to do now.

"It's me, Burton. I'm going to get you out of here."

Burton gasped, only to find a hand over her mouth, the woman leaning in a bit closer, the material of her headdress that covered her lips tickling against Burton's ear.

"You have to keep quiet. Ready?"

Burton nodded, instantly recognizing Lilli's voice. She nearly whimpered in relief at the small kiss left to her ear before deft hands reached up and unlocked her shackles. Burton cried out in pain at the sudden release of her hands, her wrists badly bruised. Realizing Lilli was no longer standing in front of her, she saw that she was releasing her cellmate, as well.

"I'm so sorry, Your Highness," Lilli said, emotion in her voice. "We didn't know."

Once he was free, he leaned heavily on her, Burton hurrying over to help with the very weak man. She met Lilli's gaze—the brown contacts giving her the creeps—behind his bent head. She could easily read the shared concern in them.

"Papa," Lilli said suddenly, confusing Burton who didn't realize there was a microphone hidden within the headdress. "We're going to need help. Send someone to meet us in the tunnel. Quickly!"

A woman on either side of the king, the three

staggered out of the cell and down the tunnel. Burton remembered it would lead past the room with all the vodka and to the armory Lilli had mentioned.

As they made their way down the dark tunnel, the only light source the small beam from a penlight Lilli held, Burton's heart raced. It was difficult not to keep looking back over her shoulder. She was terrified of what might come out of that darkness to once again grab her from behind and drag her back to the hell they'd promised her.

They passed the door where the liquor was stored when they heard shuffling ahead of them. Burton's heart stopped, but Lilli didn't seem to be fazed. Suddenly, a beam of light appeared, dimmed by the hand that partially covered it. The figure was mostly obscured in shadow, but when he spoke softly to Lilli in Chilvokian, Burton felt relieved. She recognized his voice as one of the men from the hotel. She knew he was a large man with a strong build.

The four of them made better time the last leg of the trip as the newcomer literally took the weakened and emaciated king into his arms and hurried back down the tunnel to the armory.

Once inside, Burton closed the door behind them, only then the beam of the man's flashlight fully utilized. Burton saw a shelving unit pushed aside, cement wall and everything, to reveal a secret entrance. She realized that's where she'd seen the folded pile of clothing the night she discovered the bowels of the palace.

"What is this?" she asked, walking over to it.

"It's a tunnel that links the palace to my family's distillery," Lilli explained. "It doesn't seem Bergman knows about it, and thank God my father never told Alexey."

Suddenly, a few more men joined them, ducking

slightly as they made their way through the somewhat short entrance and into the armory. One of them walked directly to the shelving filled with weapons, helping himself to anything he could carry. The second man said something to Lilli, the doctor nodding before he, too gathered weapons and ammunition.

Lilli turned to Burton. "They're going to take weapons and Arvid out of here, and you're going with them. A helicopter is waiting for you outside the distillery and I want you on it, do you understand me?"

"What about you?" Burton asked, feeling her heart begin to race.

"I'll follow as soon as I can. I have to get the remaining women out of here."

"Then I'm coming with you," Burton said stubbornly.

"Damn it, Burton, no." With pleading eyes, she took hold of Burton's arms "Please. I'm begging you," she said softly. "I can't do what I need to do if I'm worrying about you."

"*Davay zhe!*" one of the men called out, loaded down with weapons and hurrying toward the tunnel entrance.

"*Idti,*" Lilli said, waving the men into the tunnel. She turned back to Burton. "Please go with them. I've already put you through so much. I could never live with myself if you had to go through anymore…or worse."

Burton glanced at the three men as they disappeared into the blackness of the tunnel, headed to the distillery. Now, it was just her and Lilli, Lilli's penlight their only light. She watched as Lilli reached up and removed her headdress, revealing the beautiful face that she'd grown so fond of in a very short time. It was also then that she saw the long, thin plastic mouthpiece that led from one of Lilli's ears.

"I'm a grown woman, Lilli," she said softly. "Very capable of making my own decisions."

Lilli let out a heavy sigh and nodded. She brought up a hand and used gentle fingertips to touch the bruises on Burton's face. "I'm so sorry," she whispered, tears in her eyes. "So, so sorry."

Burton smiled and shook her head. "Don't be. I'm here because I want to be. I already had an out, remember?"

Without a word, Lilli reached her hand around to cup the back of Burton's head and pulled her to her. The kiss she initiated was gentle yet passionate. After a few moments, she pulled back, leaving a lingering kiss before pulling away altogether. She replaced her headdress and looked at Burton.

"Okay. then, let's do this so we can get out."

❦❦❦❦

Alexey rolled off the bed, walking naked to the chair where he'd dumped his clothing. As he dressed, he could hear the young woman he'd left on the bed also getting up, walking to what was left of her uniform. In his drunken state, he'd been too excited to wait, so had pulled out a hunting knife from the holster on his belt and sliced away her flowing skirt and black top.

He said nothing. Bare chested, wearing only his boxers and BDUs, he entered the bathroom. A glance in the mirror showed a good-looking man with an impressive physique and cold blue eyes. Moving to the toilet, he reached inside his yet-to-be-buttoned pants to relieve himself.

Always impressed with what he had to offer the ladies, he grinned, thinking of the one he'd just broken in. The reward for bringing Heinz the American was a virgin. He'd never forget that one even if she did claim it hurt.

He grinned at the memory as he finished, tucking himself back into his boxers and buttoning and zipping his pants. When he returned to the bedroom, he saw the girl trying to piece her outfit back together. Rolling his eyes, Alexey opened the closet and pulled out one of his T-shirts. He threw it at her, barking at her to put it on and get out.

Once she was gone, he washed his face and brushed his teeth before the expected knock came at his bedroom door. He had to admit, it was much nicer staying back in the palace than the shit rooms at that hotel.

Walking to the door, he opened it to see Heinz standing on the other side. "Thank you," he said, accepting the drink offered by what amounted to being his first-in-command boss.

Bergman entered the room, Alexey closing the door after him. The older man looked around before turning to Alexey, who was still shirtless. "Entertaining?" he asked.

Alexey grinned before taking a drink "You could say that."

"Pretty good, huh?" Heinz asked, glancing over at the bed, which was a mess of sheets and blankets.

"Can't complain." Alexey moved to the middle of the room and crossed his arms over a muscular chest, legs spread wide in a challenging stance. "When do they arrive?" he asked, cutting to the chase.

"The plane should be in tomorrow by ten in the morning," Heinz said, reaching out a finger to hook a pair of lace panties. He raised his hand, the torn garment dangling from his finger before he flung it at the other man. "You're too rough," he said. "It's unnecessary."

Ignoring him and letting the panties fall to the floor, Alexey asked, "How many?"

"We have sixty signed up for the basic training and we got an order in for two hundred AK-47s and eighty-thousand rounds." He brushed some lint from his suit jacket. "Too damn bad my old friend Victor Bout was stupid enough to get picked up by American DEA. His connections would be immensely helpful right now."

"That's fantastic. I'll run over to the school today and bring the inventory here," Alexey offered, taking another drink. "We're going to have to move those brats to another location soon, Heinz. We've got a whole new shipment of goods coming in, including those small tanks we ordered. Those kids are taking up space."

"And, what exactly would you recommend we do with them, sport?" Heinz asked, sipping from his own drink.

Instantly irritated, Alexey slammed his drink down on the dresser, not caring that the liquid sloshed over onto his hand and the antique wood. Standing two inches taller than Heinz, he got into his face. "You were the brains that decided to camp them out in the middle of our arsenal warehouse, *sport*."

"And, what a brilliant plan it was. Nobody has gone near that school, thinking it was abandoned and boarded up. We've been hidden in plain sight for two years, Alexey. That is, until you thought it was a good idea to blow your cover with the rebels."

Alexey had nothing to say. Running a hand through his hair, he knew there was no response he could offer. "It had to end at some time," he muttered.

"Do you realize that with our story of Arvid taking off, stealing from his people and leaving them with very little military while we tried to make things work, coupled with rebel attacks and attacks on rebels, we were the sympathetic figures?" He paused. "And now, we're the bad guys." He moved toward Alexey.

"As opposed to?" the younger man asked, a cocky eyebrow raised.

"As opposed to the country constantly unstable, uprisings from unhappy citizens as the abandoned government does its best to right itself again versus a proven coup takeover!" Heinz exclaimed, veins standing out on his neck. "Which, might I add, gets us bad attention such as from that little American reporter bitch."

Alexey waved him off, turning away from him. "We got her, Heinz. I have no idea what you're so upset about." He was stopped when suddenly his superior grabbed his chin, forcing him to look into the face of rage.

"Until when?" Heinz said. "How many Burton Blindes will it take until we have the fucking world nipping at our heels?" He released Alexey, shoving him away. "No amount of money made from sales or mercenary training classes will buy our way out of that kind of trouble."

Alexey could feel every muscle and fiber in his body stiffen, all his willpower stopping him from killing the man before him with his bare hands. He swallowed a few times, jaw muscles bulging as he tried to get his temper under control. He looked at the other man, who he wanted nothing more than to slam through the wall.

"They're all stupid," he said, voice low. "Nobody has a clue what's happened or who's behind it. It'll give us time to eliminate the problem during their confusion."

Heinz downed the rest of his drink before

slamming the glass onto the dresser top. He stormed toward the bedroom door. "It better," he growled before slamming out of the room.

Alexey stood where he was, nostrils flaring. "Bastard."

Chapter Twenty-two

The weight of yet another gun in her hand—Lilli insisting she arm herself before they left the armory—Burton couldn't wait to get home and never see another gun in her life. She'd yet to really be able to fully grieve and deal with not only what she'd seen, but the fact that she'd taken a life. Yes, she knew she'd saved lives by killing the motorcyclist, but it still weighed on her soul. She feared that when she actually did deal with it, she'd start crying and not be able to stop.

For now, she knew she had to. She had to be at Lilli's side, she had to finish this. It was no longer about a story or about a job. It was about the very soul of a nation.

They'd made their way up the spiral stone staircase to the hall that Burton knew so well, even if it did bring her nightmares. Everything was dark and quiet. They both remained near the wall, Lilli with her headdress back in place in case she had to pass as a servant girl. It would be easier to hide one of them than two. Burton's heart raced, her gun at the ready. She wasn't entirely sure what they would encounter.

They made their way down the long hall toward where Burton and Bishop's rooms had been during their brief stay. Lilli stopped, reaching an arm back behind her to stop Burton. Burton listened, trying to figure out what Lilli was seeing or hearing. Suddenly, she heard it, too. A woman crying.

"Wait," Lilli whispered. They were close to an adjacent hallway. She glanced over her shoulder at Burton and put a finger to her cotton-covered lips. "Stay here."

Burton stayed where she was, her pulse racing so hard she could hear the blood in her head. Her hand was sweating as it held on to the Glock 19. She'd received some quick instruction on how to use it. She checked behind her, the long stretch of the hallway that faded into darkness intimidating as she waited for Lilli to return.

As she listened, she heard the crying abruptly stop and a muffled protest before Lilli appeared back around the corner tugging a young woman who wore nothing but an oversized green T-shirt, one of Lilli's hands over the frightened-looking woman's mouth.

"See if we can get into one of these rooms," Lilli whispered, holding the struggling young woman tightly against her.

Burton tried a couple doors before one opened. Ironically, it was the room Bishop had stayed in. She noted randomly that he'd been given a bigger bed than she had. Lilli pulled the girl in with them then closed the door as quietly as possible.

Burton watched as Lilli spoke to the girl, her words seeming to calm her as the girl's tears stopped, though her eyes were red and puffy, short blond hair tousled. She clutched dark clothing to her body, which, upon closer inspection, Burton thought looked very much like the outfit Lilli was wearing—that of the servant girl.

"My God," Lilli said, pulling Burton out of her observations. She met the redhead's gaze. "She was just with Alexey." Lilli eyed the terrified young girl, who could not have been a day over eighteen, if that. "Son of a bitch is here."

"I know he is," Burton said. "How do you think I got here?" she asked, feeling hurt for some reason, as though Lilli should have known, though how could she?

Lilli turned to Burton and placed a hand on her arm. "I know, sweetheart. I'm sorry. I suspected, but just didn't want to believe it." She turned back to the girl and spoke to her again for a few moments. Finally, Lilli gave the girl a hug, gently brushing blond hair from her face. She turned to Burton.

"She said there are about twenty women in the building and, from what she understands, a training class coming in tomorrow morning. We've got to move now."

"Training class for what?"

"I don't know," Lilli said, facing the girl again, who looked back and forth from Lilli to Burton as though she were watching a tennis match. "That's what worries me. Let's get her out of here and find the other women." She glanced at Burton. "From her age, I'm guessing she has no sway here, or I'd send her to gather everyone. I think we're on our own."

"What about her?" Burton asked. "Poor thing looks terrified and basically is walking around half-naked."

"I know," Lilli said, putting a comforting arm around the girl's shoulders.

"Wait," Burton said, hurrying into the bathroom to see if she could find anything useful. No bathrobe or even towels that hadn't been used by Bishop. It was obvious the room hadn't been touched since their departure days before. She hurried out to the bedroom part and tugged the thin comforter off the bed, dragging it over to the girl and, with Lilli's help, wrapping it around the thin frame. "Let's get her to the tunnel."

They were about to leave the room when the

young girl stopped Lilli with a hand on her shoulder. She gesticulated wildly as she spoke quickly to her in their language. Burton waited as patiently as she could, yet again left out in the cold with the huge language barrier. She watched Lilli with her, and not for the first time that night, was charmed and awed by her and the way she interacted with these people, much like she did with Ivan and the boy. She kept her calm and oozed kindness and caring. No doubt, it made her an amazing doctor in her normal life.

"She wants to show us," Lilli said, pulling Burton out of her thoughts.

"All right. Let's get out of here."

≈≈≈≈

Freshly showered and given some clothes of Liliya's to wear, Tasha stood at a table in the middle of the bottling room with Grigoriy and one of the men who had accompanied the king back to the distillery. Grigoriy had arranged for a nurse, who had been with the group in the hotel, to look over the king and Tasha. Besides his surface—albeit painful—wounds, the king had been dangerously undernourished and dehydrated. His filthy, insect-infested beard and hair had been shaved and he'd been bathed and was now resting peacefully in Grigoriy's own bed.

Now, Tasha and the two men were looking over a map of Chilvokia. She was trying to help them locate the building where the children were being held, including her own son.

"It's always dark when they take us there," she said, "and we're always blindfolded until we're inside."

The other man, Andrei sighed and pushed away from the table as he ran a hand through his hair. "We're never going to find it."

"Just wait," Grigoriy said, glancing at the younger man over the tops of his glasses, perched on his nose. "What about the inside? Any sort of attribute of the building, color, anything?"

"Brick," she said, glancing at Andrei and seeming a bit intimidated by the big man who was obviously frustrated. "Lots of red brick. The floors are linoleum, but not in very good condition. The room where the children are kept, the only one I saw, anyway, where the younger kids are, has no furniture in it. The kids are forced to sleep on the floor with blankets and a few sleeping bags." She turned away as tears came to her eyes. She brought up a hand to cover her mouth, visibly trying to get her emotions under control. "I'm sorry." She took several deep breaths before continuing, her voice a bit shaky. "There is a wall that looks like something huge was once there but has been removed. Like," she looked around the large room, as though seeking inspiration.

Grigoriy watched as she walked over to the wall next to the bathrooms where the paint was a lighter color in the perfect rectangle shape where once a sign had hung for more than twenty years. After it had been taken down, the paint was drastically a different color due to dirt and time.

"Like this," she said, slapping the wall with her hand. "The brick is different, darker."

Grigoriy ran his fingers absently over his mustache as he tried to imagine such a room as the young woman described. What could take up such a large space of a wall? "Are there windows?" he asked.

She nodded. "Yes, but they've been boarded over from the outside. The glass is missing in many of them."

"Red brick," Andrei said, walking toward Grigoriy.

"Likely red brick would be inside, too," said the former contractor. "And, the discolored brick, something was there for a long, long time to do that." His heavy eyebrows shot up as he glanced over Grigoriy's shoulder.

The vodka maker followed the younger man as he hurried to an adjacent wall where Tasha stood, also watching him.

"Look!" Andrei said, slapping his hand on a large, rectangular board mounted to the wall where reminders, warnings, and schedules were posted with thumbtacks from the days when the distillery was still running. "If you took this down, like that there," he said, pointing to the spot Tasha had pointed out, "same effect. What if it was a blackboard? Brick building, boarded-over windows, yes, I understand that's half the country, but this"—he patted the message board again—"this makes me think it may be the old elementary school."

"But, that was abandoned," Grigoriy said, shaking his head.

"Or was it?" Tasha challenged.

※※※※

They'd learned the girl's name was Athena and Burton and Lilli followed her through the maze of halls and seemingly hidden staircases until they ended up on the fourth floor, where they were now. They were about to mount another set of stairs but Burton stopped, halting the other two women with a hand to Lilli's back.

"Hang on a second," she whispered.

Burton moved away from the other two and back down the hall they'd just traversed, hearing something she hadn't heard when they'd passed initially. It was the sound of computers and running electronics, not unlike the editing bay back during her days at the studio. She'd spent almost as much time in that room with Roger as she had in her own apartment.

Her gaze bounced around the hallway constantly as she made her way toward a door that hadn't been visible a moment before. Peeking inside, she saw that she was right. It was a dark room, perhaps the size of a very large walk-in closet, only lit by the eerie glow of four large flat-screen monitors with eight camera views per screen, which constantly changed. On the opposite wall of the screens was a desk with three towers and two small computer monitors, obviously the towers running the security system and the third she had to assume was a backup hard drive. On the corner of the desk was a docking base with six walkie-talkies plugged into it.

"What's wrong?"

Burton turned to see Lilli standing behind her. "I think I just found the way to get us out of here alive," Burton said, grinning over her shoulder at Lilli.

Before they could celebrate too much, they heard the sound of a toilet flushing nearby then a door opening. Lilli shoved Burton into the room and pushed the door closed just enough to hide them inside. Moments later, the door was pushed open and Lilli struck, cracking the butt of her gun across the skull of the man who entered. He fell like a ton of bricks, hitting his head on the leg of the desk on the way down.

Burton looked at Lilli with a mixture of shock and pride. "This Hippocratic oath is just being a little more destroyed by the moment, isn't it?" She grinned at the glare that received.

"Help me with him."

Together, they managed to carry the unconscious man to the bathroom he'd just vacated, pushing open one of the three stall doors. It took all their strength but they managed to get him seated on a toilet, his body falling over to lean against the wall.

Lilli checked his vitals and lifted each closed lid of his eyes. "He took quite a hit," she said. "Both from me and the desk leg. I'm guessing he'll be out for at least five minutes." She took in the men's room. "Definitely not enough time for us to get out before he starts the alarm."

Burton studied the dark-haired man dressed in fatigues for a long moment. Against what she really wanted, she knew they had no choice. "I say either we kill him or tie him up and put him in the security room with me." She met Lilli's gaze. "I can lead you and the others out to safety through those cameras."

"What about you?" Lilli said, already shaking her head.

"No, listen," Burton said, reaching out to place two fingers on full lips. "Did you see those walkie-talkies? All of them were accounted for, so nobody is going to be checking in with this guy," she said, patting his shoulder. "If we find something to tie him up with and gag him, stick him in the corner. He can't do a thing with a gun in his face," she added, holding up her Glock.

"Too dangerous."

"As opposed to what, Lilli? Neither of us knows this place, and according to what you've learned, we've got about twenty women to clear out and get out ourselves. What are we going to do against"—she reached inside the unconscious man's hip holster and pulled out his .44 Magnum—"Dirty Harry, here?"

Lilli leaned back against the bathroom stall wall, arms crossed over her chest. She reached up and pulled the headdress away from her mouth. "You're saying we're going to have to play a game of cat and mouse with these bastards?"

"That's exactly what I'm saying."

The man leaning against the wall moaned softly,

even as his eyes remained closed.

"And quickly!"

※ ※ ※ ※

The five men dressed in black from head to toe, brandishing the AK-47s stolen from the palace armory, made their way the half mile to the school on foot from their parked SUV. They remained completely silent, relying on hand gestures by the leader of the group, a former major in the Chilvokian army, which had disbanded after the takeover.

As they neared the dark, boarded-up brick building, they took cover behind debris and trees, inching their way forward. Finally reaching the building, the leader indicated two should join him to make their way to a boarded window in the deep shadows, the last two men offering cover fire should they need it.

They were at the part of the mostly one-story building that was two stories, likely the gymnasium. He moved his way up to the window, weapon held at the ready. He checked for any sign of crushed vegetation, for any sort of a security detail walking the perimeter, as well as security cameras, trip wires, or other such items that could give away their mission.

Seeing nothing, he reached into one of the pockets of his BDU pants and brought out a chisel. He wedged it beneath the edge of the wood covering the window and, using brute strength, worked it until he was able to dislodge it. He managed to get the entire underside up. His team member pulled out a small handheld, battery-powered saw. They met gazes for a moment, nervous the sound would bring unwanted attention. At the nod of the leader, the saw whined to life.

After several tense minutes, the bottom half of

the board fell loose and onto the ground. The saw was immediately turned off as the men listened, all weapons at the ready. The only sound was the faraway barking of a dog and a few night insects.

The leader pulled out a flashlight and clicked it on, keeping the beam low as he checked to see what was revealed. This particular window still had glass in the pane, though it was smeared with what appeared to be mud or grease from the inside.

"Damn," he muttered, realizing that the flashlight beam would never penetrate. "We're going to have to break the glass," he advised his companion. Looking around for inspiration, he ended up handing his tools over and removed his own T-shirt. Balling it up and placing it against the glass, he gritted his teeth before smashing his elbow into the padded glass. He heard a satisfying crack.

Removing the shirt, he saw he got what he intended. He put the shirt back on and took the flashlight back from his team member, using it to break out a few pieces of the glass, at least enough to be able to see what lay on the other side.

Bringing the flashlight up, he aimed the beam inside, moving it around to get a look at as much as he could.

"What do you see?" his companion whispered.

The leader gasped, his eyes growing huge. "Holy mother of God."

Chapter Twenty-three

"Okay," Burton breathed, looking around the small room. A stream of light from the security monitors spilled into the darkened room as she closed and locked the door behind Lilli, who had just taken off with a walkie-talkie. It was a risky plan but the only one she felt would really work.

She glanced over her shoulder at the man she assumed was the security guy, still out cold and wrapped up tight with extension cords they'd found in the small room she was in now, as well as a gag made from a washcloth from the bathroom and some duct tape. He'd been searched and liberated of any and everything except for pocket lint.

After the horrendous feeling, that she knew would haunt her forever, after killing a man, she was willing to take her chances with tying this guy up.

For now, she focused on the system before her. Other than the four flat-screen monitors, a keyboard also sat on the desk, black with bright yellow keys for the arrow keys. There was no mouse, so she wondered if the colored keys were how she could change views if she needed to. She had to figure out in a hurry how to follow Lilli and Athena, let alone whoever they found along the way.

Burton noticed something and hurried over to the wall at the back of the room. It was a laminated map on the wall that showed a basic outline of the palace, labeling rooms as well as fire exits.

"Thanks be to Jesus," she muttered, ripping it from the wall and looking it over before hurrying back to her seat. She checked on her "prisoner" on the way. He seemed to be coming around but was groggy and appeared dazed.

She shifted her gaze from the map to the monitor screens and saw notations for the rooms on the camera views that were similar to the notations for the printed-out rooms. Even though they were in words and terms she didn't understand, she was able to put the matching words together to get an idea of what she was looking at.

Setting the map onto her lap, she focused again on the keyboard. She glanced to one of the monitor screens and saw the tiny icon in the bottom right-hand corner of the screen of four little arrows pointing north, east, south, and west. It was a direct match to the yellow keys, so she tried one and was rewarded with the ability to toggle to another camera.

"Okay," she breathed, searching all four monitors for anything that looked like Lilli and Athena. "Come on, come on, come on," she murmured. It seemed each monitor was focused on its own floor, save for the lowest level, where Burton and the king had been held. That being said, she thought the fourth monitor was focused on Lilli's floor, but she'd yet to appear.

Sitting back in her chair, eyes trained to as many images as she could take in at once, something occurred to her. Her hand shot up to cover her mouth.

"Oh God," she breathed, considering that maybe they'd been caught. As soon as that thought had fully formed, she nearly yelled with relief when she saw Lilli and Athena hurry into view as they scurried down a hall. She laughed outright when Lilli turned to the camera and waved. She grabbed her walkie-talkie. Looking it over to make sure it was on, she pressed the button.

"Hello?" she whispered. She smiled when she saw Lilli react, obviously she'd heard it. The monitor images were silent.

"Hello!"

Burton threw the walkie-talkie up in the air, startled by the shrill response, the volume on the device as loud as possible. She managed to get it back in her hands and turned the volume wheel until it was at three rather than ten.

"Where are you and what's happening?" Burton asked into the device, her eyes glued to the little square that showcased Lilli and Athena's movements.

"Athena said we're in luck," Lilli said, her voice small and tinny from the black device in Burton's hands. "Most of the girls should be in their rooms at this time of night, considering there're not many people in the palace tonight. If we'd come tomorrow…"

Burton nodded, understanding what Lilli was intimating, even if Lilli couldn't see her. "You be careful."

༄༄༄༄

Lilli followed Athena, her heart in her throat. The only thing that made her feel somewhat better was knowing that they had an eye in the sky. She glanced at every camera they came upon, letting Burton know she was with her and making that one last connection… just in case.

As they continued, the halls became narrower, the area seeming to be older and less cared for. The lavish carpeting from the rest of the palace became hardwood floors that needed to be sanded and stained after so many years of use and neglect. In some areas, the walls needed to be repainted or cleaned. Lighting fixtures came less and less, leaving the halls dark and claustrophobic. She figured this was probably an area that had always belonged to the servants, though it didn't look like it had been inhabited in a good long time. In truth, she wasn't even entirely sure how safe it was.

As they hurried down the hall, she noted open and empty rooms on both sides, the rooms were very small and square with a small closet. There were no furnishings except for ones that had a mattress lying on the floor from time to time. Finally they stopped at a closed door near the end of the hall on the left side. Athena opened it, revealing three sets of stacked bunk beds filling the tiny space, three of the four walls lined with the beds, leaving a small square of space at the center of the room.

Three women, who lay in two of the beds, were dressed in long white sleeping gowns that looked more like something an eighteenth-century wife would have worn to bed, not young, beautiful women in the present.

"Wake up!" Athena said once they entered, keeping her tone low even as it was excited. Confusion was reflected in the women's eyes. "Wake up. We're getting out."

"What are you saying?" one of them asked, sitting up.

As Athena quickly explained the situation, Lilli checked the room. Only the black uniforms hung in the closet, the headdress scarves slung over the garments. These were young women, and there wasn't one pair of jeans or dresses or tons of shoes littering the room. *No signs of individuality, no makeup or perfumes littering the tops of the dressers that didn't exist.*

"You live here?" she asked Athena, who stood next to her. The three young women were getting up and dressing hastily.

Athena nodded. "Four of us in here are the newest girls. Our fifth, who isn't here, has been here for a while. She teaches us what to do."

"Where is she?"

"In the kitchen, I'm guessing. She helps out in there at night."

"Where are the other servants?" Lilli asked, looking from one woman to the next. "I know I've personally seen more than twenty here."

"Only on special occasions," one of the women said. "When there are people who need to be..." She exchanged a glance with the other three women, "entertained."

Lilli felt her anger rise and couldn't help but look at Athena, remembering she'd told her she'd just been with Alexey. Her blood boiled as she recalled how upset the young woman had been when they'd come across her and that she'd worn nothing more than a T-shirt and held what was left of her clothing in her hands.

As much as she wanted names and descriptions so she could go off on a neutering mission, she knew there was something else they had to do, and that was get these women out of here.

"Do you ladies know where the cells are downstairs?" she asked, meeting four blank stares. "Okay. So, none of you have been to the lower level of this place?" Again, blank stares, this time with a couple of head shakes. "All right. We've got to get out of here."

※ ※ ※ ※

The leader motioned for the final man other than himself to climb through the window. Once he was in, he checked one more time to make sure they hadn't been observed then followed suit, careful not to cut himself on the broken window.

He had to give credit to the men who had been sent with him—they'd had very little training. He was the last of the Chilvokian military and had been away on holiday in Ireland with his wife when the roundup had begun. His brothers and sisters in arms had been accused of treason by backing the king, whom they'd been told had robbed them and abandoned his country, trying to start a coup. Thousands had disappeared, never to be seen again.

Ever since, woefully lacking weapons or know-how, the people left behind had been sitting ducks to the whims of the government, which claimed to be fighting for them. He'd been grateful when Grigoriy had started a small group of rebels four years before. It had grown and included Grigoriy's daughter, who'd returned home from her career and life in the States, helping to act as a leader and a doctor.

Now, he was beyond thrilled that they were finally taking their country back.

As he shot his large body through the window, he landed in a crouch, weapon at the ready as he observed his surroundings. What he'd seen through the small break in the window he'd made had shocked him, but now, being in the room, his mind was blown.

He was surrounded by a weapons lover's wet dream. The gymnasium of the school was crammed with guns of every caliber, rounds of every size, armored vehicles, including the light tank he was crouching next to. In wonder and horror, he stood slowly. The fact that very little if any of the hardware had been used against the people pointed to two potential outcomes: a huge war of epic proportions was being planned, or the goods were being sold, which was far more alarming.

Suddenly, shots rang out and the man standing four feet away from him dropped dead. "Damn it," he muttered. How had he let himself become so complacent?

He dropped to the ground, eyes huge as he took in as much as he could in the dim lighting. He glanced around, noting another of his men lay dead a few yards away. That left three of them if the other two were still alive. He was relieved to see a terrified set of eyes staring back at him, the breathing attached to that man heavy and quick in his fear.

The leader looked away from him, glad to know he had at least one comrade left. It was too dark to see the fifth man. So, he decided to concentrate on where their enemy combatant was. He listened, nearly slowing his heartbeat to hear even better. Footsteps. He figured this man, who was doing little to hide his progress, was not trained.

He set his big gun aside and, silent as a cat, drew his pistol. He followed the footsteps, which stopped, but then there was the loud click of a fresh magazine palmed home. On his belly, he crawled toward the source of the sound, stopping to listen every few feet. As he moved deeper inside the room and farther away from the light coming in from the broken window, it was harder to see. However, after long, heart-racing moments, his eyes began to adjust and shadows began to turn into shapes that turned into both obstacles and hiding places.

He found a spot behind the large tire of a Jeep. Peering beneath the vehicle, he saw two boots scurrying to the right. They were military-grade boots and the pants were either fatigues or BDUs, different from what he and his men were wearing. He knew this was their guy.

Getting a mental image of where their attacker was, he stood from his hiding place and with handgun in firing position, fired off four quick shots. He heard a grunt then the heavy sound of a body falling to the ground. Staying put for a moment, he listened, making sure there was no one else to be worried about. Hearing nothing, he ducked and weaved his way over to the fallen gunman.

"Ellick," he gasped, looking into the eyes of the dying man. They'd been in battle together, had enjoyed meals together in the mess hall, and had swapped stories of their lives. And yet, here they sat on opposing sides. Unable to help it, he grabbed the bloody hand of his comrade and held it. "What have you done?" he asked, tears coming to his eyes.

"Denis," the man whispered. "I am sorry." He began to cough, blood spurting onto his lips and down his chin.

"Are there any more fighters?" he asked, hoping his friend would give him the gift of knowledge for old time's sake. "Ellick?" the man lying on the ground gurgled, his body spasming before he stopped moving, stopped breathing, stopped living.

Head dropping, the leader ran his hand over his hair before using thumb and forefinger to close Ellick's sightless eyes.

※※※※

Burton peered over her shoulder at the man slouched in the corner. His head was forward, chin resting on his chest.

"Crap," she murmured, leaving her post to hurry over to him. She grabbed both sides of his face to lift his head and look into his face. His eyes were unfocused and pupils dilated. "Oh God." She gently pushed his head so it would lean on the table next to him before hurrying the short distance to the security desk to grab her walkie-talkie. "Lilli?" she said into it, eyeing him.

"Lilli here."

"I think this guy is dead," Burton hissed into the small black device in her hand.

"Check his pulse, either at the wrist or at his neck," Lilli advised.

"'Kay."

Burton felt terrible bugging Lilli; she had her own worries, leading six women through the halls. They'd gathered two more, and Burton had watched the creepy parade of look-a-like women for the last fifteen minutes.

She put the walkie-talkie down and grabbed the man's wrist, using her first two fingers to feel for his pulse. It took her several tries, but finally she found it, though it was weak. She turned to grab her walkie-talkie but her gaze was caught by the monitors.

She cried out softly as she dropped the man's hand and hurried back over to the bank of screens. She could see the women were now on the second floor, but they were about to walk into a group of three heavily-armed men.

"Stop where you are!" she hissed into the walkie-talkie. "Now!"

"What's wrong?" Lilli asked.

To her relief, she saw that Lilli and her train stopped immediately. "Get out of the hallway you're in," she said, eyes glued to the men who suddenly stopped. Burton would have done anything for sound in the cameras. She sensed something was wrong.

Burton's gaze switched to the view where Lilli had been, but she was no longer there.

"Shit," she muttered, scanning each view, her hand absently going to the keyboard to use the arrow keys to change views to find her and the women. She was able to breathe when she saw they'd headed inside a large room. It must have been a ballroom of sorts at one time but now was left abandoned, furnishings covered and half the lightbulbs burned out.

She watched as the women all began to disperse and hide beneath the coverings. Burton was impressed as, within moments, it seemed there had never been anyone there at all.

"Burton?" Lilli whispered.

Burton immediately brought the walkie-talkie to her mouth, her eyes scanning the room for any sign of the women. "I'm here."

"Where are they? I can hear something outside the room."

Burton covered her mouth with her hand for a moment, watching in horror as one of the men entered the room, the barrel of his Browning pointed to the floor.

She brought the walkie-talkie up to her mouth. "Don't move," she breathed.

Chapter Twenty-four

Lilli froze, Burton's frantic whisper in her head. She hid beneath the sheet covering a table with one of the other women she was trying to guide to safety. She'd turned the volume on her walkie-talkie down to zero, just in case Burton were to accidentally say something at the very wrong time.

She turned to the girl hiding with her and put a finger to her cotton-covered lips. Tired of the ruse, she tugged the scarf away from her lower face so her companion could see her mouth. She mouthed the word for quiet, praying the other woman would get how dire their situation was.

As silently as she could, Lilli scooted to a part of the cloth where she saw there was a small tear in the fabric. She tugged the headdress off the rest of the way and focused an eye to peek out of that tear. She could see the man—whom she recognized as one of Alexey's friends—moving farther into the room. His gun was pointed down, but his finger was relaxed on the trigger, no doubt able to pull it in a nanosecond.

She watched his progress into the huge room, not entirely sure where the other five women had hidden. She held her breath as he used the nose of the long gun to poke and prod. She could feel the weight of her own gun in her palm, but she knew if she took this guy out, there could potentially be some serious ramifications. For starters, she reasoned, he was likely part of the group Burton had spotted, and they'd wonder where he'd disappeared to when he didn't rejoin them. Secondly, where could they possibly escape to once he was eliminated?

"*Blyad*," she cursed.

Somehow, Lilli managed to not yell out when she felt a touch on her arm. She checked behind her to see the woman she was hiding with. She was pointing behind them. With cat-quiet movement, Lilli scooted around the other woman and spread out onto her stomach so she could be as low as possible to look under the table covering. There, she saw what she thought she'd been alerted to. There was a door. She glanced over her shoulder at the woman who was nodding vigorously.

Lilli allowed the cloth to drop as her forehead rested silently against the floor. She knew she'd have to take the man out, and she was loath to cause more violence. What Burton had joked about earlier was true. As a doctor, she had a duty that she'd sworn her life to partake, and hurting and killing were not part of that.

But, this was also not what she'd signed up for, and she had to do what she had to do for the greater good. She took the material of her discarded headdress and wrapped it around the end of her gun into a makeshift silencer then turned to the women sitting next to her and raised her hand, all five fingers up. She made sure the woman was looking at her hand and understood as she began a silent countdown with her fingers. At one, she flew out from beneath the table and slid across the wood floor on her side, managing to get off three shots, all muffled, before the man could react. He fell to the ground without a word.

Five heads popped up, wide eyes all around. Without a word to them, Lilli sprinted across the huge room to that door, relieved to hear footsteps of the other women following her. She pulled open the door and found a staircase.

"Go!" she hissed, shepherding the women before her. She glanced back at the dead man on the floor, pausing for just a second before she ran to him and quickly searched him. She took his Browning and the extra ammo as well as a Zippo lighter. On a whim, she also took the flask he had, which from the sniff she took, was filled with the liquid fire that her family was famous for.

☙☙❧❧

Burton covered her mouth with both hands to muffle her howl of relief and celebration as she watched the door close behind Lilli. She instantly turned to the laminated map spread out across her lap to try to figure out where that door led. She saw a room and the word, *kukhnya*.

"Shit," she whispered. "What the hell does that mean?" She looked around for inspiration when she saw the captured man's phone sitting on the desk next to his gun. She grabbed it and prayed that she could get into it without being blocked by a code or password. "Thank God," she whispered when she was let in.

She logged on to an Internet search engine then examined the word again before typing it in.

"Kitchen," she read.

With her new information, she turned back to the map, dividing her attention between that and trying to follow Lilli and any other movement, especially the other men who had been with the dead man in the ballroom. She couldn't help but feel like she was in some sick game of Clue.

"Burton," was whispered across the airwaves.

Burton grabbed her walkie-talkie, looking

frantically for Lilli and the girls on the screens. "I'm here. Where are you?"

"We're in a narrow stairway," Lilli whispered. "I think we're about to enter the kitchen."

"I think so, too. That's what the map says." Burton viewed the screen. "I see a woman in there washing some dishes. She's not dressed in that weird servant's outfit but just a regular dress."

"We're going in. Where is everyone else?"

"That's what worries me," Burton said, scanning all four screens, using the arrow keys to scan through each floor. "There are a few guys in varying places on the third floor and one talking to a woman in the entryway." She glanced back to the monitor for the first floor. "Stop!" she whispered. "Someone is entering the kitchen."

Burton watched intently, sweat beginning to build between her shoulder blades and down between her breasts. She was so nervous and anxious that Lilli and the women weren't going to make it out.

"Antonia said there are stairs from the kitchen to the cellar," Lilli whispered, startling Burton.

She examined the map again, trying to find the stairs. "I'm not seeing them," she said, shaking her head. "Actually, this map shows nothing of the lower level beneath the first floor. Damn."

"We have to try," Lilli said. "I don't know any other way down."

"Agreed."

Burton sat back in her chair, letting out a heavy breath as she scrubbed her face with her hands for a moment. She glanced back at the man slumped in the corner, and to her horror, she was fairly sure he was dead. She turned away, squeezing her eyes closed for a long moment before refocusing. Checking the screen again, she noticed both the woman and the man were now gone.

"Go!" she exclaimed. "Go now, the kitchen is empty." She frantically searched to see where the pair had gone, only to find them in the dining room meshed in a heated discussion.

Turning away from that, she watched as Lilli and the girls burst out of the stairwell and into the kitchen, one of the six women taking the lead, headed toward what appeared to be a pantry. She opened the door and they all hurried in.

"Bingo," Lilli said, out of sight.

Burton let out a breath of relief. "Thank God."

༺༻

The last of the five men left standing, the leader and his companion, made their way to the door, an arsenal and three dead men behind them. He turned to his cover, nodding to indicate he was about to open the door. The other man hid behind a shelving unit, weapon at the ready as the leader kicked the door open before rushing into the hallway, sweeping his weapon in every direction.

"Clear," he said, letting the other man know it was okay to join him.

Together they made their way down the hall, passing a drinking fountain before they came to the boys' locker room. He pointed inside, indicating his companion should check it out. Without a word, he was left in the hallway. Not two minutes later, the door opened again.

"You need to come in here."

Together they entered and the leader's jaw fell open. The locker room looked like any other with cement floors, red-painted lockers lining two walls, and an archway leading to the area with four bathroom stalls and four urinals along one wall, a large tiled-off space with a half-dozen showerheads across from them.

What caught their attention, however, were all the children either lying on blankets or sleeping bags or sitting up looking back at them. There had to be more than fifty kids jammed into the center of the locker room, the benches that normally would have lined the space pushed against the walls.

"That's my son," he whispered, looking at the boy who was slowly rising to his feet, last seen when he was only four years old. Now, a five-and-a-half-year-old stared back at him.

≋≋≋≋

"You're going to need to head down that tunnel," Lilli said, pointing into the darkness beyond the moved shelf in the armory. "It'll take you to safety."

"It's so dark," Athena said, eyes wide.

"I know, but you'll be okay. Hurry!"

Once she was sure they were gone and safe, she brought the arm of the microphone connected to her earpiece to her mouth. "Papa?" She leaned back against the wall as she waited for a response. "Papa?"

"No, it's Ivan," came the tinny response.

Lilli's eyebrows fell in concern. "Is everything okay?"

"Yes. Everyone is gearing up to head to the school," he explained. "Denis found something huge there, but I'm not sure what it is. Your father put me on the radio since I can't exactly go help."

"How are you doing, buddy?" she asked, concerned that Ivan was up and around with his leg injury so new and infection such a danger.

"I'm still here."

She smiled, able to hear the smile in his voice. "All right, well I'm sending a group of women through the tunnel. Make sure they're taken care of."

Lilli stopped, her attention grabbed by what she thought were footsteps. She nearly brought up the walkie-talkie to ask Burton but remembered she was on her own. A glance behind her satisfied her that none of the women were lingering or had returned. She turned back forward and listened. She figured she must have been mistaken on footstep; she was surrounded by nothing but silence.

Heading to the door—albeit quietly—she listened again, feeling the comforting grip of her gun in her hand. More confident, she left the room, pushing the heavy door as best she could with the hand of her unhurt arm. She headed down the hall, her eyes adjusting better to the light to at least not run into the stone wall. She was about to turn the corner to the hall where the cell was that had kept King Arvid and Burton. She stopped short, eyes wide when she heard voices headed in her direction.

"Heinz wants the cells ready by tonight," a man's voice said.

"Those suckers coming for training are going to be surprised," another said, making them both laugh.

Lilli tried to calm her pounding heart. The moment the men realized the cell was empty, all hell would break loose and the likelihood of Burton and the rest of the women getting out was slim to none.

She raised her gun, cocking it as quietly as she could in anticipation of what she might have to do. She listened, her chest heaving as she breathed heavily with a heartbeat threatening to bring her to cardiac arrest.

"Hey!" a third voice said, his pounding footfalls getting closer to the cell. "They just found Devon dead in the ballroom. Come on, Alexey wants all the men he can to search the place."

She leaned back against the wall, both relieved and worried. She became absolutely terrified when she heard what one of the other men said.

"Has anyone heard from Vlad in security? Did he see anything?"

Lilli's heart stopped. She heard the men run off in the opposite direction, disaster averted with the empty cell, but a new one created with the dead guy in the ballroom. She brought her walkie-talkie up to her mouth and pressed the button to talk. "Burton?" She heard a sound come through the speaker that sounded like a static-ridden voice. "Burton?" she tried again. And, for a second time the static response. "Shit!" she exclaimed in a hissed whisper.

No doubt the reception was profoundly hampered by the stone walls. She stood there in indecision for a moment then knew she only had one option. She *had* to get the message to Burton before it was too late. She took off at a dead run back toward the room that would lead to the stairs to the upper levels of the palace.

Chapter Twenty-five

The sound of heavy booted footfalls echoed across the wood floor of the ballroom, stopping at the body briefly before moving onto a covered table. Dark material lay on the floor next to it. A hand reached down and grabbed the slightly rolled material, bringing it up to a nose to sniff.

"Gunpowder."

"What do you want to do, Alexey?" his companion asked.

The man lowered the material, letting it drop from his fingers back to the floor. "Find my sister, and kill that bitch in the cell."

☙☙☙☙

Burton's attention was torn between the weird unintelligible message on the walkie-talkie and watching as Alexey and another man stood over the dead body in the ballroom. Everything in her told her to bolt.

She pushed back from the desk with the security monitors and tucked her Glock into the back of the waistband of her pants so she could hold the .44 she'd taken off the guy slouched in the corner. It was heavy, and even though she knew more about the gun she was stowing away than the one she held, she worried this one would end up on a trip down her pant leg at a very inopportune time.

Grabbing the walkie-talkie, she hurried to the

door, pressing her ear against the wood for a long moment. Hearing nothing, she opened it a bit and glanced both ways down the hall before she jetted across to the bathroom where they'd first dragged the body of the man she was leaving behind. Her gut told her anyone would check the security room long before the bathroom, giving her a few moments to figure out what to do.

She decided on the third of four stalls and locked the door, bracing herself with hands on either wall to take a breather. She tried to ground herself, doing her best to listen beyond the bathroom. It didn't take long before she heard pounding footfalls in the hall and a door banging open, which she assumed was the security room. A man's voice yelled out a moment later and she listened as more pounding footfalls came right to the bathroom.

Burton gasped and held her breath as she reached out to unlock the stall door and allow it to open just a bit to a natural jar. She stood behind it not a second too soon before she heard someone shoving open the stall doors, one at a time, moving closer to her. She squeezed her eyes shut for a moment, preparing for her turn, which was next.

Suddenly, though not surprisingly, her door began to fly open, and she was ready. She braced against the walls and used her foot to kick the door back as hard as she could, forcing it to slam into the man, sending him flying back the few feet to the wall behind him with such force his head broke through the drywall. He slid down to his butt, looking up at her dazed and utterly confused.

In the process, his gun had flown out of his hands and skidded over by the wall, bumping against it with a lame thump. Burton grabbed it and took off, slamming out of the bathroom. The hallway was empty so she took off toward the stairs, taking them two at a time, nearly falling in her haste. Her heart was racing and she knew she had to get to a place of safety as quickly as she could.

Making it to the third floor without seeing another soul, she heard voices coming down the hall she'd just arrived at and voices traveling up the stairs behind her. Trapped, she stood frozen for a moment, not seeing anyone but knowing she had to find a place to hide. It made it even worse that she couldn't understand what was being said, so she had no idea what was going on, what was being instructed or directed.

She peeked to her left and saw a niche in the wall with a statue of an angel. Nowhere else to go, she nearly threw herself behind the huge statue, which was easily two feet taller than she was, though not quite as wide. She prayed she wouldn't be noticed. Two men came from down the hall and one from the stairs met up not more than ten yards from where she was hidden almost in plain sight.

The men spoke quietly, not that Burton could understand them, anyway, but she did understand when she heard her own name and saw one of the men give another a handgun. With that, the three split up, heading back the way they'd come.

Breathing a sigh of relief, she rested her head back against the wall for a moment to allow her racing heart to slow. She brought the walkie-talkie to her lips and, peeking out from around the statue, looked both ways down the hall.

"Lilli?"

After a moment, "I'm here. Where are you?"

"I'm on the third floor. I'm on my way to the second floor and the stairway to the basement," Burton said, ducking out of the niche and hurrying as fast as she dared to the stairs.

"Thank God they didn't find you."

"Well," Burton hedged, eyes wide as she neared the second floor. "Hold on. Going silent for a sec."

Lowering the walkie-talkie, she raised the .44 Magnum, which was uncomfortable since it was such a long-barreled, heavy gun. She reached the second floor and peeked around the corner to the endlessly long hallway of the floor she and Bishop had stayed on.

She hurried down the hall, bringing the device back up. "I'm on the second floor now and on my way. Where are you?"

"We're on the first floor almost to the kitchen stairs. I found a few more women and sent the rest on their way to the armory room ahead of us. You might run into them." There was a brief pause. "Burton?"

"Yes?" Burton responded, glancing over her shoulder as she began to jog down the hall. She could hear a change in Lilli's voice.

"I can't tell you how good it is to hear your voice. I was so worried."

Burton smiled. "Me, too," she said softly. "See you downstairs."

Tucking the walkie-talkie in her back pocket, she turned the jog into a run, for some reason her heart racing. She felt as though the Big Bad Wolf was bearing down on her, could almost feel the heat of his breath against her neck. Panic begin to set in, only to be cut with relief when she saw the end of the hall looming, the door to the stairs and escape to the left.

Wanting to cry, she was so relieved she'd reached the door, Burton grabbed for the doorknob before her hand was nearly clocked when the door exploded open, Alexey standing on the other side. He seemed as shocked as she was, but his surprise turned to rage before hers had time to turn to defense.

He swung, knocking the .44 out of her hand, the large gun skidding across the floor to come into soft contact with the wall. Burton barely had a chance to process what was happening when she found herself slammed against the wall so hard her head banged against the plaster, nearly knocking her out. He grabbed her by the shirtfront and pulled her away from the wall only to slam her a second time.

"How did you get out?" he growled, his face mere inches from hers. The wolf's hot breath was indeed upon her. "It doesn't matter," he said, not even giving Burton a chance to catch her breath, let alone speak. He grabbed her throat with a large hand and used it to hold her against the wall, his strength once again impossible to overtake. She watched in horror as he reached behind him and brought out a Bowie knife. "I don't care what Heinz wants with you," he spat. "I'm sick of seeing your fucking face. Now," he added, bringing the knife tip dangerously close to one of Burton's eyes. "I'm going to do it *my* way."

Burton felt something pressing into her lower back making an incredibly uncomfortable position all that much more uncomfortable. Confused for a few seconds, she suddenly remembered—it was her Glock. She squeezed her eyes shut and did her best not to cry out as the deadly sharp blade made a small cut on her right cheek. She could feel the tickle of blood trickling down the side of her face.

She reached her hand down, desperately trying to worm it between her back and the wall, but Alexey had her pinned not only with his hand, but nearly his entire body. It was like trying to push a brick wall away from her.

He grinned at her, so much hatred in those cold eyes it gave Burton shivers. He moved the blade to the other cheek and again, left a cut, though this time longer and even more painful. "I've been waiting so long to really, really fuck you up," he murmured, his voice sounding giddy.

She tried again to push her hips out to make room for her hand, but he wasn't budging. It was making her nauseous as she pressed against his crotch in the process. Finally, looking up into his eyes, she knew there was only one thing she could do. Using every ounce of saliva she could gather in a dry mouth, she launched the most disgusting loogie she could manage right in his face. All she needed was to startle him or make him let up just a bit. She watched in horrified fascination as it landed right on the corner of his mouth.

"You, bitch!" he roared, backing off a step and bringing up a hand to wipe it away.

That gave her all she needed. Pushing away from the wall, she reached behind her and tugged the 9mm free from her waistband and brought it around, not even aiming as she fired twice.

Alexey grunted then staggered backward, his hand on his side. His T-shirt was quickly growing a red spot, his eyes wide in surprise. He staggered backward another couple of steps before he fell to one knee.

Shocked at what had just happened, even though she'd knowingly done it, she stood there looking down at him. Shaking herself out of the shock and fear, she didn't bother to go after the dropped knife, .44, or walkie-talkie. Instead, she turned her focus to the door, reaching for it when she screamed out in surprise and pain as she was grabbed by the hair, her head jerked backward. On instinct, she sent her elbow flying back, hitting Alexey in his bullet wound in his side. He cried out and crashed to the ground.

Now in full fight-or-flight mode, Burton launched

herself at the door. She grabbed the heavy old wood door and was about to step down onto the first stair when her foot was grabbed from behind. She glanced back and saw that Alexey was holding on with everything he had, the stain on his side growing at frightening speed.

"Let go of me, you bastard!" she yelled through gritted teeth.

His grip was like a metal vice. She braced herself on the doorframe as she yanked as hard as she could, her pant leg finally free, but the inertia sent her tumbling down the stone stairs. Burton finally stopped her fall as the stairs began to turn in their spiral, hitting her head hard against the wall.

She lay there for a long moment, unable to breathe. Her lower back and neck were killing her, as was her left leg. Amazingly, she didn't seem to have broken anything, but there was no knowing that until after her adrenaline calmed. She checked the doorway, expecting to see Alexey come at her at any moment, but there was nothing, just silence.

Getting herself together, she pulled herself to her feet, crying out in pain from a badly sprained right ankle then continued to hobble down the rest of the stairs, using the walls as much as she could for balance and to keep weight off her foot.

"Oh my God, what happened?" Lilli asked, suddenly appearing at the bottom of the stairs.

For a moment, Burton thought she was a mirage and could only stare. Once Lilli reached her and touched her, she broke down in tears. "I killed him," she sobbed into Lilli's arms.

"Who?" Lilli asked gently, pushing Burton away just enough to see her face. "Oh God," she whispered. "What happened to your face?"

For a moment, not sure what Lilli was talking

about, she remembered the cuts, which sent her into fresh tears. "Alexey," she whispered. "He did this. I..." She couldn't meet Lilli's caring eyes. "I didn't have a choice." She fell back into Lilli's arms. "I'm so sorry."

"Shhh," Lilli said, holding her and rocking her slightly. "He made his own choices, sweetheart," she whispered. "Come on. Let's get out of here."

Burton nodded and pulled out of the hug. Lilli turned away, but not before Burton saw the tears in her eyes.

Lilli helped her with an arm around her waist as Burton limped along. They had to hurry, she knew, and was frustrated by the pace she was able to give, slowing them down terribly.

Once they were past the vodka room, Lilli stopped them. Burton stared at her in question even though she couldn't even see her that well in the darkness, knowing they were just a few yards away from the armory and freedom.

"Go on ahead," the doctor said. She put up two fingers to stop Burton who began to protest. "I'm going to blow up the tunnel behind us."

"No, I can help you—"

"Sweetheart," Lilli said softly, placing a hand to her jaw. "I need to be able to move fast. You're hurt and can't run." Lilli looked deeply into Burton's eyes. "I need you to go on to the distillery."

Burton met Lilli's gaze, losing herself in their green depths. She wondered absently when Lilli had chucked the brown contacts. She was glad that she had. She knew she was right, and as much as she hated the idea, she nodded. "Okay."

Without another thought, Burton grabbed Lilli and held her close. She buried her face in her neck, not caring that she was leaving blood there. She had to feel her, smell her, and know that everything would be okay. She smiled when Lilli held her just as tight.

Pulling out of the hug, she left a lingering kiss on Lilli's lips. "Please be safe," she whispered.

Lilli nodded. "I'll see you on the other side."

Burton brought her hand up and caressed the softness of Lilli's cheek. She backed away, unable to keep her eyes off Lilli, trying to hang on to the memory of what she looked like rather than what she saw standing before her, which was not much more than a silhouette.

After a dozen heartbeats, Lilli disappeared inside the vodka room. Burton turned and hurried through the last bit of tunnel to the armory and into the tunnel that would lead to safety.

Not at all familiar with the distillery tunnel, Burton had to do her best to feel her way so she didn't trip or run into anything. She was hurting badly and wanted nothing more than to sleep. She could feel the smooth stone beneath her fingertips turn into brick with slightly sharp edges of mortar from time to time.

"Ow, damn it," she muttered, one such edge slicing open her finger.

She stuck the bleeding tip in her mouth when suddenly a massive blast rocked her world. She was sent flying to the ground, landing with a painful grunt on her shoulder. She could see nothing but could hear chips of brick and stone falling all around her as well as a massive wave rush over her.

Sitting up, her heart raced as she realized the tunnel had collapsed behind her. "Lilli?" she said, slowly getting to her feet. She walked blindly to where she felt the cave-in. "Lilli!"

Chapter Twenty-six

Grigoriy pulled his Hummer up to the school, the two box trucks from the distillery arriving moments before. He'd gotten the call from Denis, and to the shock of everyone at what had been found, had rallied the troops to head to the school and get these kids and women out of there.

Climbing down from the large vehicle, he watched as men tugged the doors to the box trucks up, those inside spilling out to claim their family members and to make sure the school was guarded during the mission of rescuing these people, many of whom had disappeared two, three years before. They were thought to be dead or sold.

"Sir."

Grigoriy turned to see Denis standing next to him. "Good work. I can't believe this."

"It was a shock. We've secured the building, either taken out or restrained the enemy."

Grigoriy nodded with a smile. He'd known Denis since he'd been a boy. Even then, he'd been intense and serious, even as his father, who had been a truck driver for N7, had been light and goofy. He knew there was nobody better to make this happen, and he'd been right. The young man's father would be proud if he were still alive.

"Sir," Denis said, unwittingly breaking through the older man's thoughts. "I found—" his voice cracked. He looked away and cleared his throat. "I found Viktor."

Grigoriy's eyes grew large as his chest swelled with happiness. He took the younger man in a tight but brief hug, pounding his back a couple times with joy. They parted and he smiled, noting with surprise the tears in Denis's eyes. "I'm very happy for you. Anna will be overjoyed. She's back at the distillery."

Moments later, the front doors to the school were opened and so were the floodgates. Grigoriy watched as children reunited with their parents, siblings reunited with each other, spouses and other loved ones ran into each other's arms.

He took a handkerchief from his pocket and swiped at his eyes. He wished Liliya could see this—she knew many of these people. She'd gone to school with them, had grown up with them. He even saw a woman who had been the kids' babysitter when he and Allison were still together in Chilvokia.

"My God," he muttered, shaking his head. "How did this happen?"

※※※※

Heinz's fingers raced across the keyboard as he sent off the e-mail finalizing plans for the next day. With the new recruits coming in, there would be a lot to prepare for. He finished and hit the send button then removed his computer glasses, tossing them to the desktop. It had been a long day and he brought his hand up to rub his eyes. One thing that was nice about taking over Arvid's private quarters was that it was removed from the rest of the palace. When his day was done it was totally done. He was basically cut off from everyone else and anything happening elsewhere.

Pushing back from the desk, he got to his feet and walked across the office to the kitchen in the rooms that were more than two thousand square feet of living space. He poured himself another cup of coffee. Stirring in some cream, he laid the spoon down in the sink and headed to the door wearing his pajamas and robe. It was late and he was tired, but he wanted to work a few things out with Alexey before retiring.

Trying to suppress a yawn but failing miserably as it cracked his jaw, he reached for the doorknob and took a sip of his coffee, pulling open the door. As he stepped out into the hall, his heavy eyebrows fell.

He looked left and right and didn't see the girls who usually stood close by just in case he needed—or wanted—one of them. That was the great thing about the head scarves. It was like a surprise with each pick. Plus, they wouldn't be recognized. He had to chuckle to himself as he always thought of the American Tom Hanks movie. *Life is like a box of chocolates. You never know what you're gonna get.* The girls were the same way. He continued on, almost at the juncture that would lead out of his wing and to the rest of the palace. He stopped, coffee forgotten, as he suddenly smelled something intense and strong. It took a moment, but he realized it was alcohol, like vodka. He set the coffee cup down on a table against the hallway wall when he realized he was also smelling the acrid stench of smoke. The combination of the two was nauseating and concerning.

Quickening his pace, he hurried toward the adjacent hallway that would lead to the stairs. He noticed something small and roundish sitting in the middle of the floor. Then, too late, he noticed the trail of fire licking its way up a narrow trail on the rug, headed right for the object.

"Fuck!" he yelled, turning to run in the opposite direction as the line of flame reached the object: a grenade. Seconds later, an explosion sent him flying, his robe on fire, quickly consuming his flesh. He wasn't able to get another scream out as his lungs were consumed by the flames.

※※※※

The night was rocked with explosion after explosion, nearly sending the dark figure that sprinted away sailing through the air. They caught themselves before running even harder and faster across the grounds.

※※※※

Once again, the explosion knocked Burton to the ground as the entire tunnel shook around her, raining more debris and rock down on her. This time, the trembling in the tunnel didn't stop.

"Shit," she gasped, painfully getting to her feet as the tunnel began to further collapse around her. She ran blindly, praying she didn't run into the wall because it would likely knock her out and she'd be buried.

Her bad leg was killing her and her sprained ankle had her in tears, but she did her best not to focus on the pain. Her ankle began to give out but she pushed on, nearly yelling out in relief when she saw light just up ahead. She winced as a larger chunk of stone grazed the side of her head and bounced off her shoulder. She picked up her pace as best she could, desperately wanting out of that tunnel. She burst out through an open door into the basement of the distillery and right in the crosshairs of a woman standing with feet spread apart in an aggressive stance and both hands wrapped around a pistol.

Burton stopped, her chest heaving from her

exertion and eyes squinting from the sudden light in the room that she quickly came to realize was Grigoriy's living room.

"Wait!" she begged, raising her hands in surrender. "I'm with the good guys."

The woman slowly lowered her gun. She raised an eyebrow. "You're the American," she said simply, her accent obviously that of an Australian.

After her shock wore off, Burton realized the woman was dressed like one of those crazy servant girls. She wondered if she was one who Lilli had led to safety. "Yes. Burton Blinde."

"Angela." The woman lowered her gun. Her headdress had been removed and her short, brown hair was tucked behind her ears, though she still wore the outfit. "Sorry. I was told to keep an eye on this door."

Burton nodded, her tears continuing to fall, though now it was from fear, not the immense pain she was in. "The tunnel has been collapsed," she explained, bringing up her hand to swipe at her tears. "No need to guard it anymore."

Angela looked from Burton to the tunnel behind her and back to her face. "Where's the redhead lady?"

With that question, Burton broke down fully. She began to fall to her knees, but Angela caught her, helping her to the ground.

"It's all right," she said softly, patting Burton's back.

Now that Burton was essentially safe, everything that had occurred over the past handful of days finally caught up with her. Fearing that Lilli was gone added fuel to a very emotional fire. She could hardly breathe as her grief completely took her over. All she could see was Lilli's face, the man on the motorcycle, and the man in the security room. She knew he had died or was close to it by the time she fled. Then finally, she saw Alexey's face flash before her eyes. She felt the terror all over again and the rage and shock of learning that he was the one behind the murderous act that had changed her life forever.

Her tears continued uncontrollably as everything poured out of her. She could feel Angela holding her, but she briefly felt the coldness and loss of her comforting touch only for it to return seconds later. She was grasped tighter, her head held against soft breasts and her hair caressed as she was slowly rocked. She felt herself calming and realized she smelled a very familiar scent, as well as the smell of smoke.

Pulling away, Burton's eyes grew huge as she caught Lilli's tired and red-rimmed gaze. Her hair was loose, forming a wild mane of fire around her head. For a moment, Burton felt as though she were looking at a dream, unable to believe it until she felt soft fingers caress her cheek and even softer lips lightly touch her own.

"Hey," Lilli whispered.

"Hi," Burton said through her tears.

She pulled Lilli to her, burying her face in her neck as they held each other. She breathed her in deeply, feeling just the slightest mending of her grief-stricken heart. She had to smile internally as she thought about the therapy she was going to need after this.

"Come on," Lilli said softly, leaving another kiss on Burton's lips. "Let me look you over."

Lilli helped Burton to her feet, which were unsteady. She cried out as a shot of white-hot pain exploded from her ankle, stealing her breath. Lilli held her with an arm around her waist.

"Can you walk?" she asked.

Burton took a couple breaths, eyes closed as she

absorbed the pain, and waited for it to abate. Finally, she nodded. "We'll have to take it slow."

Angela, who stood nearby watching, hurried over and helped. Burton was grateful. With the two women on either side of her, she didn't have to put any weight on her ankle at all.

"In here," Lilli instructed, leading them down a short hall from the living area that had a bathroom on one side of the hall and a small room on the other. Inside was a small cot and cabinets that lined two of the walls with a sink and square of counter space beneath them.

Burton was helped to sit on the cot, instantly relieved to be off her bad leg.

"Thank you," Lilli said to Angela, who left.

Burton watched as Lilli went through the cabinets, pulling out ACE bandages, bottles of medications, and supplies to clean up Burton's face. The bleeding from the cuts had stopped, but she could feel the stiff stickiness of the drying blood.

Supplies gathered in her arms, Lilli hurried over to the cot and knelt down, favoring her right hand and arm. Burton watched as she held the other arm closely to her body.

"What happened?" she asked softly, seconds before gasping in pain as Lilli removed her shoe.

"I'm sorry," Lilli whispered, giving her an apologetic smile. "I know that hurts. I need to feel around, okay? Make sure nothing is broken."

Burton nodded, dreading the examination, but she knew Lilli had to. She closed her eyes, gritting her teeth as Lilli did her job as a physician. The ankle had hurt initially, but running from that blast and potential cave-in had done more damage—that she was sure of.

"Can you feel this?" Lilli asked from her squatting position at Burton's feet. She looked up and met Burton's gaze. Lilli winced right along with Burton's small cry of pain. "Guess so. Okay," she said, tenderly removing the sock and tossing it aside. "Horribly bruised," she commented, slowly turning the foot this way and that. "But, I don't think it's broken." She smiled up at Burton. "I'll wrap it to help keep it still. No crutches here, but once we get to the carrier—"

"Carrier?" Burton asked, sitting up a bit straighter. "What are you talking about?"

Lilli was quiet for a moment, tightly wrapping Burton's foot and ankle, leaving her toes free. "I called your boss," she began softly, "while you were sleeping last night."

Burton stared at her. She was filled with a mixture of emotions, the first sending a fire through her body at the memory those words brought, the memory of their night together. The second of which was confusion. "You called Everett?"

Lilli nodded, finishing up with her foot. "Don't be mad," she said softly. "He has some connections and there's an American carrier close by in international waters." She stood, reaching for the supplies she'd left on the cot next to Burton. "Also, my father told me King Arvid has been in contact with the US government to get help."

"He's here? Arvid is here?" Burton asked, spirits lifting, even as it stung like hell when Lilli cleaned out the cuts on her cheeks with peroxide.

"Sorry, baby," Lilli whispered, blowing softly over the wounds to help cool the sting. "Yes. He's here." Lilli shared Burton's smile. "And, he's quite taken with you, your dedication."

Burton's eyes were squeezed shut as Lilli applied Neosporin to the cuts on her cheeks. "And, I'm impressed as hell with his resilience," she said through gritted teeth.

"I'm sorry," Lilli said again, applying the salve to Burton's wounds. She sat back on her haunches, looking up at Burton with a critical eye. "These shouldn't scar. I truly think those cuts were simply to cause pain."

Burton nodded, able to feel the somewhat ticklish goo on her flesh. "He succeeded."

Lilli looked away then down. "I set the palace on fire, Burton," she said, her voice not much more than a whisper.

Burton stared at her for a moment, not sure she'd heard correctly. After a moment, she placed two fingers under Lilli's chin to lift her beautiful face to look at her. "What happened?" she asked softly. She kept her voice calm, despite the fact that she was shocked and not entirely sure how to feel about that action.

Lilli let out a heavy breath. "They've all done so much damage to so many people. Devastated us all, Burton," she whispered, her voice shaky with emotion.

Burton felt her own emotion grip her once again. Lilli had been so strong for her she felt she owed it to her to return the favor. She pushed aside her own reservations, blocking the thought that likely many of the men inside didn't make it out, which she knew in her heart was for the best.

"The thought of any of them escaping..." She looked away from Burton. "I just couldn't let that happen."

Burton smiled as she slowly shook her head. "I've never, in all my reporting, all my travels, all the people I've ever met, met anyone like you, Lilli." Her smile grew when Lilli met her gaze, the green depths tortured. "I used to think I was so strong, so determined." She let out a heavy sigh, suddenly feeling exhausted. "But after knowing you, even for such a short time, I have no words."

Lilli looked away, tears rolling down her cheek, which she quickly wiped away. "Thank you." She met Burton's gaze again, a small smile on her lips "I've always felt the same about you." She chuckled ruefully. "Why do you think I tried to contact you in the first place?"

Burton grinned and cupped Lilli's face, gazing at her. "You inspire me," she whispered. She brought their lips together, initiating a slow, deep kiss which lasted a few moments before she rested their foreheads together. "We're going to get through this."

Lilli nodded. "Together?" she asked, backing away just enough to look into Burton's eyes.

"Yes. Together."

Lilli's smile was brilliant, making her even more beautiful than she already was, quite stunning, in Burton's eyes. "Well, let's start by getting your face cleaned off and then getting that ankle elevated to stop the swelling. I don't think Papa has any ice packs around here, so that'll have to wait until we get on the carrier."

"What about your arm?" Burton asked, fingertips gently running up Lilli's exposed forearm.

"I dislocated my shoulder when the grenade went off in the hotel," Lilli said, lightly and gently washing away the blood from Burton's face.

"What?" Burton asked, wincing when Lilli accidentally rubbed a bit too hard on one of the bruises on her face, all thanks to Alexey.

"My brother," Lilli said with a heavy sigh. She walked over to the sink and rinsed out the bloodstained rag she'd been using, running it under hot water before returning to kneel in front of Burton to continue her ministrations. "I guess when he decided to take you, he decided the gig was up and set a booby trap." She sat back on her heels and stared up at Burton's face, gently turning it from one side to the other. "I didn't know and I...well..."

Burton saw the pain in those expressive green eyes. She cocked her head slightly to the side as she studied her. "How did this happen?" she asked softly.

"He planted a grenade—"

"No," Burton said, shaking her head. "I mean, your father seems like such a good guy, and you're an exquisite human being who has dedicated her adult life to helping people and saving lives." She shook her head. "How did this happen? How did he end up so..." She wasn't sure what to say there. No matter what she thought of the son of a bitch, she didn't want to offend or hurt Lilli.

"Evil?" Lilli supplied. "It's okay," she said with another heavy sigh, again returning to the sink. She rinsed the rag and left it to dry on the edge of the sink. She turned to face Burton, leaning back against the countertop. She held her injured arm close to her body with the other arm. "I truly believe he was born this way. I think he's a sociopath, and nothing my father ever could have done would have made a difference." She shook her head. "He was gone to us the day he was born."

"I'm sorry," Burton whispered. "I never had any siblings, and I always used to fantasize about having one. I can't imagine having that gift only for it to be so rotten."

"And, that's exactly what he is." Lilli pushed away from the counter and walked back over to the cot where Burton sat. "Lie down so we can get your foot elevated."

"What can we do about your shoulder, first?" Burton asked. "I imagine it should be in a splint or a cast or something, right?"

Lilli nodded. "Yes, but we don't have either one."

"Can it be wrapped?" Burton asked stubbornly. She pushed up from the cot, wincing as she put weight on her ankle. "What do I need to do?"

"You're stubborn," Lilli said, leaving a quick peck on her lips before she told Burton how to wrap her shoulder with the two rolls of ACE bandages they had left. "You really shouldn't be wasting these on me, though. I'd wager other folks are going to need these supplies more."

"Hush and stand still," Burton muttered.

"All right, all right." Lilli stood still as Burton got started, following instructions. "After you left St. Luke's, I lost track of you."

At the shy smile and nod she got, she ran a hand through her hair, deeply touched, stunned, and filled with an emotion she'd never fully felt before but had always wanted to. There was no way on earth she could say the words, but she allowed it to show in her eyes.

Moving so she stood in front of Lilli, she initiated a slow and loving kiss, her fingers buried in thick auburn hair. Lilli returned the kiss—it lasted several minutes. There was something different in that kiss from any other they'd shared, including while making love. It was full of promise and meaning that touched Burton deeply. Finally, when the kiss ended naturally, Burton smiled.

Lilli's smile was, yet again, big and bright. "Then mission accomplished."

Burton returned the smile and moved back around to where she'd been, continuing with Lilli's shoulder wrapping.

"Where did you go after you left the hospital?" Lilli asked.

"Well," Burton said, face twisting slightly in

exertion as she tugged the ACE bandage as tightly as she dared, "I bounced around for a bit, leaving Denver and landing at my cousin's house in Pueblo, then eventually made my way to where I live now, which is in Westcliffe." She couldn't help the smile that spread across her lips at the thought of her house and her babies, which she missed desperately. "I have a house there that I'm fixing up."

"You live there alone?" Lilli asked.

Burton nearly laughed out loud at the obvious fishing expedition in Lilli's voice. "Well," she said, teasing in her own voice, "I actually live there with another woman. And a man." She met Lilli's gaze. "My cat, Cricket and my dog, Ajax."

They met gazes, Lilli giving her a shy, rueful smile. "Oh."

Chapter Twenty-seven

International Waters – USS Brightman

"So, Commander Tennison, the Hercules has been dispatched with personnel and supplies and should arrive within the next two hours," the carrier's XO explained. "The chopper with Blinde and the king should arrive somewhere in that time frame as well."

Sydney Tennison nodded, her gaze out over the ocean. "Okay. Sounds good. Thanks, John. Keep me posted."

"Ma'am."

Left alone, the commanding officer of the aircraft carrier stared out over the sea, hands on her hips. She shook her head with a small smile on her face. She definitely hadn't seen any sort of rescue mission in her future.

~ ~ ~ ~

Burton awoke, surprised that she'd fallen asleep. She was lying on the cot on her side, squeezed between the wall and Lilli, who was pressed against her, also lying on her side, her back to Burton's front. Her ankle was killing her, but she couldn't bring herself to wake Lilli, who seemed to be sleeping peacefully.

Pushing up on her elbow, she examined Lilli's profile, so beautiful, so at peace. She brought a hand up and gently brushed soft strands of hair back from her face, tucking them behind her ear. She was surprised they'd both fallen asleep despite their exhaustion level. The cot was anything but comfortable for one, let alone two. But, after talking for an hour about Burton's house and all the things she intended to do to it over time in renovations, Burton had drifted away. Obviously, so had Lilli.

As she studied Lilli's angelic features, she once again had that feeling from earlier. Something about this precious woman, this beautiful creature made her heart expand and beat that much faster. She felt protective of her, yet so at peace around her. It felt so right to touch her and to be touched *by* her, something she didn't much allow in her life. She didn't want to leave the island and never see her again. Actually, the truth of the matter was, she couldn't even fathom the thought of that.

She used her fingertips to caress the unbelievably soft skin of Lilli's cheek before her fingers traveled down to brush against her lips, slightly parted with her deep, even breaths, which hitched slightly at the touch. Lilli began to stir. Burton smiled at the little noises she was making as she rose into wakefulness, finding it absolutely adorable.

Her attention was taken when the door to the small room opened, Grigoriy standing on the other side. Burton's hand flew back to her own side, immediately feeling guilty as she looked away, missing the grin on his face.

"It's nice to see you, Burton," he said, her gaze returning to him. "You may want to wake up my daughter. I think you both need to see this." With that, he ducked out, closing the door softly behind him.

Burton pushed the urge away to jump out of the

bed and away from Lilli, so she wouldn't totally wake to find them spooned on the cot, and stayed where she was. She took a deep breath and leaned down, murmuring in a shell-like ear. "Lilli."

"Mmm…"

Burton smiled. "Lilli," she said again, bringing her hand back up to caress her hair. "We have to wake up."

"Mmmhmm. Okay," she murmured, snuggling in a bit closer back into Burton, who was absolutely charmed.

"Lilli," she said for a third time, this time using a fingertip to tickle her ear. A shiver passed through Lilli, making Burton chuckle. "Wake up. We have to get up, now."

"Don't wanna."

"I know. I don't wanna, either, but we have to."

"Says who?" Lilli sighed, beginning to stretch, but wincing and grabbing her bad shoulder. "That was a mistake."

"Your father. Come on." Burton left a kiss on Lilli's cheek and waited for her to get off the cot—she couldn't move until Lilli did.

Lilli slowly rolled off the cot, holding her arm, her face pale. She leaned back against the counter with her eyes closed.

"Are you okay?" Burton asked softly, slowly getting off the cot in her own pain. She limped her way over to her, her fingers brushing auburn hair out of Lilli's face. "We've got to get you proper medical care, sweetheart," she said.

Lilli smiled. "Ironic, considering I'm a doctor."

"I know, but there's only so much you can do for yourself, especially with limited supplies," Burton said, indicating the room around them. "And, with only me as your nurse." She took Lilli in a delicate hug, not wanting to cause her any additional pain. "Come on," she whispered into her hair. "Let's go see what your dad wants to show us."

※ ※ ※ ※

The basement of the distillery was empty and quiet, and as the two made their rickety way up top in the elevator, the noise level grew exponentially. They exchanged a look of confusion as the elevator jostled to a stop. Burton opened the gate and the two headed toward the noise.

There were sounds of many, many people, jubilance, joyful tears, laughter, loud talking, and singing. They hurried toward the warehouse part of the distillery where the huge bay doors were located. Once the door was pushed open, Burton and Lilli stopped, eyes wide as they took it all in.

"Oh my God," Lilli whispered, her gaze scanning the room. "Alyona!" she cried, taking off toward a middle-aged woman whose long hair was pulled back into a bun. Her skin was pale, her frame unbelievably thin.

Burton's gaze was torn from the happy reunion by the hundreds of people who spilled from the large empty room outside. She saw children crying as they clung to crying adults, she saw two women who appeared to be consoling each other as they seemed to be in great pain. She was back in the world of not understanding a word anyone was saying, but looking through the eyes of a journalist, of a storyteller, no words were needed.

"They were all trapped inside the school."

Burton looked to see Grigoriy suddenly standing next to her. His hands were tucked in his pants pockets and he seemed like a proud father as he looked over the masses. He glanced at her and she met his gaze.

"There's a lot to learn, yet. We still don't know how they did it or why. But, it's safe to say, everyone had taken them all for dead. Sadly," he said with a heavy sigh, "not everyone who was taken was found. We don't know why or where they went."

"Were they sold?" Burton asked quietly, feeling emotional with Grigoriy's information and her own deep fears about the fate of some.

He shook his head. "I don't know. I imagine over the next several months we'll be finding out more than we care to know." He looked at her again, a sad smile on his lips. "The nightmare they've been through. Far worse than any of us who remained on the outside."

"There are so many," Burton said, not entirely sure how to feel. She knew that she and Lilli had a little something to do with all of it, and it felt amazing. Long ago this had stopped being about a story. Those around her rejoicing in their freedom and rejoining their loved ones was unlike any story, any job, and anything she'd ever felt before.

Something caught her attention, and to her surprise, King Arvid was making his way into the room. She was stunned to see his head and beard had been shaven, but he had a bit more color even as he was still dangerously thin, just like many of those celebrating.

She felt a hand on her arm and turned to see Grigoriy, who was gently pushing her back toward the door.

"Best to get out of the way," he suggested.

As people realized who he was, a silence spread throughout the crowd, people stepping back to allow him a path. Some bowed, others stood in defiance. Burton was concerned when she saw the angry looks many of the people began to shoot his way upon recognition. She felt protective and was about to head into the crowd in case he needed her, but again, Lilli's father stopped her, his hand gently grasping her arm.

"Wait," he said.

A man who looked to be in his forties stormed over to Arvid, his face red and rage in his eyes. He began to yell at the king, followed by a few other men.

"*Izmennik!*" The first man began to push the king, who staggered backward. "Izmennik!"

The crowd began to grow excited, some trying to push the men away, some joining in, yelling in the face of the terrified-looking man, one woman delivering a vicious slap that left a cut on his pale cheek.

Burton watched in horror. She again tried to run toward the fray but was stopped. She looked back at Grigoriy, angry.

"No," he hissed. "No."

Suddenly, the chaos was instantly quieted by the sound of a gunshot. Burton was terrified that Arvid had been shot, but instead saw Ivan standing at the edge of the crowd, his arm raised and a pistol pointed at the ceiling.

"*Net!*" he yelled over the sudden silence. He glared at everyone, lowering the gun to point at the crowd.

Burton shrugged Grigoriy's hand away as she ran over to Ivan. It looked as though he were about to collapse, the bandage wrapped around his leg growing a crimson patch. He looked at her with wide, frightened eyes. She smiled at him.

"Burdon," he said, a small smile curving his own lips.

She reached for the gun, which after a moment, he handed over. "Thank you, Ivan." She helped lower him so he was seated on the cement floor, his face pale. "It's okay. You did good."

She saw, to her relief, that Arvid was being led from the crowd by Lilli and the woman she'd been so happy to see. For just a moment their gazes locked until Lilli looked away, helping the monarch to reach her father. Burton wished she knew what Lilli was saying as he turned on the quieting crowd. The room was mostly silent other than for the cries of a few frightened children.

Lilli's voice was loud and firm as she spoke and gestured to Arvid. Burton assumed she was explaining to them all what had happened to their leader, nothing like what they'd been taught to believe over far too many years.

She felt such pride, watching as the people not only calmed down but looked sheepish, the men who had begun the trouble looking away, one leaving the building. As everyone seemed to absorb what the situation was, slowly, a few at a time, the crowd began to make their way over to where Grigoriy had pushed the king behind him to shield him. Not long after, a whole new round of joyous cries rent the air, bringing tears to Burton's eyes.

She felt a hand on her shoulder and looked up from where she squatted next to Ivan. Lilli smiled down at her. She got slowly to her feet, wincing at the scream of her ankle. She was about to speak but stopped when a new sound caught her attention. From her last night with Bishop, she recognized it as the rotors of a helicopter.

"You ready to get out of here?" Lilli asked.

Burton let out a heavy sigh with a nod. "Yes." She smiled, though it was sad. She couldn't help but feel like a cheater, like she was giving up on the people just found, by leaving.

"Hey," Lilli said softly, a hand coming up to rest

against Burton's jaw. "It's okay. It's really okay."

They both turned to see Grigoriy and Arvid step up to them, the crowd back to mingling and reuniting with each other. "Do you both have everything? The pilot is ready to leave."

Burton looked down at herself and raised her hands before slapping them back to her thighs. "Yep."

Lilli stepped up to her father and took him in a tight hug. She murmured to him in their language; he nodded at whatever she said and held her just as tight. They shared a quick peck on the lips.

"Thank you," Grigoriy said to Burton, coming toward her and taking her into a hug. "Without you, none of this would have happened."

Burton smiled into the hug. She surprised herself by leaving a kiss on his grizzled cheek, which made his eyes shine. She handed him the pistol she'd taken from Ivan moments before. He took it and tucked it into the waistline of his pants.

The two men turned to each other, exchanging a quick hug and a handshake.

"Is he coming with us?" Burton asked.

"Yes," Lilli said, taking Arvid's arm. "He needs proper care, far more than I can give him here, and we want to make sure he's safe."

Burton nodded, moving around to his other side. With all their injuries, walking was slow going, but the crowd once again quieted down and parted for them. Burton received many pats on the back and a few kisses of gratitude. She looked at every face she passed, just in case she never saw the people of this wonderful place again. They were young, they were old, and everything in between. They were underfed, malnourished, and looked sickly, but the one thing she saw in the eyes of each and every one was something she hadn't seen since she'd arrived: hope.

Touched by this, and the fact that they believed she had anything to do with it—even if she had, it was hard to process and absorb—made her feel strong and weak at the same time. Strong to know she'd taken the conscious step to stay behind, but weak because she felt like she was about to fall apart at any moment.

They finally made their way through the crowd and out of the warehouse, applause and cheers behind them. It brought back that moment in the newsroom for her when she'd returned to get her things after the explosion that had killed Roger. Admittedly, this time around it was profound in a way she knew would take a long time to fully wrap her mind around.

Outside, the morning was chilly but the sun was out and the sky was bright blue. It was a beautiful day and it gave Burton some of that hope that she saw so much of moments before.

Sitting in the middle of the empty parking lot was the same blue helicopter that had been on the rooftop of the hotel just days before. The rotors were still spinning, the pilot in his seat with headset in place. He watched as the trio neared the helicopter, followed by Grigoriy and some of the people.

Together, Burton and Lilli helped Arvid climb into the chopper, his weakened state making it difficult for him. Finally, they got him seated and belted safely in. Burton was the one in after him, so she took the seat next to him, leaving Lilli to climb in and sit across from them.

From where she was belted in, she reached over to extend a hand to help Lilli climb in when out of the corner of her eye, she saw Grigoriy thrown to the ground. Her eyes grew in horror when she saw Alexey standing behind him. He was pale, his shirt half-covered in blood, and his eyes were terrifying. He was extremely unsteady on his feet, and she couldn't breathe as she saw him raise her own Glock and take a shot. Fire ripped through her arm as she watched Lilli yanked out of the helicopter by the back of her shirt and thrown to the ground.

"Lilli!" Burton screamed, her voice all but swallowed by the sound of the rotors.

Alexey aimed his gun again. From where she lay on the ground, Lilli kicked one of his legs out from under him, knocking him to his knee. The shot went wide and caught the side of the helicopter.

"Go!" Lilli yelled, the pilot meeting her gaze as he looked back over his shoulder through the open door. "Go!" she yelled again, waving her hand for emphasis.

Burton watched and was horrified as the helicopter lifted off the ground.

"No!" she screamed, ignoring the intense ache and pain in her bleeding arm as she tried desperately to unbuckle her seatbelt.

"No, Burton!" Arvid growled, holding her trembling hands still. "No. You'll get yourself killed. There's nothing we can do."

As the helicopter lifted higher and higher, time stood still as Alexey turned and got to his incredibly unsteady feet, one hand held over his side wound. He aimed the Glock at Lilli. In that second, she tilted her head up at Burton, their gazes locked. Tears streamed so hard down Burton's face, her vision was beginning to swim. She blinked furiously, not wanting to lose their connection. So much passed between them in that moment, so much she wished she'd had the courage to say. She saw it plainly written in Lilli's beautiful green eyes.

I love you.

"No!" Burton screamed again as Lilli's head jerked and her eyes closed.

She was sobbing as she continued to watch. She could hear nothing, but saw Grigoriy aim the very gun she'd handed him not ten minutes before at his own son and pull the trigger. Alexey fell to his knees then flat onto his face

The helicopter was now at an altitude too high for her to see anything but ants on the ground and toy cars and buildings.

Burton felt an arm reach around her shoulders and her head gently placed against a thin shoulder in comfort. She continued to sob, the pain in her arm throbbing with every beat of her heart.

"We've got to put pressure on that wound," the pilot called back to them. "Here." He tossed back a towel from the cockpit.

Arvid grabbed it and wrapped it around the bullet wound as tightly as he could, which made it hurt even more. Burton didn't care. Let it bleed…

Chapter Twenty-eight

Denver International Airport – Two Weeks Later

Right arm lightly wrapped after surgery eight days before at a hospital in Germany for her gunshot wound, Burton made her way from the train that had taken her from the terminal to the baggage claim. She was dressed in a fresh pair of jeans and a sweater, all brought to her while she was in the hospital by military personnel. Her own clothing had been stained with blood, hers and Alexey's.

She felt essentially like a zombie as she made her way with the herd of people up the escalator from the train to the floor above where she'd be met by Everett, she was told. She'd all but shut down emotionally.

After two days on the aircraft carrier, she'd been flown in what they'd called a "prop job" to Germany to Landstuhl Regional Medical Center where she was debriefed about the bad actors in the Chilvokian coup, her wounds treated, and was allowed to rest. From there, she'd been sent back to the States and finally to Denver. It had been a whirlwind trip, and she was definitely ready for the merry-go-round to stop so she could get off.

Reaching the top of the escalator, she, like those fellow travelers around her, was surprised to find a wall of media and press. People with cameras hitched upon their shoulders, others holding microphones with banners announcing CNBC, MSNBC, NBC, CBS, ABC,

CNN, and many local stations.

Burton looked behind and around her for a celebrity or sports figure when the crush of press was suddenly on her, her name shouted at her as well as questions. Utterly confused, she brought her hand up, trying to block the blinding light from the cameras, looking desperately for a friendly face.

"Get out of the way! Move, asshole!"

Burton was stunned at the voice and then stunned again when she saw the person attached to it push through the crowd. "Simone," she breathed.

Simone, looking as elegant and beautiful as ever, smiled at her. "Welcome home."

For the first time in days, Burton felt like she was able to let go. She collapsed into her old friend's arms and allowed her emotions to rise to the surface. She held on to Simone, clutching her satin blouse in her fists as she cried. She could hear the soothing words that were murmured in her ear, could smell the soothing scent of her friend's perfume, and could hear an endless symphony of camera clicks from the sea of press that surrounded them.

After several moments, Burton calmed down and pulled out of the hug, looking around at all the eyes—human and camera—that were on them. "Where's Everett?" she asked.

"Fuck him, I wasn't about to let him come get you after everything you've been through," Simone said, grabbing Burton's hand on the uninjured side and tugging to lead them through the throngs of media and fellow travelers.

They were followed to the automatic doors that let them out into the cool afternoon, though there was a small group of brand new reporters in the parking lot to meet them.

"No comment!" Simone said, brushing them aside, her stride insistent and unstoppable until they reached her Stingray.

Once safely inside, Burton glanced at Simone, who was already eyeing her with concern.

"Are you okay?" she asked.

"Where the hell did they come from?" Burton asked, indicating the few that had followed them and continued to take pictures. "I'm not Lindsey Lohan, for Christ's sake!"

Simone reached over and took Burton's hand in her own and bestowed a kind smile. "You've been gone. You have no idea how much this story has spread across the world,"

Burton stared at her, stunned. "How?"

"Bishop Fromminger for one," Simone said, starting the ignition of the small car. "Katherine Dennison, for two," she added, glancing over her shoulder as she backed out of the space. She met Burton's shocked gaze. "Yes, it's a good story, but believe it or not, the world has been worried as hell about you."

"What?"

"You've topped the news for weeks, Burt," Simone said,

Burton looked out the window, watching the familiar scenery of Denver pass by as they drove. She was lost in her own thoughts and mind, not even thinking about where they were going. Her physical wounds had all healed, save for her arm, which no longer hurt. She'd been instructed to see a doctor in a week to get her stitches looked at and removed in another two weeks beyond that if everything looked okay. Inside, however, that was a whole different story.

"I thought Everett was supposed to come today," she said at length, her voice quiet and flat.

Simone peeked at her before returning her focus to the road. "No," she said, shaking her head. "There was no way I wanted his to be the first friendly face you saw. Not today."

Burton studied Simone's profile for a long moment. A slow and very small smile spread across her lips. "Thank you for that."

Simone met her gaze and her smile. "What are friends for?"

☙☙☙☙

Forty minutes later, Simone pulled the little sports car into a well-established neighborhood of well-kept homes with well-kept yards in Castle Rock, thirty-five minutes outside of downtown Denver.

Burton looked around, surprised, really. Simone had always been into the hip parts of downtown Denver living, surrounded by the noise, people, and shops. She never pictured her in the suburbs.

Simone pulled into a cul-de-sac then into the driveway of one of the four houses. It was a two-story with rock face and a portico over the dark red-painted front door. She reached up to push a button on the remote clipped to the sun visor. A moment later, the garage door gracefully slid open revealing a white Explorer parked on one side.

Simone pulled slowly in to park next to it. She stopped the car and cut the engine before looking at Burton. "I want you to stay the night with us, Burt," she said softly and shrugged. "I don't feel you should be alone tonight." The softest, sweetest smile crossed her lips. "And, I really want you to meet Hannah."

Burton recognized the feelings behind that kind of smile; she recognized the joy in Simone's eyes. She looked down at her hands resting in her lap then nodded, returning her gaze to her old friend. "I'd love to."

The house was quiet and very well-kept. It had modern furnishings and features, including the long, narrow gas fireplace that burned cheerily in the wall beneath the mounted flat-screen TV.

"Hey, baby," Simone called out as they entered the house through the washroom, which took them to a gourmet kitchen. Simone removed her jacket and tossed it and her purse across the granite peninsula.

"Hiya, gorgeous." Out of the TV and fire-lit living room walked the beautiful Asian woman Burton recognized from the picture she'd seen in Simone's work area at the station. She was dressed casually in sweatpants and an oversized T-shirt on her petite frame, her long black hair pulled back in a ponytail. Even without any makeup on, she was quite stunning. The two shared a quick kiss and the woman looked at Burton with a welcoming smile. "It's really nice to meet you, Burton. Like the world, I've heard so much about you lately."

Burton gave her a small smile in return. She felt a bit awkward and out of place. "It's nice to meet you, too, Hannah." She glanced at her friend, who was absolutely beaming as she stood next to her wife, her hand resting on Hannah's lower hip. "I never knew anyone could tame this tiger," she added, attempting to add some levity to the situation.

"And nobody ever will," Simone laughed. She kissed Hannah again. "I'm going to get her settled upstairs, baby." She grabbed Burton's hand and tugged. "Come on."

Burton was led from the open kitchen-living room configuration up the stairs to the second floor where there were four bedrooms and an open loft space. She had to smile as, in the loft, she saw bookshelves lining the wall, but rather than books, there was every type and color of makeup and beautification product anyone could think of. Paul Mitchell would be in heaven, she thought to herself.

"What do you think of our house?" Simone asked, leading Burton to the bedroom halfway down the hall.

"This is so nice, Simone," Burton said, meaning it. "Very beautiful." She smiled at her friend, one of the more genuine smiles she'd given in weeks. "I'm so happy for you. Hannah seems wonderful, too."

"She's wonderful, Burt," Simone said, flipping on the light as they entered the room. It was a guest room with a queen-sized bed covered in a homey quilt. The motif was rustic and comfortable, warm and welcoming. "This room has its own bathroom, so anything you need should be in there," she said, walking to the opened doorway of the bathroom and flicking on the light. "Hannah put clean sheets on the bed today and there's clean towels, shampoo, soap, even a new toothbrush."

Burton felt overwhelmed as she stood at the center of the room and hugged herself, not sure where to look first or what to think or feel. She looked down at the floor, hard wood with a large throw rug covering a good portion of the room.

"Thank you, Simone," she said quietly. "After everything, you didn't have to do any of this."

"Hey," the makeup artist said softly, walking over to Burton and gently rubbing her upper arms. "The past is the past. At the end of the day, you're my friend and I love you. I can't quite wrap my mind around what you've been through, but it's profound and it's taken a heavy toll on you." She looked Burton over. "I've never seen you so thin." She looked into her eyes. "I hardly recognized you at the airport."

Burton gave her a rueful smile. "To be honest, I hardly recognize myself. I just feel tired."

Simone wrapped her in a warm hug, holding for a long moment before she let her go with a kiss to her forehead. "You get some rest, okay? We'll talk in the morning."

Burton nodded and watched as Simone left the room, closing the door softly behind her. With a heavy sigh, she looked around the lovely room, feeling warm and safe yet deeply empty.

Walking over to the bed, she sat down, hands falling limply in her lap. Her frame seemed to give out on her as she slowly crumpled sideways, bringing her legs up to curl into as tight a ball as she could. The tears came quietly, simply rolling down her cheek and to the quilt beneath her.

≈≈≈≈

Simone was quiet for so long, Burton wasn't entirely sure her friend had heard everything she'd just said over the past forty minutes. As they drove from Simone's house to Burton's, she eyed Simone in the small confines of the Stingray. She was surprised when she saw the silent tears that flowed down Simone's cheeks.

Simone sniffled then said softly, "Burton, would you reach inside the glove compartment and grab me a tissue, please?"

Burton did as she was asked, tugging a tissue free from the small packet of Kleenex. She handed it to Simone and put the packet back, the glove box closing with a click. She remained silent as Simone wiped her eyes and face then blew her nose.

"I'm sorry," Simone finally said, balling the tissue

up and dropping it in her lap. "I had no idea you'd gone through that." Her eyes glistened. "I'm so sorry. I think we all had this romanticized vision of what you were doing, you know? Wolf Blitzer during Desert Storm, safe, watching from a distance." She shook her head as she focused on the road before them. "I had no idea." She reached over and took Burton's hand in her own, lightly squeezing her fingers. "I'm here for you, Burton. We all are."

※ ※ ※ ※

Two hours of light discussion and catching up later, Simone pulled onto the dirt road that would lead to Burton's house. Lee Ann told her she'd meet them there with her babies. Burton couldn't wait to see them, hold them, and be surrounded by their noises, smells, and love. She'd been gone nearly a month, due to her time in Germany, yet it may as well have been a year.

"This one?" Simone asked, pointing to the house at the end of the lane.

"Yes," Burton muttered absently as she sat slightly forward in her seat. There were cars lining her driveway and the dirt road in front of her house. "What the hell?" She looked at Simone when she heard a soft little chuckle come from her. "What's going on?"

Simone met her gaze for a moment before turning the Stingray into her driveway behind a pickup truck. "I told you we were all here for you."

Burton climbed out of the low-slung car and walked with Simone to her own front door. Simone reached ahead of her and turned the doorknob, pushing the door open to reveal a crush of people inside who began to cheer as soon as Burton stepped her shocked self inside. She first saw Lee Ann and her husband, then Theresa and two of her and Roger's children. Alongside them stood Everett and several of Burton's former KNWZ colleagues. Joining the crowd was her boss from the library and many of the patrons she'd helped so many times. She was stunned to see her cousin Louis walk up to her with a wide smile and Colorado's own Governor, John Hickenlooper waiting to shake her hand.

"Welcome home, baby girl," Lee Ann said softly, a hand on Burton's shoulder.

Chapter Twenty-nine

Lounging on her couch with Ajax curled up at her feet and Cricket on the back of the couch—both stuck to her like glue all day—Burton sipped the wine Lee Ann had brought with her during the day's welcome home celebration.

After a couple hours of mingling, catching up, laughing, and—most importantly—finding great distraction, everyone had gone except for Lee Ann. Left alone, they'd opened up the Riesling she'd brought and sat down to relax. A very cool evening had settled over them, and Burton started a fire in the fireplace.

"You should be so proud of yourself, kid," Lee Ann said from where she sat in the armchair perpendicular to Burton on the couch. "I absolutely cannot believe that you left here Lulu Librarian and ended up Rambo."

Burton gave her a small smile, the wine helping to warm and calm her. She took a sip before responding. "I don't intend to tie a headband on anytime soon." She reached up and ran her hand down Cricket's soft fur. "I missed these guys so much. Everything with them is so simple. It's about love, nothing else, you know?"

"I do." Lee Ann raised her glass. "To the furry people."

Burton smiled and raised her own glass. "Hear, hear." She grew silent as she stared into the flames. She hadn't told anyone about Lilli, not even Simone. She just couldn't bring herself to share such a special and lovely person with anyone. Someday, she hoped she'd be able to, but not yet. Right now, she needed to be selfish with the memory of Lilli and what they'd shared on so many levels.

"There's such a difference in you, Burton," Lee Ann said softly, all teasing out of her voice. "So much sadness in your eyes."

Burton took a deep breath and ran her hand through her hair as she stared into the flames. "Yeah," she said. "I know."

Lee Ann was quiet for a moment then got to her feet to walk over to the coffee table where the bottle of wine sat. She poured herself another glass and topped off Burton's. "Remember that e-mail you sent me? About that woman, Alison Lange?"

Burton watched her as she put the bottle back down in the bucket of ice to keep it chilled and sat back down, bare feet tucked beneath her. She felt emotion trying to tug at her sleeve again but swallowed it back.

"Yeah." She took a sip from her refreshed drink. "What did you find?"

"She was murdered."

Burton stared hard at her, unable to blink. "What?"

"She was murdered," Lee Ann said again. "I have the file for you, but a guy by the name of Jasper Carvel was an opportunistic piece of shit and saw his opportunity. He forced her to drive him all the way to Fort Collins. An hour that bastard had a gun pointed at her." She met Burton's shocked gaze. "Two days later, the burned-out car and body were found close to the Wyoming border."

Burton looked away, caught somewhere between laughter and tears. "She didn't leave them," she whispered. She shook her head and met Lee Ann's confused gaze. "She didn't leave them, didn't abandon them." She brought a hand up and covered her mouth as her mind spun with the new information. "So much damage done," she whispered. "Such a senseless act." She looked at Lee Ann again. "Do you know where she's buried?"

"I do, but what's all this about? Who is this chick?"

Burton sipped her wine as she once again stared into the flames. "It's closure," she said softly.

"Well," Lee Ann said at length, "I have a surprise for you." She set her wineglass down on the coffee table and pushed up from the chair. "I'll be right back."

Left alone, Burton let out a heavy sigh and took a drink of her wine. She was definitely feeling the effects, and it felt good to a degree. It felt good to be home, surrounded by all of her personal things, and especially, her animals. Their warmth, love, and enthusiasm in seeing her after such a long time helped to center her a bit.

Lee Ann walked back into the room with a large, yet thin wrapped box and a much smaller rectangular wrapped box on top of it. She set them on the coffee table. She grinned at Burton as she reclaimed her wine and her seat. "A few of us went in together."

"What did you do?" Burton asked suspiciously, sitting up with feet on the floor and wineglass on the coffee table next to the festively wrapped boxes.

The small box proved to be a brand new phone. Her smile was huge as she took the gadget out of its wrappings. Since she'd lost her phone in the stairwell after Alexey abducted her, she hadn't had one in all the time since. Very kind people had let her use theirs or the phones on the base she had stayed at in Germany to speak to those back home.

"Same phone number and everything, of course," Lee Ann said, grinning from ear to ear as she watched. "The guy at the store was able to get all your information, pictures, and everything switched to this phone because of the cloud."

"Thank you so much," Burton whispered, in awe. "And a red case, too."

"Yeah, we all know how obsessed you are with the damn color."

Burton smiled as she gazed at her friend, truly touched and happy. "Thank you."

"You got it. The phone is from me and Phil. But this"—she patted the larger box—"is from Everett and Simone and a couple others at KNWZ."

Burton set the phone and its wrappings aside and tore into the colorful paper that covered the second box. When she saw the picture on the box, her eyes grew wide. "A laptop?" she asked, stunned as she met Lee Ann's gaze.

"You're pretty damn loved, my friend," Lee Ann said as she sat back in her chair and sipped from her glass. She had a smile on her face that looked smug and satisfied.

"I can't believe this." She tore the remaining paper away until the box was fully revealed. After she'd been taken, she'd never seen any of her belongings again and had no idea what had become of her computer. Likely it had been destroyed, but whatever happened, she'd never see it again, no doubt. "This is so kind of all of you. Truly, I'm deeply touched."

Burton pushed up from the couch and walked over to Lee Ann, who also stood. They shared a tight embrace, Burton smiling up at her.

⁂

Burton had been home for nearly a week, and it had been five days she'd needed. Her former therapist who she'd been seeing for her PTSD after the car explosion had sent her to see Dr. Tiffani Brackrog, or "Dr. Tiffani" as she'd asked Burton to call her. She specialized in grief counseling and grief management. She'd seen her three times already, and she'd been very helpful, working with Burton on something she called Mindfulness and the three by three by three, both of which were coping techniques.

Today was the first Monday since she'd returned home and her first day back to work at the library. She and her boss, Sally Estrada had a wonderful conversation at her welcome home party, and whereas Sally had once been essentially cool to her presence, she seemed to have warmed up with a greater understanding of who Burton was.

Burton always felt like Sally thought she was a joke, a journalist who ended up working as a librarian. She wasn't sure if Sally saw her as a sellout or felt she had no business working in the library system. Either way, Burton did feel they'd come to a new understanding and mutual respect.

She parked her Jeep, which Lee Ann had driven down to her house, in her usual spot and cut the engine. She sat there behind the wheel for a long moment staring at the building through the windshield. She was filled with a mixture of feelings. She was looking forward to the distraction as well as working with her coworkers and the patrons again. She enjoyed her job.

Gathering her purse and keys, she opened the Jeep's door and climbed out. It was a cold late-September day, and she felt warm and comfortable in a long skirt with brown leather knee boots beneath it and a cream-colored sweater. Her hair was up and her makeup was light. She admitted, she looked every bit the librarian, but she just wanted to blend in, become absorbed back into her life.

She entered the building, smiling at the woman who sat at the front to help direct patrons. "Good morning, Faye," she said, heading to the back where the employee break room was and where she could leave her peacoat and purse, tucking her phone in the pocket of her long, flowing skirt.

She smiled and waved to a few coworkers she passed as she headed to her desk. She was only supposed to be gone for a week and ended up being gone for a month, so Sally had no choice but to bring someone in from another library temporarily. That certainly helped with her workload, but she knew she'd still have a lot to catch up on.

Once she arrived at her desk and reached around the monitor to turn it on, she had to smile as Helen Hollis walked up to her, a welcoming smile on her lips.

"It's so good to have you back! Oh my goodness," Mrs. Hollis gushed. "I've been so worried about you!" She reached across the desk and took both of Burton's hands in her own. "Here I thought my little friend had my back to get me new Nora books." She smiled and shook her head. "All the while, she's Jane Pauley!"

Burton burst into laughter. "I don't know about that. I always wanted to be Barbara Walters, though," she said with a wink.

Mrs. Hollis laughed too, squeezing Burton's hands before letting them go. "Well, whoever you are, I'm glad you're back. I need my Nora!"

As the day went on, Burton enjoyed herself and though, yes there was a lot of work to catch up on, it did wonders to keep her mind busy and emotions on track. She was able to fully focus on what she was doing and actually go an hour or two without thinking.

She hoped that such a good day would lead to

some actual sleep that night. She wasn't convinced but was hopeful.

※※※※

Burton pushed her cart through the grocery store, her boots squeaking on the floor from the wet trail left by customers tracking in snow from the parking lot. Halloween was in two weeks, and the store was decorated festively for the holiday along with offers of endless bags of candy and treats for trick-or-treaters. Burton fingered a bag of bite-sized Hershey bars when her phone rang.

Reaching into her purse, which sat in the front of the cart, she saw that it was Everett. "Good afternoon," she said.

"Hey there. Great job on the statement you sent us last week. Not sure if you saw, but it's been passed around the networks, including CNN and MSNBC."

"That's what I heard," she said, eyeing a box of brightly colored foil-wrapped Cadbury Scream Eggs and deciding on the spot she'd have to check those out. "It was the best way for me to go. I just don't have it in me to do interviews, yet." She let out a heavy sigh. "If at all."

"I know, Burt. You did good. Listen, speaking of, I got an interesting phone call today. I didn't want to just give out your phone number, so figured I'd run it by you, first."

"Okay." Burton leaned against the shelving unit behind her, crossing her free arm over her chest. "What's up?"

"The White House is bringing King Arvid of Chilvokia in to meet with Obama."

Burton's heart began to beat a little bit faster at the mention of the monarch's name. "Oh. Okay."

"They want you there, Burt. I guess the king has something for you."

"Oh," she murmured, suddenly feeling a bit faint. "Okay."

"Listen, think about it, okay? I'll text you the number they gave me for you to call and discuss details. I think this would be really good for you, Burton. Maybe offer a bit of closure. If nothing else, you certainly deserve the recognition."

She let out a shaky breath, suddenly feeling emotion prick the backs of her eyes. "Okay. Send me the number."

An hour later Burton pulled into her driveway, taking it slow so as not to skid on the ice at the turn from the road. She'd intended to put some salt on that spot but had forgotten. She parked in front of the garage beside and slightly behind the house as she always did.

Cutting the engine, Sarah Brightman's sultry "Anytime, Anywhere" cut off midsong. She grabbed her purse and slung it across her chest so it wouldn't slide off her shoulder as she carried in grocery bags.

Ever since her brief phone call with Everett in the store, her mind had been in a terrible state, at war with the need to shut down and the desire to see Arvid again, such a good man, and hopefully find some peace finally in everything that happened.

Her emotions were deeply unsteady as she carried in the four grocery bags. She took several deep breaths, trying to calm herself and push it all away. She didn't want to have to deal with it yet again. She felt that's all she'd been doing in the past month: dealing.

"Watch out, babies," she said, pushing in between an excited Ajax and curious Cricket as she walked over to the kitchen counter and set her bags down. She had one more trip to make to grab the final bag and the twelve-pack of diet Dr. Pepper from the back of the Jeep.

As she went back outside, she let the cold air rush over her, enjoying the invigorating nature of it. She closed her eyes and inhaled the clean, fresh mountain air. It helped and she felt better than she had mere moments before. She found the simple life she'd created for herself calming and peaceful. She craved that peace again. Dr. Tiffani said it would come in time, but the smallest—or biggest, like today—thing could shake her to the core. She hadn't felt like herself since the day before she'd left for her flight to meet Bishop in London.

Grabbing the final groceries, Burton headed back inside. She flicked on the small flat-screen TV mounted over the fridge in the kitchen then headed to the living room where she got a fire started before giving her babies some love. After that, she headed back to the kitchen to put groceries away.

"Not," she muttered, noting a talk show on the screen that she had no desire to watch.

She grabbed the remote for the TV and changed the channel. The scene that immediately popped on the screen was a car chase, though it wasn't two cars: it was a car and a motorcycle.

As Burton watched, everything slowed down, her brain seeming to have a full minute to process everything it was seeing. She tore the messenger bag off her shoulder and reached inside it, feeling the cold steel of the gun on her fingers.

Ivan had nearly reached the child as the motorcycle bore down on him, the driver seeming intent on running him or the child over.

With an inhuman roar, Burton stood and aimed the 9mm, clicking off the safety with her thumb as she fired three rounds, hitting the driver in the chest. He reacted to each one, the bike giving in to gravity and skidding as the back wheel continued to turn. The man with the AK-47 fell to the ground and rolled, his gun flying in the opposite direction.

"Die, you fucker!" Burton screamed, firing the remainder of her clip into the gunman, his body jumping with every shot that hit its mark.

Burton gasped, stumbling backward to crash into the stove, her heart racing, chest heaving as her breathing came in quick, unstoppable breaths. The tears were immediate and so fierce she could hardly breathe. She collapsed to the floor, her emotions completely out of control. Her heart began to race so quickly, she honestly worried she was about to have a heart attack.

Ajax walked up to her sniffing at her hair and nudging her as he whined. He lay down next to her, chin resting on his paws.

Burton was only vaguely aware of her dog's presence as she continued to sob.

"Remember, Burton," Dr. Tiffani had told her during their last session. "Find an object. Focus on it. Three by three by three..."

Burton tried desperately to stop the tears that kept flowing. She crawled over to the cabinet and used the counter to help herself stand. Chest still heaving, she looked around, trying to find something, *anything* to focus on. She noted the coffee cup sitting upside down in the strainer that she'd washed that morning after her cup of coffee. Grabbing it, she placed it on the counter before her.

"It's white," she mumbled through her tears, observing the cup. "It has a red handle and in black letters, it says, 'got Xena?'" Her head fell as a new wave of panic and tears swept over her. "Damn it!" she yelled, slamming her fist on the counter, sending Ajax scampering out of the room. She forced her breathing to slow as much as she could, again focusing on the mug. She picked it up. "It's smooth, it's cool to the touch..." Another bout of fresh tears. "It's a cylinder." She closed her eyes as she held the mug against her chest, her breathing slowing as her emotions began to calm. The tears slowed from sobs to silent tears rolling down her cheeks to simply being caught in her eyelashes. "Okay," she whispered. "Okay, calm, calm. Okay..." She set the mug on the counter and ran her hand through her hair. "We can do this. We got this."

Letting out several more deep breaths until she felt calm and in control, Burton grabbed the remote and turned to the TV again, switching the channel back to the talk show.

Chapter Thirty

"I have to say," Lee Ann commented, looking briefly at Burton who sat in the passenger seat, "I didn't expect you to head to an airport so quickly after you came back."

Burton chuckled, meeting her gaze. "Hey, when the president and a king call, you kinda don't have a choice."

Lee Ann smiled. "Not a bad gig, either. First class all the way, huh?"

"That's what my boarding pass says," Burton said, patting her messenger bag, which held the printed-out pass. "You're sure you don't mind watching Ajax and Cricket? Again?"

"I don't mind." Lee Ann reached over and patted Burton's hand. "This is important stuff."

※※※※

"I'd like to extend my greatest gratitude and thanks to President Obama, the American people, and the leaders and people all around the world for the help of your time and resources in rebuilding our beautiful country. And I must say," King Arvid said, running his hands down the svelte figure he cut in a well-fitted suit, "I know I needed to lose a few pounds, but this was not the way to do it."

He paused as the gathered audience, press, and president laughed at his comment. He placed both hands on the podium, glancing to his right and holding the gaze of the young woman who sat there for a long moment.

"Today, I'm deeply pleased to acknowledge a very special young woman," he continued, again glancing at her. "She is one of the bravest souls I've ever known. To the people of America and the world, I'd like to introduce you to Burton Blinde. She is a young woman who came in search of a story that her journalistic nose led her to. What she found..." He paused for a long moment, looking away from all the eyes and cameras on him. After a moment, he cleared his throat and returned to the microphone on the podium. "What she found was far more than she should ever have had to bear. But, what she did was not merely 'bear' it, she jumped in and she helped to save a nation, save a people, and save a king."

Arvid turned to the woman sitting to his right again, this time extending a hand. She stood and walked toward him, dressed in green as applause throughout the room, including from the president sounded. The king embraced her tightly for a long moment, which she returned. Once he stepped back, he smiled at her before leaning down to place a kiss on either cheek.

"Today, I wish to bestow Burton with the medal of the Golden Shield," he said, bringing the velvet jewelry box up from the podium. "This is the highest medal I can offer from my kingdom. It's given for the highest valor and sacrifice of my people."

"We're watching right now as the monarch is placing the medal on the blue ribbon around Burton Blinde's neck," explained the reporter. "You can see tears in King Arvid's eyes as he's doing this. An extraordinary moment for an extraordinary young woman..."

The two figures stood watching the television, the taller with an arm around that of the shorter and smaller. A hand came up to ruffle the short locks of auburn, growing back after an emergency shave.

"*Idti k ney.*" The figure leaned over and placed a kiss on the other's head.

※ ※ ※ ※

They walked together in silence, Arvid with his hands tucked behind his back. The two were wrapped in jackets as they strolled around the Rose Garden, Secret Service standing discreetly by. Burton could still feel the heaviness of the medal around her neck, something she was deeply touched by and proud of. She absently reached up a gloved hand and touched the spot where it hung beneath her jacket.
"It's so good to see you, Burton," the king said, smiling down at her.
She returned the smile as she met his gaze. "You look really good, Your Highness," she said, feeling silly using such a title yet sensed it was the right thing to do.
He waved her off. "Arvid. With all we've been through together, you're the last person I want formalities with." He brought his hands out from behind his back and grabbed her hand, placing it at the bend of his arm as they continued to stroll. "If I had a daughter, Burton, I could only hope she'd be just like you." Again, he bestowed a smile down at her. "Your own father must be very proud."
She smiled and shook her head. "I don't have one. But, my friend's husband is."
Arvid chuckled, patting Burton's hand with his own. "I hope you'll come back and see us. I know many of the folks would love to see you again, to thank you." They strolled in silence for a moment before he added, "I think you'd be surprised to see all the progress that has been made. So much has been rebuilt. Grigoriy is back in the vodka business."

Burton smiled at that bit of news, but it didn't reach her eyes. She was glad he was doing well, but his loss was her loss, a loss she'd never get over.

※※※※

"That is absolutely gorgeous," Sally Estrada said tilting the velvet box this way and that. "I can't believe he awarded you such an honor." She smiled at her employee, softly closing the box containing the medal and handing it back to Burton. "Really a special moment to watch, I have to say." She gave her a shy smile. "We set up a TV here in the library and watched it with the patrons."

"Are you serious?" Burton asked, hugging the velvet box to her chest.

"You should have seen Helen Hollis. She was a mess." The women laughed as they stood in the employee break room. Sally sobered and gave her a genuine smile. "We're all very proud of you, Burton. What you did was remarkable, and I know I don't know the half of it."

"Why do you say that?" Burton asked, leaning back against the kitchenette counter. Today, she was in another of her long, flowing skirts and boots with a button-up satin blouse.

"I can see it in your eyes," Sally said softly. "There used to be such a light there, and now..." She shook her head. "So much sadness all the time." Her smile grew into a warm, motherly one. "You're such a young woman with so much life ahead of you. I hope you find your light again." With a quick, one-armed hug, Sally headed toward the door before stopping, her hand on the doorframe. She turned back. "Merry Christmas on Sunday, Burton. Go have fun with your friends in

Denver."

Burton chuckled. "Merry Christmas, Sally. I'll do my best. Have a good weekend and I'll see you Monday."

Burton watched her go then looked down at the dark blue velvet box that bore the Chilvokian crest. She let out a heavy sigh and went to her locker to return the box to her purse.

The day had been long but good overall. She was, once again, glad to be back at work. She hadn't fully decided what to do for the holiday weekend, even though she'd been invited by both Simone and Lee Ann to join them. She hadn't committed to either and considered perhaps spending the holiday weekend quietly at home with Cricket and Ajax.

Wrapped up in her peacoat, she headed out into the cold afternoon, though it hadn't begun to snow yet. They were forecasted to have a white Christmas, so that would be nice. She started her Jeep and got the heater going as she scraped ice from her windows. Finished, she climbed inside the SUV and tossed the scraper to the passenger-side floor.

"Brrr, brrr, brrr," she murmured, rubbing her hands together. She'd forgotten her gloves that morning and was definitely paying for it now.

Moments later, she was on the road and headed home. She turned up the volume as Sarah Brightman's "Delivery Me" began. She sang along, though certainly not well as she headed home. The traffic on the Friday before Christmas was fairly substantial, even for Westcliffe's standards. Finally, she was on the outskirts of town and hers was the only car on the road as she neared the turnoff to the street that would take her home.

Burton smiled when she saw her house down the lane, happy to be headed home for a couple days. The smile began to falter, however when she saw a gray Ford Explorer parked out front.

Eyebrows drawing, she pulled into her driveway, tires crunching on the packed snow from the storm two days before. She pulled up to her usual spot, only then noticing that someone was sitting on the stoop by the kitchen door. Cutting the engine of her Jeep, she opened the door and only got one booted foot on the ground before her heart stopped as she glanced out at the person.

She couldn't take her eyes off of her as she slowly climbed out of the Jeep. Her mind raced, confusion gripping her. She didn't even close the door to the SUV or grab anything from inside as she slowly walked over to the stoop, the figure standing as she neared.

Dressed in jeans and hiking boots and wrapped in a heavy quilted winter jacket, her auburn hair in a pixie cut, stood—

"Lilli?"

"Hi," Lilli said softly.

Burton couldn't speak, could barely breathe. Her legs gave out on her and she began to collapse to the ground, her shock so profound. Lilli rushed to her and caught her, both falling to the ground on their knees. Burton stared into the intensely beautiful green eyes and felt an instant wave of grief wash over her.

The tears came so quickly, so hard that she didn't have time to attempt to stem them. She felt Lilli's arms around her and was suddenly filled with anger. She pushed at Lilli, months of grief and the horrific images that had haunted her since the day it happened flashing before her eyes.

"Why did you leave me!" she wailed. Everything she'd felt, tried to push away, or tried to deal with came at her full throttle in a torrent of emotion and sobs. She tried to push Lilli away, fists beating at her shoulders and upper chest. Lilli said nothing—simply took it and let her get it out, but refused to let go of her.

Finally, Burton's energy was gone and she fell against the other woman, who wrapped her arms around her and held her tight. Burton grabbed fistfuls of Lilli's jacket, clinging to her as she cried.

"You died," Burton murmured weakly.

"No," Lilli said into her ear. "I'm alive and I'm here with you. For so long I didn't know that I had, but I survived."

Face wet with tears and vision blurry, Burton tried to blink away her emotion as she pulled back enough to examine Lilli's face, also wet with tears. "You're here?" she whispered. "You're really here?"

Lilli nodded, fresh tears sliding down her cheeks. "I'm here."

Burton grabbed her in a hug that was painfully tight, her hand cupping the back of her head, almost like a drowning man clinging to a buoy. "Lilli..." She felt like she was in a dream, like at any moment she'd wake up and start the grieving process all over again. So many times she'd seen Lilli in her dreams, so many times she'd woken up heartbroken and alone. Now, she could feel the solid form against her, smell the familiar scent of her hair and skin. She released a long breath, releasing a lot of her pain at the same time.

She pulled out of the hug again, not releasing Lilli, but she had to look into her face, had to see her eyes again. She had to know that she was really real and not her own heart's greatest desire come to torment her. She brought a hand up, cupping Lilli's cheek, Lilli leaning into the touch as those eyes slid closed. It was then that she saw the scar above her left eyebrow, a scar that hadn't been there before. It was a scar that held her heart.

Leaning up, she placed a lingering kiss on that scar before her lips found Lilli's, the softness so familiar to her, even in the short time she'd experienced it. In that brief touch, she felt so much of her shattered world come back together and right itself. She couldn't move away, couldn't end that connection.

Arms wrapping around Lilli's neck, she initiated an insistent kiss, claiming what she thought she'd lost, not only Lilli the woman, but also a part of her own soul. Lilli responded, the kiss quickly growing possessive and passionate, both breathing heavily.

After long moments, Lilli pulled away, her hand mirroring Burton's to cup Burton's jaw. She stared deeply into pained brown eyes, reaching up to brush dark strands of Burton's hair out of her face. "Can we go inside?" she asked softly.

Without a verbal response, Burton got to her feet, tugging Lilli by the hand. She reached over to her Jeep and pushed the door closed before leading the way to the back door of the house.

Burton felt like she was in a daze as she picked through the keys on her key chain to find her house key. After several fumbled attempts with shaky hands, she finally got the door unlocked and pushed it open. Ajax and Cricket were there to greet her, Ajax's tail wagging even faster when he saw a new friend as Lilli followed Burton inside.

"Down, guys!" Burton exclaimed, trying to get Ajax to stop jumping on Lilli, who she struggled to take her eyes off of.

"It's okay. What's your name, sweetheart?" Lilli said, reaching down to pet the dog's head, her other hand reaching out to Cricket, who had jumped onto the kitchen counter to get a better look at the newcomer.

"I'm sorry," Burton said, amused and charmed that her animals were as enamored as she was.

"Don't be. They're beautiful," Lilli said, meeting Burton's gaze. "And so are you. God, I've missed you."

Without a word, Burton shrugged out of her jacket, laying it across the breakfast bar as she walked to Lilli, unzipping her heavy jacket and helping her out of it, revealing a cream-colored sweater before she placed Lilli's jacket atop her own. She needed a hug but not through six inches of padded jackets. She wrapped her arms around Lilli, holding their bodies together, relishing in the warmth and closeness.

They stood there, doing nothing more than just holding each other. Burton could feel Lilli's breath against her neck, Lilli's breasts pressed to her own. Again, suddenly she found it hard to breathe, her heart racing though for a very different reason.

She turned her head and, almost by magnetism, found Lilli's lips again. This kiss, however, was soft and slow, a reconnection. At the first touch of Lilli's tongue against her own, she let out a soft sigh, her hand finding its way into the short hair she wasn't used to. In that moment, it didn't matter as she felt the soft strands against her fingers. The kiss came to a natural end and she looked into Lilli's eyes, seeing her own desperate need for healing in the green depths.

Taking Lilli's hand, she led her from the kitchen up the stairs and down the hall to her bedroom. She crawled across the comforter, Lilli following until Burton lay on her back, Lilli hovering over her on her side as they continued their kissing. Again, Burton buried her fingers in auburn locks as Lilli reached down to place her hand on Burton's hip. Their movements were slow, each absorbing the touch, feel, and reunion.

Burton sighed into the kiss again as Lilli urged

her to bring her leg up, her still booted foot flat on the bed. Lilli's hand slipped beneath the skirt to caress a bare upper thigh, adding more intimacy to the moment.

Lilli left Burton's mouth and began to explore her jaw and neck, leaving a trail of kisses and whispered words of love. Her head fell to the side as Lilli's kisses teased the opening of her blouse, nudging the material slightly aside to lightly nip at her cleavage.

The sudden need to feel Lilli against her gripped Burton. She reached down and urged the redhead to return to her mouth. Their kiss was passionate, but gentle and filled with tenderness. Lilli's hand caressed Burton's breast before resting on her hip once more. In time, the long kiss came to a natural end and Lilli lifted herself so she could look down at Burton. They shared a long gaze filled with intensity. She needed to know that Lilli was really there. Seeming to understand this, Lilli smiled down at her before leaving a final kiss on her lips and sitting up, pulling Burton along with her.

They shared another quick kiss before Lilli reached the hem of her sweater and tugged it over her head, revealing a green-and-cream-colored bra, her beautiful breasts cupped lovingly in it, the creaminess of her cleavage beckoning to Burton. Even so, she reached up and began to unbutton her own blouse, shrugging the soft material off her shoulders once she was finished. She tossed the blouse aside then crawled off the bed to remove her boots, Lilli doing the same before shoving her jeans down and kicking them off. Burton allowed the skirt to slide down over her hips and legs once she'd unbuttoned and unzipped it. She watched as Lilli hooked her thumbs beneath the waistband of her panties, pushing them down over womanly hips until they too fell to the floor, followed by Burton's.

Naked, Burton climbed back on the bed, met

almost instantly by Lilli. The immensity of what she felt was almost overwhelming. She was aroused and had tremendous desire for Lilli of course, but it was so much more than that. She needed to feel her, touch her, connect with her, and validate that it had all been worth it

Lilli moved so she was lying atop Burton, their nakedness pressed together in a way that made them both moan at the full-body contact. Their kiss was hotter than it had been before, their need amped to a new level.

Burton buried her hand in Lilli's hair as once again her mouth found Burton's neck and throat, licking and kissing a trail down until the warmth of her mouth and tongue engulfed both of Burton's breasts, one at a time, causing Burton to get lost in the physical and emotional. She felt like she wanted to cry, but held it back, instead focusing on the feel of Lilli's tongue running down her inner thigh, Burton falling fully open to her.

"Lilli," she whispered at the first touch of the firm tongue against her greatest need.

Her hips began to move with the slow but steady rhythm that was quickly set. She reached down to touch any part of Lilli that she could. It didn't take long before her body exploded, releasing not only her passion, but all that she'd been holding in for the past four months.

The tears came swiftly, and she couldn't stop them if she wanted to. She was aware of Lilli moving away from her only to move back atop Burton, holding her tightly to her.

"It's okay," Lilli whispered, raining kisses all over Burton's face. "It's okay."

Burton rolled her eyes at her own behavior as her emotion calmed. "Why is it every time we make love tears are involved somehow?"

Lilli grinned. "Because we're that awesome."

Burton's smile was quick as everything negative seemed to drain out of her. She trailed her nails up Lilli's back as she leaned up to capture soft lips. Lilli moaned into the kiss. She ran her hand down Burton's thigh, gripping it to pull it up farther along her hip as she adjusted them so they were pressed together in the most intimate way.

Burton gasped at the white-hot bolt of pleasure that shot through her as Lilli began to move her hips, rubbing her clit against Burton's. Opening her thighs wider, Burton gave Lilli more access. Her fingers roamed restlessly across the smooth plain of Lilli's back and down to a firm behind before making their way back up and entangling in the short hair as they kissed.

Lilli placed her hands on the bed on either side of Burton's shoulders and raised herself up as she increased her thrusts. Burton brought her hands up and cupped Lilli's breasts, which caused the auburn-haired beauty's head to fall and eyes to close as Burton pinched her hard nipples. Her hips began to move faster, Burton moving with her.

As her pleasure grew, so did Burton's moans and whimpers. She released Lilli's breasts and hugged her so she fell on top of her, both holding on to each other as Lilli continued to thrust into her. Her whimpers and heavy breathing were buried in Burton's neck, which amplified Burton's desire.

Finally, and without warning, Burton's release claimed her with a loud cry, her back arching and fingers digging into Lilli's behind. Almost simultaneously, Lilli joined her, slamming her hips into Burton, grinding against her to milk any pleasure she could, making Burton gasp.

They held on to each other for a long moment, trying to catch their breaths. Burton's heart raced and she almost felt faint from breathing so hard. As she calmed, she caressed Lilli's back and hair.

At length, Lilli moved off Burton, rolling to her back and covering her face with a hand. "My God," she panted, her other hand slapping against her stomach.

Burton smiled, completely understanding as her legs fell limp to the bed. She reached blindly for Lilli's hand, which was given to her. They lay there, briefly, in silence. She glanced at Lilli, still in shock at the completely unexpected events of the last hour. After a moment, Lilli met her gaze.

"Do you mind if we cuddle?" she asked.

Burton chuckled, utterly charmed. "Come on, let's get under the covers."

❧❧❦❦

Burton's eyes slowly opened to find herself looking right into the face of an angel. Lilli lay on her side facing her, her eyes closed as she appeared to be sleeping deeply. The smile that spread across Burton's face was unstoppable when she realized it hadn't been a dream after all. She was about to reach out for her when she realized with a small gasp that night had fallen.

"Crap," she whispered, slipping out of bed as quietly as she could.

Dressed in only her robe, Burton padded downstairs only to see a very forlorn-looking Cricket and Ajax lying on the couch looking at her.

"I'm so sorry, guys!" she exclaimed in a whisper.

Hurrying to the kitchen, she flicked on the light, confident that it wouldn't bother Lilli upstairs. The animals followed her as she walked to their food bowls. Night had fallen already, and she was about four hours past their dinnertime.

A scoop for each, she gave them some loves as they raced to their empty bowls to dig in. Standing back to let them eat, she grinned at them, filled with so much love. That love would grow when she heard someone enter the kitchen.

Turning, she saw Lilli padding toward her, dressed only in Burton's unbuttoned shirt. She had to admit, Liliya Novikoff was the most stunning and sexy woman she'd ever seen.

"Hey," she said, moving toward her.

"Hey, yourself. Why did you get up?" Lilli asked, reaching out to tug Burton's robe belt free, the two sides falling open. She entered Burton's personal space, opening the ends of the shirt she wore so their naked flesh pressed together. She hugged Burton beneath her robe.

Burton let out a sigh of happy contentment. "I always feed these guys when I get home," she explained, returning the embrace, her fingers combing through soft strands of short, auburn hair.

"Oops," Lilli chuckled. "I guess you were a little distracted."

They stayed quiet for a long time, just holding on to each other. "Why did you cut your hair?" Burton asked at length, thinking she probably knew the answer but wanted to know.

"They had to shave part of my head when I was rushed into surgery to remove the bullet, so they just went ahead and shaved my whole head," Lilli explained softly.

"I'm sorry I left you," Burton whispered. "I'm so sorry. I should have—"

"No!" Lilli grabbed Burton's face in both hands and forced her to look at her. She shook her head and repeated it. "No." She used one of her hands to caress her cheek. "I wanted you to go. There was absolutely nothing you could have done, and he may have shot you again." She brought Burton's face to hers and placed a lingering kiss on her lips. "It's over. No more of that from you. Okay?"

Looking into Lilli's eyes, she indeed saw that it was over. She felt so much leave her shoulders for the first time since everything had happened. She nodded. "Yes. Okay."

Lilli hugged her again, resting her head on Burton's shoulder. "I'm so glad I'm home," she murmured. "I had a lot of healing to do, but I did and here I am."

"Are you?" Burton asked, her voice sounding small, like a little girl. "Home?"

Lilli lifted her head again and met Burton's gaze. Something passed between them, no words needed. "Yes. I'm home."

Burton's former smile returned. "I love you."

"And I love you." Lilli stepped back from her, taking her hand. "Let's go to bed."

Led out of the kitchen, Burton glanced out the living room window as they headed to the stairs. She stopped Lilli with a tug of her hand. Together they watched as the snow fell.

"Merry Christmas, Lilli," she whispered, coming up behind her and wrapping her arms around her waist.

Lilli's head leaned back against Burton as she covered her arms with her own. "Merry Christmas."

Epilogue

"Good morning to you! Good morning to you!" Lilli sang, laughing when Ajax became even more excited as he and Cricket followed her to their food bowls.

Padding over to them in a tank top and Burton's Denver Broncos cotton pajama pants, she filled the bowls with a scoop each of the respective food then moved on to the coffeemaker to get the brew started.

She hummed softly to herself and reached into a sugar bowl on the breakfast bar where they kept odds and ends, such as loose change, a partial roll of TUMS, and a few hair ties. She fished one of those out and gathered her shoulder-length hair back in a ponytail. A glance outside brought a smile to her face. It was a gorgeous and bright late-spring day—a perfect day for a road trip.

Returning her attention to the coffeemaker, which had begun to sputter and cough to life, she reached up to the cabinet for their favorite mugs and set them down on the counter. At that moment, Burton entered the kitchen, dressed in a similar fashion.

"Coffee's almost ready, baby," Lilli said, meeting Burton halfway across the room for a quick kiss.

"Sounds wonderful," Burton said, headed to the fridge, opening the freezer side.

"I thought you already had breakfast this morning," Lilli said with a sexy little grin.

Burton returned it over her shoulder from where

she stood, the fridge side now open. "Hey, now. Can I help it if your breasts were lying there exposed, the beautiful morning sunlight shining on them like a beacon?"

Lilli laughed, reaching for the bottle of flavored coffee creamer that Burton was extending to her. "No, I suppose not, and I'm certainly not complaining." She poured them both a cup of coffee as the maker gurgled to a finish. "It's a beautiful day today."

"I know. I'm *so* happy the hospital finally gave you a weekend off," Burton said, letting the doors close before she walked to Lilli, wrapping her arms around her waist and smiling at her. "Are you sure you still want to go today?"

"Absolutely," Lilli said with a nod, locking her hands lightly behind Burton's neck. "It's time."

"Okay."

They shared a quick kiss and tight hug.

"I'm glad you'll be going with me," Lilli murmured into it. "Thank you so much for finding out for me."

༺༻༺༻

"Okay, we are now on Turkey Creek Road," Lilli said, glancing from the GPS on her phone screen to the map she'd printed out at home before they left. "It shouldn't be far now."

"I think I see it," Burton said, maneuvering the Jeep to turn onto the road they needed to be on. "Yup, there it is."

Moments later, Burton found a place for them to park. She glanced at Lilli after reaching into the backseat behind her to grab the bouquet of flowers. "Are you ready, baby?"

Lilli looked out her window, taking several deep

breaths before she met Burton's gaze. "Yes."

"Let's go say hi to your mom."

They shared a quick kiss before each opened a door, climbing out of the Jeep, the doors slamming shut with finality.

About the author

Kim Pritekel was born and raised in Colorado, where she still lives, loving the blue skies and the beautiful Rockies. She's been writing since she was a child and has created a career as both a novelist filmmaker. You can find out more at http://www.kimpritekel.com/ or at Kim Pritekel on Facebook

Check out Kim's other books.

Zero Ward - ISBN - 978-1-943353-19-4

Danny Felts grew up in the heart of the Midwest on a dairy farm, expected to follow in her mother's footsteps and marry a farmer and become a mother. Danny had other ideas. As World War II heats up, she makes a decision that will change her life forever as she becomes a lie, serving with the Seabees in the Navy as Daniel Felts.

Kate Adams is about to graduate high school in her prestigious and elite San Diego neighborhood when she's dragged to the USO for a dance with friends and servicemen. There, she meets the person that will catch her eye and her heart, only for jealousy and vengeance to tear her apart.

Are Danny and Kate strong enough to win the battle within and fight for their love?

Connection- ISBN - 978-1-939062-24-6

Julie Wilson lives a charmed life as a beloved teacher and aunt in the small town of Woodland. Close to her brother and guardian of two adorable Yorkies, she loves her life, the only negative being ex-boyfriend, Ray who can't seem to understand the phrase, "We're done." Believing that's her only problem, Julie has no idea what hell awaits her during a normal summer afternoon.

Remmy Foster is the quirky, friendly drifter who has never found roots after a difficult childhood, as well as the difficulties her very special gift brings into her life. Though she may call it exploring, the truth is she's running from ghosts that haunt her every step.

After a chance meeting with Julie while hitchhiking, Remmy will be thrown head first into darkness she could never have foreseen, regardless of her abilities. As the clock ticks, life and death is on her shoulders to make the right connection.

Warning - Some scenes may be too intense for some readers.

1049 Club - ISBN - 978-1-939062-97-0

Almost two hundred souls, one plane, six survivors, endless heartbreak.

When flight 1049, headed from Buffalo, NY to Italy falls from the sky, a firestorm of drama, pain, angst and sorrow ensues. Can an author, a business owner, a teenager, good ol' boy, veterinarian and ruthless lawyer survive? Better yet, can those left behind?

1049 Club is a story of survival, love, deep regret and miracles. Can the living make peace with the presumed dead? Can the presumed dead make peace with the lives and loves they thought they had before?

CPSIA information can be obtained
at www.ICGtesting.com
Printed in the USA
LVHW04s0950300718
585356LV00004B/449/P